Captive of the Heart

Molly gasped as Ben Cantrell materialized out of the darkness. "What . . . what are you doing here?"

"Looking for you," he told her. "Are you meeting someone?"

"No! I . . . I just wanted to be alone for a few minutes." She laid a hand on her racing heart as he moved closer.

"They say you're going to marry Harry," he said angrily. "Are you?"

"I . . . I don't think that's any of your business, Ben Cantrell."

"Maybe it is my business, Molly Wade," he mocked.

"Why would it be?" Her heart was pounding now.

"Because," was all he said as he swept her up into his arms . . .

BELOVED OUTCAST

BELOVED OUTCAST

VICTORIA THOMPSON

PAGEANT BOOKS

With thanks to the counselors at Family and Children's Services of Blair County: Executive Director Jacquelyn Sutton, Domestic Abuse Project Coordinator Joanna Watts, and Domestic Abuse Project Caseworker Beverly Moss-Oswalt, and to my agent, Cherry Weiner, for convincing me I could do it.

PAGEANT BOOKS
225 Park Avenue South
New York, New York 10003

PAGEANT and colophon are trademarks of the publisher

Cover artwork by Greg Golbronson

Printed in the U.S.A.

First Pageant Books printing: April, 1989

10 9 8 7 6 5 4 3 2 1

PROLOGUE

MIRIAM RODE LIKE the wind, heedless that her long black hair had pulled loose and was whipping across her face, conscious only of the warm, sensuous feel of the pony's bare back between her legs and her fingers curled tightly in the animal's thick mane. The pounding of the pony's hooves as he galloped fearlessly into the night beat through her, and she remembered other wild rides long ago. As a child she had always ridden bareback, her family too poor to spare her a saddle. A bitter smile curved her lips as she realized she would never be poor again.

Using her hands and her voice, she just barely managed to get her "borrowed" pony to pull up at the crest of the next hill. While he blew and

1

snorted, Miriam stared down into the small valley at the ranch buildings huddled there.

Hardly more than shadows in the darkness, the buildings were nevertheless as clear as day to the girl who saw them more with her heart than with her eyes. The hulking barn; the bunkhouse, empty now but that would shelter the hired hands at a busier time of year; the ranchhouse, actually nothing more than a one-room cabin where the man lived with his son. Not an impressive layout, yet Miriam gazed down at it with a longing that made her weak. Stifling a sob, she kicked the pony into motion and rode slowly into the ranch yard.

Tying the poor beast to the corral fence with a piece of rope, she stole silently up to the door of the house. She paused only a moment before knocking, tentatively at first and then more boldly.

"Sam! Sam, it's me," she called, a note of urgency in her voice.

She heard movement inside, and she pictured the man rising, half-awake, and clumsily pulling on his clothes. A voice asked, "Pa? What's she doing here?" and the man called Sam answered, "I'll take care of it, Ben. Stay in the house." Then the door opened, and Sam was there.

He was a tall man, his sun-bleached hair lightly touched with silver and sleep-tousled. He was still buttoning his shirt, a look of bewildered alarm on his bronzed face. The face was still handsome, even after thirty-five years spent working out of doors. The lines time and weather had etched around his eyes and mouth only added character, and the bright blue eyes looking down at her were those of a man who was still a boy at heart.

"Miriam, what is it? What are you doing here at this time of night?"

"I had to see you, talk to you. Please, Sam," she entreated, grasping his arm.

"Sure, honey, sure," he soothed, as he closed the cabin door behind him. "Let's go over to the bunkhouse so we won't disturb Ben." He reached out and caught the girl protectively to his side as they made their way across the darkened yard.

Just inside the bunkhouse door he stopped and turned her toward him until the moonlight fell full on her lovely face. "Now tell me, darlin', what is it that's so urgent?" he asked, faintly amused at her serious expression. She was so young, he thought. Nothing could be as serious as all that.

"You love me, don't you, Sam?"

"You know I do, sweet girl, more than anything in the world," he assured her, a tender smile curving his lips. Her eyes, almost black in the moonlight, looked enormous in her fragile face, and he wondered what could have happened to frighten her so.

Suddenly, with something like desperation, she threw her arms around his neck and pulled his mouth to hers. Caught off guard, he hesitated only a moment before responding to her kiss. They clung together for a long time, his strong arms molding her willing body close to his. Her restless hands found their way under his dangling shirttail and began to explore the sinewy strength of his back and sides, sending a shudder of desire through him.

"Love me, Sam, love me," she begged, drawing him toward the nearest bunk.

"No darlin', no," he said hoarsely, his regret obvious. "Not like this. It isn't right. When we're married . . ."

"It wasn't right the other time, either," she said, her voice sharp with frustration, "but that didn't stop you then. Is it only all right when you want it but not when I do?"

Sam groaned, caught between reason and desire, but Miriam kissed him again. This time she used her tongue, as he had taught her, and sank her small, white teeth into his lower lip while her hands moved deftly over the buttons on his pants. This time he did not resist when she drew him toward the bunk, and he tumbled down with her willingly.

With trembling hands, he bared her small, firm breasts to his feverish exploration and, at her urging, lifted her skirts, gasping when he found her naked beneath her petticoat. They came together in a frenzy of need, clinging to each other as the wave of passion lifted them higher and higher and then brought them crashing down again.

It was a long time before either of them stirred. At last Sam's rasping breath slowed to normal, his heart quieted in his chest, and he found the energy to lever himself up onto his elbows. Looking down at the girl's sweet face, so content now, he smiled and gently smoothed back the damp hair from her forehead. "Now do you believe I love you, little one?" he teased.

Her passion-glazed eyes suddenly cleared, and he saw something very akin to fear in them. "Oh, Sam, will you always love me?"

"Of course I will," he promised, a little puzzled and even worried now. Why was she still so upset?

"Even if I did something bad? Something terrible?"

"You could never do anything very bad," he said, stroking his callused fingers across the satin of her cheek.

"Oh, but I could! I did!" she replied, tears sparkling in her eyes. "I promised to marry Franklin Hoskins."

Sam's whole body went rigid with shock and with the tidal wave of anger that followed. "Well, you can just unpromise him, then. What in God's name possessed you to do a damn-fool thing like that?"

Wincing under the force of his rage, Miriam squeezed out two tears, but she could not give in to his pain or her own. Resolutely, she opened her eyes again. "I can't."

"Can't? Can't or *won't?"* He scrambled to his feet, hastily rearranging his clothes.

"Sam," she pleaded, the silver tears rolling down her face. "I can't be poor. I told you that before. I just can't be poor anymore."

"So you'll sell yourself to Hoskins? You're no better than a whore!" His eyes raked her body, still wantonly exposed. "Cover yourself," he snapped, jerking her skirt contemptuously over the long, shapely legs she had so recently wrapped around his own. "What in the hell did you come here for, anyway?"

Grasping the front of her blouse together with trembling hands, she sat up. "I had to see you, to tell you . . ."

"And what was all this about?" he demanded, gesturing toward the bunk where she still sat, his pain now overtaking anger as the reality of her betrayal began to set in.

"I needed you."

"Needed me?"

"I love you, Sam. I can't give you up!"

He stared at her, wondering how she could say these things to him. "Well, if you think you can ride out here everytime you *need* me after you're married, you can think again. I'm not some stud who'll service you whenever you get an itch between your legs. You marry Hoskins, you'll never see me again."

"Sam, please . . ."

"Miriam, darlin'," he tried, softer now, more reasonable, controlling his anger with a mighty effort, remembering she was only eighteen. "You're young, too young to have good sense, I reckon. Think this over. Go back to Hoskins, tell him you changed your mind. We'll forget this ever happened. You'll see, I'll make you happy."

But she could not believe him. She knew only

one thing brought happiness, and Sam Cantrell did not have it. Rich Franklin Hoskins did. Shaking with the force of her emotions, Miriam turned her dark eyes up to the man she loved, the man she would always love. "I can't," she replied in an agony of despair.

Sam looked down at her for a long moment, trembling with an agony of his own. "Then to hell with you," he said.

Chapter One

✦ ✦ ✦ ✦

MOLLY HAD NEVER seen a hanged man before, and she didn't want to go see one now. Unfortunately, she did not have a choice. Rattling along in the back of the wagon, she straightened her shoulders and tried valiantly not to cry. She had to set a good example for her little sister, Julie, who was only ten and scared stiff. Twelve-year-old Molly put a comforting arm around Julie's shoulders and swallowed hard against the lump in her throat.

It was bad enough seeing a dead person at a funeral, all laid out in nice clothes in a pine box. But to see somebody dead, just hanging from a tree with a rope around his neck and his face all black and . . . Molly shuddered. It was especially bad because she knew Mr. Cantrell. Nice Mr. Cantrell. Not that she knew him well, but he didn't seem like the kind of person who would kill a man or burn down somebody's barn for no good reason. Molly didn't know for sure, though. Maybe Sam Cantrell was only nice to children.

She did know about his son, Ben. Ben didn't deserve to be an orphan. She would never forget the time mean old Harry Hoskins had dipped her pigtails in the inkwell at school. She had been much younger then, and her hair had been bright yellow. Not only had her mother had to cut her hair, but the ink had ruined the only decent dress she'd owned. Since her father refused to buy her a new one, she'd had to wear the stained one for half a year until she had finally outgrown it.

The teacher had been afraid to punish Harry because Harry's father was the richest man in town. Franklin Hoskins owned the bank and a ranch, and he was chairman of the school board, so Harry had gotten off scot free. Except for Ben Cantrell.

Ben was four years older than Molly. When he found out what Harry had done, he fought him. Harry was a year older than Ben and bigger, but it had been a pretty even match, all things considered. Although Molly hated fighting, she had gotten some satisfaction out of Harry Hoskins's black eye.

No, Molly decided, Ben didn't deserve to be an orphan, and he certainly didn't deserve to have his father hanged.

"I don't know why we have to see this," Molly's mother was saying to her husband from where she sat beside him on the wagon seat. She was a small-boned woman, gaunt and aged beyond her years by hard work and the secret shame of her marriage. She spoke in the soft voice she used when she wanted to reason with her husband without incurring his wrath.

"I told you before, woman, these young-uns got to see what happens to sinners. They got to see God's judgment on those who work iniquity," Elijah Wade explained impatiently. Then he chuckled, a sound that sent shivers up Molly's spine. "You should have been there, Hannah. Sam Cantrell sure put up a fight. Took four men to hold him while we got the noose around his neck. He cursed us all, too. Might've scared me if I didn't know he was a low-down murdering barn burner. Reckon he wouldn't have come with us so peaceable if he'd known he wasn't never gonna make it to jail. His boy was ready to shoot us all, swore his pa hadn't been out of the house all night, couldn't have burned that barn. Cantrell just patted the boy on the shoulder and told him not to worry, the law would take care of everything."

"Why didn't you let the law take care of it, Elijah?" Hannah Wade asked her husband plaintively. It was the closest she could come to openly criticizing his taking part in a lynching.

Wade, a scrawny, banty rooster of a man, bristled at the implied criticism. "Hell, the sheriff was in San Antone. No telling when he'd be back. Cantrell could've broke out by then and—

been long gone. We all knew he was the one shot Fletcher and burned his barn. Who else could it've been? Everybody knows how Cantrell and Fletcher fought the other day. Cantrell sneaked out last night to burn Fletcher's barn, wanting to get even. Fletcher caught him and ended up dead. Don't take a judge and jury to figure that out."

"It's just so hard to believe," Hannah said. "Sam Cantrell has always been such a gentleman. Never once knew him to get in a fight."

Elijah's eyes narrowed. "You talk like you knew him pretty well."

"No better than you did," Hannah assured him hastily. "I saw him at church and in town a time or two."

"He lived pretty close. Maybe you saw him more often. Maybe he came by when I wasn't home—"

"Pa," Molly said in a frantic effort to distract him, "why was it you thought Mr. Cantrell burned the barn?"

Wade glared over his shoulder at his older daughter. "I told you before, don't interrupt."

"I'm sorry, Pa, but I've been so curious about Mr. Cantrell. What made him change?"

"Don't nobody know for sure. Past couple months he's been taken by the devil, though. Drinking like a man possessed and fighting with anyone didn't have the sense to get outa his way. Always did know those Cantrells would come to no good." He paused thoughtfully. "Reckon the boy'll pull up stakes now. Sure-wouldn't mind having use of Cantrell's land. No, sir, wouldn't mind at all," he mused.

Molly winced. She had often heard her father curse Sam Cantrell for having a better piece of ranch land than he did. She didn't dare point out that Elijah had come first and taken first choice but had simply chosen poorly. Or that Sam Cantrell was a better rancher, so his small herd increased while Wade's herd scattered and died.

Cantrell had even been planning to take cattle north to Kansas this spring and sell it for cash money, something her father couldn't do. Her father had always been jealous of Sam Cantrell's "luck." Molly sighed. Now he didn't have to be jealous anymore.

"What the hell?" her father said fiercely, and slapped the reins, urging the horses faster. Jolting in the back of the wagon, Molly could not see what had alarmed him until he finally brought the team to a lurching halt. Cautiously, she and Julie rose up on their knees and peered over the side.

They had arrived at the scene of Sam Cantrell's execution, but no body was hanging from the huge live oak tree. Instead, a wagon was parked beneath its spreading branches. Lying in the wagon was a blanket-shrouded bundle that could only be Sam Cantrell. Standing beside the wagon were Ben Cantrell and Nathan, the Negro man who worked for the Cantrells.

"What do you think you're doing, boy?" shouted Wade.

Ben Cantrell squared his shoulders and threw

back his head defiantly. He had grown almost a foot in the six months since school ended. In those months, doing a man's work had put a man's muscles on Ben's lanky frame.

"I'm giving my pa a decent burial," Ben replied, his voice deeper now than Molly remembered, his tone sure and firm.

Elijah Wade sputtered in his rage, rising up to stand in the wagon box. "We left that body hanging for a reason, for an example—"

"You lied about my pa, and you killed him for that lie, but you won't shame him anymore. I'm going to take him home now. You want to stop me, you're gonna have to murder me, too."

Wade stood for a moment, literally shaking with fury, but he made no move to stop the boy. Ben watched him for a few minutes, as if judging the man's potential danger, and then, deciding he had none, turned and climbed up into his wagon seat. Nathan joined him, and when Ben flicked the team into motion, Elijah seemed to come to life.

"You'll be sorry for this, boy!" he shouted, shaking his fist at Ben Cantrell's back. "The sins of the fathers are visited on the children! The Cantrell name is no good around here anymore! You'd best hightail it out of these parts where no one knows you're the son of a murderer!"

There was more, but Molly was no longer listening. This was the first time she could remember seeing anyone defy her father, and she watched, mesmerized, as the Cantrell wagon with its sad burden drove out of sight.

Molly had read all the fairy tales and knew all about the knights in shining armor who rescued fair maidens and about the princes who married poor girls. Ben Cantrell hardly qualified as either a knight or a prince, except that today he had stood tall and straight, incredibly handsome in his patched range clothes, his beautiful blond hair curling out from under his hat, his sky-blue eyes flashing in the sunlight, and he had faced down the fire-breathing dragon and won!

Molly could love a man like Ben Cantrell. A man like Ben Cantrell could rescue her from the home of that very dragon. A man like Ben could keep her safe all the days of her life. Something—she thought it must be her heart—quivered in her chest, and she knew she was in love. She loved Ben Cantrell with every bit of her twelve-year-old being, and she swore no matter what might happen, she would love him until the day she died.

Ben Cantrell did not look back as he rode away. It was crazy, he thought bitterly. Yesterday he would have been terrified of a man like Elijah Wade. He guessed he'd grown up a lot in the past twenty-four hours.

He and Nathan did not speak until they got back to the ranch. Nathan said he would build a coffin, and Ben numbly nodded agreement. His own job was a bit more difficult: preparing his father's body for burial. It was hard, the hardest thing he had ever done, especially when he looked at the poor, bloated face, not his father's face at all anymore.

But at last Sam Cantrell was in the ground, the final shovelful of dirt thrown on. Nathan read some passages out of the Bible while Ben stared dry-eyed at the naked mound of earth. All his tears had been shed earlier that morning when the preacher came to tell him what had happened.

Ben had sobbed like a child then, pouring out his grief, while Nathan and Reverend Bates offered what comfort they could. Losing his father was bad enough, a crippling blow to a boy who could not even remember his mother, but the shame of the way his father died made it infinitely worse. Only his anger at the injustice of it all kept him from wallowing in self-pity.

Ben straightened his shoulders, vaguely aware Nathan had finished his reading. Where had the former slave learned to read? Ben wondered irrelevantly. There was much Ben did not know about the black man whom his father had brought home with him at the end of the war, much that might explain the fierce loyalty and unlikely friendship between a Texan and a Negro.

"What you gonna do now, Massa Ben?"

Ben blinked in surprise. Nathan never called him anything but plain old "Ben." Sam was "Massa Sam," even though he had never been Nathan's master in any sense of the word. Now Ben realized the title and the responsibility had passed to him. "What did you say, Nathan?"

"What you gonna do now? You gonna run off like that no-account white-trash Mr. Wade said, or you gonna stick?" Nathan's words were a challenge.

"I'm gonna stick, Nathan," he replied, the vow coming readily to his lips, as if he had spent weeks considering his options. "I'm gonna run this ranch just like Pa would have, and I'm gonna make a success at it. I'll show folks around here they can't beat us Cantrells."

Nathan nodded his approval. "Your pa was gonna take a herd north this year."

"Then I will, too. We'll hire us some men, go on a cow hunt—"

"Won't be easy. Not many men'll work for a kid and a nigger."

"We'll hire some men," Ben repeated, ignoring Nathan's prediction. "We'll find somebody's been to Kansas, so's he can lead the way, tell us what to do. We got the money for an outfit and grub," he added bitterly, remembering the mortgage his father had taken out on the ranch, a mortgage from Franklin Hoskins. Hoskins had been in the posse last night. What did the banker expect Ben to do now?

He could pay off the mortgage, of course. The money was still there, hidden behind a loose stone in the fireplace. Ben could still see his father putting it there. "We'll take us a herd north, boy," he had said, "and make us some real money. Then we'll fix this place up proper, build on another room." Ben had not understood. Their house was perfectly good, and the place looked fine as far as Ben could see. At first he had thought his father's plans somehow involved Miss Miriam, the schoolteacher, but then she had married Mr. Hoskins, so it couldn't have been that.

Ben hadn't questioned his father's plans, though, and later Sam seemed to forget all about them. In the past few months, Sam Cantrell had changed. Usually peaceful and friendly, he had become truculent, drinking and fighting as never before. The fighting made him a suspect in the Fletcher killing and ultimately led to his death.

Ben had never known what caused the change in his father, but he did know one thing: hanging was a high price to pay for being in a bad mood.

He wasn't going to let them get away with it, though. They'd murdered his father, but they'd pay for it someday. Ben Cantrell was going to find out who the real murderer was. He'd bring the man to justice and clear the Cantrell name, even if it took the rest of his life. And even if it took more than that.

Chapter Two

❖❖❖❖

MOLLY FINGERED the length of satin ribbon covetously. She really wanted the pink, but it wasn't practical. She had nothing to match pink. No, the blue would match her best dress, and she could either use it in her hair or make a bow for the collar of the dress. "I'll take the blue, Mrs. Wells," she said to the storekeeper's wife.

"That's nice," Mrs. Wells said. "It matches your eyes, Molly."

Molly smiled. At sixteen she was well aware of what matched her eyes, which was why her best dress was blue. "What are you going to get, Julie?"

"I can't decide," her younger sister replied with a frown, examining all the geegaws displayed in the glass case.

The girls didn't get the opportunity to make such a decision very often. For the first time in longer than Molly could remember, their father had given them each a dime and told them they could buy whatever they wanted with it. She guessed he was feeling prosperous since he had sold some cattle this year. Both girls knew the chance to buy themselves a treat probably would not come again soon, so they were lingering over it.

"Take your time," Molly advised. "If I know Pa, he won't be along for quite a while." Molly waited until Mrs. Wells had wrapped up her

ribbon and handed it to her. Placing it lovingly
in her pocket, she strolled over to the door,
which stood open to the warm afternoon sunshine.

For a few minutes, she watched the Saturday
traffic moving in the dusty street, the wagons
clattering past carrying families come to town for
their weekly visit and the cowboys on horseback
come to squander their wages on the pleasures
of the flesh. Molly wasn't exactly sure what
"pleasures of the flesh" were, but she'd heard
her father say it often enough to know that was
what the men did.

She was enjoying the colorful scene when she
saw him. *Him*, Ben Cantrell, in person. For one
awful moment she thought her heart might actually burst, and she put a hand over where it
had swelled in her chest as she watched Ben
riding down the street.

He looked different from the way he had the
last time she had seen him, but of course he
would. She hadn't seen him for over a year, and
that time she had caught only a glimpse as he
had ridden by their wagon on the road. In fact,
she could count on the fingers of one hand the
times she had seen him in the four years since
his father had died. She remembered every single time, though, just as she remembered how
much she loved him.

The older she got, the easier it was to love
him, too. Sometimes she wondered how she
could really be in love with someone she hadn't
even spoken to in over four years, but she was.

She knew because of the way her stomach sort of ached whenever she thought about him and the way her heart was pounding ominously in her chest at the mere sight of him.

He was just arriving in town, and her hungry gaze followed him as he rode up to the livery stable and dismounted. He was more handsome than ever. His golden hair had darkened a little over the years, she noticed when he took off his hat for a moment to wipe his brow, but it was still more gold than brown. The skinny, gangly boy she remembered from school had grown tall and straight. The broad shoulders straining the seams of his shirt tapered down to a narrow waist and hips, and he had the long, muscular legs of a rider. Even from here she could see the white flash of his teeth as he smiled at something the man with him had said.

Suddenly Molly realized this was her big chance. Every other time she had seen Ben, she had been with her parents. Her father, of course, had ignored him or else muttered some insulting remark that Ben had pretended not to hear, and Ben had walked or ridden on by without so much as a glance in her direction. But today was different. Today her father was over at the saloon, bragging about selling his cattle, and her mother was visiting one of the ladies in town. Molly was free to waltz right out there on the street, and if she just happened to pass Ben Cantrell, well, common courtesy demanded she say hello to her old school friend, didn't it?

Excitement bubbled up inside of her, and she

glanced at Julie impatiently. She'd have to take Julie with her, or else the girl would complain that Molly had left her all alone in town and her father would be angry. "Haven't you decided yet, Julie?" she asked.

"Not yet."

"Well, hurry up!" Molly turned back to check on Ben's location. He was still at the livery. She'd have to watch where he went so she could time things properly. She only prayed he didn't go into the saloon, the only place in town where she wouldn't be able to follow him.

In front of the livery stable, Ben laughed at one of Johnny McGee's raunchy observations and stepped aside as a wagon rattled up to the building. The man driving it had been in the posse that hanged Ben's father. "Afternoon, Ben," the rancher said stiffly.

"Afternoon, Riggs," Ben replied.

Neither man smiled, and Riggs climbed down from his wagon. When he had given instructions to the boy who came for his horses, he turned back to Ben. "I hear you're doing well."

"Can't complain."

"Glad to hear it," said Riggs. "Your pa . . . would be proud of you."

"Yeah, if he was here to see me."

Riggs's face turned dull red, but he stood his ground. "We can't change the past, no matter how much we might want to, Ben."

"Do you want to?"

"A lot of us do." When Ben did not reply, he

said, "If you ever need anything, let me know. We're neighbors, after all."

"Are we?" Ben challenged.

Riggs sighed. For a second he looked as if he would say more, but then he turned away and headed up the street.

"Sonofabitch," Johnny muttered.

"Ain't it funny how they all try to be friends? Must be their consciences. You figure it keeps 'em awake nights, knowing they killed an innocent man?"

"What keeps 'em awake is wondering when you're gonna get your revenge," Johnny said. "They still can't figure why you didn't run off after your pa died."

"Yeah, I reckon it sticks in their craw to see me still here and 'doing well.' "

"Didn't nobody expect a sixteen-year-old boy could run a ranch. You showed 'em, though."

"And I'm gonna keep on showing 'em until one of them finally tells the truth."

Johnny slapped him on the back. "Come on, we came to town to have some fun. Let's get a drink."

Ben grinned knowingly. "Are you sure it's a drink you want, or is it the red-haired girl who'll be bringing it to you?"

"Both," Johnny replied cheerfully.

From what Ben knew about Johnny and women—and he knew a lot, considering Johnny had taken Ben to his first bordello—Ben decided he wouldn't hold him up.

"You go ahead. I've got some errands to run first."

"I ain't too sure about leaving you on your own hook. What if you run into somebody—"

"Go on," Ben said. "I'm a big boy. I can even cross the street by myself now."

Johnny snorted. "Don't be too long, or I'll have to come looking for you."

Ben laughed out loud. "The only place you're gonna be looking this afternoon is under Annie's skirt, and I promise I won't be there."

Johnny told Ben in no uncertain terms what he thought of his ancestry and his moral turpitude before Ben gave him a friendly shove to send him on his way. Then he crossed the street, all by himself, and set out for the general store to put in his order.

Molly watched him cross the street with a sense of panic. He was coming right this way, and here she was, stuck in this stupid store! "Haven't you made up your mind yet?" she snapped at Julie.

The girl was holding a tucking comb in one hand and a length of ribbon in the other. "No . . ." Julie replied thoughtfully.

"Get the ribbon," Molly urged.

"But I don't want to get the same thing you did," Julie complained.

"Then get the comb!"

"But I'm not wearing my hair up yet."

"Then get something else!" Molly cried in exasperation. Ben was taking his time, but he would be passing the store any minute. If she didn't get out soon, she'd miss her chance.

"Here, I'll help you decide," Molly offered, hurrying over to the counter and quickly surveying all the delights it held. "How about that?" she said, pointing at a small, japanned box.

"I don't have anything to keep in it."

"Then how about the doll?"

"I'm too old for dolls."

Molly swallowed her frustration. "Then why don't you get ten sticks of candy," she suggested with false brightness. "You can eat one every day for ten whole days!"

"But then they'll be gone, and I won't have *anything!*" Julie wailed.

"Then don't get anything! See if I care! I'm tired of waiting for you to make up your mind. I'm going to find Mama!"

"Go ahead," Julie sniffed, and turned back to her trinkets.

With an exasperated huff, Molly straightened her bonnet, whirled around, and ran smack dab into what felt like a wall of granite.

Like a rubber ball, she bounced back again. Two large hands reached out to catch her, but they missed, and she fell flat on her bottom onto the dusty floor.

With an outraged gasp, Molly looked up to see who on earth had been so clumsy as to run right into her, but the gasp strangled in her throat.

"I'm awfully sorry, miss, but you came so fast, I didn't have time to duck." Ben Cantrell looked down at her with an apologetic smile. "Are you hurt?"

Molly thought she might very well die, but she decided not to say so. Not knowing what else to do, she covered her humiliation with anger. "You always were a clumsy oaf, Ben Cantrell."

Ben blinked in surprise and then leaned over, squinting to make out the girl's face in the dim interior light. "Molly?" he asked at last. "Molly Wade, is that you?"

"Yes, it's me." Molly wondered dismally what kind of a picture she made, sitting on the floor with her bonnet half-off and her skirt . . . Oh, good Lord! Her skirt! Frantically, she pushed it down to cover her ankles, but she could tell by the way Ben was grinning that she was too late. He had already gotten an eyeful of her legs.

"Here, let me help you up," he said.

Molly stubbornly ignored his outstretched hand, not really trusting herself to take it. She'd already made a big enough fool of herself. If the touch of his hand was going to make her swoon, she didn't want anyone to know about it. Tucking her feet beneath her, she prepared to stand under her own power.

Ben didn't give her a chance. He reached down, grasped her by the elbows, and lifted her to her feet. Molly thought she must have gotten up too fast. That would account for the way her head was spinning. It didn't account for the way her heart was fluttering against her ribs like a trapped bird, though, or the way Ben's hands burned like firebrands against her arms.

A full minute passed before Mrs. Wells tactfully inquired, "Are you all right, Molly?"

Without thinking, Molly breathed, "No." Ben was still holding her, still staring at her like she were the most interesting thing he'd ever seen. She didn't want him to stop.

"Molly?" Julie's concern cut through the fog.

"Oh, I mean, yes, I'm fine," Molly stammered, jerking free of Ben's grasp at last. Her whole face was flaming now, and she ducked her head, pretending to brush her skirt, in order to hide her embarrassment.

Ben was starting to think *he* would never be fine again. How could all this have happened to little Molly Wade? She had been frozen in his memory as a skinny, pigtailed little girl, all knees and elbows with a pair of big blue eyes. The pigtails were gone, the skinny had filled out rather nicely, and the big blue eyes were even prettier than ever. How could he have been living in the same county with her all these years without ever having noticed her before? Well, he had noticed her now, and things were never going to be exactly the same again.

"I'm awfully sorry I bumped into you, Molly," he lied. He wasn't a bit sorry, but he knew from the furious way she was brushing her skirt that he had better pretend to be. "Seemed like you were in a powerful hurry to get somewhere. Can I walk you there, to make up for it?"

Molly's head came up in surprise. Oh, Lord, he was tall! So much taller than she remembered. She didn't think the top of her head even reached his chin. He was handsome, too, even more handsome than he looked from a distance. And she loved the way his eyes crinkled at the corners when he smiled.

For a minute Molly thought she might die of sheer happiness as she contemplated the vision of walking down the street on Ben Cantrell's strong arm. Another vision intruded, however—the vision of what her father would do if he saw them together. "No!" she said, too sharply. "I mean, no, thank you," she amended, seeing his disappointment. "I don't think . . . I mean . . . my father . . ."

She didn't have to explain any further. Ben's face hardened, and his beautiful smile faded. She could feel his withdrawal, although he did not move a muscle. At that moment, Molly would have done almost anything to put the smile back on his face. Anything except brave her father's fury.

For the first time in four years, Ben felt the pinch of his restricted position in the community. Bitterness left a sour taste in his mouth as he stepped back, silently telling her he understood and would respect her wishes.

"Molly?" Julie said tentatively. "I've decided. I'm going to get the ribbon after all."

"That's nice," Molly said, not really caring and unable to tear her gaze from Ben's face. She was vaguely aware of her sister paying for her ribbon, and then Julie was tugging at her sleeve.

"We'd better go," the girl was saying, and Molly nodded absently. She allowed Julie to lead her past Ben to the door.

Ben nodded and tipped his hat as she went by. "It was good to see you again, Molly," he said.

"Yes," she whispered sadly.

When the girls had gone, Ben walked over to the door and watched until they disappeared around a corner. Lord, but she was a cute little thing, he thought with a grim smile, slender but round in all the right places. And those eyes! They almost looked too big for her face, and they revealed every thought going on inside her pretty little head. She had liked him, too.

That shouldn't have surprised him. He had already discovered he could get most girls to like him if he put his mind to it. For some reason he had never quite understood, girls seemed to think he was attractive, and that went for the nice girls as well as the chippies. Of course, the rule only held true in other towns. In this town, nice girls had never dared to notice him, at least not openly. He had never minded until today.

"She's a pretty girl, isn't she?" Mrs. Wells commented.

"Who? Oh, you mean Molly." He pretended to think it over. "Yeah, I guess she is sort of pretty. She's changed a lot from when we were in school together. I hardly recognized her."

"So I noticed," Mrs. Wells said with a knowing grin.

* * *

"Oh, Molly, he's awful handsome, isn't he?" Julie whispered when they were far enough away from the store for it to be safe.

"I didn't notice," Molly lied.

"You did so," Julie insisted smugly. "I think if he had asked *me*, I would have walked out with him, even if Pa did give me a licking. It would be worth it."

"But he might've taken it out on Ma instead," Molly reminded her, and Julie sobered instantly.

"Well, anyways, you got to talk to him."

"Yes, and now everything's ruined."

"Ruined? What do you mean?"

"I mean I used to dream about him because of the way he stood up to Pa that time, remember?"

Julie nodded.

"He wasn't real, though, just a dream. But now . . ."

"Now he's even better than a dream," Julie said. "He'd take care of us, I know he would. Did you see how big and strong he is? And remember how he fought Harry Hoskins when we were little?"

"Yes, I do. He likes to fight, Julie, like Pa does—"

"Ben wouldn't hit a woman. I know he wouldn't," Julie insisted.

"You don't know anything about him," Molly reminded her sternly, "and we aren't likely to ever find out, anyway. We'll probably never get another chance to even talk to him again."

Julie's acceptance came reluctantly. "I wish—"

"Wishing won't change anything, so you'd better quit thinking about him," Molly said, but the warning was really for herself. Julie was right, the real Ben was better than Molly's dreams, bigger and stronger and more handsome. He had spoken to her and touched her and made her feel like a grown-up woman. Would she ever be able to forget about him now?

"Where the hell have you been?" Johnny inquired when Ben finally joined him in the saloon. Johnny was standing at the far end of the crowded bar, and Ben had to make his way past several men whose greetings he acknowledged with a stiff nod.

"I told you, I had some errands," Ben replied, motioning to the bartender for a beer. He wasn't telling the entire truth. Like a fool, he'd gone roaming around town for a while after he'd finished up his business, hoping to catch another glimpse of Molly Wade. He hadn't, though, and now he wanted a beer. Several beers.

"You look sort of peaked," Johnny observed. "Did something happen?"

Ben waited until the bartender set the beer down in front of him and walked away. "Yeah," he replied. "I met a girl."

"It's about time. What's her name?" he asked, taking a sip of his own drink.

"Molly Wade."

Beer sprayed everywhere as Johnny choked. The bartender hustled over, cursing, to wipe up the counter, so it was a few minutes before they were alone again. When Johnny had recovered, he turned to Ben in dismay. "Tell me I heard you wrong. Tell me she isn't any kin to Elijah Wade. Please tell me that, Ben."

Ben couldn't help but grin. He had known what Johnny's reaction would be. If anything, Johnny would be more worried about the situation than Ben. Ever since he had met Johnny on his very first trail drive, the man had made it his bounden duty to look after Ben. It wasn't because he was that much older, just a few years. It wasn't that he was that much more responsible, either. In fact, if the truth were told, Johnny was really the one who needed looking after.

But Ben didn't mind Johnny's concern. Johnny was his friend. For some reason, the two of them had hit it off right away, and Johnny had attached himself to Ben like a blood tick on a fat hound, quitting the job he had held for three years with Big Jim Harris down in Uvalde and coming back to Hoskinsville with Ben. Ben never had understood why. Johnny could have been foreman of some big ranch if he'd wanted to, but he stayed on with Ben. Most times it was just the two of them, now that Nathan had passed on. In the spring, they'd hire on a few extra hands to help with the branding and such, but the rest of the time they ran Ben's place together, and Johnny seemed more than satisfied. Ben had a feeling that if he ever wanted to get rid of Johnny, he'd have to shoot the poor fellow. In fact, Johnny had even said so, more than once.

"She's Elijah Wade's daughter," Ben informed him.

Johnny winced like a dog passing peach seeds and swore eloquently. "If they put your brains in a jaybird, he'd fly backwards, Ben Cantrell. There's a million girls in this world. Why'd you have to pick the only one you sure as hell can't have?"

A very good question, Ben admitted silently, and shrugged.

"Be careful what you say," Johnny warned, lowering his voice. "The old fart's right over there." Sure enough, Elijah Wade sat at a corner table with two of his cronies. He was acting like he was having a good time, but even still he looked cross and tight-lipped, like his bowels had been locked for a couple of days. You couldn't tell anything from his expression, though, because he always looked sour. Observing that Molly must not take after her father at all, Ben turned back to Johnny. "Where's Annie?" he asked to change the subject.

Johnny grinned. "I left her upstairs. She's resting up for next time."

Ben laughed, shaking his head in wonder. "As much as you like poontang, you ought to find yourself a nice girl and settle down. You could have it every night."

Johnny's brown eyes widened in horror. "That just shows how much you know about nice girls. Besides," he added with a good-natured grin, "who'd have an ugly plug like me?"

Another good question, Ben decided. Johnny wasn't exactly a prize. His hair was all right, dark black and curly, but his face looked like something God had put together in the dark, the eyes too small, the nose too big, mouth too broad. Still, a girl in Dodge City had once told Ben that Johnny was so ugly he was cute, and it had been apparent to Ben down through the years that she wasn't the only one who thought so.

Ben diplomatically changed the subject from Johnny's looks, and they whiled away the rest of the afternoon in the saloon. Ben waited patiently while Johnny went upstairs and paid Annie another visit, then they strolled over to the hotel for supper. Afterward they claimed two chairs in the shade of the hotel porch so they could sit and watch the town heat up for Saturday night before they went back to the saloon.

Johnny dug around in his teeth with a broomstraw for a while before going back to the topic he'd been putting off discussing with Ben all afternoon. "That Wade girl," he began without preamble. "You'd better stay away from her."

When Ben didn't answer, Johnny felt free to continue. "If the old man ever catches you making eyes at her, he'll have you stuffed and mounted. You can take it as gospel."

"I'm not afraid of Elijah Wade."

"Then you oughta be," Johnny warned. "It ain't what he can do to you in a fight that you gotta be worried about, anyways. It's the way he can turn folks against you."

Ben frowned. Johnny was right, of course. As long as he stayed in his place, the people of Hoskinsville tolerated his presence. But he'd better not try to go courting their daughters.

"Besides," Johnny went on, "you don't want to get mixed up with any nice girls. That's why I left Big Jim Harris, you know. Did I ever tell you he had *five* daughters?"

In point of fact, Johnny had given Ben this astonishing piece of information at least a hundred times, but Ben was not one to quibble.

"Five daughters," Johnny reiterated, "and each one uglier than the last. The oldest one had her eye on me, too. Yes, sir, that filly was dragging her rope for sure, and I knew if I didn't get away soon, I was gonna step right in it. Nice girls or not, they've got their little ways of making a man do what he's got no intention of doing, and that's God's truth."

Ben didn't comment, but he knew Johnny was right, at least about the Harris girls. In fact, Big Jim had even invited Ben to come down to Uvalde for a visit, bragging that he had five pretty daughters who'd like to meet him.

"It's plain as a wart on a billygoat's nose," Johnny was saying, but broke off when he heard Ben swear softly. "What is it?" he asked in alarm. Ben looked like somebody'd just dropped a hammer on his toe.

"It's her," Ben whispered, not even moving his lips. "In the wagon."

Sure enough, the Wade family was riding by on their way out of town. Like the other families who had come in for the day, they were leaving before the cowboys could commence celebrating their day off.

Molly sat on a seat in the wagon bed, facing the rear. From there she could scan the town without being observed by her father, who was driving. Julie sat beside her and, by unspoken agreement, was helping her look.

Julie's elbow dug into her ribs, but Molly didn't need the nudge. She had seen him already, sitting on the hotel porch with the same man he'd been with earlier. Her mouth trembled at the corners, wanting desperately to smile at him. She wanted even more desperately to wave but didn't dare to do either. Instead she sat perfectly still, clutching her hands together in her lap and watching him for all she was worth.

Heaven only knew how long it would be until she got to see him again. Her father rarely brought them to town, and even when he did there was no guarantee she'd see Ben. Her heart ached, and she blinked back the sting of tears. It wasn't fair. It wasn't a bit fair. Pa would say it was God's will, but Molly didn't believe God could be so cruel. She had loved Ben for so long. It just didn't seem possible nothing could ever come of it.

Ben didn't move, didn't even bat an eye, until

the wagon had disappeared from sight. "Isn't she the prettiest girl you ever saw?"

"As pretty as a red heifer in a flower bed," Johnny agreed grudgingly. "And if you had the sense God gave a ripe gourd, you'd forget you ever saw her."

The Wades were halfway home and Molly was still lost in her own misery when the trouble started. Her father turned to her mother on the wagon seat. "Where were you all day?"

"I went to visit Ethel Davis," Hannah said.

"That fat cow. I'll bet she didn't have nothing good to say about me, did she?"

"She asked how you were is all."

"I reckon you talked all afternoon about 'how I am,'" Elijah snarled.

Julie reached for Molly's hand. They could both smell the sickening-sweet odor of whiskey on him. The two girls sat as still as stones while the wagon clattered along the rutted road. Julie closed her eyes, praying for a miracle Molly knew would not come. Molly had stopped asking for it years ago.

"We talked about folks in town, mostly," Hannah was saying, her voice falsely cheerful as she tried to lighten her husband's mood. "Miriam Hoskins stopped by. You should have seen the dress she was wearing. I'll bet it cost a hundred dollars."

"Old Hoskins can afford to dress his whore up

real fine. The old bastard lives like a king off our sweat and blood, stealing from us every chance he gets. You probably think I should buy you fancy dresses, too."

"I don't need fancy dresses."

"Damn right you don't, a hag like you. You're so ugly you're lucky you ever got a man to marry you. You know that, don't you?" he taunted. "You're lucky to have me to take care of you and feed you and keep a roof over your head."

"Yes, Elijah, I'm very lucky," Hannah said meekly.

Molly cringed at her mother's humiliation. Mama wasn't ugly at all. If she weren't so thin and had some nice clothes . . .

"Damn right you're lucky, and don't you forget it. What did the Hoskins whore want with the likes of you?"

"She came by to see Ethel. She invited us to a quilting bee the church ladies are having."	.

"How'd she expect you'd come to a quilting bee? I guess she thinks I haven't got nothin' better to do than cart you around the country-side so you can kick up your heels. And what about your family? Who's going to take care of your children? Who's going to—"

"Pa, don't!" Molly cried, grabbing his arm.

"Shut up, you little bitch. Stay out of this." His shove sent her sprawling among the sacks of flour and coffee stacked neatly in the wagon bed.

Julie was crying silently, the tears making wet tracks down her cheeks, and helped Molly back up onto the seat. Molly put her arm around her sister, and they clung to each other as the tirade continued.

"You probably think I believe those lies about a quilting bee," Elijah was saying. "I know why you really want to get out of the house."

"I never asked to go," Hannah said patiently.

"Not yet, you didn't, but I know what's in your mind. You've got a man somewhere, don't you? You're wanting to go off and wallow with him, and you think you can trick me into taking you into town so you can do it. You filthy, lying whore!"

Smack! The blow almost knocked Hannah from the wagon seat.

"Mama!" the girls cried, catching her as best they could while she fought for balance. Blood spurted from her nose, and the girls watched helplessly as she tried to stanch it.

"Stay away from her, you hear?" he bellowed at Molly when she tried to place a comforting hand on her mother's shoulder.

Julie pulled Molly back down to the low seat in the wagon bed. The younger girl was sobbing quietly now, and she held Molly fiercely. Above them their father's voice droned on with accusations and degrading profanity. In one breath he accused Hannah of having a dozen lovers; in the next he told her she was too ugly for a man to look at.

Hannah huddled on the seat defensively, braced for the intermittent blows that punctuated his harangue.

"Pa! Someone'll see you!" Molly cried when

he grabbed a fistful of Hannah's hair and started shaking her.

"Then they'll know what a worthless bitch I married, won't they?" he said, but he let her go.

The ride home seemed endless, and Molly wasn't looking forward to their arrival. In the privacy of his own house, Elijah Wade could do whatever he wanted to his lawfully wedded wife. When the wagon finally stopped, he sent the women inside to prepare his supper. Julie ran on ahead to find some rags with which to clean her mother up while Molly helped her into the house.

"You girls go on up to bed now," Hannah said the instant they were in the house.

"But Ma—"

"Here, take these biscuits." Hannah handed Molly a tin containing the leftovers from the morning meal. "I'll bring you something later when he's asleep. Go on now before he sees you still here."

Knowing their presence only made things worse, the girls hastily climbed the ladder to their bedroom loft. There they huddled together long into the night and tried to ignore their father's curses and their mother's cries and the thud of flesh against flesh.

"Why doesn't she leave him?" Julie whispered brokenly as she sobbed against Molly's shoulder. "Why doesn't she take us away?"

"She can't. You know she can't."

"We could take care of her," Julie insisted. "We're older now. We could work."

"Doing what? Dancing in a saloon?"

"We could clean somebody's house or cook. . . ."

"Oh, Julie." Molly sighed in despair. How many times had she made the very same arguments to her mother? "Even if we could find work, he'd come after us, and he'd kill her. He said so. You've heard him say it a hundred times."

Julie's thin body shuddered on a new sob. "Maybe we could get away. . . ."

"How, Julie? How?"

They jumped at the sound of shattering glass. "Elijah," Hannah wailed. "That was my mother's mirror."

"Now you won't have to see how ugly you are, you stinking whore."

Julie's voice strangled on a new sob. "Can't we get away? Can't we go *somewhere?*"

Molly tightened her embrace. "Yes, *we* can, you and me," she vowed rashly. "I'll get you out of here somehow, Julie. *I promise.*"

"I feel like a jackass in the wrong stall," Johnny complained as they walked into the schoolhouse. A community dance was under way, an event everyone in the area would attend. Such dances were held several times a year, but Ben and Johnny preferred riding a hundred miles to attend such functions in places where they were unknown and appreciated simply as eligible young men.

Ben ignored Johnny's complaint and searched the crowd for Molly. "She's not here yet. Let's go get some punch," he suggested.

"Punch? There's whiskey outside," Johnny said hopefully.

"Not tonight. We have to act respectable."

Johnny rolled his eyes but didn't bother to complain again. It wouldn't help, he knew. He'd been griping all afternoon, and it hadn't done a lick of good. He'd tried to convince Ben he was crazy to come to something like this, where he could see the girl but couldn't talk to her, couldn't even let on he knew her. It would be torture, but Ben just wouldn't listen to reason. In the three months since he'd first seen the Wade girl, he hadn't talked about anything else, and he wasn't about to pass up an opportunity to see her again, even if looking was all he'd get to do.

The two men took their punch and moved to a far corner where they could observe the people coming and going in the room. Ben stared intently at the door while Johnny glowered at the occupants of the room.

Suddenly Johnny sucked in a ragged breath. "My God, there she is."

"Where?"

"Over by the punch table," he said, turning in the opposite direction and draining his punch cup.

Ben looked and looked. "There's nobody over there but Mr. and Mrs. Hoskins."

"That's who I mean. *Her.* Mrs. Hoskins."

Ben looked at the Hoskinses again and then

back at Johnny's expression of profound misery. "Have you got an itch for Miriam Hoskins?" he asked incredulously.

The unflappable Johnny McGee turned crimson and tried to take a drink. Finding his cup empty, he cursed softly and glared at Ben, who was beginning to look very amused.

" 'If they put your brains in a jaybird, he'd fly backwards,' " Ben quoted gleefully. " 'There's a million girls in the world. Why did you pick the one girl you sure as hell can't have?' Good Lord, Johnny, at least Molly's single!"

"Shut up," Johnny hissed, but Ben wasn't about to be discouraged, not after having listened to Johnny's warnings for the past three months.

"You want to meet her? I'll introduce you," Ben offered, taking another look at Mrs. Hoskins. The years had been kind to her, that was certain. When he had known her, she had been just a girl, but she hadn't changed much. She was still slender as a reed, willowy and graceful and pretty as a picture. No, he amended, she was beautiful, the way only a mature woman can be beautiful. Marriage had improved her, especially a marriage to the richest man in the county. Franklin Hoskins owned the bank and several of the stores in town and even a ranch, although rumor had it he had turned the ranch over to his son, Harry, a while back. Hoskins had taken good care of his bride, if the silk dress she was wearing was any indication. She made all the other women in the room look dowdy by comparison, although they, too, were rigged out in their Sunday best.

"Go to h— You *know* her?" Johnny asked.

"Of course I know her. She used to be my teacher in school."

"Liar! She's too young."

Ben glanced back at the lady in question and decided it *would* be hard to believe. "Oh, she's not much older than I am, probably about your age. Even so, she was my teacher the last year I went to school. In fact," he went on with delight, having recalled a delicious detail with which to taunt his friend, "my father courted her before she married Hoskins. She might have been my *mother!*"

Johnny winced, but Ben was merciless. "See, you never would have stood a chance with her. She likes older men."

"Yeah, and rich ones, too," Johnny added bitterly.

Ben clapped Johnny on the back. "Come on, let's see if we can't find you somebody just as pretty. Somebody with bad eyes, too, who won't notice how ugly you are," he added, hoping to tease Johnny out of his despondency. A fine pair they made, Ben reflected as he pretended to search the crowd for this mythical nearsighted girl. That was when he saw Molly.

She had just come in with her family. The four of them were hovering in the doorway, waiting to be acknowledged. Molly had taken off her bonnet, so now he could see that the years had turned her yellow hair the color of raw honey. It was still as thick and lustrous as he remembered, even more so now that the childish braids had been replaced by a grown-up style. Her blue eyes were eager, hopeful. He imagined her life at home with Elijah Wade was far from pleasant, and the prospect of a dance would be one very bright spot in an otherwise dull existence. Ben's lips drew back into an unconscious smile.

Molly nervously smoothed the material of her dress, her best dress, and glanced around. She had been attending these dances ever since she could remember, but until recently they had been no more than interesting diversions for her. In the past year or so, however, everything had changed. Suddenly she wasn't a little girl anymore, hanging around the fringes of activity. Now she was a young lady who found herself very much in demand as a dancing partner. All the eligible young men sought her out and even argued over who would have the honor of her company. In a country where simply being young and female was quite enough, Molly was pretty into the bargain, and she had found to her amazement that she was considered a prize.

"The other girls are looking at you," Julie reported.

"They'll probably be counting how many different men I dance with and gossiping about it," Molly said with dismay.

"I'll be counting, too, so I can tell you later," Julie said with a conspiratorial smile.

"You'll warn me if I'm flirting too much, won't you?"

Julie nodded vigorously. "Pa'll let you know, too, I reckon."

"That's why I want you to tell me first, so I won't have to listen to him ranting and raving about how I carried on."

"Oh, he won't mind so long as you're carrying on with Harry Hoskins."

Molly frowned. "He never has anything good to say about anyone else. This fellow's lazy, and that one is worthless. The only one he likes is Harry."

"He doesn't like *Harry*," Julie corrected. "He likes Harry's money and Harry's ranch and Harry's father's bank."

"I know." Molly sighed.

"I guess we're lucky Harry likes you."

"Yes, we are." Ever since they had discovered Harry's interest in Molly, he had assumed the role of rescuer, at least in Julie's mind. The girl dreamed of the day Molly married Harry and took Julie away to live with them.

"Ask him about his house tonight," Julie urged. "Find out if he has a room for me."

"I . . . I will," Molly promised. Dutifully, she scanned the crowd for Harry. That was when she saw Ben.

He was staring at her with such intensity, the hairs on the back of her neck prickled. Oh, dear heaven, why was he here? And why was he looking straight at her?

"Now what in the hell is *he* doing here?"

Molly jumped guiltily, imagining for one horrible moment her father was addressing her.

"So far, he's just standing around, looking," replied the man to whom he was speaking.

"Well, he'd better not try to do anything more than look," her father grumbled, and then he and his companion wandered off.

Molly suddenly realized Julie was holding her arm in a white-knuckled grip. "Oh, Molly," she whispered, "Ben Cantrell is here. He came to see you. I know he did."

"Hush!" Molly hissed back, praying no one had heard her.

Their mother hurried over to them. "Do you girls see that boy over there, the tall one with yellow hair?"

Julie had the presence of mind to look puzzled. "Which one, Mama?"

"The tall, blond one in the brown shirt, over in the corner. Ben Cantrell. You might remember him from school, though he's changed some." Mrs. Wade sighed, her nervous hands fluttering in a warning motion. "Now listen, you girls stay away from him. If he tries to talk to you, just walk away, pretend like you don't hear him. You understand?"

Molly understood perfectly, but Julie asked, "Why? What's he done?"

Mrs. Wade looked pained. "It's not him, it's his pa. They hanged him, remember?" She glanced surreptitiously in her husband's direction and continued in a fervent whisper. "Your pa'll be real mad if you have anything to do with him."

"But it's not fair," Julie whined, and Molly

realized her sister was speaking on her behalf. "He's the best-looking boy here. All the other girls will get to dance with him."

Mrs. Wade shook her head vigorously. "No, he won't dare. None of the other girls will be allowed to dance with him, either."

Molly took a deep breath and asked the question to which she dreaded hearing the answer. "What would happen if he did ask someone?"

"I reckon some of the men would . . ." She gestured vaguely with her hand.

"Would what?" Molly insisted.

Mrs. Wade shook her head. "I'm not sure, but they'd teach him a lesson, not to come around respectable people. They might even horsewhip him."

Molly felt the blood rush from her head, and Julie's hand tightened reassuringly on her arm again. She would have to be careful, so careful. If she even so much as smiled at him, if he thought for one minute she liked him and decided to take a chance . . . Molly shuddered.

The music was starting up, and the young men were seeking partners. Molly did not dare glance over to see if Ben had moved. Instead, she accepted the first offer she received and moved woodenly to join one of the forming sets. By rote, her hands and feet went through the motions of the dance, and her lips smiled stiffly. When that dance was over, she went from one partner to the next, through dance after dance, never allowing herself so much as a glance at Ben Cantrell.

Much later she managed a moment alone with Julie. "What's he been doing?" she asked.

"He's just been watching," Julie said, knowing instantly who "he" was. "He hasn't asked anybody to dance or anything. He just stands there. I don't think anybody else has noticed, but I'm pretty sure he's watching you."

Molly barely stifled a groan, although she couldn't help the warm glow Julie's theory gave her. She was foolish to think he had come tonight, had risked the displeasure of the whole community, just to see her, just to watch her dance with other men. She would let Julie think it, though. After all, Julie was a child and tended to be overly romantic.

"I'm glad he's not dancing with anyone else," Molly said, and then blushed at Julie's knowing grin. "I mean, I don't want to see him get in trouble," she amended. Julie's grin never wavered. Harry Hoskins came over then and asked Molly for a waltz, so she had no further opportunity to convince Julie of her unconcern.

Molly knew she should have been glad Harry Hoskins had finally claimed her. She also knew she should smile at him and say something clever, but instead she asked, "Did you know Ben Cantrell is here?"

Harry seemed a little startled at her distress. "Did he say anything to you?"

"No, oh, no," Molly assured him hastily, recalling her mother's prediction of the trouble Ben would be in if he did such a thing. "It's just, I saw him, and . . . well, I've never seen him at a dance before, not since his father . . ."

Harry nodded. "A lot of people don't approve of his being here."

Molly looked up at Harry, really looked at him. Not as tall as Ben, he was still taller than average. His dark brown hair curled slightly, giving him a rakish air, and his brown eyes always twinkled with laughter. He was certainly attractive, but Molly found him more pretty than handsome, and he seemed soft, somehow, not strong like Ben. Was that good or bad?

"I think it's terrible the way people treat Ben," Molly heard herself saying, and noted with alarm the way Harry's eyebrows rose in surprise.

"His father was a murderer, or so they say."

"Do *you* say so?"

"Molly," Harry explained patiently, "Mr. Cantrell had argued with the man. They'd had a bitter, ugly fight, in front of witnesses. The next night, the man's barn is burned. When he came out and caught the burner in the act, he was killed. Who else could have done it? The man didn't have another enemy in the world."

"What if it was somebody who wanted Mr. Cantrell to get the blame?" Molly asked, voicing aloud for the first time an idea that had haunted her for a long time.

"Why would somebody want to do a thing like that?"

"Maybe somebody who wanted to see him dead, maybe somebody who wanted his land . . ." She stopped, wondering if Harry knew she had described her own father.

"Why would somebody go to all that trouble? Why not just kill Cantrell outright if he was the one this mysterious person wanted to get rid of?"

"Because," Molly insisted, certain she was more than a little right, "if he killed Mr. Cantrell and then took his land, people would figure it out, but if he fixed it so Mr. Cantrell got killed another way, a legal way, no one would ever suspect."

Harry stared at her for a long moment. "Did you know my father holds a mortgage on the Cantrell land?"

Molly gasped in surprise at the implication of his question. "No, no, I didn't. I'm sorry, I didn't mean . . ." Again she stopped, unwilling to admit she had just accused Harry's father of murder. It would be bad enough if Harry had known she was actually thinking of her own father.

They danced on in silence until she found the courage to say, "I still don't think it's right for people to blame Ben. After all, whether his father was guilty or not, he didn't do anything."

Harry smiled down at her tolerantly. "You're a very soft-hearted girl, Molly. That's one of the things I like about you. Now if I can just get you to start feeling sorry for *me* instead of for every Tom, Dick and Har—Ben who comes along.''

"You aren't exactly the type of person people usually feel sorry for, Harry Hoskins.''

Harry assumed an injured expression. "I'll bet every man in this room would feel sorry for me if they knew that while I was dancing with the prettiest girl here, all she could talk about was some other fellow. Sometimes I think you're still mad at me for dipping your pigtails in the ink-well.''

Molly made herself smile. In truth, she sometimes still was mad at him for that. "You ruined my dress.''

"Your hair, too, as I remember. I always regretted spoiling your hair. It grew in even prettier, though,'' he remarked with offhanded charm.

Molly hadn't forgotten he had just referred to her as the prettiest girl in the room, either, and she felt herself warming to him, forgetting what a mischievous little boy he had been. He wasn't Ben Cantrell, but he was very nice all the same. Besides, if she couldn't dance with the best-looking man in the room, she should be grateful for the second-best-looking one. She gave him a small conciliatory smile.

"Can we go home now?'' Johnny asked Ben in exasperation. At first he thought Ben had not even heard him. His friend was still watching the Wade girl, and Johnny had to admit she was worth watching, especially the way she glided around the floor with the Hoskins boy. They made a nice couple, what with him all slicked up like an advertisement in a Monkey Ward's catalog and her looking good enough to eat. But watching them couldn't be easy for Ben, and Johnny was starting to think they'd better get out of there before Ben did something stupid.

Ben hadn't heard Johnny's request to leave. He was too busy remembering with satisfaction the time he had beat up Harry Hoskins for dipping Molly's pigtails in the inkwell. Funny, he'd forgotten all about it until this minute. He couldn't even remember why he'd done it, why he'd felt duty-bound to defend Molly. She had been nothing to him then except another little girl in a school full of them. But she'd looked so sad when she'd come to school the next day with her hair hacked off short and the back of her dress stained black, and Harry had laughed at her.

Ben had known better than to pick on Harry, having been beaten by him more than once, but this time he hadn't taken time to think. He'd just mowed into Harry and had the very satisfying experience of blackening his eye before the teacher broke them up. Pa hadn't even whipped him for fighting in school when he'd heard the reason for it.

"Ben," Johnny tried again, jarring Ben back to the present. "Let's get out of here."

Ben nodded absently, knowing Johnny was right. They had overstayed their welcome, and people were starting to look askance at the two nattily dressed men who had stood watching them all night. The music stopped, and Hoskins tucked Molly's hand into the crook of his arm and led her over to the punch table. Ben wondered for the thousandth time what it was about the way Molly moved that was so wonderful.

She turned slightly away from Hoskins to take a sip of her punch, and her gaze clashed with Ben's. He knew instinctively she had been looking for him, even though she had very carefully avoided him all night. Those big blue eyes widened even further, and the punch cup paused, resting against her sweet little mouth. It would be sweet, too. Ben was sure of it.

Oh, Ben, Molly's heart cried in that one brief moment of communion. He really had been watching her, just as Julie had suspected. She was sure because she had felt his eyes on her all evening and because he did not look the least bit surprised now. Oh, Ben, I'm sorry. Quickly, before anyone could notice where she was looking or why, she turned back to Harry, smiling at whatever he was saying although she hadn't heard one word.

"Let's go," Ben snapped, jealousy burning like a hot iron into his soul. Johnny had been right; he never should have come. Ben was halfway to the door before Johnny could close his mouth and catch up.

Muttering imprecations against people who couldn't make up their minds, Johnny followed Ben out to where their horses were tied. At least

Ben had learned his lesson, Johnny reflected. They wouldn't ever have to go through something like this again. Johnny hadn't enjoyed it, either, having to watch Mrs. Hoskins being fussed over by her husband. It was one thing to admire somebody from afar. It was quite another to be held captive in the same room and have your nose rubbed into the fact that you just weren't good enough to merit a glance.

Unfortunately Johnny had underestimated Ben's capacity for pain. As much as Ben hated the thought of it, as many times as he called himself a fool for doing it, he went to the next dance and the next and the next. Spring became summer and changed to fall. Winter dragged by, and when warm weather made socializing convenient once more, he went again.

Molly changed little as the months went by, except to grow progressively more lovely. Occasionally their eyes would meet across the room, and Ben would imagine he saw sadness in hers. Johnny had tried to tell him he was a fool to think Molly Wade would regret not being courted by the town outcast. Johnny alternately cursed him up and down and tried to reason with him. Neither approach did any good.

In the spring they took a herd up the trail and sold it in Dodge City. Ben had a mortgage payment due, or at least that was the excuse he used. Actually he had more than enough money cached to pay the mortgage three times over, but he didn't like for people to know he was well off. They already had enough reason to hate him.

Besides, he got a kick out of making Mr. Hoskins
at the bank think he was barely scraping by. For
some reason the old goat seemed almost disappointed each year when Ben came in to make his
payment, and Ben enjoyed disappointing him.
He had not forgotten Hoskins had been in the
posse that had hanged his father.

Johnny hoped the trip to Dodge would help
Ben get Molly Wade out of his system. Indeed,
Ben hardly mentioned her in all the three months
it took them to get there. Johnny had high hopes
until they arrived at the Pleasure Palace, and Ben
picked a girl with hair the color of raw honey.
She wasn't nearly as pretty as Molly Wade, but
even a blind man could see the resemblance.
Johnny was so disgusted he almost forgot why
they'd come.

Chapter Three

+ + + + +

"THEY SAY HE'S going to marry her," Johnny said.

He and Ben were watching Harry Hoskins
waltz Molly around the schoolhouse floor. Fall
had stripped the leaves from the trees, and their
trip to Dodge was fading to a dim memory. This
time when Ben had announced his intention to
attend the dance, Johnny didn't even bother to

argue. He'd heard a rumor he thought might have the power to bring Ben to his senses at last.

"*Who* says he's going to marry her?" Ben asked.

"Folks," Johnny replied vaguely. "Look at them if you don't believe me."

Ben *was* looking. Molly had always been popular, never sitting out a single dance, and Harry Hoskins always claimed more than his fair share of those dances. Something had changed, though, and even Ben could see it. Now Hoskins was claiming her for practically every other dance, and he did so as if it were his right.

Still, Ben couldn't believe she was going to marry him. In spite of Harry's proprietary air, something about the way Molly looked at him was wrong. That day in the store, a day almost a year and a half ago, she had looked at Ben quite differently. The moment was branded into his memory, and to the last day he lived, he would never forget the expression in her eyes. He did not see that expression when she looked at Hoskins. No, Molly wasn't going to marry Harry Hoskins, not if Ben had anything to say about it.

Molly knew Ben was watching her. She had forgotten how disconcerting he could be. In the months since he'd left for Kansas, she'd even managed to convince herself she really didn't love him, but the way her heart lurched when she first saw him come in tonight proved otherwise.

She was having a difficult time concentrating

on anything but Ben's presence, and to her dismay she discovered her distraction had allowed Harry to start in on the topic she least wanted to discuss.

"Not many men my age own their own ranch," he was saying. "Of course, it won't really be legally mine until I marry, but for all practical purposes, I own it already."

He was hinting again. Molly could have groaned aloud. "Why doesn't your father just go ahead and give you the ranch?"

"I told you, he wants me to get married, the sooner the better."

"But why?" she insisted. "I mean, you're still young. Surely you don't want to get tied down yet."

A shadow flickered across Harry's face. "Can't you guess why, Molly? I thought everybody knew. As soon as my father noticed I was a man, he sent me out to the ranch to live. He couldn't stand to have me in the same house with Miriam."

"Miriam? You mean . . . you and Miriam . . .?" she asked, shocked.

"Of course not," Harry snapped. "We were friends, but my father is insanely jealous of her. He . . . " He paused, getting hold of his temper with visible effort. "Anyway, my father felt that if I were safely married, I would cease to be a threat, so he's holding ownership of the ranch out to me like a carrot on a stick."

"Oh, Harry, I'm sorry."

"Don't be sorry. I'm really very lucky, all things considered. When I own the ranch, I'll be free of the old bas—the old man once and for all." He smiled provocatively. "Now if I can just find the right girl to share it with me . . ."

"I hope you do," she replied, fighting a surge of panic. Hinting, he was always hinting, and she knew she was an idiot to hesitate. As Harry's wife she would have everything she'd always dreamed of, a nice home, pretty clothes, and a husband everyone respected. Most of all, she'd have a place for Julie to live, a place where they could both be safe. Then why did the prospect frighten her so much?

Harry frowned at her expression. "I never should have let you start talking about love. Really, Molly, you set too much store by it. We like each other, and we get along fine. That's more than most married people have. We'll learn to love each other."

Molly gave him a rueful smile. The first time Harry had proposed, she'd waited in vain for a declaration of undying devotion. Although Harry thought she was the prettiest girl in Texas and was more than eager to have her share his life and his bed, he didn't love her. In fact, he didn't set much store in love at all, and his arguments made more sense than she liked to admit. Still, she hadn't quite been able to completely accept his logic, so he'd started trying to convince her they would come to love each other in time. She wanted to believe him, but how much time would have to pass before she felt the same longing for Harry she had always felt for Ben Cantrell?

The dance ended, but Harry did not release her hand. "I'll get you some punch," he said, leading her over to the table.

"Thank you," she murmured, wondering why she felt so resentful of his gentlemanly offer. Perhaps it was because he never asked. He always said "I'll get you this or that," not "Would you like something?" or "You're cold," not "Are you cold?" and "It's late. I'll take you home," instead of "Are you ready to leave yet?" Any other girl would have been thrilled at his solicitude. Why did Molly find it stifling?

"Are you young folks having a good time?"

Molly jumped at her father's question.

"Yes, sir, we are," Harry replied. "If you don't mind, I'd like to drive Molly home after the dance."

"Don't mind a bit," Elijah said, giving Molly a warning glance. She tensed at the alcoholic glitter in his overbright eyes, but she easily read his silent message. For reasons she had not yet fathomed, her father desperately wanted Harry Hoskins as a son-in-law, and he expected Molly to do her part.

Everyone, it seemed, wanted her to marry Harry. Harry wanted it so he could get his ranch. Julie wanted it so she could have a home. Her father wanted it for God only knew what. Why couldn't Molly want it, too?

As Harry ladled out some punch, Molly glanced around the room, easily finding Ben Cantrell in a far corner. He was still watching her, and the expression on his face sent a shiver of apprehension up her spine. He wanted her, too. Dear heaven, didn't anyone care what *she* wanted?

Harry claimed her for the next dance, a rousing reel that fortunately made conversation impossible. When it was over she excused herself to go outside, but instead of heading for the privy, she sought the solitude of the dark shadows at the rear of the schoolhouse.

Here the crowd noise was a dull rumble, and she breathed deeply of the cool night air. Overhead, the stars twinkled serenely, mocking her own turmoil.

"Molly?"

Molly gasped as Ben Cantrell materialized out of the darkness. "What . . . what are you doing here?"

"Looking for you. Are you meeting someone?"

"No! I . . . I just wanted to be alone for a minute." Molly placed a hand over her racing heart. Her breath snagged in her throat as he moved closer.

"I've been watching you with Harry."

"I know."

"They say you're going to marry him."

"They do?" she asked in alarm. Were people gossiping about it already?

"Yes, they do. Are you?" He sounded angry.

"I . . . I don't think that's any of your business, Ben Cantrell."

"Maybe it is my business, Molly Wade," he mocked.

"Why would it be?" Her heart was pounding now, and her breath came in quick gasps.

"Because maybe I've had my eye on you, too, and maybe I thought you liked me more than a little. Maybe I thought that some-day—"

"Ben!" she pleaded.

In the next instant his arms were around her, rough and insistent. A startled sound escaped her lips, but he smothered it with his own. Terror boiled up in her like a tidal wave.

"No!" she cried, breaking free.

"Molly!" Her name was a supplication, full of agony and despair, stopping her flight.

"I . . . you frightened me," she accused breathlessly.

"I'm sorry." This time his hands were gentle as they reached for her. This time his lips were tender, barely touching hers, teasing and tasting and tormenting. Her fear transformed into the tingling tremors of excitement.

He breathed her name. Timidly she lifted her hands to his shoulders. His arms tightened around her, and his mouth opened over hers, hot and urgent. Terror surged again, but when she struggled, he didn't let her go. "Now are you going to marry him?" Ben demanded.

"Molly? Molly, where are you?" Harry called from the other side of the building.

Molly looked up at Ben. Fear and desire warred for preeminence.

"Are you?" His hands tightened on her arms, hurting her, and panic surged again.

"Yes!"

She jerked free and ran.

Stunned, Ben watched her go. What a fool he was! Did he think one kiss would work a miracle? Did he think she could forget he was the town outcast? Did he think she would come to him when she could have the son of the richest man in town? All that dreaming and mooning over her must have softened his brain.

He stood there for a long time, absorbing the pain of her rejection and cursing his own stupidity. When Johnny found him, he was almost calm again.

"You were right, Johnny," he said. "I never should have kept coming to these dances."

"You mean—"

"I'm through acting like a gold-plated idiot. Let's get out of here."

Johnny gave a silent sigh of relief. He wanted to know what had changed Ben's mind but decided this was probably not a good time to inquire. "I'm right behind you, partner," he said, and followed Ben into the night.

*   *   *

"Charge it to my account," Ben told the store-keeper's wife as he started to pick up the last bag of flour to carry out to his wagon.

"Are you boys going to the box social on Saturday next?" Mrs. Wells asked.

Ben glanced at Johnny, who was standing in the doorway of the store waiting for him. Johnny refused to meet his eye, so Ben looked back at Mrs. Wells. She was a small, stout woman with bright eyes and a perpetual smile. "No, we hadn't heard about it. What's a box social, anyway?"

Mrs. Wells laughed her astonishment. "I guess it's been a while since we've had one around here if you can't recollect it. A box social is when all the women and girls make box suppers and the men bid on them. The highest bidder gets to eat supper with the girl or woman whose box it is. We're trying to raise money for the school. Miss Ferguson, the new schoolmarm, has lots of fancy ideas for new books and such. The social was her idea, although most folks think it was a good one."

"I'm sure it is," Ben agreed, glancing at Johnny again. Surely his friend knew about the social. Johnny was the biggest gossip in the county. Why hadn't he said anything?

"You boys come along," Mrs. Wells urged. "We can always use two extra men."

"Maybe we will," Ben said, hoisting his flour sack. "Afternoon, Mrs. Wells."

"Good day to you both," she called as they left the store.

Squinting in the bright spring sunlight, Ben caught Johnny's sheepish expression before his friend turned away and headed toward the buckboard into which they had just loaded six months' worth of supplies. Johnny had known about the social all right.

"You ever been to a box social?" Ben asked idly. He hefted the flour sack onto the top of the pile in the back of the wagon and began adjusting the tarp to cover it all.

"Sure," Johnny replied too casually. "We had lots of 'em back in Uvalde. Big Jim Harris's daughters were good cooks, and they figured it was a good way to trap a man."

Ben tied down the tarp and moved around to the wagon seat. "Funny we hadn't heard about this one. The way you keep up with news, I'd've thought you'd know all about it."

Ben waited until Johnny had climbed up onto the seat before doing so himself. When Ben had the reins in his hands, Johnny cleared his throat uncomfortably. "Oh, I reckon I must've heard about it. I guess it just slipped my mind."

Ben released the brake and slapped the team into motion. "Johnny, I'm over Molly," he lied. "Didn't I stay away from her all winter? I'm not going to make a fool of myself anymore, so you can stop acting like a mother hen."

"I wasn't worried about you. I was worried about me."

"You? What've you got to be worried about?"

"Well, at a box social, a fellow can bid on a woman's box, and then he gets to spend some time with her. Don't forget, you ain't the only one who's had his eye on a filly he can't have."

"Good God almighty," Ben muttered. "You wouldn't be crazy enough to bid on Mrs. Hoskins's box, would you?"

"I don't know, so I figured I better not take the chance." Johnny's obvious misery made Ben sorry he had accused his friend of being a mother hen.

They rode on for several miles. Johnny rolled a couple of cigarettes, and they smoked in companionable silence as they passed first the Hoskins ranch and then the Wade place. As always, the road to the Flying W ranch made Ben think of Molly with her huge blue eyes and her honey-colored hair and her vital woman's body.

Even the months away from her had not dimmed his memories. Molly was like no other girl he had ever known, and in spite of his determination to forget her, she still haunted his dreams and turned up with alarming frequency in his waking thoughts, too. She was, he knew, something unique and special, although he could not have said in what way.

"She ain't engaged yet," Johnny remarked.

"Who?"

"Molly Wade. I saw you mooning when we passed her road," Johnny explained with some disgust. "I don't know if Harry hasn't asked her yet or if she hasn't said 'yes' yet, but I do know they ain't announced anything."

Ben couldn't believe it. He could still hear her

desperate "yes" echoing in his head all these months later. She had seemed so determined, so sure. Why hadn't Harry asked her? What was he waiting for? And if he had, why weren't they engaged? Could Molly have turned him down after all?

Ben smiled slowly, unconsciously. "So you say that at a box social, any man who bids on a girl's box gets to eat supper with her?"

"It sounds immoral!" Molly objected with a frown. "Almost like the fellow is *buying* you!"

Daisy Ferguson smiled knowingly. "Yes, it does. Isn't it deliciously wicked?"

Molly wasn't so sure. She had an idea her father would think the whole thing was just plain ordinary wicked and put a stop to it instantly—or at least make sure she and Julie didn't participate. Molly studied the new schoolteacher for a long moment, noting the mischievous gleam in her green eyes. The two girls were sprawled on Daisy's bed in their nightdresses, enjoying their privacy in Daisy's rented room where Molly had come to spend the night with her new friend. "You say you've done this before?"

Daisy nodded, her bright red curls bouncing enthusiastically.

"What did the preacher there say about such goings-on?"

"He loved it. We raised enough money to put a new roof on the church."

"I hope Reverend Bates is that broad-minded," Molly said doubtfully.

"He will be," Daisy assured her, waving away Molly's concern with a flick of her elegant hand. Molly so admired Daisy's polish and sophistication. Although the schoolteacher was only a year older, she struck Molly as having decades more experience. Molly knew Daisy had benefited from a finishing school education. What Molly couldn't figure out was why a girl with so many advantages would have come all the way to west Texas to teach school for twenty-five dollars a month.

"I don't like to brag," Daisy was saying in the well-modulated voice Molly envied, "but at the social I was telling you about, my box brought five dollars."

"Five dollars!" Molly exclaimed.

"Yes, five dollars. Nobody else's brought anywhere near as much." Daisy hugged her pillow and sighed. "I wonder if anyone around here has that kind of money."

"Harry does," Molly replied.

"Harry isn't going to bid on anyone's box but yours," Daisy scoffed. "That man is absolutely devoted to you. I can't understand why he hasn't already proposed."

"He's . . . well, I've asked him to wait a while," Molly said uneasily.

"Wait? Whatever for?"

"We're both young. I'm not eighteen yet, and—"

"Do you want to die an old maid? Harry might get tired of waiting, you know. One of your friends might steal him out from under your nose," she warned with an impish grin. "Besides, he gets a ranch as a wedding present."

"How did you know that?"

"Everybody knows. You're crazy not to snap him up. Men are fickle. Best get his ring on your finger as quick as you can."

Molly frowned as she considered Daisy's advice. Julie had been telling her the same thing for months, and her father had become almost irrational on the subject. If he ever found out *she* was the one who was dragging her feet, he'd make their lives a living hell.

Ignoring the lump of apprehension forming in her stomach, Molly changed the subject. "So who do you hope bids on your box?"

"I haven't decided yet, but I saw the handsomest fellow in the mercantile this morning. He was tall and blond, and he had shoulders as broad as a barn door. And his eyes! I never saw eyes so blue, like the sky when the sun comes out just after it's rained."

Molly smiled, but her lips felt stiff. Daisy's description sounded altogether too familiar. "Did you find out his name?"

"Mrs. Wells called him Ben. Do you know who he is?"

"Ben Cantrell," Molly said, no longer able to keep her smile in place as she remembered their last meeting. "He probably won't be at the social."

"Why not?" Daisy demanded in outrage. "How do you know?"

"Because he's . . . because of his father," Molly hedged. Briefly she told Daisy the story of Sam Cantrell's lynching.

"But that was years ago. Surely people don't hold it against him."

"Some do," Molly said, thinking of her father.

"No young women do, I'll bet." The sparkle was back in Daisy's green eyes, and Molly tasted the bile of pure, unadulterated jealousy.

"He used to come to the dances sometimes, but he doesn't socialize anymore," Molly warned, knowing that if Ben did show up at the social and Daisy got to dance with him, Molly would just die.

Oblivious to Molly's concerns, Daisy smiled smugly. "I bet he'll socialize with me."

"I feel like a jackass in the wrong stall," Johnny complained as they joined the crowd already gathered at the schoolhouse for the box social.

"You say that every time," Ben reminded him.

"It's true every time," Johnny grumbled. "I don't know why I let you talk me into this."

"I didn't talk you into anything. I told you you could stay home if you wanted."

"Oh, yeah, stay home and let you get into God only knows what kind of trouble."

Ben sighed impatiently. "I'm a grown man, Johnny. You don't have to hold my hand every-where we go."

"Even a grown man can act like a fool where a woman's concerned," Johnny replied, and the shadows in his brown eyes reminded Ben that Johnny spoke from personal experience. "There's plenty of folks around here who'd like nothing better than a good reason to run you out of town on a rail."

"Maybe I'll give them one tonight."

Johnny groaned, but he followed Ben into the schoolhouse, where the women were stacking their boxes on the raised platform at the front of the room. The smell of fried chicken and freshly baked bread was almost overpowering. Molly Wade was the first person Ben saw.

He hadn't seen her in months, and she stood with her back to him, but he still would have known her anywhere. She was wearing a blue dress and her lovely amber hair was pinned up, exposing a length of alabaster neck above her high collar. For a minute he simply stared.

Molly nervously smoothed down the skirt of her new dress and shared a look of suppressed excitement with Daisy Ferguson.

"You look lovely," Daisy assured her. "I can't believe you made that dress yourself."

Molly couldn't, either. The dress was the most beautiful thing she had ever owned. The blue watered floral print matched the blue of her eyes exactly, and the soft cotton fabric clung faithfully to her tightly laced curves. Although the style was the traditional "wrapper" and not anything fashionable like Daisy's moss-green bustled gown, Molly had used a new pattern this time, one that featured the flattering Watteau pleats in both the front and back and gave the dress an elegant fullness. From her white eyelet neck ruffle to the toes of her new high-button shoes, Molly felt totally gorgeous.

"My father almost had apoplexy when he found out I needed ten yards of material for it," Molly confided.

"It serves him right," Daisy said. "After all, he was the one who decided you needed a new dress to bring Harry up to scratch."

Molly winced. She knew tonight was the night. She couldn't put Harry off any longer without taking the risk of losing him. She had to think of Julie, and maybe if she pleased her father by marrying Harry, things would get better for her mother. Even Harry would be happy because he would get the ranch and the freedom he wanted so badly. Everyone would be pleased by her engagement. Why did the thought terrify her so?

"How does my hair look?" she asked Daisy, placing a hand over the anxious flutter in her stomach.

"It looks fine," Daisy said, but Molly barely heard as she considered the ordeal ahead of her.

Suddenly Julie appeared beside them. *"He's here!"* she announced, her eyes wide with apprehension.

"Harry?" Molly asked, wondering why Harry's appearance would have alarmed her sister.

"No, *Ben Cantrell!*"

Daisy's face lit up like someone had struck a match inside her head. "He is? Where?"

But she had already found him, standing with his friend Johnny by the door. "Oh, he's looking this way," Daisy exclaimed in an excited whisper, flashing the two men a radiant smile.

Molly turned cautiously, as aware of Ben's presence as if he had sent a bolt of electricity streaking across the room toward her. Yes, there he was, looking more handsome than ever, if such a thing were possible. He was wearing a bright yellow double-breasted shirt with mother-of-pearl buttons and brown nankeen pants. His hair looked like spun gold in the fading rays of the sun, and he held a spanking-white Stetson in his hand.

"Julie, take me over and introduce me," Daisy said, grabbing the younger girl by the arm.

"I couldn't!" Julie insisted, digging in her heels when Daisy would have used force. "I can't talk to Ben Cantrell. My pa would skin me alive!"

"Molly, you know him, don't you?" Daisy entreated, but Molly only shook her head, unable to speak because of the constriction in her throat. Ben *was* looking their way, straight at Molly, and all she could think was that Daisy had been right about the color of his eyes. They were as bright and blue as the cloudless Texas sky.

"Oh, sweet Savior," Molly murmured. She wanted to shout at Ben, tell him to leave, tell him not to do whatever it was that had brought the strange, determined glitter to his beautiful eyes. Would he try to talk to her again? Would he try to kiss her? Oh, please don't, Ben! her mind cried, but her heart said something entirely different.

"He's still looking at you," Julie whispered.

"Let's go outside," Molly said to Daisy, who was watching Ben with eager interest.

"Why?" she asked, her green eyes narrowed in concentration. "I want to see what Mr. Cantrell intends to do, and he certainly looks like he intends to do *something*."

"I'll go outside with you, Molly," Julie offered, taking her sister's arm much as Daisy had taken hers moments before. Molly balked when she realized their course would take them directly past where Ben stood, but Daisy made the same discovery at the same instant and changed her mind about accompanying the Wade sisters.

"Well, if you won't introduce me to him, at least I can pique his interest," Daisy announced, grasping Molly's free arm and starting for the door.

Molly had no choice except to follow. She felt the color coming to her cheeks even as the blood rushed from her head. The air inside the schoolhouse seemed to evaporate as her lungs strained for breath. Dear heaven, he wasn't even going to step out of their way! He stood his ground, his long legs braced as if expecting a fight or a challenge and his broad shoulders squared with the same determination glimmering in his eyes.

Closer and closer they came, until Molly had to lift her chin to maintain eye contact. Her heart quivered like a dying bird. Her knees grew rubbery and threatened to give way, but somehow they continued to function, carrying her closer still.

Then, to her eternal amazement, his finely molded lips twitched and then stretched into the most tantalizing smile Molly had ever seen.

"Hello, Molly," he said. His voice was deep, like the rumble of distant thunder warning of the storm to come.

The sound shook her to her toes. Her heart turned over in her chest and quit beating altogether, and her breath seemed permanently lodged somewhere beneath it. But in spite of all that, her own lips somehow trembled into an answering smile. "Hello, Ben."

Julie yanked her arm, and in the next second they were past him, on their way out the door.

"Good heavens," Daisy said a little breathlessly. "Did you see the way he was looking at you, Molly?"

Oh, yes, she had seen. "He was only being friendly. We knew each other in school."

"Pshaw! If a man ever looked at me like that, I'd curl up and die! You sly thing, Molly Wade. Do you have *two* fellows on your string?"

"I don't know what you're talking about," she said evasively. "Oh, there's Harry." Molly waved, more grateful than she could have said for an excuse to escape Daisy's questions. She hurried to Harry's side, leaving Daisy and Julie in her wake.

Ben was still grinning long after Molly was out of sight. Johnny poked him in the ribs. "Did you see the redhead? She was giving you the eye. She's the one we saw in the store the other day."

"What redhead?"

Johnny swore.

"Now, how am I supposed to tell which box is Molly's?" Ben asked, glancing at the prodigious stack of box suppers spread out at the front of the room. Several women were helping to arrange them in an orderly fashion and accepting new ones as they came in.

Johnny sighed gustily. "It ain't too hard. You look around to see which girl's blushing and trying to act unconcerned," he explained with a fatalistic air. "But I don't think you'll have to work much to figure out which one's Molly's. My guess would be the one with the bow on it that matches her dress."

Sure enough, one of the boxes sitting at the very front of the stage sported a swatch of fabric identical with the material of Molly's dress. Ben smiled. "Reckon she wanted me to know which one was hers?" he asked Johnny, who swore again.

"Let's go outside," Johnny urged. "The smell

of chicken in here is getting my stomach all excited.''

Ben was only too happy to oblige. After all, Molly was outside, wasn't she?

Molly caught sight of her father watching her and Harry with narrow-eyed calculation, so she allowed Harry to walk her a little away from the crowd. Her father wouldn't mind such a liberty tonight, not when he was expecting her to encourage Harry's proposal.

"Now how am I supposed to know which box is yours?" Harry asked, tucking her arm through his as they strolled along.

"I marked it special. It matches me." Molly's smile felt a little forced, and she hoped she sounded more enthusiastic about the evening to come than she felt. She couldn't help worrying about Ben Cantrell and wondering what he was up to. What if her father had heard him speak to her? And what if her father had heard her reply! She shuddered at the thought.

"You're cold," Harry said. "I'll take you inside."

"No, I'm fine, really," she said with irritation. Why did he always think he knew what was best for her? He was always telling her how she felt and what she wanted and what she thought, just like her father . . .

No! Harry wasn't like her father, not at all! He was nice and polite and considerate. He'd never hurt her, she was sure he wouldn't. If only he didn't try so hard to control her . . .

"How much are you going to bid for my box?" she forced herself to ask.

"Oh, I don't know," he teased. "Fifty cents?"

Molly managed a coy pout. "Daisy Ferguson said somebody back east bid five dollars for her one time."

"Oh," Harry said as if comprehension had just dawned. "For *her*. I was thinking about fried chicken, but if we're talking about how much Molly Wade is worth, well, I'll have to give this some thought. . . . *Ouch!*"

"Serves you right," Molly said, unrepentant for having pinched him. "You know what I meant."

"And you know I only meant a little of your precious company," he defended himself, rubbing his arm gingerly.

"Humph," Molly said, maintaining her outrage with effort. Flirting with Harry was hard work. Would being married to him be even harder?

"Five dollars, huh? I guess I could manage six or seven," he allowed with a placating grin. "Would that bring back your smile?"

Molly made herself smile. "I'll even save you the first dance."

"The first and last and a lot of them in between," he warned.

"All right." A cold shiver of dread raced over her, and she called herself a fool. She should be glad to marry a man like Harry. She wanted to get away from her father, didn't she? She wanted to have a house of her own and a husband and children. What was wrong with her?

But she knew what was wrong. From the corner of her eye she caught sight of Ben Cantrell watching and waiting. Awareness tingled over her. Why didn't Harry excite her the way Ben did? But Ben frightened her, too. As much as she resented Harry's domineering attitude, she feared Ben's roughness even more.

"Look, they're ready to start the auction," Harry said, directing her back toward the school.

Ben waited until Molly had gone inside with Harry. He had watched their every move, seen their every exchanged glance, and he knew beyond doubt that Molly Wade still did not love Harry Hoskins. Harry's feelings were more difficult to read, but Ben was pretty sure Harry wasn't head over heels, either. The hot wave of jealousy he had felt upon first seeing them together ebbed into a mild irritation. Harry would be a minor obstacle. Now he only had to get around Molly's father. And Molly.

"Ben, Johnny, good to see you." Ben looked up to see Mr. Wells, the storekeeper. A tall, balding man, Wells took his avocation as mayor of Hoskinsville quite seriously, and smiled almost as much as his wife did. Ben allowed him to pump his hand vigorously. "We've missed seeing you boys around. I'm glad the warm weather brought you back."

"We're not always sure of our welcome," Ben said.

"Nonsense." Wells clapped a hand on Ben's shoulder, then leaned closer and lowered his voice. "Nobody holds the past against you, Ben. . . . Well, maybe a few do," he allowed at Ben's skeptical look, "but *only* a few, and nobody pays them any mind anymore. You're as welcome here as anyone else."

"I'm glad to hear it," Ben replied, knowing he would need more than a welcome before the night was over.

"Good. I hope you plan to bid on a box supper."

"Oh, we do," replied Ben. Beside him, Johnny grunted disapprovingly, but Ben ignored him.

"Let's get inside, then," Wells urged. "Of course, they can't start without me since I'm the auctioneer."

Chuckling with him, Ben and Johnny moved toward the schoolhouse. The area just inside the door was jammed, and Ben squeezed in and stepped immediately to one side to make room for those behind him. Someone jostled him, and he in turned bumped someone else.

"Excuse me," he said, turning quickly to come face to face with Miriam Hoskins. He had taken her arm automatically to keep her from falling, and when he saw the shocked expression on her face, he thought he'd hurt her.

"Miz Hoskins? Are you all right?"

She blinked, and her dark eyes kindled with

an emotion he didn't dare name. For a moment he thought . . .

"Ben?" She blinked again. "Ben, you look so much like your father," she said breathlessly.

His father, of course. He should have known. But why would Miriam Hoskins still look so stunned to be reminded of Sam Cantrell after all this time?

Her dark eyes cleared, and he could see the effort with which she gathered her composure. "You've grown a lot since I taught you in school."

"And you haven't aged a day," he replied. She hadn't, either. In fact, she looked even better than he remembered. Franklin Hoskins had taken great care of his young bride.

"You're gallant," she said, but her voice sounded hollow. Once again her eyes clouded, and although her face was as smooth as a child's, suddenly she looked a hundred years old.

"Miriam!"

She jumped and turned abruptly away toward where her husband was standing in the crowd. "I'm coming," she called, moving with swift grace toward him. She didn't even glance back at Ben, who saw the rough way Hoskins took her arm to drag her off to the other side of the room. Over his shoulder, Hoskins sent Ben a look of such malice that Ben started. In an instant he changed his mind about the kind of care Miriam had received from her husband. Ben suspected that marrying the richest man in town hadn't brought her the happiness most girls dreamed such money will buy. Was that what Molly dreamed of? Was that why she let Harry Hoskins court her even though she didn't love him?

"What did she say to you?" Johnny demanded, having wormed his way through the crowd just in time to witness the end of Ben's little scene with Miriam.

"Nothing much. She thinks I look like my father."

"She sure jumped when her husband called her." Johnny was holding his temper with difficulty. "And did you see the way he grabbed her arm?"

"Bankers aren't known for being kind-hearted."

"Sonofabitch," Johnny muttered, watching Miriam's face pale under her husband's whispered reprimand.

But they had no further time for conjecture—the auction was starting. At Mr. Wells's command, the two sexes split up. The men clustered in the center of the room where they could better see the boxes being offered for sale. The women gathered in small groups around the edge of the room to gossip about who bid on whose box and how much each one brought. Molly stood with Daisy, Julie, and a few other girls she knew from school. Luckily they were all too giddy with anticipation to notice her lack of enthusiasm.

The initial bidding was sluggish, the men being shy and reluctant to commit themselves unless they knew to whom the box belonged. But

Mr. Wells wasn't about to let the auction flop.

"Come on, gents," he cried in mock despair, holding up the latest offering. "I can smell fried chicken and apple pie in this one, and I happen to know the lady who made it is single."

"A dollar," someone called.

"Only a dollar? Remember the children," Mr. Wells scolded. "They need new books."

"A dollar and two bits."

The crowd was warming up, and when a cowboy came forward to claim his prize and discovered he had won the company of a lady old enough to be his grandmother, everyone roared in approval. After that Mr. Wells had little trouble getting bids, and each new pairing brought another wave of raucous laughter.

Ben waited patiently, studying the crowd from his position near the back of the room. Johnny stood beside him, ready for trouble and expecting the worst to happen at any moment.

"Five dollars," came the latest bid, drawing a murmur from the crowd. No box had yet brought more than three.

"Oh, God," Johnny mumbled.

"What's wrong?"

"Will you cover my bid?"

"Cover? I thought you—"

"Will you or not?" Johnny demanded.

"Sure," Ben said, not yet realizing the implications.

"Six dollars," Johnny called, drawing the amazed attention of everyone present.

"Seven dollars!"

Ben's gaze darted to the opposite side of the room where a red-faced Franklin Hoskins stood glaring at Ben and Johnny. Ben felt the first stirrings of alarm. Despite Johnny's vows to the contrary, he had decided to bid for Miriam Hoskins.

"Eight dollars," Johnny countered, assuming the innocent expression for which whores in three states adored him.

"Do you know what you're doing?" Ben hissed.

Johnny flashed his reckless grin. "It's for the kids."

"Twenty dollars!" Hoskins called, and the crowd murmur grew momentarily deafening. Ben noticed with concern that Miriam Hoskins's perfect face had gone chalk white, and her dark eyes were glazed with what could only be called terror. Catching Ben's eye, she sent him a pleading glance that he interpreted easily.

"Twenty-five!" Johnny called before Ben could stop him.

"Fifty!" Hoskins replied, and the crowd roared its approval.

"Johnny, stop!" Ben grabbed his arm and gave it a warning shake. "Look at her face!"

He did. "Oh, shit."

"Fifty dollars is the bid," Mr. Wells was saying, obviously ill at ease with the undercurrents. "Going once, going twice . . ." He paused, and Johnny clamped his lips together to keep from raising. "Sold to Franklin Hoskins."

Although his face was still red, Hoskins managed a magnanimous smile as he stepped up to claim his prize. "It's for the children, after all," he said, waving in acknowledgment to the crowd's applause.

"Sonofabitch," Johnny muttered again, and Ben agreed wholeheartedly. A swift glance at Miriam showed she was holding on to her composure with difficulty, and Ben wondered what price she would pay for Johnny's innocent adoration. He only hoped Johnny didn't guess the extent of her terror. The poor fellow was going to be miserable enough just for having embarrassed her with his impulsiveness.

When everyone had settled down again, Wells held up the next box, and a little old lady standing near Ben's elbow announced, "That one's mine, and even though I ain't as pretty as Miz Hoskins, I got a few more years' experience cooking than she does, so I expect I oughta raise a few dollars myself."

"Five dollars," Johnny called, his grin back in place, although Ben could see it did not reach his eyes.

Ben gave Johnny an approving slap on the back, knowing his friend was trying to cover his indiscretion by pretending generosity for a worthy cause. No one raised his bid, so Johnny moved forward to claim his supper and his lady. The crowd was only too anxious to forget the awkwardness of the last bid, so they cheered him lustily, willingly accepting the fiction he had created.

Ben shook his head in admiration when

Johnny peeked into the box and whooped with delight at its contents. The fellow was a born actor.

The bidding went on and on. Two little boys went together to buy their mother's box. The redheaded schoolteacher earned twenty dollars for the cause from the spirited bidding of a dozen cowboys. Gradually the pile of boxes dwindled, and at long last Wells picked up the one with the blue bow.

Ben watched Molly's face and realized Johnny had been right: he would have known simply from her expression the box belonged to her. She looked toward Harry, who'd also had no trouble identifying the box, and her look bore the same sort of pleading Miriam Hoskins's had earlier. She knew! Somehow she knew Ben was going to bid for her, and she was asking Harry to win. Harry flashed her a reassuring smile, and then, as if drawn by the force of his will, her gaze found Ben.

He looked carefully for signs of fear, but he saw none. So much the better, Molly Wade, he thought. I'm going to have you either way.

Harry opened the bidding at five dollars, and it quickly went up to ten since the remaining cowboys also had no trouble identifying to whom the box belonged.

Molly listened with mounting anxiety. She had been a fool to put that rose on the box. The idea had seemed so clever at the time. She had fashioned the flower originally out of scraps from her dress as a hair ornament, but then she had thought of using it on her box. She intended to make things easy for Harry, but she hadn't known Ben Cantrell would be there tonight.

"Twenty dollars," Ben said, deciding to eliminate the less serious bidders quickly.

Harry was standing near the front of the room, and his head jerked around in surprise. His expression was almost comic, but he recovered quickly. "Twenty-five," he called in challenge.

"Thirty."

Molly saw movement out of the corner of her eye and turned to find her father bearing down on Ben Cantrell. Her heart jumped to her throat, but before she could cry out a warning, Reverend Bates caught her father's arm and stopped him in his tracks. She never learned what the minister said to calm the savage fury on her father's face, but whatever he said, it worked a miracle. Elijah Wade was still angry but somewhat mollified; he stepped back and observed the rest of the bidding with a jaundiced eye.

"Fifty," Harry called.

Good Lord! She must have missed some bids. How could they have gone so high without her hearing? The men had all stepped back so they could watch the two competitors, and a diagonal aisle had formed down the center of the room between Harry in the front and Ben in the back. The two were grinning at each other, oblivious to their audience.

"Fifty-five," Ben countered.

Wouldn't they ever stop? But of course they wouldn't. Neither of them would give in until one of them had spent every cent he had. She couldn't let this go on any longer. Without conscious thought, she waded into the sea of males, pushing through them almost unheeded until she reached the clear space in the center of the room. Her gaze went from Harry to Ben and back again. To which one should she appeal? Which one would be most malleable?

Her gaze settled on Harry. "Sixty," he said, and then caught sight of her, a bright splash of blue among the men's darker clothing.

"Sixty-five," Ben called, and Molly winced.

Harry opened his mouth to counter, but Molly sent him a look of abject supplication and shook her head frantically. Please don't! Oh, Harry, please don't! her heart cried. He paused, and she could see his inner struggle, but—as she had guessed—his innate gallantry won out. Not able to cause her distress, he closed his mouth and shrugged in good-natured defeat.

"The bid is sixty-five. Do I hear seventy?" Mr. Wells prodded the crowd. Harry turned back to face him and shook his head. "Sixty-five. Going once, going twice, sold to Ben Cantrell."

A lusty cheer went up around her, but Molly barely heard it through the roaring in her ears. Ben Cantrell had paid sixty-five dollars—more than two months' wages for an ordinary cowboy—just for the privilege of eating supper with her. Never in her wildest dreams had she dared imagine such a tribute, but if she had, she would have imagined feeling honored instead of terrified. What would happen now? What would people say? And what would her father do to her and to Ben?

Ben marched down the aisle, nodding and pausing occasionally to shake hands with someone who felt compelled to congratulate him on his perseverance. He passed her with a proprietary grin and strode confidently up to claim his victory. Molly watched with growing apprehension as he counted out the proper number of gold coins, stuffing a handful back into his pocket. Obviously, he had come prepared to bid much higher even than he had, if necessary. Ben wanted her, and wanted her badly. The knowledge brought a new wave of apprehension.

Mr. Wells handed Ben his box supper. "I guess we all know who this belongs to," he said with a wink in Molly's direction. Her cheeks burned, and she knew she must be scarlet. With everyone who lived within a hundred miles staring at her, it was no wonder. Vaguely she noticed Harry frowning in the background, obviously displeased but helpless to do anything. And then all she saw was Ben.

He sauntered back to where she stood, tucked his box supper under one arm and offered her his other one. His smile was wide and cocky, and she might have refused to go with him had she not seen the momentary flicker of uncertainty when she hesitated. Underneath his bravado, he was as nervous as she! The knowledge gave her new courage, and she slipped her hand into the crook of his elbow.

He started toward the rear of the room. Molly

assumed he would just lead her to a spot out of the way where they could watch the rest of the bidding, as most of those who had already been paired up were doing, but he did not stop. He led her on, out the door, down the few steps into the schoolyard, and away.

"Where would you like to go?" he asked, and once again she was struck by how deep his voice was. Her fingers unconsciously tightened on his arm.

"Anywhere," she replied, hoping she didn't sound as quivery as she felt. Here in the twilight, he seemed so much larger than she remembered. "Someplace close."

Ignoring her wishes, he took her farther out into the yard to an ancient cottonwood. The white cottony puffs that gave the tree its name were just starting to open, giving the old tree a grayed look, as if it were showing its age.

"How about here?" he asked.

"Fine," she said, even though the spot was much too isolated and the shadows much too deep. She glanced at the bare ground in dismay, thinking of her new dress and wishing she had a blanket on which to sit.

Seeing her dilemma, Ben said, "Wait a minute," and quickly unknotted the yellow silk scarf he wore at his throat, shook it out, and spread it on the ground.

"I'll ruin it," she protested, thinking of the dirt that would be ground into the delicate fabric.

"Better than ruining your pretty dress."

He'd noticed! she thought wildly, the lavish

compliments Harry had paid her earlier in the
evening fading into insignificance. Pleased beyond reason, she gathered her skirts and lowered herself carefully onto her makeshift seat.
She pulled her knees up in front of her and
locked her hands around them.

Ben crouched beside her, setting the box down
in front of him. "Well, now, let's see what I paid
so dearly for," he said, gently plucking the cloth
rose out of its bindings and laying it aside so he
could work the string loose. "I hope it's not cold
sandwiches."

"Why did you do it?" she asked, no longer
able to control her curiosity.

"Do what?" he asked with maddening unconcern, still engrossed with the string.

"Why did you make a spectacle of me and
yourself and poor Harry? Why did you spend a
fortune for—"

"Fried chicken," he announced. "And biscuits,
and potato salad and apple pie. Tell me, did you
make all this yourself, or did your mother make
it, hoping to catch you a husband?"

"I made it myself," she said, not bothering to
conceal her annoyance. "You didn't answer my
question."

He lifted his sapphire gaze to hers, and once
again she felt the jolt that had jarred her when
she had first seen him that evening. His eyes
were clear and glittering, all trace of amusement
gone. "I wanted to talk to you."

"You could have done that for free!" she
pointed out, but he shook his head.

"The last time I tried, you ran away."

"You frightened me."

"I didn't mean to. What did I do that scared you?"

"You . . . you hurt me," she said, unconsciously rubbing her arms.

"I'm sorry. I was feeling kind of desperate. Doesn't Harry sometimes get a little rough when he kisses you?"

"*No!*" She didn't want to say she hardly ever let Harry kiss her.

Ben's eyebrows rose. "Maybe he doesn't like you as much as I do."

Her face heated. "Harry is a gentleman."

"A gentleman who never hurts you."

"Yes."

"Molly, I'd never hurt you either."

His gaze was so intense, Molly could hardly breathe. She wanted to believe him but how could she?

"So," he continued, "you're going to marry Harry because he's a gentleman."

Dropping her gaze, she stared blindly at the flowers swirling in the print of her skirt. She wanted to explain how things were; she had to make him understand. "I *have* to marry him."

"*Have* to?" he echoed snidely.

"No! I didn't mean . . ." Her cheeks were scalding, but her embarrassment turned to anger when she looked up and saw his amusement. She blurted, "My father's making me!"

Ben's magnificent eyes narrowed in speculation. Absently he picked up a biscuit and polished it off in two bites. "How is he making you?"

"He . . . he just is," she insisted.

Someone came out of the schoolhouse, and Molly glanced over in alarm, but it was only the first of the diners seeking a good picnic spot.

"The auction must be over," Ben remarked, picking up a chicken leg. He offered it to her, but she shook her head. The way her stomach felt, she didn't dare eat anything. More people came out, and the schoolyard began filling up.

Molly looked at Ben again. He had devoured the chicken leg and was scooping himself out a piece of apple pie. "You're a good cook, Molly."

She was glad he was enjoying the food; he'd paid enough for it. But then she remembered he hadn't cared about the supper at all. "Did you really?"

"Did I really what?" he asked, rummaging in the box for a fork with which to eat his pie.

"Did you really buy my box just because you wanted to talk to me?"

His lips twitched again, but this time he didn't smile. "Yeah, I did."

"What did you want to talk about?"

"Oh, things," he said, tasting the pie. "Mmmm, you *are* a good cook, if you were telling the truth about making this."

"What thinigs?" she asked impatiently.

He chewed thoughtfully and swallowed. "Oh, I don't know. I suppose I was wondering what you'd say if somebody besides Harry Hoskins asked you to marry him."

Chapter Four

✦✦✦✦✦

As soon as the words were out of his mouth, Ben wanted to snatch them back. Molly grew suddenly frightened, like a doe cornered by a hunter in the instant before he pulls the trigger. If he wasn't careful, she'd run from him again. In a desperate attempt to put her at ease, he tried a reassuring grin. " 'Course, I knew if I asked you that, you'd slap my face, so I thought of a few other things I'd ask you instead."

"What?" she asked warily.

Now Ben was caught. He picked up another biscuit and popped it into his mouth whole, chewing slowly so he would have time to think. Her eyes had darkened like a stormy sky, and she still looked ready to run. He swallowed the biscuit with difficulty.

"I've been wondering what you were thinking that day I knocked you down in the store," he improvised.

Molly released her breath in a relieved sigh. "I was thinking how much you'd changed since . . . since the last time I'd seen you."

"Changed good or changed bad?"

"You're taller," she hedged.

"Do you like tall men?"

"I've always liked you, Ben."

He nodded sagely. "Ever since I beat up Harry Hoskins for dipping your pigtails in the inkwell."

He remembered! "You were my hero then," she said, wishing she could still see him that way.

Immensely pleased, he sat down out of his crouch and thumbed back his fancy white Stetson. "A hero, huh?"

"I thought you were so brave, especially because Harry was bigger than you. I've always wondered why you fought him over *me*."

Ben shrugged. "You looked so sad when you came to school the next day. I knew you were embarrassed because your dress was stained and your hair was short . . . although you did look awfully cute."

The blush his compliment inspired spread quickly, warming her to her toes. She watched him watching her, enjoying his frank admiration. "I thought I looked like a boy."

"An awfully pretty boy."

Oh, Ben! her heart cried, weeping for the love that could never be. Impulsively she said, "After you fought Harry, I always looked up to you, but I really thought you were a hero when you . . ."

"When I what?" he prompted, leaning closer.

Her breath caught at his nearness. The heat from his body seemed to radiate across the small space separating them, warming her in the oddest places. "I don't want to . . . I didn't mean . . ."

"When I what?" he insisted, and she knew he would not rest until she told him.

"I'm, sorry . . . I . . . When you stood up to my father that day."

His puzzled expression slowly cleared as he remembered. "The day my father died."

"I'm sorry," she said again, instinctively laying a comforting hand on his arm. "I shouldn't have said anything."

"It's all right," he said, covering her hand with his own.

His palm was rough and callused, but his touch was gentle. It sent a tingle up her arm and straight to her heart, where it jarred loose the secret she had kept hidden there so long. "I never saw anybody stand up to my father the way you did. You were just a boy, but you made him back down. You were so brave, just like Sir Lancelot."

"*Who?*"

Molly could have bitten her tongue. What had possessed her to say such a thing? Suddenly aware of the way her fingers were clutching his arm and the way his fingers were clutching hers back, she tried to withdraw her hand, but he would not let her go.

"Who's this Sir What's-his-name?"

"A knight . . . of the Round Table . . . King Arthur's court," she mumbled, knowing he must think her an idiot.

"A knight in shining armor? Is that how you see me, Molly?"

She had once, but how silly it sounded when spoken aloud. "Ben, please," she begged, pulling on her hand in an agony of embarrassment.

This time he let her go and sank back onto one elbow, stretching his long legs out in front of him. "A knight in shining armor," he repeated, apparently delighted. "And are you a princess in distress, Miss Molly?"

Molly had rarely felt more distressed, but she wasn't about to admit it. She tucked her hands in her lap for safekeeping. "Anyway, I thought you were brave."

Ben frowned. "It wasn't so much brave as knowing I was right. My pa was innocent."

Molly looked up in alarm. "Do you have proof?"

"I sure do. He *couldn't* have done it because he was home with me the whole night. He didn't leave the house one time, but they wouldn't listen to me when I tried to tell them."

"Why did he go with them then?"

"He wasn't afraid. They said they were taking him to jail, and he thought the law would straighten it out. He wouldn't even let me go along." Even after six years, Ben's anger was palpable.

"But they thought they were right."

"Not all of them," Ben contended. "At least one of them knew he was hanging an innocent man."

"What do you mean?"

"One of the men in the posse was the one who killed Fletcher. He framed my father for the crime and talked the others into the lynching."

Ben's eyes were terrible, full of pain and fury and an awful determination. Molly was trembling now, but still she asked the question she most feared. "Do you know who did it?"

His lips pursed, as if he were debating his response. "It's pretty easy to figure out," he said at last. "The killer was somebody who stood to gain from my pa's death."

"Or from Mr. Fletcher's," Molly tried.

Ben shook his head. "Fletcher didn't have an enemy in the world, and nobody profited from his death. I already thought of that and checked it out. No, my pa was the one they wanted."

Did Ben share her suspicions? Did he, too, think Elijah Wade was the killer? "But who gained something from your father's death?"

"Nobody, because the killer was counting on me to leave town. He probably hopes I still will. He'll show his hand someday, and when he does . . ."

Ben's voice trailed off ominously, and fear snaked through her. "Do you know who he is?"

He studied her for a long moment, his eyes narrowed speculatively. "You know something, don't you?" he said. "Something your father told you?"

"No!" she cried, jumping to her feet in panic.

By the time Ben was on his feet, too, Harry was by her side. "What did he say to you? What did you say to her, Cantrell?" he demanded furiously.

"Nothing!" she said, but she was trembling from her unspoken fears.

"You son of a . . ." Harry's fist connected with

Ben's chin before either Molly or Ben could even register his intention.

"Harry!" she screamed in protest, but she was too late. Ben collapsed backward in a heap.

"Ben!" someone hollered, and Johnny McGee was there, his fists clenched, every inch of his compact body tensed for conflict.

Molly grabbed Harry and hung on, clinging the way she had often clung to her father in his fits of rage.

He shook her off. "Get up and fight like a man!" he shouted at Ben, who had pushed up on one elbow and was rubbing his chin.

Ben's gaze flickered from Harry to Molly and back again. "I got no fight with you, Hoskins."

"You insulted Molly."

"Maybe you oughta check with her about that first."

"I don't have to."

"He didn't, Harry," Molly cried. "It wasn't anything like that." But she knew he wasn't listening. Like her father, he refused to listen to reason. All her nebulous fears about Harry coalesced into grim certainty.

A crowd was forming around them, and her father broke through. His face was flushed and sweating, and she knew he had been drinking. "What'd he say to you, girl?"

"Nothing, Pa. This is all a mistake."

"Cantrell, are you gonna fight?" Harry asked again, his rage a quivering presence.

"I don't think fighting will solve anything, Harry," Ben said to Molly's amazement.

"Harry, please," Molly said. "You're making a scene."

Controlling his temper with a visible effort, Harry straightened, pulling down his vest with a jerk. "Come on, Molly." He took her arm. For an instant, she considered resisting but quickly realized she would only be making a bigger scene. Reluctantly she once again surrendered to Harry's will and allowed him to lead her away. As Harry forced a path through the crowd gathered to see the excitement, Molly glanced back and saw Ben still studying her, as if nothing were more important to him than figuring out what was in her mind. She gave him an apologetic look in the last instant before the crowd closed around him again.

Above the sound of murmured comments she heard her father's shrill voice. "What do you expect from the son of a murdering barn burner? We should've run him off years ago instead of giving him a chance to defile our daughters!"

A strangled sound escaped her, and Harry, all solicitude, slipped his arm around her shoulders. "It's over now, dear. Everything is fine."

"All right, the show's over," Mr. Wells was saying, doing his duty as mayor. "Everybody get back to your suppers now. We've got some dancing to do in a little while." Molly also heard Reverend Bates urging people to disperse. She was afraid to turn around to see if they were obeying for fear she might catch sight of Ben again. She didn't know if her fragile composure could stand it.

Still lying on the ground, Ben ignored Elijah Wade's continuing taunts, allowing Reverend Bates to take the man in hand and conduct him away. Conscious of the disapproving expressions of the people around him, he ignored them, too, until they drifted off. Only then did he struggle to his feet.

"Whoa, partner," Johnny said, rushing to assist him. "Maybe you oughta stay down a while."

"Hoskins does pack quite a punch, but I'm all right," Ben said, although he had to blink a few times before the world came straight again.

"What in the hell was going on? I was watching you every minute, and I didn't see a thing!"

"I just said something that scared Molly."

"Scare her? What the—"

"Now, boys, you two settle down."

Ben glanced around in surprise to see the old lady whose supper Johnny had bought. She was the only other person left under the cottonwood tree, and she seemed intent on taking charge. "John, go back and get our supper and bring it over here. We'll eat with your friend since his partner's done deserted him."

"You don't have to—" Ben tried to protest, but she was having none of it.

"Go on now, John." Johnny obeyed, clearly in agreement with her plan to provide Ben com-

pany. Ben would have preferred being left alone
to consider what had happened between him
and Molly, but he guessed he would have plenty
of time later for contemplation. He figured he
had best make himself scarce before the dancing
started, or he would be tempting fate where Elijah Wade was concerned. The little coyote was
drunk enough to start something right here, and
Ben didn't want to have to fight Molly's father
on top of everything else.

"Oh, Molly, what happened?" Julie asked,
taking her sister in her arms the instant Harry
led her out of the crowd.

"Nothing, nothing," she said, wishing someone would believe her. "Ben and I were talking,
and—"

"What did he say to you?" Harry demanded.

Molly took a deep breath to steady herself.
"We were talking about when Ben's father got
killed, and—" Her voice broke when she remembered how close Ben had come to confirming her
worst fears. He knew! She was sure he did. Was
that why he was pursuing her? Did he hope to
use her to gather evidence against her own father?

"Good God," Harry was saying. "What a
thing to talk about to you. No wonder you were
upset."

"Come over here," Julie urged, leading her to
where a blanket was spread on one side of the
schoolhouse. "You can eat with us."

Through her tears, Molly saw the contents of
Julie's box supper spread out on a blanket, and

she realized Harry had bought Julie's supper when he did not get hers.

She sank gratefully onto the blanket and let Julie pet her and Harry fuss over her while she regained her composure. After a few minutes, Julie turned to Harry and said, "Would you get Molly some punch, please?"

When he was gone, she took Molly's hand. "What really happened? What did he really say?"

"Nothing, Julie. Harry hit him for no reason!"

"He was *defending* you."

"I didn't need defending. Julie, listen to me. I was wrong about Harry. He's just like Pa."

"No, he isn't! He's nice and gentle. He'll protect you."

"I don't want a man who protects me with his fists."

"Then what *do* you want?" Julie asked in exasperation.

"I want . . ." She paused, picturing Ben lying on the ground. She could still hear him saying, "I don't think fighting will solve anything." "I want a man who's brave enough *not* to fight."

Julie's eyes widened, but before she could respond, Harry returned with the punch, and they had no further opportunity to discuss the matter. Molly sat and watched Julie and Harry eat their suppers in the growing darkness, unable to swallow a bite herself. From surreptitious glances, she saw the crowd around Ben had dispersed. Her father had returned to the whiskey barrel and was imbibing freely. What would happen when they got home and Molly told him she couldn't marry Harry Hoskins? Her blood ran cold at the mere thought, but she also knew she couldn't give herself to Harry, not now. She would much rather face her father's wrath than condemn herself to a life of misery.

By the time people started returning to the schoolhouse for the dancing, Molly had recovered enough to fool everyone except Julie into thinking she was fine. She avoided her sister's concerned gaze as Harry escorted both of them inside. But she did manage one last glance at the old cottonwood tree.

The first few hours of dancing seemed endless, and Molly let Harry claim her for almost every set since her other partners seemed intent on questioning her about her encounter with Ben. Fortunately, after a while, people finally accepted her reticence and dropped the subject. So long as she didn't let herself think, she could pretend everything was fine and forget the trials that still lay ahead.

When the fiddlers announced they were taking a break, Molly was swept from the room by the other girls, who wanted to take this opportunity to "freshen up." Daisy Ferguson talked nonstop as they made their way to the school's privies, which had been designated for use by the ladies. The line was long, and Molly stood back, allowing others to go ahead while she listened to Daisy brag about her conquests of the evening.

Julie stayed loyally by Molly's side. Molly knew her sister hoped for a minute alone with her and was prepared to wait for it. By the time Molly's turn came, the music had already resumed and most of the others had returned to the school. Julie and Daisy came out of the twin doors of the privy at the same time. "They're starting!" Daisy said in dismay. "I promised this dance to that tall fellow I met at church last Sunday."

"Go on, then," Molly urged. Daisy needed no further encouragement.

When the sisters were alone, Julie took Molly's hands. "How are you doing?"

"Fine, really. Have you seen Ben anywhere? I've been afraid to look for him."

"No, I haven't seen a sign of him. He must've left."

Molly sighed, partly relieved and partly disappointed. Would she ever have a chance to tell him how sorry she was? But she had others to think of, too. "Have you seen Mama?"

"Not for a while."

"Go look for her, then. See how she's doing. I know she'll be worried about Pa and what happened with me."

Julie frowned, and Molly could sense her sister's reluctance to leave her alone. "I told you, I'm fine. I need a few minutes by myself. I'm getting so tired of smiling and pretending."

Nodding her understanding, Julie gave Molly's hands a squeeze and darted off back toward the schoolhouse as Molly closed herself inside the darkness of the privy. Had the atmosphere been even a tiny bit more pleasant, Molly would have been content to remain there for the rest of the evening. Unfortunately, even her desperate need for privacy could not overcome her other sensitivities, and after only a few minutes she was forced to leave her refuge.

Now the schoolyard was virtually deserted. Even the group gathered around the whiskey barrel had dwindled to a mere handful. Seeking to avoid her father, who was bound to be among them, she walked around the rear of the building, planning to enter on the other side. What she had not planned on was seeing the old cottonwood tree again.

The sight of it silhouetted against the darker night sky stopped her. For one sweet moment, she imagined Ben and herself seated beneath it again, only this time she would do things differently. This time when he opened her box, she would take the chicken leg he offered, and they would talk and laugh about pleasant subjects.

Picturing the scene so vividly in her mind, she could actually see Ben's strong hand removing the rose she had made from the box and . . . The rose! In the excitement she had forgotten all about it. She had, of course, intended for Harry to give it back to her when he bought her box, but things hadn't worked out exactly according to plan. She imagined the rose now lying unheeded in the dirt beneath the old cottonwood, and a shaft of longing pierced her. If she could take nothing else away with her this night, at least she could have the rose.

She hurried over to the tree and began searching in the shadows. When a cursory inspection proved futile, she carefully gathered her skirts and stooped down, using her hands to feel for it. Once and then again she went over the area where they had sat, but it simply wasn't there. Rose, box, and even Ben's yellow silk scarf were gone.

Suddenly the loss assumed far greater importance than it merited, and the tears she had fought all evening stung her eyes with renewed vigor. Rebelling against them, she surged to her feet, scrubbing her eyes with both hands and fighting the sobs forming in her throat.

"Looking for something?"

She whirled. Ben was standing no more than three feet away. "You scared the life out of me," she said, laying a hand over her pounding heart.

"I'm sorry. I figured you knew I was here."

"No, I . . . I didn't see you. It's dark." He took a step toward her, and her heart convulsed in her chest.

"I didn't mean to scare you earlier this evening, either. I meant it when I said I'd never hurt you."

"You didn't scare me," she lied.

"Don't worry. We won't talk about that anymore. I want to ask you something else."

"What?"

"If you're going to marry Harry, why aren't you engaged yet?"

"I . . . I put him off."

His eyes glittered in the moolight. "Last fall you told me you were going to marry him."

"I changed my mind."

"Why?"

She shook her head, not knowing how to answer.

"Why?" he insisted, reaching for her. "Was it because I kissed you?"

"Yes . . . No! I don't know!" Panic welled in her, and she wrenched out of his grasp.

"Molly, wait!"

She ran, heading for the distant copse of trees behind the school where she had played as a child, Ben following close behind.

"Molly!"

She snatched up her skirts and ran faster. The trees loomed large in the shadows, promising a hiding place, but just as she reached them, Ben's hand caught her arm. He was only trying to stop her, but his feet tangled in her skirts and the impetus of their movement hurled them to the ground. He twisted quickly so he fell first, carrying her and cushioning her with his body, but they rolled, and when they stopped in the stygian darkness of the trees, he was on top.

She fought like a trapped animal, wildly, frantically, but he captured her hands easily and rendered her helpless beneath him.

"Let me go!" she begged breathlessly.

"Tell me why you won't marry Harry, and I will."

"You're hurting me!"

His grip gentled instantly, but he did not let her go. "Why did you put Harry off? What are you scared of, Molly?" he taunted. "Are you thinking about spending the next forty or fifty years with a man you don't love? Are you thinking about what Miriam Hoskins's life has been like?"

She had, of course, many times. "Ben, please!"

"Or have you been thinking about knights and princesses and happy endings? Have you imagined how you'd feel if the man you truly loved came for you?"

"Let me go!"

"Why? So you can run to safety? I don't think you really want to get away from me, Molly."

"I do, I do!"

"Then why didn't you run to the school?"

Molly froze. Why *hadn't* she run to the school instead of here where no one could see or find them? "I don't . . . Please, Ben, let me go."

"I will if you tell me who you *really* love."

"I . . . I love you, Ben," she said, past caring for the consequences. "I love *you!*"

His whole body went still above her. Even his breathing stopped as he absorbed the knowledge. "Molly," he whispered reverently.

Slowly, ever so slowly, his mouth came down to hers. She could have turned away. She could

have struggled or called for help. Someone
would have heard. Instead she waited, holding
her breath for the moment she had dreamed of
for almost half her life.

His kiss was pure magic, a tender touch, a
tasting, a mingling that gradually deepened into
possession and claiming and conquest. Her very
bones melted with surrender.

When at last he lifted his mouth from hers,
they were both breathless once again. "Let go of
my hands," she whispered, surprised to discover he still held her. His grip became a caress
and slid lovingly away. Freed, she lifted her arms
and slipped them around his neck. "Ben," she
said with wonder in the second before their lips
met again.

Now she knew why kissing Harry had held no
attraction for her. Love was what made the difference between pressing mouths together and
real kissing. Love, the mystical, glorious, fantas-
tic emotion that changed every aspect of life.

Love and Ben, the two most important forces
in her world, soon blurred and then blended
into one as his kisses went on and on. She
opened her mouth instinctively, granting him
full access. At first she found the invasion
strange, but when his tongue tangled with hers
in a sensuous duel, she began to realize the
depths of pleasure her body could experience.

Questing to learn more, she grew bolder, exploring him with her hands, discovering the in-
tricate mass of bone and muscle that made a
man. His strength awed her. He had the power

to do with her whatever he would, yet he leashed it into tenderness. His touch was gentle, his hands exploring her body with an eagerness surpassing her own. His promise echoed in her mind: "I'll never hurt you." This was the man she had waited for, the man she could trust.

Her breasts seemed to swell, straining against the fabric of her dress and aching for comfort. When his seeking palm brushed one ruched nipple, she gasped and lifted herself to him again. Needing no further encouragement, he filled his hands with her, stroking and kneading and caressing until they both lost patience with the fabric separating skin from skin.

His mouth moved hungrily along her bare throat, taking what little was available while he struggled unsuccessfully to find an opening to her bodice. By now she was too lost to be of any help, her fingers clumsy with the need to hold him closer. No longer capable of conscious action, she could only react to his urgings.

Barred from her breasts, he sought a more accessible prize. Beneath her skirt only one thin layer of cloth covered her, and it was no barrier at all against his caress as he found and cupped the center of her need.

She cried out at the invasion, but he soothed her fervently. "I'll never hurt you, Molly. I only want to love you."

"Yes," she whispered. She wanted so desperately to be loved.

His hands moved on her, and she lifted her hips to increase the glorious pressure. The world was swirling now, tumbling over itself in its hurry to reach the goal to which he was pushing her.

This time he had no trouble with fastenings. The simple drawstring slipped through his fingers, and he easily slid the cotton drawers from her hips. His palms were rough against the silk of her skin, and the contrast sent tremors of awareness streaking over her body. She obeyed those hands mindlessly, opening to him, welcoming him, waiting while he loosened his own clothes.

When his probing, throbbing hardness snagged on her innocence, she knew one lucid moment of sanity. "No, Ben, wait!"

"We've waited too long already," he said hoarsely. "You're mine now, aren't you?"

"Yes . . . yes, I am."

"Then show me, Molly. Love me."

"I don't know how."

"I'll teach you."

And he did. Easing past the fragile barrier, he claimed what she had long dreamed of giving him. The pain was fleeting, but she barely heard his mumbled words of concern. Filled with him, she could concentrate only on the wonder of it. The pleasure was secondary until he began to move within her and her body responded of its own accord. Discovering the ancient rhythm, she began to move with him.

"Molly," he said as if to confirm the unbelievable, and she responded, "Ben." Even her dreams had not prepared her for the richness of reality. His weight, his strength, his scent, his power, all overwhelmed her and transformed their dark and secret hideaway into a treasure trove brilliantly lit by their shining, sparkling love.

Lights danced behind her eyelids, like fireflies gone mad, blinking and teasing as the pressure built. The rhythm grew more urgent, striving toward the invisible goal. She raced to meet it, charging heedlessly into the heat and the light, faster and faster, and then she was there, in the midst of the explosion. Suns burst inside her in a shower of flame and sparks, and she cried out in wonder. Ben echoed her cry, shuddering above her when the explosion caught him, too.

He collapsed on her, his blessed weight pressing into her. She clung to him, trying to maintain the fleeting sense of unity; but in spite of her efforts, it slowly began to fade as the heat of their passion cooled inexorably. With another murmur of concern, he rolled away from her, his breath ragged. For a long moment he lay still beside her with one arm thrown across his eyes.

Molly watched him with growing concern. Why didn't he say something? And what did one say after sharing such a fearsome intimacy? She felt as if she had been stripped naked, both physically and emotionally. She had never been so vulnerable, and the gentle quivering of their lovemaking's afterglow gradually became a nervous tremor.

With growing apprehension, she began to realize the magnitude of her act. She had surren-

dered her most precious possession to a
stranger. Who was Ben Cantrell, really? Was he
the boy whose fighting she had feared, or was
he the gentle man who had refused to fight? Was
he a man she should flee or a man she could
trust?

A few moments ago the answer had seemed
so simple. She had been his completely, but now
the bond between them was broken. She
watched the uneven rise and fall of his chest.
Oh, please, Ben, she begged silently. Please tell
me you love me! Please make everything all
right!

Ben waited for his body to calm. He had things
to say to Molly, demands to make, but he must
say and make them rationally. She was his now.
She would be wary, even frightened, but he
could ease her fears. He had no intention of
letting her go, not after knowing her love. Harry
Hoskins would never have her.

The thought touched off a raging jealousy, a
jealousy he had ruthlessly held in check, never
daring to acknowledge it. Only now that he
knew Molly truly belonged to him could he indulge his fury. She loved Ben, yet she had been
willing to sell herself to another man in exchange
for what she imagined would be an easy life and
condemn all three of them to misery. Anger and
frustration roiled with him, and he closed his
hands into fists. He wanted to shake her when
he thought how close she'd come to ruining
three lives, and he forgot his resolve to be rational.

He lifted the arm from his eyes to find Molly watching him. "Well, I guess you won't be marrying Harry Hoskins now, will you?"

Molly stared at him in horror. He'd used her, ruined her, and all for *revenge*. With a tiny cry, she scrambled to her feet. Remembering at the last moment to snatch up the undergarment she had so recklessly discarded, she raced back to the safety of the schoolhouse.

"Molly!" he called, too surprised at first to react. When he finally realized she intended to escape him, he lunged up but had to stop and rearrange his clothing before he could go after her. By then she had disappeared from sight. "Molly!" he tried again, but got no response.

Aware of her disheveled appearance, Molly headed straight for the privy. Locked inside, she pulled her drawers on over her shaking limbs, acutely aware of the sticky residue between her legs which she knew must be her virgin's blood. The tears she'd held back all evening fell freely now, and she made no attempt to stop them. She covered her mouth with both hands to stifle her sobs and surrendered to despair.

Ben Cantrell had his revenge. If she married Harry, he would know she'd betrayed him with Ben. If she jilted Harry, he would be humiliated. How could she have been such a fool?

Ben slowed his pace as he neared the school, not wanting to attract attention. It wouldn't do for someone to ask him why he was running

around in the dark calling Molly's name. Seeing
no sign of her outside, he went to the spot by the
old cottonwood from where he had watched the
first part of the dance through one of the windows. He'd seen Molly dancing every dance
then, but now she was not even in the room.
Where could she have gone?

Inside the school, Harry escorted Julie back to
her seat when the latest reel ended. "Where do
you suppose Molly could be?" he asked for the
tenth time in as many minutes.

Julie had tried to make light of Molly's pro-
longed absence, knowing her sister needed time
alone, but now even she was beginning to
worry. "I'll go check on her," she offered. Harry
discreetly left her at the door, knowing he could
not follow her all the way to the women's out-
house.

Julie quickened her step as soon as she left the
circle of light from the doorway, hoping to escape her father's notice. So far this evening she
had been lucky. After the altercation with Ben,
he had sought the comfort of the whiskey barrel
and had not paid his daughters the slightest notice since.

"Molly? Molly, are you in there?" she called as
she approached the twin doors of the necessary.

Molly swallowed the last of her sobs and began scrubbing the moisture from her face. "Yes,
I'm here. Just a minute."

When she opened the door, Julie pulled her out and tried to make out her face in the fading moonlight. "You've been crying."

"Only a little. I must look terrrible."

"Your hair's kind of messy, but at least you don't have to worry about your face being red." Julie had often complained of how unfair it was that Molly's eyes and nose never reddened no matter how hard she wept, while Julie's turned scarlet at the first teardrop.

"Help me fix it," Molly said, turning her back so Julie could make the necessary repairs to her coiffure.

"Heavens, you've got grass in your hair. What were you doing in there?"

"I . . . nothing," she stammered, wondering if the back of her dress were grass-stained and dirty. Would everyone see the evidence and know what she had done? If so, she didn't dare go back into the brightly lit schoolhouse. "I was leaning against the wall. There must have been something on it. Is my dress dirty?"

"I can't tell," Julie said as she removed and replaced hairpin after hairpin. "There now, that's better," she said when she was finished. With capable hands she began to brush at the back of Molly's dress.

"Molly? Are you all right?" Harry's voice came to them across the schoolyard from a respectable distance.

"Yes, I'm fine," she replied as cheerfully as she could manage, glad to hear the hoarseness of her tears had faded from her voice. "I felt a little faint, but it passed. Go back inside, Harry. We'll be along in a minute."

"If you aren't feeling well, you shouldn't go back to the dance. I'll take you right home," he said.

Molly was too weary even to feel irritated at his presumption. Thinking only of the dangers of being seen in public in her present condition, she said, "Oh, thank you. Could you fetch your buggy right away?"

Instantly she realized she had jumped from the frying pan into the fire. The last thing she felt capable of doing was putting up a good front for Harry on the long drive home. New tears stung her eyes, but she blinked them away. She would simply have to be much sicker than she had thought, too sick even to talk. In truth she did feel ill. If she had eaten any supper, she surely would have lost it by now, and she was starting to shake again. Her father expected her to get Harry to propose tonight, too. She actually groaned at the thought.

"Molly?" Julie asked in alarm.

"I'm feeling worse all of a sudden," she said quite truthfully. "Would you come with us?"

"Of course. I'll go tell Mama we're leaving. Will you be all right while I'm gone?"

Molly nodded numbly, knowing she would never really be "all right" again. When Julie had gone, Molly sank back against the wall of the privy and closed her eyes. In the distance she heard the clatter of a running horse on the hard ground. Someone was riding away, riding very fast, as if the hounds of hell were at his heels. Damn you, Ben Cantrell, she thought. I hope they catch you, too.

It seemed an eternity before she heard Harry's buggy pull up in front of the school. Julie had just returned to help her walk the short distance to it when a man's shout brought their heads up in surprise.

"Look! Fire!"

Sure enough, in the distance they could see a golden glow lighting the horizon.

"Harry, that's your place, isn't it?" someone else yelled.

"Yes, it is," Harry replied in alarm.

"Fire!" The shout carried, repeated by a score of voices. Inside the schoolhouse, the fiddling ceased with a discordant screech, and people began spilling out the door.

Quickly the men mobilized. Ever in control, Harry told Julie to use his buggy to take Molly home. He would ride in one of the wagons now filling with men who would fight the fire. Their families would go home alone in their own wagons. In a matter of minutes, every able-bodied man was gone, racing toward the false dawn on the northern horizon. Dazed, Molly watched them go.

"Mama!" Julie called, catching sight of the familiar figure in the crowd. "I told some of the men to take our wagon. Harry left us his buggy."

Mrs. Wade made her way over to the two girls. "Have you seen your pa? I couldn't find him any— Molly, what's the matter?"

"I told you, she's sick, Ma," Julie replied for her, pushing her sister ahead of her toward the waiting buggy. "After what happened, is it any wonder?"

"No, it isn't," Mrs. Wade said with a worried glance at the distant glow. "What do you suppose is burning?"

Molly's gaze followed her mother's. She didn't know the answer, but she did know that all her own dreams had gone up in smoke already this night.

In spite of her emotional exhaustion, or perhaps because of it, Molly slept only fitfully once she was safely in her own bed at home. Her dreams were haunted by visions of fires and Ben Cantrell, and the slamming of the front door just minutes after dawn woke her instantly.

"Where is everybody? Where's my breakfast?" her father demanded.

The hairs on the back of Molly's neck prickled in warning at his tone. She was out of bed and throwing on her clothes within seconds, and Julie was right behind her. From the loft they shared in the two-room cabin, they could hear her mother hurrying from the other room in which her parents slept.

"Elijah, I didn't hear you," Mrs. Wade said breathlessly, shrugging into a tattered robe.

"It's a fine thing. A man is up all night fighting a fire, and his woman can't even have a hot meal waiting for him when he comes in."

"I'll have something right away. I didn't know when you'd get home," she said. Molly heard the sounds of her mother stirring the fire, coaxing a flame from the coals.

"So now I know what you do when I'm not here. You sleep like the lazy bitch you are."

"Elijah, it's four o'clock in the morning," her mother protested.

Molly and Julie exchanged a glance. It was always the same. He came in looking for a fight, and no amount of reason or logic would dissuade him. Their only hope was to distract him. Not bothering with shoes or stockings, Molly hurried down the ladder as soon as she was decently clothed.

"Morning, Pa," she called, knowing that as his favorite, she had the best chance of warding off the pending violence. "Tell us all about the fire. We could hardly sleep for worrying."

The look he turned on her was so vicious she halted midway down the ladder, her heart in her throat. For one awful moment she thought he must know about her and Ben.

"It was Harry's barn," he said.

"Poor Harry," she replied through stiff lips. The loss of the barn was unfortunate, but Harry could afford a new one. In fact, he had recently mentioned wanting to tear the old one down so he could build one. At least the house he was so proud of hadn't been harmed.

"Don't look like that boy's gonna be thinking about a wedding for a while," her father was saying, making her realize why he was so irritated. "He's got more trouble'n you can shake a stick at."

"What do you mean?" she asked, forcing her feet to continue down the ladder. He doesn't know about Ben, she told herself sternly, so quit shaking. He's mad because he thinks the fire will delay Harry's proposal. If she could calm him down, everything would be fine.

"I mean somebody set the barn on fire apurpose, that's what. Somebody who wanted us to know it, too."

Molly gave her mother a nervous glance, glad to see she had the fire going in the fireplace. If she was quick enough with breakfast, maybe . . .

"How do you know the fire was set?" she asked, taking a seat opposite her father at the table in an attempt to keep his attention away from his wife.

"Because whoever did it spread a trail of coal oil way out into the yard, dropped a cigarette on it, and watched it go. He left the can sitting there, too, so's even if we was slow-witted, we could've figured it out." Her father scowled. "Sonofabitch," he muttered.

She could smell the whiskey on him and wondered who would have taken liquor along to fight a fire. Perhaps he had taken it himself. "But who would want to burn Harry's barn? He doesn't have an enemy in the world," she asked, uneasily aware of having heard those same words spoken only last night when she and Ben were talking about the late Mr. Fletcher, another victim of barn burning.

Her father looked up and grinned maliciously. "Harry's got one enemy. He made him last night, fighting over you, girl."

"No!"

"Yes," her father said. "We talked it over while we was waiting for the fire to burn down. Even Harry agreed it couldn't be nobody else. Like father, like son, I say. Just like Sam Cantrell, he got his revenge by burning the man's barn."

"But he didn't! He couldn't!"

Her father's bloodshot eyes turned cold again. "How do you know what he could and couldn't do?"

They both jumped at the sound of the coffeepot clattering to the floor. Julie had followed Molly down from the loft and now stood staring at the pot she had just dropped.

"Dammit, girl, can't you do anything right?" Wade shouted, bolting from his chair. "Look at that mess! And what about the wasted coffee? You think I work from morning to night just so you can throw it on the floor?"

"I'm sorry," Julie mumbled, hastening to clean up the mess.

"She didn't mean it," Mrs. Wade said, stepping between the girl and her father.

"It was an accident, Pa," Molly said, hurrying to his side. The hand she laid on his arm was trembling, but he was too furious to notice. "You were telling me about Ben Cantrell. You said even Harry thought he did it."

"That's right," he said, turning his anger back on her as she had hoped. "Some of us wanted to go get him right then, and teach him what happens to a bastard who thinks he can get away with a trick like that."

Molly fought down her panic. "But you didn't, did you?"

Her father snorted in disgust. "Sheriff Bigelow wouldn't let us. Said he'd go after the kid himself. Said after what happened with Sam Cantrell, he didn't want no lynching."

Wade stalked away, toward the cabinet where he kept his liquor supply. Molly placed a hand over her pounding heart, hoping her terror did not show on her face. She had no reason to feel kindly toward Ben Cantrell this morning, but she also knew he was innocent of the crime of which he'd been accused. He couldn't possibly have set the fire because he'd been with her. The distance to Harry's ranch was simply too great. Apprehensively, she watched her father pull a jug of moonshine from the cabinet, uncork it, and take a long swallow.

"Pa," she protested weakly. "You shouldn't drink on an empty stomach. You know what'll happen. . . ."

"You let me worry about my stomach, little girl. You'd better look to your own self."

"Wh . . . what do you mean?"

"I mean you got to get yourself married.

There's lots of girls'd love to hitch up with Harry Hoskins. If you expect to get him, you'd better hustle your bustle."

"He's going to ask me soon," she tried, wondering how long she could keep up the charade.

"Soon ain't good enough. I got a loan due. Ol' Hoskins ain't gonna wait forever."

So that was it! He thought Harry's father would forgive his debt if she and Harry were married. But why would he think such a thing? Mr. Hoskins was hardly the sentimental type, and he detested Elijah Wade.

"Where's my breakfast, woman? I'm getting tired of waiting," he shouted. Suddenly Molly saw everything plainly. Even though her father had no logical reason to expect Hoskins to forgive his debt, he had convinced himself it would happen if only Molly could catch Harry as a husband. She should have known since she knew her father's twisted way of looking at things. He saw the world as he wanted it to be or as it suited him to be, never letting reality distract him.

"The coffee's still boiling," her mother told him, "but I've got some mush for you."

She set the bowl and a spoon on the table and hurried away to finish the preparations. Stomping over to the table, he pulled out his chair with a scrape and collapsed onto it. He took one spoonful of the mush and spit it out with a curse. "What is this shit?" He scooped up the bowl and hurled it at her mother, who ducked, covering her head. The bowl smashed against the wall, and steaming mush flew everywhere. "I wanted eggs!"

"We don't have eggs!" her mother shouted back. "You wouldn't let me buy any when we were in town."

"That's right, blame it on me! Everything's always my fault. Nothing's ever your fault, you lazy good-for-nothing bitch!"

Molly watched as one in a trance. How many times had she witnessed this scene? Too many to count, she thought numbly. She caught Julie's eye and motioned for her to start edging for the door and safety.

"I'm not lazy!" their mother was saying. "I work harder than anyone around here."

"Pa, don't!" Molly cried, racing to stop him as he lunged for her mother. Molly caught his arm, but he shook her off, sending her flying across the room. She slammed into the wall and recovered just as he reached her mother. "No, Pa!"

Hannah scrambled out of the way, but she wasn't quick enough. He caught her unbound hair and yanked. She went backward with a scream, his fist pounding into her as she fell. Molly was on him in a second, trying to hold him, trying to fight him, trying to do anything to make him stop. He spared her only a glance as he backhanded her across the face.

Stars burst before her eyes as she collapsed in a heap on the floor. As if from a distance, she heard her mother's cries of pain and the dull

thud of fist against flesh. Dear God, when would
it ever end?

"Molly, get up, *hurry.*" Julie's voice beside her
ear was urgent. Responding to the urgency, she
let her sister help her up. Stumbling, she somehow made it to the door, and Julie half carried,
half dragged her to refuge in the barn. Sobbing
now with pain and frustration, Molly slumped
down to the floor as Julie pulled the barn door
shut behind them.

"Did he hurt you? Your nose is bleeding
some," Julie said, going to her knees beside her.

Molly swiped ineffectually at the red trickle.
"Oh, Julie, I've ruined everything."

"Don't be a goose," Julie scolded, lifting her
skirt and using a corner of her chemise to dab at
the blood. "You know you can never stop him
once he starts. And if we're there, watching, he
only gets worse."

"I didn't mean *that,*" Molly said, gratefully
allowing Julie to mother her. "I mean our plan.
I ruined our plan. I ruined everything."

"You're talking crazy. Harry isn't going to forget about you because his barn burned down.
You'll still get married, and then I can come live
with you, and Ma can, too, if she will, and we'll
all be safe. We might have to wait a little longer
than we thought, but it'll work out. You'll see."

"You don't understand. Last night . . . Ben
Cantrell . . ." She couldn't finish the sentence,
couldn't bring herself to tell sweet, trusting Julie
what an idiot she had been.

"Harry wasn't mad at you for having supper with Ben," Julie assured her. "Oh, he was mad at Ben, but not at you. He knew you were only trying to make peace."

Molly sobbed again, and Julie took her in her arms. "Everything'll work out, you'll see. Maybe this is the last time we'll ever have to see them fight."

Molly clutched her sister fiercely to her and choked on another sob. How could she explain to poor Julie that because of what she had done with Ben Cantrell, *nothing* could ever work out now?

Chapter Five
✦ ✦ ✦ ✦

BEN WAS SITTING on the front porch of his cabin, his chair tipped back so he could watch the sunrise, when he saw Johnny hightailing it for home, his horse kicking up dust in his haste. Ben frowned, sensing trouble. After a sleepless night spent thinking about Molly's perfidy, the last thing he needed was trouble.

He'd found more than his share when he'd heard Molly asking Harry to take her home. How could she have lain with Ben one minute and gone off with Harry the next, as if nothing had happened? He'd been asking himself that question all night, and he was no closer to an answer now than when he'd first ridden away from the school hours ago.

He rose wearily as Johnny's mount skidded to a halt in the ranch yard. "They're coming for you, partner," Johnny shouted as he swung down from the lathered horse and loped over to where Ben stood on the porch.

"Who's coming for me?"

"The sheriff and maybe a posse, too."

Dread slithered over him. "A posse? What on earth for?"

"For the fire. Didn't you see it? Harry Hoskins's barn burned to the ground last night." As Johnny came closer, Ben noticed his soot-stained face and smelled the smoke on his clothes. "It broke out along about midnight, and all the men went over to fight it, but we were too late, so we let it burn and did what we could to keep it from spreading."

"What does that have to do with me?"

"The fire was set deliberate. Whoever set it made damn sure we'd notice, too. There was a lot of talk about who could've done it, and you can bet everybody remembered you and Harry had a fight last night. They also remembered you wasn't anywhere around when the fire got noticed, and you didn't show up to fight it, either. Where'd you get to, anyways? You said you was gonna stay put right outside until the dancing was over."

Johnny sounded aggrieved, and Ben couldn't

blame him. "I went home . . . along about midnight. I must've left right before the excitement."

Johnny swore eloquently. "You sure picked a great time to leave. How're we gonna prove you didn't do it?"

"How are they gonna prove I did?" Ben countered, but he suspected that Ben Cantrell, son of a murdering barn burner, would be judged guilty even without evidence. Johnny's scowl confirmed his suspicions.

"We gotta get out of here. We can't let 'em take you. They'll lynch you just like they lynched your pa."

Ben stiffened in silent rebellion at the very thought. "Nobody was killed, was they?" he asked. Johnny shook his head. "Then they won't have an excuse to hang me."

"They don't need an excuse. You've seen the way Elijah Wade looks at you, and you should've heard the stuff he was spouting last night. If Bigelow hadn't been there, he would've talked the rest of them into coming after you with a rope."

Ben knew Johnny was trying to scare him into being sensible, but his words had exactly the opposite effect. "Did they think I'd go as quietly as my father did?"

"How the hell should I know what they thought? All I know is we gotta get you out of here before they come."

"I'm not going to run, Johnny."

"Being innocent won't protect you. That's

what your father thought, and look what happened to him!"

"I'm not going to make the same mistake my father made," Ben said. Was that dust he saw in the distance? More riders were approaching. Bigelow hadn't wasted any time. He hurried into the house and took the Winchester from its place over the mantel.

"Ben, don't be a fool!"

"I'd be a fool to run, Johnny," he said, checking the loads in the rifle. "Then they'd be sure I was guilty."

Swearing a blue streak, Johnny hurried over to the far corner and snatched up a shotgun.

"You don't have to stay if you don't approve," Ben told him.

Johnny explained in extremely colorful terms exactly what he thought of Ben's plan. Then he said, "I'll back your play, though God only knows why I bother with such a simple-minded jackass."

Grinning, Ben set the Winchester aside for a moment in order to strap on his gunbelt and check the loads in his pistol. By then they could hear the muffled thud of horses' hooves outside. Cautiously, Ben peered out to see who had come for him, and to his surprise he saw only two men, Sheriff Bigelow and Reverend Bates.

"Hello the house!" called Bigelow, giving the traditional western greeting.

Ben and Johnny exchanged a surprised glance, and after retrieving the Winchester, Ben stepped unhesitatingly out onto the porch. "Morning, Sheriff," he said. Johnny followed him and took up a position on the opposite side of the porch.

The sheriff noted their defensive stance and their hardware. He ostentatiously placed both of his hands on his saddle horn—in plain sight and away from his gun. "I see you boys were expecting me."

"What's this all about?" asked Ben.

"I guess Johnny told you about the fire."

Ben nodded.

"Well, there's some folks think you had a good reason for setting it."

"Are you one of them?"

Bigelow shrugged. "Burning Harry's barn like that seems a pretty stupid thing to do, and I ain't never thought you was stupid, Ben."

"Then why are you here?"

"Like I said, some folks think you set the fire. I figure the best way to clear your name is to let the judge hear the evidence and rule that there ain't enough to charge you with. Luckily Judge Gordon'll be by here on his circuit any day now."

"Are you arresting me, then?" Ben asked, feeling a trace of the impotent fury his father must have known at being falsely accused.

Bigelow glanced at the preacher in silent appeal. "Ben," said Reverend Bates, "the sheriff doesn't want to arrest you, but we both feel you might be better off in jail than out here by yourself."

"Better off in jail!" Johnny echoed in outrage.

"So they can come and lynch him without no trouble?"

"I figured you'd worry about lynching," the sheriff said. "It's only natural. I was worried, too, especially when I heard some of the talk last night. That's why I came alone except for the preacher here. I wanted you to know I aim to protect you any way I can."

"Protect!" Johnny scoffed. "In jail he'd be a sitting duck."

"No," Reverend Bates contradicted gently. "In jail he'd be guarded by the sheriff and his sworn deputies. Out here you'd only have each other."

"Wait a minute!" Johnny snapped.

"Johnny," Ben cautioned him again, beginning to see the wisdom in the sheriff's plan. "He's right. We've got to sleep sometime, and if a mob was to surround this place, we wouldn't stand a chance."

Johnny's homely face turned beet red in indignation. Ben appreciated his loyalty. He certainly didn't relish the idea of going to jail, but he didn't want a mob to drag him out of his bed in the middle of the night, either.

"You won't be under arrest," the sheriff hastened to explain. "We'll call it protective custody. I won't even take your gun."

"And what about *my* gun?" Johnny demanded.

Reverend Bates smiled slightly. "We assumed you'd want to go along and help guard your friend, Johnny."

Somewhat taken aback, Johnny looked to
Ben for a decision. Ben had already made up
his mind. This wasn't like what happened to his
father. This was to *prevent* what happened to
his father, and Ben well knew there was still at
least one man out there who'd like to see the last
of the Cantrells swinging from a noose. "All
right, Sheriff. We'll go along with you."

Johnny swore, briefly and succinctly, but his
shoulders drooped in resignation. "I hope we
ain't making a mistake."

"You'll want to get some things together," the
sheriff told them. "Like I said, the judge probably won't be here for a couple of days yet."

Ben and Johnny had to turn out the spare
horses and take care of a few chores before they
could leave. The sun was already high by the
time they were ready to head for town. As they
were mounting for the trip, the sheriff turned to
Ben with a speculative gleam in his eye. "You
wouldn't happen to remember exactly where
you were between eleven and twelve o'clock last
night, would you?"

"Matter of fact," Ben said bitterly, "I do."

"Bigelow's got Ben Cantrell locked up in the
jail," Elijah Wade reported to his family the next
day at dinner. One of their cowboys had carried
this bit of juicy gossip back with him from the
range.

"Then they must have some proof he did it,"
Mrs. Wade replied. She seemed relieved.

"What proof could they have?" Molly asked, watching her mother moving carefully as she carried a steaming bowl of beans to the table. Her face bore the marks of the savage beating she had taken the day before, and she moved stiffly, guarding her battered body against any jarring motion. Molly and Julie ached to help her, to ease the burden of her chores, but their father would never permit them to. They knew from experience that their solicitude would only bring on renewed violence.

Elijah was grinning, oblivious to his wife's discomfort, his actions of the day before forgotten in an alcoholic haze. "I don't reckon they need too much proof. He had the reason to do it, and he left the dance in plenty of time."

Molly winced, knowing Ben *hadn't* left the dance at all, not until moments before the burning barn was noticed and certainly not in time to have set the fire. "What's going to happen to him?" she asked, hoping her father would not sense the depth of her concern.

"The circuit judge is coming in a day or two. I reckon they'll try him, and he'll go to prison."

"Prison!"

"He destroyed a man's property. You ask me, we oughta just shoot him and get it over with. He's a bad seed. 'The sins of the fathers are visited on the children,' " he quoted piously. "Didn't I tell you he'd come to no good?"

He had indeed, on many occasions, but Molly had never guessed how ruin would be thrust upon Ben by circumstances. Forcing herself to eat lest someone notice her distress and ask the reason for it, Molly somehow got through the meal and the rest of the afternoon and evening.

Her father was unusually jovial, apparently cheered by the prospect of seeing Ben Cantrell eliminated once and for all. Of course, prison wasn't quite as final as hanging, but it would do for now. He made several pointed references to the choice Cantrell range land that would soon be available. By the time Molly and Julie retired to their loft for the night, Molly was literally sick with apprehension.

She lay perfectly still until she heard her father snoring in the other room. Then she turned to Julie in the darkness. "Pa sure seems happy about Ben getting arrested."

Julie sighed wearily. "Yeah, but what can you expect? He's been harping about Ben Cantrell for years, ever since Mr. Cantrell got hanged."

"Do *you* think Ben set the fire?" Molly asked, wanting an unbiased person's opinion.

"I don't know. I mean, if he was mad at Harry, why didn't he just go ahead and fight him when he had the chance? He's bigger, and he probably would've won. I kind've thought Ben didn't want any trouble at all. Seems likely he wouldn't, after what happened to his pa and all. I can't believe he'd go out and set a fire, especially when everybody was bound to think it was him."

"That's what I thought, too," Molly said with relief, hoping other people would see things as clearly as Julie did. "But who else could've done it?"

The straw mattress crackled as Julie rolled over to face her sister. "I been trying to figure it out myself, but I can't think of anybody, unless . . ."

The hairs on the back of Molly's neck prickled in warning. "Unless what?"

"Unless . . . I know this sounds crazy, but . . . Oh, I can't even say it!"

"Unless it was the same man who killed Mr. Fletcher, and he wanted folks to think it was Ben," Molly said quietly.

This time Julie's sigh was shaky. "I reckon it ain't as crazy as I thought."

"But who could it be? Who would still want to hurt Ben after all these years?"

Julie did not reply for several minutes, and when she did, her voice was only a breathy whisper. "Somebody who wants his land, maybe."

Molly's own breath lodged in her throat. After a moment she let it out slowly, seeking some semblance of calm. "Julie," she said as if changing the subject, "did you see Pa the night of the social?"

"Sure," she replied warily. "He was there when Harry knocked Ben down."

"No, I mean later, like right before we saw the fire and when the other men loaded into wagons and set out for Harry's place."

This time the silence stretched even longer. "No," she said at last, her reluctance obvious. "I didn't see him at all, and neither did Mama."

Neither girl spoke again, each afraid to voice the unspeakable. As if to deny her own suspicions, Julie rolled over again, putting her back to Molly. After what seemed a long time, Julie's regular breathing told Molly she was asleep, but Molly bore a burden too heavy to be surrendered to sleep.

Ben Cantrell was going to stand trial for a crime of which he was innocent. She was certain he wouldn't go to prison if he could help it, which meant he would have to tell his story at the trial. She would probably be called as a witness, too. Having sworn before God to tell the truth, she would be bound to tell exactly what had happened, to ruin herself and her reputation forever.

And her father! God in heaven, what would he do when he found out? If an imagined transgression could send him into a murderous rage, what would he do to her and to the rest of the family when he heard this?

Quaking in terror, she considered her options. Running away was one, but where could she go? With no money and no friends to help her, she would be helpless out in the world. Staying was not an option, either, not when she knew the fate awaiting her if her sins became public knowledge. She knew she must have a third option, but only after a long period of terrified soul-searching did she discover it.

It was risky, and it might not even work. What if she took the chance and had to testify anyway?

What if her father caught her? What if . . . ? The possible consequences were too horrible even to imagine, but after a good hour of frantic internal debate, she knew she had no other choice.

Slipping from her bed, she dressed quickly in a dark skirt and shirt and tucked her hair beneath a broad-brimmed hat that had once belonged to her father. Pulling the chin strap tight, she snatched up her jacket and shoes and stole down the ladder.

Praying with every step, she sneaked out of the cabin and across the yard to where a few horses were kept handy in the corral. Only when she was outside did she stop to put her shoes on, slipping them over her bare feet since she had been in too much of a hurry for stockings.

With softly spoken words, fearing discovery at any second, she coaxed one of the horses from the corral, a big buckskin who could travel far and fast. She led him into the barn for saddling. Working by feel because of the darkness, she got the animal ready and mounted. Every movement, every sound, was like a shout summoning those who would stop her, those who would demand to know her purpose in leaving the house in the dead of night. Even her own heart seemed bent on sounding an alarm as it pounded against her ribs with the force of a triphammer.

But no one heard and no one came and no one stopped her. In an agony of apprehension, she walked the horse away from the ranch buildings until she felt safe in kicking him into a lope.

After a mile, her heart slowed down to a dull thudding, and gradually, as the road slipped by beneath the buckskin's feet, she began to forget the terrors behind her and consider those ahead.

What if they didn't believe her? What if she still had to testify under oath? What if even that wasn't enough to save Ben? The only question she did not ask herself during the long, lonely ride was why she was risking everything to help Ben Cantrell.

The moon rose, a yellow sliver of light, but she needed no illumination to find her way. The road stretched clearly before her, a pale strip of beaten earth between twin expanses of lush spring grass that looked black beneath the twinkling pinpricks of stars. She urged the horse into a run, knowing any danger she might face from a fall was small compared with the danger of arriving back home after everyone was up.

Alternating the buckskin between an outright run and a ground-eating lope, she reached town in good time. The stars told her she still had several hours of safety left. Hoskinsville nestled snugly on the prairie, an orderly collection of wooden structures dominated by the bank, the mercantile, and the mansion Franklin Hoskins had built his bride on the outskirts of town. Two of those three buildings belonged to Hoskins, but Molly spared not a thought for the man who controlled most of the wealth in the county. Instead she headed straight for the alley behind Main Street, which would take her to the back of the jail.

Here the darkness was almost complete, and she slowed her horse to a careful walk. Going by instinct as much as anything else, she found the adobe building in which Ben Cantrell was imprisoned. She left the buckskin ground-hitched in the alley and felt her way to the window, which she knew opened into the tiny room where the sheriff kept a cot for his own personal use. Surely he would be sleeping in the jail tonight, guarding his important prisoner.

Taking one last look around, Molly determined she was entirely alone in the streets of Hoskinsville. No sound reached her ears save the rush of her own blood. Lifting a trembling hand, she tapped lightly on the windowpane.

The noise was like a gunshot in the velvet stillness, and Molly jumped, certain lights would go on everywhere as honest citizens roused to discover who had disturbed their slumber. But no lights came on, and no one roused, and she was forced to repeat her tapping, this time rattling the pane with the force of her blow.

From inside she heard a slight noise, a scraping sound, and then she saw the flare of a match. Sheriff Bigelow's broad face appeared in the glow, his eyes wide as he peered around. Molly tapped again, just loudly enough to draw his amazed attention. She wasn't sure he saw her because at that instant the match flame touched his fingertips and he dropped the stick with a curse, plunging the room into darkness again.

Molly held her breath, expecting to hear him sounding an alarm, expecting someone to come running down the alley to catch her and drag her into the light. What are you doing here? they would want to know, and Molly had no answer, or at least no answer she could give.

In front of her the window sash slid up, the sound like thunder to her supersensitive ears. "Who's out there?" demanded Sheriff Bigelow.

"Shhh!" she hushed him, new terrors of discovery shivering over her. "It's Molly Wade. Please, Sheriff, I have to talk to you."

"Molly Wade?" he repeated incredulously in a voice that sounded like a shout to Molly. "What on earth? . . . Wait a minute while I get my pants on." Muttering imprecations, he stumbled around, each bump and noise feeding Molly's steadily growing panic. After the longest minute of her life, he said, "Don't you want to go around to the door?"

"No, I can't! I can't let anyone see me. Please, Sheriff, I have something real important to talk to you about. About Ben Cantrell. Can't I come in the window?"

He muttered something that sounded like "hell fire," but he lifted the sash all the way and reached out a hand to her. "You know I'd lose my job if anyone found you in my room in the middle of the night, don't you?"

"I don't expect anyone to find me," Molly replied, forcing her quivering legs to negotiate the climb through the window.

As soon as she was inside, the sheriff shut the window, pulled the battered shade, and lit the lamp. Molly blinked in the sudden brightness.

Sheriff Bigelow looked slightly ridiculous in his blue jeans and red long-handled underwear. His gray-streaked hair was standing up in spikes, giving her a hysterical urge to laugh. She might have done so if the expression on his face hadn't been so forbidding.

"Now what's all this about Ben Cantrell?" he demanded, obviously unhappy with her melodramatic entrance.

"Is it true you've got him locked up here?"

"He's not locked in, but I've got him here for safekeeping until the judge comes tomorrow."

"Then you really are going to try him for burning Harry's barn." The knowledge sank in her stomach like a lead weight. Some part of her had clung to the hope it was all a mistake.

"We're going to have a hearing first, let the judge hear all the evidence so he can decide if there's any reason for a trial," he explained, his shrewd eyes narrowing as he studied her in the light. "Say, maybe you'd better sit down. You're shaking like a leaf."

Knowing she was violating every rule of decorum, Molly sank gratefully onto the sheriff's rumpled bed. "Thank you," she murmured. Then, unable to delay another second, she said, "Ben didn't do it. He couldn't have."

"And what makes you so sure?" the sheriff asked skeptically.

"Didn't he . . . didn't he tell you where he was when the fire started?"

"No, he didn't. Said he couldn't tell me without ruining somebody's good name."

Molly stared at him in disbelief. Why would Ben have chosen to protect her? Only knights in storybooks exhibited such chivalry, and Ben Cantrell was no knight, as she had learned to her sorrow. Whatever his reason, she knew he would not continue to protect her if it meant going to prison. Sooner or later he would have to tell the truth. Her only hope was to beat him to it.

"Ben couldn't have burned Harry's barn because he was with me when the fire was set."

Sheriff Bigelow's murky brown eyes widened perceptively. *"You?* Why was he with you? And where?"

Molly swallowed down the lump forming in her throat. "We were out in the trees behind the schoolhouse. I . . . I saw him when I went outside, and I wanted to talk to him about what happened earlier," she said, giving him the explanation she had carefully rehearsed on her long ride in. "I didn't want to be seen talking to him, so we went off a ways. He was pretty mad at Harry, and I calmed him down. We had a long talk, and then . . . then I went back to the schoolhouse, and he rode off. A few minutes later— not more than ten, I'd say—I heard somebody yelling about the fire."

She paused, trying to decide if the sheriff believed her story, but his expression told her nothing. "Don't you see?" she tried desperately. "He couldn't have set the fire because he was with me when it was being set. He couldn't possibly have done it!"

The sheriff leaned back against the wall and

crossed his arms over his chest. "Well, then, you can testify to that at the hearing, and Ben'll go free."

"No, I can't!"

"Why not?"

Molly swallowed again. "My pa . . . he'll *kill* me if he finds out."

Bigelow studied her for a long moment and then said, "What were you and Ben doing out in the trees?"

"Nothing! I told you! We were talking!" Molly felt her face grow hot, but she refused to drop her gaze.

"Did you ride in here all by yourself tonight?" he asked suddenly.

"Yes," she replied, puzzled by the question.

"That's a long ways for a girl to come all by herself. You took quite a chance, and all for a man you were just talking to."

The words were softly spoken, but they hit Molly with the force of a blow. The sheriff knew what she had done with Ben, and if he knew, *everyone* would know. No one would believe her carefully constructed story, especially when Ben Cantrell told what had really happened. "I . . . I don't want to see an innocent man go to prison," she tried.

"An innocent man you're in love with."

"*No!*" she cried, jumping to her feet. She *didn't* love him, *couldn't* love him, not after the way he'd used her.

"Hey, now, I didn't mean to make you cry," the sheriff said in dismay.

Only then did Molly realize she was crying. Angrily, she swiped at the tears. "Do you at least believe Ben didn't start the fire?"

"I didn't believe it before. All I needed was some proof, and now you've given it to me . . . unless you're lying to protect him."

"Why would I lie? Why would I say we were together if we weren't? Ben Cantrell is nothing to me."

The sheriff's bushy eyebrows lifted, but he did not dispute her claim. Instead he said, "Only thing I can't figure is how we're going to get him out of this if you won't testify, and he won't say your name in court."

"Can't *you* tell the judge? Can't you explain how things are?"

"The law don't work that way, honey."

More tears slid down her cheeks, but Molly barely noticed them as despair claimed her. Her wild ride had been for nothing. If she wanted to save Ben—and she wouldn't be able to live with herself if she didn't—she would still have to step forward when the time came. Her life would be ruined. She could already hear her father's shrill accusations: Whore! Bitch!

And what would become of Julie and her mother when she brought her father's wrath down on their heads?

"There now, don't take on so," Bigelow urged, patting her shoulder awkwardly. "I know how you feel. I sure wouldn't want any daughter of mine to stand up in court and say she'd been off in the woods with a man. I wish there was some way. . . . Wait a minute, maybe . . ."

"What?" Molly asked, grasping at this straw.

"One time I saw it done. What was it called again? Some fancy legal name I can't recollect. A witness couldn't come to court, so he wrote down what he was going to say."

"Could I do that? Could you read it and not give my name?"

"I don't know about that, but I could sure try. In fact, I could explain everything to the judge. He's really the only one has to see it anyway since this ain't a regular trial. Judge Gordon is a fair man. I don't think he'd want to see you ruined for no good reason."

"Oh, Sheriff Bigelow, how can I ever thank you?"

"Don't start thanking me 'til this is all over. I may not be able to keep you out of it after all, you know. Wait right here. I'll fetch a pencil and paper so you can write everything out."

Molly did as he instructed, and when she had finished writing her somewhat edited version of the events of that evening, she handed them to the sheriff to read.

"Sounds fine to me. Just sign your name at the bottom."

When she had, he said, "I reckon Ben'll be mighty grateful for what you did."

"I didn't do it so he'd be grateful." In fact, she suspected he might even be disappointed because she had cheated him out of the opportunity of shaming her publicly. "I'd better be going if I want to get home before everybody wakes up."

"Don't you want to see Ben before you go?"

"Oh, no!" Ben Cantrell was the last person she wanted to see, tonight or ever again.

Bigelow was startled by her vehemence. "I'll tell him what you did."

"Fine," Molly said without much enthusiasm. "Thanks for all your help, Mr. Bigelow." Hastily, before he could say anything else, Molly climbed back out the window. Her horse was waiting where she'd left it, standing three-legged and dozing. She mounted swiftly and guided the animal out into the street. The position of the moon told her she had plenty of time to get home before daylight. If no one had seen her leave and if no one saw her return, she would have passed the first obstacle of the perilous course she had set for herself.

Inside the jail, Sheriff Bigelow listened to the fading sound of hoofbeats and then turned and walked into the main room of the jail. The door to one cell stood open, and faint sounds of snoring came from within. The sheriff slipped quietly inside and shook the man sleeping on the bottom bunk.

Ben was instantly awake. "What? Is somebody here?"

"No, son. Everything's quiet," Bigelow assured him in hushed tones. He didn't want to wake Johnny McGee. "I did have a visitor, though. Molly Wade was just here."

"Molly?" Ben looked around in disbelief. "It's the middle of the night."

"Yeah, she didn't want anybody to know she came. She told me you two were together the night of the social. Said you couldn't've set the fire."

Ben swore in exasperation. "Why'd she do a damn fool thing like that? I wasn't going to tell anyone it was her. Her reputation'll be ruined."

"She said she didn't want to see an innocent man go to prison."

"Damn," Ben said in wonder. Why had she risked everything to save him? Didn't she know Harry wouldn't have a thing to do with her if he knew? Of course she did. That's why she'd come at night when no one would see her. "But what about the hearing? She doesn't want to testify, does she?"

"She wrote out her statement for me. I'm going to give it to Gordon. If he's as much of a gentleman as he should be, he'll accept it without making her tell the story in court."

In the bunk above, Johnny's snores suddenly ceased with a startled snort. "What's going on? Is it trouble?" he asked in alarm.

"No, everything's fine," Ben assured him. "The sheriff just came to see if we were tucked in."

"Sleep tight, boys," Bigelow said with a grin, turning to leave. "Gordon ought to be here tomorrow sometime."

Ben lay back in his bunk. In a few seconds Johnny was snoring again, leaving Ben alone with his thoughts, and his thoughts centered on one subject only: Molly Wade.

Why had she come? Why had she risked her reputation for him when she didn't really care about him? Or did she? After all, she *had* made love with him. She must have some feelings for him. A girl like Molly wouldn't give herself to just any man. On the other hand, afterward she had run like a scared rabbit, straight into Harry Hoskins's arms.

None of it made sense, no matter how many times he tried to figure it out.

Molly was beginning to think she would never feel anything except totally terrified ever again. The days since the fire seemed like one long nightmare. She had worried over every word, every glance, every gesture, wondering if someone had guessed her secret. Miraculously, in spite of her odd behavior, no one seemed aware of the momentous change in her, the change that had occurred the night she'd lain with Ben Cantrell. Still, she knew her ordeal was far from over. Everything depended on Judge Gordon now, so she waited helplessly, fighting the nausea of her fear and struggling to appear normal to the rest of the world.

Then, when she thought she could hear nothing worse, her father announced they were all going to town to hear Judge Gordon try Ben. She'd tried to beg off, but her father was adamant. This was one of the moral illustrations he thought would benefit Molly and Julie, like going to see Sam Cantrell hanging from a tree. Arguing was futile, like talking to a fencepost.

Molly wasn't sure which she dreaded more, actually being there or having the sheriff come to the house to fetch her to testify. As they arrived in town, she decided she would far rather have been at home. Everyone who had been at the box social and others besides had made the trip. From her seat in the back of the wagon, Molly tried to guess how many of them were as anxious as her father was to see Ben hang.

She caught sight of Harry standing outside the schoolhouse where Judge Gordon held court when he came to town. Harry's expression was grim as he talked with his father and some other men, but when he saw her family's wagon pulling up to the building, he excused himself and hurried over to help her out.

"I didn't expect you to be here," he said, handing her down first and then Julie.

Her father didn't give her a chance to reply. "We came to show you our support," he said, giving Harry a slap on the back. Molly knew Harry did not relish such familiarities from her father, but he took it with good grace.

"I appreciate your concern, but I don't think Molly should be exposed to this unpleasantness."

For once Molly could appreciate his protective attitude. She only wished his fears for her sensibilities were justified.

If he knew the kind of "unpleasantness" she had been subjected to in the confines of her own home, he'd probably faint dead away.

"Molly wanted to come, didn't you, honey?" her father was saying.

Molly did not reply, but Harry was much too distracted to notice. Just then his father called him and motioned him to go inside.

"Looks like things are getting under way. If you'll excuse me, I'll see you later."

With renewed trepidation, Molly allowed herself to be herded into the schoolhouse along with the rest of the spectators. Claiming a privilege to which Molly no longer had a right, her father procured them seats near the front, right behind the Hoskins family.

The room was filled beyond capacity, every square foot crammed with spectators, and more were stationed outside the open windows to hear every word. Molly glanced around furtively, but she saw no sign of Ben. Clutching her hands together, she waited, only vaguely aware of the desultory conversation going on around her. After a few minutes she sensed a change in the crowd noise. It swelled to a crescendo and then died away, and she knew Ben had arrived.

For one long moment she closed her eyes, bracing herself for the sight of him. Would he be in chains? Would he be cowed? Would all the attention humiliate him? Slowly, she turned to the sound of booted feet making their way through the press to the front of the room.

As always, the sight of him stunned her, and for a few precious seconds she was aware only of how wonderful he looked—not bound, not cowed, and not embarrassed at all. He marched in with what could only be called disdain, looking neither to the right nor to the left, as if refusing to acknowledge those who had come to see his downfall. The sheriff walked behind him, followed by a scowling Johnny McGee. The three took their seats on the bench reserved for them at the front of the room.

The judge came in, and there were a few moments of confusion during which Molly managed another glance at Ben.

"He's wearing a goddamned gun!" her father whispered in outrage. "What in the hell is Bigelow thinking of?"

Franklin Hoskins turned around in annoyance. "Wade, there are ladies present," he snapped.

Her father's face grew dull red, but he bit back whatever reply he might have wanted to make. The judge was banging his gavel for silence.

"I'd like to think you all came just to see my pretty face or because you're interested in the cause of justice," Judge Gordon said, "but I reckon I know why you're really here, so we'll get to it first thing. Sheriff, take the stand and tell me what you know about the fire at Harry Hoskins's ranch last Saturday night."

The crowd murmured its approval as the sheriff made his way to the witness chair. Molly, however, watched Judge Gordon, wondering if he had read her statement and what he intended to do about it. He was a dignified-looking man with iron-gray hair and a respectable paunch beneath his black judicial robes. His dark eyes seemed capable of seeing into a person's soul and determining whether or not he was telling the truth. She prayed he had seen the truth in her version of the story.

Molly listened to the sheriff's testimony with a curious sense of detachment, as if she had somehow left her body and was observing the event from some distant place. Bigelow's voice seemed to come from far away as he droned on, reciting the facts of the case.

When he was finished, Judge Gordon considered the matter in silence for a moment. "So you're saying that whoever set the fire must have left the social well before eleven o'clock—at least an hour before the fire was spotted by the people at the school—in order to have ridden the distance to Mr. Hoskins's ranch, set the fire, and for the fire to have grown large enough to be seen from so far away. Am I correct?"

"Yes, Your Honor. That's about the way I've got it figured."

"Now I'd like to ask you what made anybody think Ben Cantrell might have been the one to set the fire."

The sheriff shifted on his chair and tossed a disgruntled look at the spectators, who had started to murmur. "He and Harry Hoskins had a little disagreement at the social. They both bid for the same young lady's supper, and Cantrell won. Later they had some sort of argument, and Hoskins knocked Cantrell down."

"Did Cantrell fight back?"

"No, he didn't. He said he didn't want any trouble with Harry or something like that."

Molly shivered slightly and felt Julie's comforting hand on her arm.

The judge scowled at Sheriff Bigelow. "Are you telling me you think a man who refused to fight when he had a better than even chance of whipping his adversary would get revenge by sneaking away and burning the man's barn?"

"I don't think any such thing, Your Honor," Bigelow replied, his disgust evident. "I asked Mr. Hoskins who might've had a reason to do him harm. Ben Cantrell was the only one he could think of, and nobody could remember Cantrell being at the social after the dancing started around nine o'clock."

"I see," said the judge, plainly not seeing at all.

The judge didn't think Ben was guilty! Molly felt one small strand of tension in her loosen.

"Did you have any other reason for thinking Cantrell had set the fire?" the judge asked.

"Like I said, I didn't have any reason at all, but Mr. Hoskins and some others remembered that Cantrell's father had been hung for burning a man's barn, and—"

"I'm not interested in something that may or may not have happened in the past," the judge said coldly. "I'm interested in proof. Do you have any proof that Ben Cantrell burned Harry Hoskins's barn?"

"None at all," the sheriff reported, and the crowd murmur swelled to a roar.

The judge banged his gavel on the desk to restore order, but the audience was slow in responding. "If you folks want to see this, you're going to have to keep quiet!" he shouted, and at last they did. "Thank you, Sheriff. Now I'd like to call Ben Cantrell."

Molly's heart convulsed, and for one horrible second the room grew dim. She forced herself to take a deep breath and let it out slowly. By the time Ben had taken the stand, she was fairly certain she would not faint.

"Now I know everybody's wondering why you wouldn't fight with Harry Hoskins," the judge was saying. "I don't think it has much bearing on the case, but I'll ask you anyway. Why wouldn't you fight?"

Ben's face was expressionless, his eyes cold. "I didn't want to cause any more trouble. The young lady in question had already been embarrassed enough."

The young lady. Dear heaven! He wasn't even going to say her name! Another strand of tension relaxed.

"Did you harbor a grudge against Mr. Hoskins for knocking you down?" the judge asked.

"I wasn't too happy about it, but I didn't blame him much. I probably would've done the same thing in his shoes."

The judge nodded thoughtfully. "Now we come to the question of where you went after the fight. Did you leave the social?"

"No, not then. I didn't leave until around midnight," he replied, starting another crowd murmur that the judge rapped to silence.

"But the sheriff said no one saw you there."

"I wasn't inside at the dance. I figured if I went inside, I might start more trouble, so I stayed out. I was waiting for my friend, Johnny McGee. I figured we'd go home together when the dance was over."

"Did anyone see you?"

Molly held her breath as she waited for his answer.

"One person did."

"And what were the circumstances?"

Molly waited, half expecting Ben's cold gaze to settle on her, but he studiously avoided looking in her direction.

"The person saw me standing there and came over to talk."

"It's funny nobody saw the two of you together," the judge remarked.

Ben shifted on his chair much as Sheriff Bigelow had done earlier. "This person didn't want to be seen with me, so we walked off a ways, back behind the school."

"Where it's dark and you were unlikely to be seen by anyone else, is that correct?"

"Yes, sir," Ben replied with obvious reluctance.

"How long were you back there?"

"I don't know exactly. Maybe fifteen or twenty minutes."

"And then?"

"And then I left. I went on home."

"And the other person?"

"She went back to the dance."

She. The word was like an explosion in the room, and Molly was not the only one who felt the blast. Judge Gordon had to pound his gavel for a full minute to restore order. The crowd quieted only grudgingly.

"Do you know what time it was when you left the dance?" the judge asked when he had regained control of his courtroom.

"From the stars, it was close to midnight."

"Midnight, eh?" Judge Gordon pretended to consider this information. "Then if you were at the schoolhouse until midnight, and the person who set the fire would have had to leave well before eleven o'clock, you would've had a difficult time setting the fire, wouldn't you?"

"Your Honor!" Harry was on his feet, his face scarlet. "We only have his word for all of this. Who is this mysterious female he was with?"

"Sit down, Mr. Hoskins," the judge commanded sternly, pounding his gavel. Harry sat down stiffly, his expression murderous. Molly was trembling again, knowing Harry would not rest until he learned the identity of the mystery woman.

Turning to Ben, the judge said, "You may step down now. Sheriff Bigelow, would you come back, please?"

The sheriff resumed his place in the witness chair. His expression was smug, and for the first time since she had first heard of Ben's arrest, Molly began to believe things might work out.

"I understand you had a visitor the other night at the jail."

"Yes, I did. A . . . a woman came to see me. She wanted me to know Ben Cantrell couldn't have set the fire because he was with her at the dance when the fire was set." The sheriff grinned at the stir his statement caused.

"Are you prepared to name this woman?"

"No, Your Honor, not at this time."

"And why not?"

"Because she specifically asked me not to. You see, like Ben said, she didn't want anyone to know she'd been with him the night of the dance. It could prove very embarrassing to her."

"Your Honor!" Harry was on his feet again. "Surely you aren't going to accept the testimony of an anonymous witness!"

"I most certainly am not," the judge replied solemnly. "I have in my possession a sworn statement from this person which confirms the testimony Mr. Cantrell gave."

"Then I demand you call her to the stand!"

"Mr. Hoskins, you are out of order! You have no right to demand anything. This is a hearing, not a trial, and I make the decisions here. I know who this lady is, and I have decided no purpose will be served by revealing her identity unless this case goes to trial, which . . ." He paused dramatically, frowning his displeasure with the

entire proceeding. "Which I think is totally un-
necessary considering the accused has an alibi.
According to this lady, Cantrell left the dance
only moments before the fire was noticed, and
no one has been able to produce a shred of evidence to prove he had a thing to do with it. I
must therefore conclude that the fire in Harry
Hoskins's barn was set by a person or persons
unknown. Next case."

No one had the slightest interest in the next
case, and pandemonium broke out. Everyone
around Molly jumped up, effectively blocking
her view of Ben. She used these precious moments to gather her composure and deal with
her overwhelming sense of relief. She could
hardly believe it was over. Ben had testified, he
had spoken about her, but he had not mentioned
her name, had not even hinted at her identity.
Whatever his reasons for doing so, he had protected her. The knowledge left her weak.

"Molly, are you all right?"

Harry's voice close to her ear jarred her back to
the real world. "Yes, no, I . . . I'm still not feeling very well from the other night," she said
quite truthfully, although she couldn't help wondering how long she would be able to extend
this mythical illness.

"Your face is flushed. Come on, let's get you
outside into the air." Harry helped her to her
feet. She was vaguely conscious of Julie taking
her other arm and of her parents and Mr. and
Mrs. Hoskins coming along behind.

* * *

Ben watched her leaving on Harry's arm, his eyes narrowed as he fought the jealousy boiling up in him. Whatever hope she had given him by making her statement to the sheriff was now dashed. Regardless of her feelings for Ben, Molly Wade obviously had no intention of losing her chance at a rich husband.

Numbly, Ben shook the hands offered to him and accepted the congratulations of those who came to assure him they had believed him innocent all along. Ben smiled his thanks in spite of his skepticism. When the last well-wisher had drifted away, the sheriff clapped him on the shoulder.

"See, son, I wasn't the only one who thought you didn't do it."

Ben didn't want to argue with the man to whom he owed so much. "I don't know how to thank you, Mr. Bigelow."

"Just stay out of trouble from now on," the sheriff said with a grin.

"I don't usually go looking for it, but it still seems to find me somehow."

"I'll keep his nose clean," Johnny offered, shaking the sheriff's hand and earning an affectionate cuff from Ben.

The room was almost empty now, and Judge Gordon, who had long since given up hope of restoring order and recessed his court, stepped down from the front platform to offer Ben his own congratulations.

"I appreciate what you did," Ben said.

"No decent man would've done any different," the judge demurred. "I've known her old man for a long time, and I wouldn't want to bring his wrath down on her head."

Sheriff Bigelow sighed, and Johnny scowled. Ben knew his friend had wanted Molly to take the stand. Johnny still thought she was cowardly for not stepping forward, and he refused to hear arguments to the contrary. He was afraid her anonymity would leave doubts in the minds of some people, people who might take it into their heads that Ben was guilty after all.

"I reckon you boys'll want to head on home," the sheriff was saying.

"Yeah, we've neglected our work long enough," Ben replied. "Although we did enjoy your hospitality."

"We sure did," Johnny agreed. "It was a treat not having to eat our own cooking."

Ben and Johnny were still smiling when they left the schoolhouse, but the sight of Harry fussing over Molly wiped all signs of happiniess from Ben's face. She was sitting in her father's wagon, and Harry hovered nearby, surrounded by Molly's family and his own. They would be griping to each other about the dreadful miscarriage of justice. Setting his jaw, Ben turned toward where his horse was tethered and made his way out of town without so much as a backward glance.

* * *

Molly winced at the open hostility directed toward Ben's departing back. Apparently no one in the little group clustered around her believed in Ben's innocence except her. Or if they did, they were unhappy about it.

"I can't believe Judge Gordon would be a party to such a thing," Harry said. "Imagine having a witness who won't come forward."

"I figure she's a married woman," Elijah speculated.

Miriam Hoskins gasped slightly at the theory, drawing a sharp look from her husband, but Molly barely registered the exchange. "What makes you think so?" Molly asked.

Elijah Wade drew himself up to his full height, preening under the sudden attention of the entire Hoskins family. "It stands to reason. Why else would a woman be afraid to be seen with Cantrell? He's been messing with somebody's wife. She didn't want him to be tried because he would've had to say her name to save his neck."

"I think you may have something there, Wade," Mr. Hoskins said, rubbing his neatly cropped beard thoughtfully and giving his own wife a sidelong glance. Molly had always thought him a fine-looking man with his immaculately tailored clothes and his dark, slightly graying hair and beard. Only his eyes had put her off. They were cold and hard, like dark brown marbles placed in his head in error by a careless creator. If eyes were the windows of the soul, as Molly had read somewhere, then Franklin Hoskins's soul had been boarded up.

She listened to the continuing conjecture about Ben Cantrell's married paramour with growing alarm. "I think you've all lost sight of the important thing here. We still don't know who set Harry's barn on fire or why."

"Molly's right," Harry said. "You're all assuming there really *is* a woman, and I'm still not sure. I'm going to talk to the judge later when he's finished for the day. I'd at least like to see this statement she supposedly made."

A frisson of alarm shot through Molly, but she reminded herself sternly of how careful Judge Gordon had been to protect her. Surely he wouldn't reveal her name to Harry, of all people.

An uncomfortable silence fell, until at last Molly's mother said, "Elijah, maybe we ought to get Molly on home. She's looking mighty peaked."

Harry responded before Elijah could. "Yes, of course. We're being very thoughtless to keep her sitting here."

Harry and his father shook hands with Wade and stepped back while Miriam bid Molly, Julie, and Hannah farewell.

As the wagon rattled away, Molly raised a hand in answer to Harry's wave, but her attention was on the couple behind him. Franklin Hoskins had pulled his wife aside and was saying something to her, something that made her lovely eyes go wide with fear, something that made her shake her head violently, and something that made her finally wrench away from him in alarm.

Chapter Six

✦ ✦ ✦ ✦ ✦

MOLLY TOOK A deep breath and fought the wave of nausea that threatened to send her running for the weeds. After breakfast, she and Julie had come out to hoe the garden patch, and the combination of the sun and the work and the cornmeal mush in her stomach was proving disastrous.

"Molly, are you all right?" Julie called from the other end of the garden.

"Yes," she replied, working her hoe blindly in an attempt to allay Julie's concern. In the six weeks since Ben's trial, Molly had become a constant worry to her sister, one more thing for Molly to add to her burden of guilt. Destroying Julie's chances for a normal home life with her after she married Harry had not been enough. Now Molly's continuing illness had the girl fretting day and night. When Julie found out the reason behind the illness . . .

"Molly!"

Molly barely made it to the weeds. Julie came after her, reaching her just as she finished retching. Molly knelt in the grass, trembling and gasping.

"You're sick," Julie accused, dropping down beside her. "You shouldn't be working. Let's go inside. Mama'll make you some chamomile tea and—"

"No! We can't tell Mama I'm sick."

"Why not?"

"Because . . ." Molly wiped a shaking hand across her mouth. "Because I'm not really sick."

"Don't be silly, of course you are—"

"No, I'm not, I'm . . ."

"What? What's wrong with you?"

"I'm . . . I'm going to have a baby."

Julie's mouth dropped open. "You're crazy! How could you have a baby?"

"The usual way people get them."

"But how? With who?" Julie insisted. "Not . . . not Harry?"

Molly shook her head vigorously.

"Then who?"

"Ben Cantrell."

Totally stunned, Julie sank back on her heels.

"I'm sorry, Julie. I didn't mean to tell you, but . . . I'm so scared. I had to tell *somebody*."

"When did it happen?" Julie asked, still unable to comprehend completely.

"The night of the box social. Remember you left me outside, and I was out there a long time?"

Julie nodded slowly. "You were with him then?"

"Yes." Ashamed, Molly buried her face in her hands.

"I can't understand this. Why would you . . . with *Ben Cantrell?*"

"I don't understand it, either. It seemed so right at the time. He said some things. . . . I thought he loved me and . . . But he was only using me to get revenge on Harry."

"Revenge? How would that—?"

"Don't you see? I can't marry Harry now because he'd know I'd been with someone else."

"Oh." Gradually Julie managed to put all the pieces together. "That's why you've been avoiding Harry, not letting him call and pretending you're sick and—"

"I'm not pretending."

"—and *you're* the 'mystery woman'!"

Molly nodded.

"How on earth did you talk to the sheriff?"

"I snuck away in the middle of the night. I thought sure somebody'd see me, but nobody did."

"Good Lord," Julie marveled. "But how do you know you're going to have a baby?"

"I know from back when Mama was, a long time ago. You were awful little then. Do you remember?"

"No. What are the signs?"

"She was tired a lot and sick to her stomach. She lost her breakfast most days, and her monthly stopped. I heard her talking to another woman about it after church one Sunday."

"But she never had a baby. What happened to it?"

Molly swallowed hard against the bile rising in her throat again. She couldn't tell Julie the whole truth, how their father had beaten their mother until she'd convulsed in the agony of a miscarriage. "It came too early, and it died."

Julie nodded absently, more concerned with the problem at hand. "Did you miss your monthly?"

"Twice now. Oh, Julie, what am I going to do? When Pa finds out—"

"You have to tell Ben."

"I can't do that! He won't care anyway."

"Are you crazy? Of course he will. It's his baby, too."

"Men don't care about babies."

"Well, Ben Cantrell cares about *you*, no matter what you think. I've seen the way he looks at you when he thinks nobody's watching. He'll come for you. I know he will."

Molly shook her head miserably.

"Aren't you even going to try?" Julie demanded.

"I can't face him. What if he laughs at me? What if he—"

"Then *I'll* tell him."

"Don't you dare!"

"Molly, what's happened to you? You used to be so brave about things. You always protected me and took care of me and—"

"Being brave won't solve this, Julie. *Nothing* can solve this."

Julie made a disgusted noise and rose to her feet. "Get up and get back to the garden," she said, stomping off toward the barn.

Wearily, Molly got up and retrieved the hoe she had dropped in her haste. The long rows of fledgling vegetables swam before her for a moment, but she fought off the dizziness and began to chop at the weeds.

Ben squinted in the late morning sunshine as he stepped out of the house. Johnny and his two new hired men were waiting for him over by the barn. On Saturday they always made a trip to town. Ben had on a new shirt and vest, and he was looking forward to a lively evening away from the ranch.

"Pssst!"

At first Ben thought he'd imagined the sound. No one was in sight.

"Pssst! Ben! Over here."

He caught a glimpse of a girl's face and honey-colored hair peeking around the corner of the house, and his heart turned over. "Molly?" he asked, hardly daring to hope she had come to him after all these weeks of silence. Hastily he ducked around the side of the house, but the girl he found there was not Molly.

"Ben, I have to talk to you," she said.

"You're Molly's sister, aren't you?"

Julie nodded nervously. "I don't want anybody to see me."

"What are you doing here?"

"I have to tell you something, something about Molly."

"Wait here. I'll get rid of the others."

Ben loped over where the men waited and made up some excuse about remembering a har-ness he needed to take to town to be repaired. With some reluctance, they went on ahead when he promised to meet them later.

"What is it? Why didn't she come herself?" he demanded the instant he found Julie again.

"She was afraid. She thinks you don't like her anymore."

Ben frowned. "She was the one who went off with Harry Hoskins after . . . after we . . ."

"I know what happened between you two at the social. Molly told me, but she thought you were just trying to get revenge on Harry."

"*Revenge?* Where'd she get a fool idea like that?"

"I knew she was wrong," Julie said smugly. "I knew you liked her. You do, don't you?"

"Why did you come here?" Ben hedged.

"Because Molly's in trouble."

"What kind of trouble?"

"She . . . she's going to have a baby."

"A *baby? My* baby?"

"Of course your baby," Julie snapped in annoyance. "She doesn't think you'll care, though."

"She doesn't . . . Has she lost her mind?"

"She's awful scared, Ben. She's not thinking very straight."

"I can see that. What does she want me to do?"

"She doesn't want you to do anything. She didn't even want me to tell you about it, so I guess it's up to you now."

"Where is she?"

"At home. I figure the best thing is to just go and get her."

"Shouldn't I try to talk to her first? We could meet someplace and—"

"No, she's scared, and she doesn't trust you anymore, and if Pa caught her meeting you . . ." Julie shuddered. "You'd best just go get her and be done with it."

"I reckon your pa'll put up a fight."

"You won't let him stop you from taking her, will you?"

"Not on your life, little Julie," he said. "Nothing's going to stop me from having her now."

Molly was sweeping the front porch when she saw Julie sneaking back from the barn. Julie had ridden away earlier, and Molly hoped the ride had made her sister feel better. The thought of Julie still being upset with her was more than she could stand.

"Where you been, Julie?" Elijah Wade demanded. He was sitting on the porch steps, recovering from a hangover so he would be in fit shape to go into town for another binge.

"I was out in the barn," Julie replied as if that were a perfectly satisfactory answer, and breezed on into the house.

Sensing Julie was up to something, Molly started to follow her, but the sound of hoofbeats in the ranch yard stopped her. To her horror, Ben Cantrell rode right up to the front porch, bold as you please.

Elijah jumped to his feet. "What the hell do you want?"

"I came for Molly," Ben replied.

Molly's heart was pounding a mile a minute, and she couldn't seem to get her breath. What did he mean, he'd come for her?

"*Molly!*" Elijah echoed incredulously. "You must be outa your mind. I've got half a notion . . . Where's my rifle?"

"Pa, don't!" Molly cried, but he was already in the house. A second later he came back brandishing a Winchester.

"Get off my property, Cantrell!" Elijah shouted.

Molly didn't think the gun was loaded, but she wasn't sure. "Pa, put that thing down before you hurt somebody."

"I'll hurt somebody all right. I'll blow his damn head off."

"Elijah!" Hannah flew out the door and almost got the gun away from him, but he flung her off, slamming her against the house.

"Wade, that's enough," Ben said, his voice ringing like steel. "Let Molly come with me, and there won't be any trouble."

"Trouble! I'll show you trouble! What makes you think she'd go with the likes of you, anyway?"

"She's carrying my child."

As if from a distance, Molly heard her mother's gasp and her father's curse. The world started spinning, and through the maelstrom she saw her father's face contorted in rage. "Whore! Bitch!" The rifle butt came up, and she screamed, throwing her hands up to protect her head. Then suddenly Ben was there, wrenching the rifle away and silencing Elijah's stream of curses with his fist. The blow sent the older man sprawling onto the porch.

"If you ever lay a hand on her again, so help me God, I'll kill you," Ben swore, tossing the rifle out into the yard. "Molly, get your things and come with me. Now."

Molly lifted a trembling hand to her throat as she looked from Ben's determined face to his clenched fists and then at her parents. Her mother slumped against the side of the house, but her eyes were bright, sending her a silent message of encouragement. Her father sat stunned just where Ben's punch had sent him.

If she stayed, her father would kill her or at least make her wish she was dead. She glanced at Ben's clenched fists again. If she went with him, would her life be any better?

Julie appeared in the doorway carrying a blanket-wrapped bundle. She took in the scene at a glance and thrust the bundle into Molly's hands. "I packed all your things. Now go!"

Molly hesitated only a moment, then impulsively threw her arms around her sister, bundle and all. "Thank you," she whispered in the second before she let Julie go and turned to her mother.

"Mama, I—"

"Don't touch her," Wade ordered Hannah. "You're no daughter of mine, you cheap slut. You'll never set foot in this house again, you hear? And nobody in this family'll ever speak to you again. You're dead to us. Do you hear me? *Dead!* And as for you, Cantrell, we should've hanged you when we had the chance. You're nothing but a lowdown son of a . . ."

Molly couldn't listen anymore. She let Ben take her arm and lead her away. Tears were streaming down her face as she looked back at the only home she could remember. As awful as her life there had been, she had known love there, too. Her mother waved, and Molly waved back, choking on a sob. Would she ever see her mother again? Or Julie? And if she did, would they be allowed to speak to her? And what would their lives be like without her?

They reached Ben's horse, and he lifted her effortlessly into the saddle. She saw him frown when he noticed her bare feet, and she tried to hide them beneath the tattered hem of her skirt. Then he swung up behind her and kicked the animal into motion.

"Good-bye Molly! Be happy!" Julie called, braving her father's wrath and earning a sound cursing for her trouble.

Molly tried to speak, but tears clogged her throat and the sound came out as another sob. Ben's arm slipped around her, drawing her against his chest, where she poured out her grief and pain as they rode away.

Ben glanced back over his shoulder to make sure Wade wasn't going after the rifle again. The old bastard still sat on the porch, cursing a blue streak while the two women stared after them. The longing in their eyes was poignant, and Ben knew an urge to go back for them, too. Unfortunately he suspected he'd more than have his hands full with just Molly.

He patted her awkwardly, feeling helpless in the face of her near hysteria. On the ride over, he had imagined her reaction would be relief or resignation or maybe even happiness. He had no idea how to deal with a woman's tears. "Don't cry, Molly. I'll take good care of you and the baby, too."

Mention of the child sent her into fresh spasms of weeping, and Ben gave up trying to comfort her. By the time they had covered the few miles to his ranch, Molly's tears had subsided into an occasional hiccup. "Here we are, Molly. Your new home."

Molly looked up in alarm, rubbing the moisture from her face with the back of her hand. "I thought—I mean, aren't we going to . . . ?"

"Going to what?"

Molly's fears bubbled up again. Had she presumed too much? "I thought we'd get married first."

His astonishment was almost comic, but he recovered quickly. "I figured you'd want to change your clothes and get cleaned up before we went to town."

Her relief quickly gave way to self-conscious-

ness at her appearance. She was wearing a shirt
made from a flour sack and a skirt that anyone
else would have consigned to the rag bag long
ago. Her feet were bare and dirty from working
outside all morning, because she dared not wear
her one pair of shoes for fear of ruining them. "I
. . . Yes, thank you, I'd like to change."

Suddenly she was aware of Ben's arm around
her. In her grief, he had been nothing more than
a solid presence on which to lean, but now he
was a man again. The man who had come for
her. The man with whom she would live and
share a bed, the man whose children she would
bear, whose child she already carried.

And he was a stranger.

"I'll hurry," she said, wiggling free of his embrace and sliding down from the saddle.

"Molly!" he cried in alarm when she stumbled
as she hit the ground, but she was up in an
instant and heading for the house at a near run,
clutching her bundle to her breast.

The house was small, only one room. She
slammed the door behind her and looked in vain
for a lock. Panting, she glanced around for something with which to secure the door but found
nothing. Then she heard Ben's horse heading for
the barn and realized he had no intention of
following her.

She sagged against the door and took a deep
breath. She was behaving like an idiot. What
was she afraid of, for heaven's sake? Ben
wouldn't hurt her. *Ben wouldn't hurt her.* He'd
promised to take care of her, hadn't he?

Willing herself to calmness, she looked around. Her new home, Ben had said. She wasn't sure what she had expected his house to be like, but certainly not like this. The place was neat as a pin, the bed made with precision square corners, all the cooking utensils hanging neatly on pegs, dishes stacked on shelves in an open cupboard. The table was scrubbed white and the floor swept clean. The furniture was mostly handmade but sturdy and comfortable, and a cook stove stood in one corner. What a luxury!

Her gaze trailed back to the bed built into one of the other corners. The *only* bed. It seemed narrow for two people to share. For an instant she tried to imagine what it would be like to lie down with a stranger. A strange man. She shivered.

"Molly, do you need some water?"

Molly jumped. Dragging her attention back to the present, she looked around again, this time for bathing facilities. She saw a tub propped in one of the corners and thought she could improvise a quick bath. "Yes," she called. "Is there any hot?"

"Afraid not." He was on the other side of the door. "Can I come in?"

She pulled the door open and stood back as he carried in two buckets of water and set them down near the stove. When he turned to face her, his expression was wary, and his blue eyes took her in from head to bare toes.

"I . . . I must look a sight," she said, fumbling with her bundle.

His mouth quirked. "I was thinking how pretty you are."

She resisted the impulse to hurl herself into his arms, and fought the lump in her throat. She couldn't let him see her cry anymore. He'd lose patience with her and get angry. She managed a smile. "I'll look a lot better when I get cleaned up."

"I hope my heart can stand it."

Her heart did a little flip, and for the life of her she couldn't think of a single thing to say. Her toes curled on the wooden floor, and she shifted her bundle again.

Ben cleared his throat. "I've got three men working for me right now, but they're all in town today."

"Oh."

"I . . . maybe you'd like to be alone now."

"Yes, I would."

"Oh."

He didn't move for a minute, and when he did, he came right toward her.

She jumped back like a scared rabbit, but he was only heading for the door. He frowned at her nervousness. "I told you I won't hurt you, Molly. You don't have to be scared anymore."

"I'm not." She straightened her shoulders and stood taller.

"Holler if you need anything."

"I will."

She closed the door behind him with a sigh. When would she stop panicking every time he came near her? Why couldn't she believe him when he promised not to hurt her?

Shaking off her disturbing thoughts, she forced herself to walk over to the bed and set her bundle down. After all, she had a wedding to prepare for.

A little less than an hour later, clad in her blue watered floral dress with the Watteau pleats, she opened the cabin door. "I'm read—"

Ben was standing no more than three feet away, leaning up against one of the porch supports. He let out a low whistle.

"The dress is a little wrinkled," she said uncertainly. "I couldn't find an iron."

"I'll buy you one. I reckon there's a lot of things you'll be wanting. We're not set up for a woman around here."

"Everything's very nice, really. Nicer than I expected." And so clean, she thought. He didn't really need a woman at all. She wanted so desperately to please him, but whatever could she do to earn her keep?

"Well, you tell me anything you want."

"All right."

He looked her over again, much as he had done before, inside the house, only this time she felt more confident about her appearance. "You were wearing that dress the night we . . ."

Molly's face flamed. Did he think she'd worn it on purpose? "It's the only nice dress I have."

"The *only* one?"

"I had another one, but when I got this, I gave

it to Julie. Pa doesn't . . ." She stopped, too ashamed to tell him the whole truth.

"He doesn't see any reason to waste good money on clothes for you. I figured as much from the outfit you had on before." He sounded angry.

"I don't need a lot of fancy clothes."

"You ought to have some decent ones, anyway. I'll buy you some when we get to town. Come on, I've got the wagon hitched."

Molly followed reluctantly. Why was he so angry? Did he think she'd be a burden to him, always demanding he buy her this or that? She didn't dare ask her questions aloud, however. She couldn't risk making him even madder. He helped her up onto the seat of the buckboard, and they set out in silence.

The ride into town seemed endless to Molly, for whom the whole day was assuming an air of unreality. Since she had given herself to Ben Cantrell, her whole life had taken such a bizarre turn she could no longer remember what "normal" felt like. Now here she was, pregnant, disowned by her family, and on her way to marry a man she barely knew. It was the kind of experience one hoped to awaken from, discovering it had been a nightmare.

"I guess Julie told you about the baby," she said when she could stand the silence no longer.

"Yeah, she did," he replied bitterly, making Molly sorry she had introduced the subject. "If you weren't planning to tell me about it, what *were* you going to do?"

"I . . . I don't know."

"Were you going to marry Harry and tell him the baby was his?"

"No! I haven't even seen Harry since we . . . since . . . for a long time."

"You were quick enough to go off with him that night after you left me."

"I had to go home! My dress was dirty and my hair was a mess. If I'd gone back to the dance, everyone would have known what happened!"

"I would've taken you home if you'd given me a chance, but you ran away."

"I didn't want to hear you gloat about how you'd used me to get back at Harry."

"Get back at Harry? What on God's earth would make you think a thing like that?"

"You said it yourself! You said, *'Now* you won't be able to marry Harry.' "

He muttered something unintelligible. "That's not what I meant."

"What did you mean?"

He hesitated so long, she began to think he wasn't going to answer. "I meant that Harry couldn't have you because you belonged to me. And you do belong to me, Molly."

He didn't sound too happy about it. Molly clutched her hands together in her lap and looked away. What on earth had she gotten herself into?

Ben took the back roads to Reverend Bates's house, hoping to avoid the Saturday afternoon crowds on Main Street. They left the wagon out front and proceeded up the walk. Molly sighed with relief when the minister answered the door.

"Molly, Ben, what a surprise," he said, obviously puzzled at seeing the two of them together. "Please, come in.

"What can I do for you?" he asked when he had seated them in the parlor.

"We'd like for you to marry us," Ben said belligerently.

Reverend Bates could not hide his astonishment. "But I thought . . . I mean, I had no idea you two were even . . . Well, what do your parents think about all this, Molly?"

"My father threw me out of the house, Reverend Bates, and told me never to come back."

Reverend Bates needed a minute to recover from his shock. "This is no way to start a marriage. The first thing we must do is reconcile you and your father, and then we must—"

"We don't have time to wait," Ben said. "We need to get married today, right now. Will you do it or not?"

"I really don't think—"

"Please, Reverend Bates," Molly said, feeling the all-too-familiar sense of panic rising up in her. "I have to go with Ben. If you won't marry us—" Her voice broke as she considered the possibilities. She just didn't think she could endure any more shame.

"There now, don't cry, Molly," Reverend Bates urged. "Of course I'll marry you, if that's what you want. I must say, neither of you looks very happy about the prospect, though. A wedding should be a joyful occasion, and—"

"We'll be real happy if you just get on with it," Ben said grimly.

"Certainly. If you'll excuse me for a moment, I'll get my book." He went to a desk in the corner and found the book he sought in one of the drawers. "Now then, if you'll both step over here." He motioned to the far end of the room where there was space for all three of them to stand together.

Ben took Molly's elbow as they walked over, but his touch was as impersonal as his expression. If he was so unhappy about this, why was he doing it?

Reverend Bates cleared his throat and began. "Dearly beloved . . ."

Once again Molly felt a strange detachment. The minister's voice sounded hollow and far away.

"Join hands, please."

Ben seemed startled that her hand was like ice, but she felt cold all over in spite of the warmth of the spring day.

"Do you, Ben, take this woman . . ."

When had she become a woman? She still felt very much like a little girl in so many ways, helpless against the forces moving around her.

"I do," Ben responded.

"Do you, Molly, take this man . . ."

Did she have a choice? There were more promises, promises she wasn't sure she could keep.

How could she pledge herself to a man she hardly knew, a man she sometimes feared? But she could and she did, because she had no choice.

"I do," she said, and Ben's eyes glittered with what might have been triumph.

"Do you have a ring?"

"No," Ben said, "I forgot. Do we have to have one?"

"You can get one later," Reverend Bates assured them both, and went on with the ceremony.

"I now pronounce you man and wife. You may kiss the bride."

Molly lifted her face to Ben's, vaguely curious as to what he would do. It didn't matter, of course. She felt as if all this were happening to someone else.

He bent down and touched his lips to hers, gently and briefly. Her eyes fluttered shut as she accepted the kiss, but when it ended and her eyes opened again, the room tilted dangerously.

"Ben!" she cried, or tried to before everything went black.

When she awoke, she was lying on the sofa and Mrs. Bates hovered over her. She was wearing a hat and was dressed for the street. Obviously she had just come home.

"She's coming around," said the minister's wife. "I can't understand why you didn't wait until I got home. Were they really in that big of a hurry?"

"Yes, they were," Reverend Bates said, glancing at Ben in disapproval.

Ben was oblivious. He hung over Mrs. Bates's shoulder, a worried frown marring his handsome face. He looked agonizingly concerned, Molly noted. "What happened?" she asked.

"You fainted," Mrs. Bates said, "or at least that's what I assume from the story these two told me. Brides often do, you know. How do you feel?"

"A little light-headed."

Mrs. Bates frowned. "When was the last time you ate?"

Molly tried to remember. "Breakfast, except I threw it up."

Mrs. Bates's eyes grew wide, and she exchanged a knowing glance with her husband. "Then I expect it wasn't only nerves that caused you to faint. Young man," she said, turning to Ben, "you had better take your wife out and feed her."

"Yes, ma'am, I will," Ben said.

"Where's that glass of water, Alex?"

Reverend Bates handed it to her, and Mrs. Bates helped Molly take a few sips. "Yes, I'd suggest a nice dinner at the hotel restaurant," she said when Molly was finished. She helped Molly sit up.

Molly still felt woozy, but she didn't think she'd lose consciousness again. What a scene she must have made, and who had carried her to the couch? Was Ben angry? She couldn't tell.

"Do you think you'll be all right now?" asked Mrs. Bates.

"Yes, I'm feeling much better." Except for being embarrassed half to death. Imagine fainting just as Ben kissed her! "Thank you both, for everything."

"You still need to sign the marriage certificate to make everything official," Reverend Bates said.

When the formalities had been taken care of, Molly saw Ben slip some money into the minister's hand. Then he escorted her back outside.

"We don't really have to go to the restaurant," she said as he helped her back up into the wagon.

"Don't you like their food?"

"I . . . I don't know. I've never eaten there."

He was so surprised he forgot to let go of her arm. "Never? Where does your family eat when you come to town?"

"We pack food. Pa doesn't think—"

"Don't tell me. I can guess." His fingers squeezed her upper arm. "I'm not your father, Molly, and I'm taking you to the restaurant."

"All right." How much did it cost to eat in a restaurant? And how much money did Ben have? Her father had always called him shiftless and no-account, but his ranch looked prosperous and well cared for, unlike the Flying W.

Ben found a place along the street to leave the wagon. Molly tried not to stare as they entered the hotel. She had never actually been inside, and Ben hustled her through the lobby too quickly for her to get more than a brief impression of idle men seated on worn furniture reading newspapers.

The dining room was a revelation, too. She'd never seen so many tables and chairs gathered in one place. Most of them were empty now, since it was midway between the dinner and supper hours. Ben directed her to one in the corner, far from any other diners, and seated her with her back to the room.

"What'll it be, folks?"

Molly glanced up to see a middle-aged woman she knew from community functions. She had graying hair and a sagging figure behind her full apron. Molly couldn't quite recall the woman's name, but she obviously recognized Molly. Her gimlet gaze darted back and forth between her and Ben.

Ben ignored her curiosity. "What have you got today?"

"Fried steak and pork chops. The steak is tough, but the chops are lean."

"Molly?"

"The chops, I guess," she said, hoping she was doing what he expected of her. She wished she knew how much the meals cost. Perhaps she had made a wrong decision.

"I'll have the chops, too," Ben said. "And bring us both some coffee. Or would you rather have tea?" he asked Molly.

"Tea, I think," she said, hoping it would settle

her stomach. It was starting to feel jumpy again, although the tantalizing aromas from the kitchen were making her remember how hungry she was. Odd how she had forgotten all about food until now.

The waitress waited another moment, as if expecting them to say more, then Ben sent her on her way with a cold-eyed stare. "Nosy old biddy," he remarked.

"I guess we have to expect folks to be curious. Nobody's ever seen us together before."

Ben frowned. "I wish I'd thought to get you a ring. Then people would know they'll be seeing us together from now on."

Molly rubbed her bare left hand self-consciously. "Does it really mean that much to you?"

"Yes," he said, leaning across the table. The fading sunlight glistened on his golden hair and his eyes were the color of a stormy sky. "I want everyone to know you're my woman now, my *wife*."

His intensity made her uneasy. "You say that like you think I belong to you."

"We belong to each other, you and me and the baby. I've wanted to have a family for as long as I can remember. I hardly even remember my mother, and I've been alone for the past six years. I know you never would've married me if you hadn't been in trouble, but I'll take you any way I can get you."

"Ben, please, not so loud."

He straightened, surprised. "I'm sorry. I just want you to understand how I feel."

Molly shivered slightly, not certain she wanted to be privy to all his emotions.

The waitress brought their coffee and tea. She took the opportunity to study both of them, as if she could read their thoughts and discern the meaning of their presence there together. She went away disappointed.

Ben made a visible effort to be more pleasant. "I didn't ever thank you for telling the sheriff I was with you the night of the fire."

Molly's face flamed, and she dropped her gaze to the tea in front of her. "I couldn't let you go to prison."

"Why not?"

"Because . . . because I couldn't." She was being foolish. Ben was her husband now. She had no reason to keep her feelings a secret any longer. She looked up at him again. "Because I care about you."

At long last his angry expression faded into the softness she had once seen and loved. "But you thought I'd used you just to get revenge on Harry."

"I still couldn't let you go to prison. But there's one thing *I* don't understand: why didn't you tell the sheriff yourself?"

"Your reputation would've been ruined."

"But I thought you were mad at me for going off with Harry."

"I was."

"Then why would you care about my reputation? You could've gone to prison!"

His mouth twitched into a genuine smile. "I guess I care about you, too."

For the first time in the six weeks since she and Ben had made love, the knot of tension that had bound her heart loosened completely.

"I thought you might be mad about the baby," she whispered.

"Mad?" He was genuinely astonished. "Why would I be mad?"

"Some men . . ." She thought of her father and the way he had kicked and punched her mother until he'd killed her baby. "Some men think children are a burden."

"I don't." He reached across the table and grasped her hand. "I want this baby more than anything else in the world."

She stared at their clasped fingers. "But everybody'll know why we got married. Won't you be . . . embarrassed?"

His fingers tightened. "I'll be proud. Every man dreams of giving his woman a baby the very first time."

Molly's breath caught as his words scorched through her and settled in her belly in a white-hot flame. Before she could recover, the waitress arrived with their food. The woman found their expressions fascinating. Molly smiled when she thought of how shocked the waitress would be if she had overheard their conversation, too.

"This looks good," Ben said, glancing down at

the heaps of pork chops and fried potatoes when the waitress had gone.

"I can't believe we forgot to eat. I wasn't even hungry until now."

"I guess we were both too nervous."

Molly's fork stopped halfway to her mouth. "Were *you* nervous?"

He gave her the grin she liked so well. "Sure. I never got married before."

Ben was nervous! She could hardly credit it. She had been scared witless, of course, which was probably as much to blame for her fainting as pregnancy and lack of food. But *Ben?* He was so big and strong and so . . . *dauntless.* How could a little thing like marrying Molly Wade unsettle him?

But perhaps he didn't consider it a little thing. Perhaps he considered it as momentous as she did. She watched him cut a bit of meat and lift it with his fork. "Eat," he commanded her with a wink just before he popped it in his mouth.

Suddenly remembering her own fork still poised in midair, she obeyed him, chewing slowly and praying her errant stomach would cooperate. To her surprise, she was able to finish the entire meal and a slice of apple pie as well. Following western custom, they ate in silence, and as soon as they were finished, Ben said, "Let's go over to the store. I want to get you a ring and whatever else you need before we go home."

Home. The word struck a sour note. Where

was her home now? But she managed a smile and allowed Ben to conduct her back through the hotel lobby onto the street. The supper hour was near, and most of the ranchers in town for the day had headed on home. A few cowboys still lingered on the sidewalks, but the rest had already made their way to the saloons. Molly saw no one she knew well enough to speak to, although she was painfully aware of the stares she and Ben were attracting. By tomorrow everyone within a hundred miles would have heard how she ate supper with Ben Cantrell and walked down the street with him and went away in a wagon with him. Hopefully, the news of their marriage would travel with equal swiftness.

Mrs. Wells was all smiles as they entered her store. "Hello, Molly, Ben." Her eyebrows lifted, but she seemed more inquisitive than surprised. Perhaps the news had already spread this far. "You're just in time. I was getting ready to close up."

"I'm sorry," Molly said. "I didn't realize it was so late."

"Don't worry about it. What can I do for you?"

"We need a few things," Ben said as they moved up to the glass counter where the more valuable items in the store were displayed. "First thing is a wedding ring."

"A wedding ri— Are you two—? Are congratulations in order?"

Ben nodded proudly, slipping his arm around Molly's waist. Molly's cheeks warmed with mingled pride and embarrassment.

"When's the happy day?" Mrs. Well asked, plainly delighted.

"Today," Ben said.

Mrs. Wells's smile froze. "Today? You're *eloping?*"

"We already eloped, but we forgot the ring, so if you'll . . ." He motioned to the glass case.

"Oh, yes, of course." Mrs. Wells hastily pulled out a tray of rings and set it before them. Most of the rings were cheap trinkets, but one row was exclusively plain gold bands. "Let's see now, this one should fit." She pulled one out and handed it to Molly.

With hands that shook slightly, Molly slipped it on her finger. The fit was perfect. The gold glinted provocatively in the late afternoon sunlight. She would have liked to admire it longer, but acutely aware of her audience, she took it off and gave it back to Mrs. Wells. "It's fine."

"Maybe you'd like one with a stone in it," Ben suggested.

Certain a stone would cost too much, Molly shook her head. "A plain one is fine. It's exactly what I want."

"Would you like to wear it?" Mrs. Wells asked.

Molly simply stared back. What should she say?

"Or maybe," Mrs. Wells suggested slyly, "you'd like Ben to put it on your finger later, when you're alone."

"Yes," she said impulsively, looking to Ben for approval.

The smile he gave her rekindled that white-hot flame in her belly, and her heart quivered in reaction. His eyes promised that "later" would be very interesting indeed.

"I'll wrap the ring up for you," Mrs. Wells said. "Can I show you anything else?"

Ben shook his head slightly as if to clear it and turned back to Mrs. Wells. "Molly needs a flat-iron and some clothes. What have you got ready made?"

"Not much, I'm afraid. Some of the things on the shelf over there might fit her, though. Depends on what you're looking for."

"Nothing fancy," Molly hastened to assure her. "Maybe a house dress."

Ben frowned his disapproval and followed her over to the counter. Molly quickly found a simple shirtwaist and skirt she thought would do very well. When she would have walked away, Ben caught her arm and hauled her back.

"What about this?" He held up a violet-sprigged calico.

"I really don't need—"

"I'm going to burn every one of your rags when we get home, Molly, so if you don't want to go around stark naked—"

"Ben Cantrell!" Her face was flaming, but she snatched the dress from his hands and held it up to see if it would fit. It *was* pretty. Too pretty for housework, but the choice was so limited. . . .

Refusing to meet his eye, she folded it carefully and laid it over her arm with her other selections.

"How about something fancy?" he taunted.

"I told you, I don't need anything fancy."

"Mrs. Wells, Molly wants something nice, for dances and such, but you don't have anything here," Ben said, ignoring Molly's dismay.

"I have some new patterns and some lovely material," Mrs. Wells said, coming over to join them in the dry goods section. "This rose taffeta would look lovely on you."

The bolt of fabric she produced made Molly's mouth drop open. It was exquisitely lovely, but it certainly cost at least a dollar a yard, and any dress design suitable for such fine material would require upward of twenty yards. "I don't think—"

"What kind of patterns have you got?" Ben asked.

Mrs. Wells's smile grew even broader than usual as she observed the battle of wills between the newlyweds. "This is a popular style," she said, selecting a pattern from the box. "It would show off your figure beautifully."

Her figure! Dear heaven, she wouldn't have her figure much longer, would she? But she couldn't say such a thing to Mrs. Wells, not on her wedding day. "I . . . I don't know."

"We'll take it," Ben said.

"Ben, you don't even know how much it'll cost," she protested.

"It doesn't matter. Nothing is too good for my bride."

"You're a lucky girl, Molly," Mrs. Wells said as she bustled away to cut the material.

"Ben," she whispered as soon as Mrs. Wells

was out of earshot, "that taffeta probably costs at least a dollar a yard. The dress will cost over twenty dollars!"

He shrugged as if twenty dollars were not enough to keep a whole family fed for several months. "I'm not poor, Molly, so stop worrying. And stop looking so injured. Most people are happy when they get a present. Some of them even say 'thank you.' "

Oh, dear, she'd displeased him when all she wanted to do was prove how careful she could be. "I'm sorry, Ben. I didn't mean . . . Thank you."

He sighed with what might have been disappointment and walked back to the front counter, where he told Mrs. Wells to charge everything to his account. Molly followed, appalled at the way she had destroyed the warmth that had been developing between them. She would have to do much better than this if she didn't want Ben to regret marrying her.

When Mrs. Wells had wrapped their purchases, she wished them happiness and sent them on their way with a cheery wave. Ben put the package in the back of the wagon and helped Molly onto the seat. They were several miles out of town before she worked up enough courage to speak.

"I'm sorry. I know I was rude back there in the store. It's just . . . I'm not used to getting presents."

To her surprise, Ben yanked on the reins, bringing the buckboard to an abrupt halt.

"Dammit, Molly, stop apologizing for everything!"

"I'm sorry," she blurted, and instantly covered her mouth lest she apologize for apologizing again.

He drew a ragged breath. "You're my wife now, Molly, and I'm going to take good care of you. You're going to have everything you need, no matter what your father would or wouldn't have bought for you. I suspect Elijah Wade is a tight-fisted old skinflint who pleaded poverty so you wouldn't make him feel guilty for not even putting shoes on your feet—"

"I have shoes!"

"—but I'm *not* Elijah Wade."

Before she could think, his free hand snaked around her, and he hauled her against his chest, pressing his mouth to hers. She knew one moment of total shock before her body responded of its own accord. Her hands slid up from their defensive position to entwine around his neck, and her lips opened beneath his. The flames inside her flickered to vibrant life, heating her blood and sending it roaring through her veins.

"'Molly, Molly," he chanted against her cheek. "I've wanted to do this all day. I thought I'd never hold you again."

She'd forgotten what he was like, so strong, so warm, so powerful, a force with which to be reckoned. No wonder she had been so helpless to resist him that night. She felt helpless now, too, and the sensation frightened her. Did she dare trust him yet?

Before she could decide, the wagon lurched, almost sending them sprawling backward. Ben heaved on the reins, releasing her so he could use both hands. "Whoa! Hold up there," he called, settling the animals.

By the time he had them under control again, Molly's breathing had almost returned to normal. Ben gave her a lopsided grin. "I reckon we'd better wait 'till we get home for any more of that."

Still holding the reins securely in both hands, he gave her a quick peck on the mouth and slapped the team into motion again.

Home! Dear Lord in heaven, she had forgotten all about what would happen next. They were about to start their honeymoon!

Chapter Seven

✦✦✦✦

BEN FELT A surge of anticipation as he guided the buckboard into the twilit ranch yard. The buildings were dark, and no one was there to welcome him home, but for the first time since he could remember, he didn't mind one bit. Tonight Molly was with him, his wife Molly, the mother of his child. He was no longer alone.

Molly would share his life, and she would share his bed. His body tightened at the thought of having her softness beside him every hour of every night, her sweet mouth, her satiny skin, her lush breasts, and the blessed haven of her womanhood. All of her belonged to him.

He shifted on the seat and resisted the urge to whip the horses into a run. They'd be there soon enough, he told himself, and they had the whole night ahead of them—the rest of their lives ahead of them, in fact. Would a lifetime be long enough to get his fill of Molly Wade? To learn all the secrets her woman's body held? To sate the desire raging within him?

He checked the horizon where the edge of the sun still lingered. How long until he could suggest going to bed? And how would he wait until then?

Molly felt a surge of apprehension as they approached the ranch buildings. Now her life as Ben's wife would really begin. Soon, much sooner than she would have wished, it would be time to go to bed. The strange ache between her thighs frightened her. What did it mean? And how could she possibly feel desire when she was scared enough to curl up into a ball?

Frantically, she tried to recall the details of the night she and Ben had made love hidden in the trees behind the school house, but her memories were only images and sensations at once vivid and vague. She'd known acute, mind-numbing pleasure, but the agonizing pain of wounded pride blurred the edges of her recollections.

Tonight would be different, though. Tonight she was Ben's wife. He'd risked death to take her from her father's house. Surely he wanted her. Surely he cared for her.

She sensed the tension in him when he stopped the wagon just outside the barn. He barely glanced at her as he jumped down and came around to help her. His hands grasped her waist, but he released her the instant her feet touched the ground, and he would not meet her eye.

"I'll put the buckboard away and take care of the horses. Why don't you go on in the house? Here, you can unpack your things." He handed her the package from the back of the wagon.

It felt awkward in her hands, the weight of the flatiron shifting beneath the layers of fabric. Reluctantly, she moved away as he led the horses into the barn.

The house was dark and uninviting, but she quickly lit a lamp. In its golden glow, she set her new bundle on the bed beside the one she had carried in earlier that day. The skirt and shirt she had been wearing lay across the neat coverlet, and Molly remembered Ben threatening to burn her "rags." He was right, of course. Most of her things *were* little more than rags. She gathered them up, folded them neatly, and, for the time being, at least, tucked them under the bed, out of sight.

Then she unwrapped the new things. She shook out the violet dress and held it against her, imagining how it would look. Even the shirtwaist and brown skirt seemed elegant compared with the things she had hidden under the bed. And the rose taffeta! Good heavens, she had never expected to own anything half so beautiful in her whole life. She trailed her fingers across the fine fabric, savoring its crisp texture. She'd rustle when she walked, and people would turn their heads to look. No one would doubt that Molly Wade was loved when they saw what a magnificent dress her husband had bought for her. She would start on it first thing tomorrow. Perhaps she could have it finished in time to wear for church next Sunday.

She found a place in the cupboard for the iron and hung her new clothing on the pegs near the bed next to Ben's spare shirts and pants. The sight of their clothing in such close proximity was disturbingly intimate, reminding her of things she was trying not to think about. Resolutely, she turned away and began to rewrap the taffeta for safekeeping when she remembered one other purchase they had made.

The ring! Where was the ring? She searched through the folds of taffeta, ran her hands all over the bed, and even looked under it, but the ring was nowhere to be found.

"Ben!" she cried, heading for the door. "Ben, I can't find—"

She collided with him just outside.

"What's the matter?" he asked, taking her arms.

"I can't find the ring! It wasn't in the package, and I looked everywhere, and . . ."

He was smiling. He led her gently back into the house. "I have it."

"Oh," she said, feeling foolish.

When they were inside, he fished in one of his vest pockets and pulled out a small box. In it was the gold band. He took it out and tossed the box onto the table. "We're alone now. Would you like me to put it on your finger?"

The tension she had sensed in him before vibrated between them like a living thing. The hand she held out was less than steady. He took it carefully, as if it were something extremely fragile and precious, and slid the golden band onto her third finger.

They both stared at it for a heartbeat or two, and then Ben bent and kissed it. His gesture touched her very soul, and the last of her restraint shattered. With a tiny cry, she threw herself into his arms. His mouth crushed hers, but she welcomed his ferocity, clinging to him with the desperation born of her driving need for his love.

Their kiss was long and wild. His hand found her breast and kneaded it, sending bursts of pleasure spiraling through her. The ache between her thighs intensified, sending a searing heat radiating through her.

When he lifted his mouth from hers so they could gasp for breath, his eyes gleamed with the same look of triumph she had seen when she had promised to be his wife. "It's a little early, but it's been a long day," he said hoarsely. "Maybe you'd like to turn in now."

So soon? All her fears came rushing back, quenching the rush of passion, and she jerked out of his arms in alarm. "It's . . . it's broad daylight!"

His eyebrows lifted skeptically as he glanced outside. Twilight shadows hovered just beyond the lamplight. Her whole body pulsed in reaction when his smoldering gaze touched her again, but she couldn't surrender. She knew no decent woman would feel the things she was feeling, and he already thought her easy. "Are you hungry?" she asked too brightly. "I can fix you something."

"We just ate, Molly."

"How about some coffee? I can have it ready in no time."

He caught her arm when she would have gone to the stove. "Molly, I don't want food and I don't want coffee. I only want you. You don't have to be afraid."

"I'm not afraid," she said, but even she could hear the tremor in her voice.

"Nervous, then. You don't have to be nervous. It's not like we haven't done this before."

"That's right," she said, stung. "We did it before, and now you think . . . you think I'm . . . Well, I'm not! And I won't do it, not in the daylight. It isn't decent!"

She tried to break his grip, but he held her easily, pulling her against him. "What in the hell are you talking about?" he demanded.

"Don't swear at me!" she said, frightened that she might have made him mad. She struggled, but he tightened his grip.

"I'm not swearing at you, and hold still! What are you talking about?"

"You know what I'm talking about."

"I guess I do, but you're not making a lick of sense. If you don't want to go to bed with me, just say so!"

That, of course, was the real problem. She did want to go to bed with him, desperately, but she couldn't admit it. And now, like a fool, she had made him angry. "You're hurting me," she tried, remembering the ploy had worked once before and praying it would again.

He released her instantly, throwing his hands in the air. She gasped, cringing instinctively, but he hardly seemed to notice. Oblivious to her fright, he turned on his heel and stormed out of the cabin.

Shaking, she grabbed the edge of the table for support. For one awful moment she had thought . . . But he had only been showing his contempt. He wasn't raising his hand to her, at least not yet. But now she had driven him away. Weak with relief and despair, she sank onto a chair and buried her face in her hands.

Ben went for a long, hard ride, and the sky was full dark when he returned. He was calmer and pleasantly tired, but he still could make no sense of Molly's behavior. One minute she was melting in his arms and the next she was acting as if he had small pox. And all that talk about making love in the daylight was ridiculous. He'd done it in the daylight lots of times, although the circumstances of those times might well be considered indecent by some.

Then again, maybe she wasn't being ridiculous. She was, after all, a good girl, a churchgoing girl. Sure, she'd given in to him that night, but she wasn't the kind to do it with every Tom, Dick and Har . . .

And good girls were funny about sex. Hadn't Johnny told him so a hundred times? Maybe he'd been too rough with her. Maybe he'd been too quick to assume she wanted it.

Sighing with disgust, he slowly made his way across the yard to the cabin. This time a faint glow shone from the front window, but he didn't feel any more welcomed than he had when the window was dark.

Molly had left a lamp burning low when she had gone to bed. A quick glance told him she was asleep or pretending to be. He blew out the light and undressed quietly, stripping down to his drawers. He would rather have fought a grizzly bear than climb into that bed beside her knowing he couldn't touch her, but he did so. Not touching her was fairly easy. She was squished up about as close to the wall as she could get without crawling into a knothole. He turned his back to her and sighed again.

Molly's eyes popped open in surprise. She waited, staring into the darkness, but he didn't move. She'd been lying there for over an hour, tensed for the sound of his return, and for the last ten minutes she had been petrified while she waited for the moment when he would climb in bed and reach for her. Except he obviously had no intention of reaching for her.

Was he still angry? A chill slithered over her at the thought, but she had to know. "Ben?" she whispered.

"What?" He sounded infinitely weary.

"I'm sorry."

Something in him snapped, and he whirled on her. "If you say that one more time, I swear I'll . . ."

The words died in his throat when he saw her flattened up against the wall, her eyes wide with terror, the covers clutched defensively to her chest.

"Molly?"

She didn't even blink.

"Molly, honey." He reached out to graze her cheek with his fingertips, and she flinched. "What's wrong? You act like you think I'm going to take a stick to you or something."

She shuddered, but she still didn't blink.

"I told you I wouldn't hurt you, and I meant

it. All I want is . . ." No, he wouldn't beg. He swallowed with difficulty. "You're my wife now. It's not a sin if we make love, even in the daylight."

She thought that over for a minute. "All right."

"What do you mean, 'all right'?"

"I mean if you want to, go ahead."

He muttered a barnyard curse. "I don't just want to climb on top of you. I don't want you to *let* me; I want you to *want* me."

Molly finally blinked as she absorbed this information. "Oh . . . then . . . I do."

"You do what?"

"I do want you."

Her confession exploded inside of him, but he somehow managed to rein in his enthusiasm. Go easy, he told himself sternly. Don't scare her. Using every ounce of self-control he possessed, he stretched one arm out to her. "Come here, then."

She bit her lip, but she hesitated only a moment. Cautiously, she closed the space between them and slipped into his arms.

Easy, partner, easy. He touched his mouth to hers experimentally, once and then again. The third time her lips softened. He pulled her a little closer, deepening the kiss. Her body was stiff, but soon it, too, surrendered to his tender onslaught. Tentatively, her hands touched the bare skin of his shoulder, and he fought down a moan.

Molly marveled at the feel of him. Somehow

she had expected his skin to be harder, rougher than hers, but he was so smooth, so tempting. Without conscious thought, she began to explore, sliding her hands downward until she encountered the crisp, curling hairs that blanketed his chest. Fascinated, she trailed her fingers through them until she found one flat, male nipple.

She felt the rumble beneath her hand in the instant before it became a groan. He groped for her breast, cursing the fabric that blocked his way.

"Molly," he gasped, "can we get rid of this thing?"

But he was already fumbling with the buttons at her throat. She helped as best she could, and then before she knew what he intended, he pulled it off over her head. Dear heaven, she was naked! Thanking God for the darkness, she was only vaguely aware that Ben was struggling out of his single remaining garment.

When his arms closed around her again, the overwhelming sensation of flesh against flesh smothered all her remaining inhibitions. His hands roamed at will, tracing the mounds and valleys of her body until he forced a moan from her throat, too. Fires flickered everywhere now, searing her, melting her.

Coaxed by his magical fingers, her ache became a throbbing, pulsing need. "Ben, please," she murmured, not certain what words to use.

He needed no words. He loomed over her, a darker shadow in the dark night. This time no barrier blocked his way. This time he claimed her swiftly, surely, sinking into her satiny depths with a sigh of near anguish. She wrapped her legs around him to hold him close, knowing she needed his nearness more than life itself. He *was* life, vital, vibrant, indomitable. How could she ever have resisted this glorious union?

He moved slowly at first, stroking her cautiously, but her need was already too great for caution. She grasped his hair-roughened flanks to urge him on. Uttering a strangled gasp, he responded, plunging into her with a ferocity she eagerly met. Thrusting, churning, twisting, she clung and clawed in a frantic attempt to get closer still. The pleasure welled inside her, bubbling, boiling, seething, until it erupted into spasms of purest ecstasy that shook them both to their very souls.

A few minutes later, when their breathing had almost returned to normal and the spasms had died away to an occasional ripple, Ben still lay on top of her, resting his head against the pillow of her breast. Blissfully exhausted, Molly stroked his hair, smiling when his tongue flicked out to tease her nipple.

She loved him. The knowledge came to her with a certainty that made her previous infatuation fade into insignificance. Only a woman could love a man, and only tonight had she truly become a woman.

But did he love her? He surely cared for her. Hadn't he said so himself? But love . . . love was another matter entirely. Love was all-consuming. Love would bind them together as nothing else could. If Ben did not love her yet, she would *make* him love her. She would give him no other choice. "I'm going to be a good wife to you, Ben. I promise."

She could feel his smile against her love-dampened skin. "I don't think I could stand it if you got any better."

She gave his hair a playful yank. "I didn't mean *that*."

His hand caressed her hip. "What else is there?"

"Lots of things."

"Like what?"

His palm was tantalizingly rough, scraping seductively up to her waist and back down almost to her knee and then starting the journey all over again. "Uh, like . . . like . . ."

"Hmmm?"

His stroking was hypnotic. Her brain ceased to function as sensation took control. "Ben, I . . . What's happening?"

"I don't know, but I hope it's the same thing that's happening to me."

She felt him harden against her thigh. "Can we . . . ? I mean, *again?*"

"Please, God, yes," he murmured as he rose up to cover her mouth with his.

Ben awoke slowly, conscious of bright sunlight in his eyes but knowing such a thing was impossible. He never slept past dawn. He tried to roll over, but something was holding his arm, pinning it to the bed. Reluctantly he lifted his eyelids and came face to face with Molly Wade.

No, Molly Cantrell, he thought with a smile. How many times had he dreamed of waking up like this with Molly in his arms? He sighed contentedly, stirring the wisps of honey-colored hair resting on her cheek. She muttered something in her sleep and rolled over on her back, freeing Ben's arm. He propped himself up on it so he could study her while she slept.

She was even prettier than he remembered. In the morning light she looked almost perfect, with her mouth still reddened from his kisses and her long chestnut lashes brushing her lightly tanned cheeks. Up this close he could see a faint smattering of freckles across her upturned nose. He knew a powerful urge to kiss them, but he didn't want to waken her just yet, not until he'd looked his fill.

His gaze strayed lower, down the creamy softness of her throat to where the coverlet left her breasts partially exposed. His hand hovered at the edge of the quilt as he debated pulling it back. She *was* his wife now, he reminded himself, and after all the things they'd done last night . . .

Had they made love three or four times? He'd lost count. In any case, neither of them had any secrets left from the other. Actually seeing what he already knew so well was simply a formality.

Gently, and ever so carefully, he lifted the coverlet and pulled it down, down and down, past the swell of her breasts with their delectable pink nipples, past the curve of her waist, past the flat plane of her belly, past the nest of russet curls, past her long, shapely legs, down to where her delicate toes curled in protest at the cool morning air.

The sight of her stunned him. How could someone so beautiful truly belong to him? But she did. And more than that, she carried his child. There, inside her wondrous body, his seed had taken hold, and soon the whole world would know. Awed, he placed his hand on her belly, just above the russet curls, where his baby slept.

She stirred slightly and then started, coming fully awake in an instant. "What . . . ?"

So many impressions registered at once that Molly couldn't comprehend any of them. She was in bed, naked, with Ben Cantrell, and his hand was . . . Oh, where were the covers?

Ben grinned at her distress. "Embarrassed? I'll cover you up." He pushed up and lowered himself until his body covered hers completely. "How's that?" he asked wickedly.

"Ben," she protested, but the protest held no conviction. Her outrage stood no chance against his provocative smile, and her nerves were already tingling with awareness. With his golden hair falling across his forehead and the gilt stubble on his lean cheeks and his blue eyes dancing with mischief, he was irresistible. "I . . . you . . . you were looking at me and . . . and touching me," she accused.

"I was saying good morning to our baby, Mrs. Cantrell. Now I'm going to say good morning to you, *in the broad daylight.*"

She tried to remember why the idea had seemed so shocking the day before, but her brain refused to cooperate. It obediently turned to mush the instant Ben's lips touched hers and did not recover until long minutes after she and Ben had gasped out their release.

"I'm glad to know you're a woman of your word, Mrs. Cantrell," he murmured into her hair sometime later.

"Hmmm?" she asked lethargically against his shoulder.

"You promised to be a good wife to me, and you're certainly off to a fine start."

"You're easy to please. I thought you'd at least expect me to cook."

His wonderful eyes widened in mock surprise. "You can cook, too?"

She stuck her tongue out at him and pushed up on one elbow. "Now what do you like for breakfast?"

"You mean besides what I just had?"

Molly yanked on a chest hair this time, and Ben pretended to be severely injured, insisting she kiss it and make it better. After a few more minutes of playful wrestling and cuddling, Ben allowed as how they probably ought to get up before noon. Pulling out of her embrace, he swung his legs over the side of the bed with an exaggerated groan.

Molly watched in fascination as he stood up,

unashamedly naked. Everything about him pro-
claimed his blatant masculinity, from his broad
shoulders to the thatch of straw-colored hair on
his chest to his long muscular legs. There was
one part of him, the most masculine part of all,
that she only dared glance at, but when she did,
she felt an unmistakably feminine reaction.

"Aren't you getting up?" he asked when he
got his pants on. The question was innocent
enough, but she saw the teasing twinkle in his
eye.

"Not until you're gone," she informed him,
adjusting the covers more modestly over her bosom.

"I wasn't going anywhere."

"Ben . . ." she said in warning.

"Well," he allowed, "I guess I do need to get
some water so we can wash up a little."

"And shave."

Ben grinned wickedly. "I thought I'd wait 'til
a little closer to bedtime before I shave."

When Ben had brought back the water, Molly
washed and dressed in her new violet dress and
basked in Ben's blatant admiration. The rest of
the morning passed blissfully. Molly fixed Ben a
mountain of flapjacks, which he devoured
with—so extravagant!—honey instead of the
usual molasses. They laughed and teased and
touched and kissed, intoxicated with each other's presence. Finally, Ben remembered he had a
few chores he should attend to out in the barn
while Molly cleaned up from their meal.

Molly actually hummed while she washed the

dishes, *her* dishes in *her* home, the home of *her* husband, a husband who adored her. They'd gotten off to a rocky start, but things were going to work out fine from here on. She just knew it.

When she had washed everything in sight and made the bed and had the cabin just as neat as Ben had left it the day before, she began casting about for something else to do. She wanted to keep her promise to be a good wife. Coming across a bag of dried apples, she remembered how much Ben had liked her apple pie the night of the box social. Would he like her to make some especially for him? With a grin, she decided to ask him.

It was almost noon, and the bright sunlight made her squint as she stepped out into the yard and started for the barn. The sight of a rider coming hell-bent for the ranch stopped her, though, and she waited, shading her eyes with her hand as he approached.

She knew a moment's alarm when she thought it might be her father, but she soon realized it was Johnny McGee. Had he heard about the wedding? And why was he coming so fast?

The moment he saw her, his mouth dropped open in astonishment, and he reined up so quickly his horse reared, almost unseating him. No, she decided, he hadn't heard about the wedding. He launched himself from the saddle and strode over to her menacingly. With his unshaven cheeks, his bloodshot eyes, and his rumpled clothes, he looked like the wrath of God, and Molly felt a frisson of fear at his murderous glower.

"What in the hell are you doing here?" he demanded, but he didn't wait for an answer. "Haven't you caused Ben enough trouble? Were you here with him all night? Is that why he didn't come into town? Don't you know your pappy'll kill him when he finds out you're here, or is that what you've been wanting all along?" He grabbed her arm, and she cried out in alarm. "I've got a notion to—"

"Johnny!" Ben called, sprinting across the yard toward them, but Johnny didn't let go of her. Although she was quaking inside at the cowboy's threat of violence, she tried to meet his fierce glare squarely.

"Johnny, Molly and I got married yesterday," Ben said.

Johnny had already opened his mouth to reply before the meaning of the words sank in. His momentary shock gave Molly the chance to pull free of his grasp.

"Married?" he repeated incredulously.

"Yes, married," Molly affirmed righteously. Under different circumstances, she would have found his expression amusing. He looked very much as if he had been poleaxed.

"*Married?*" He turned on Ben in outrage. "Do you know what you've gotten yourself into? What's her pappy gonna say? He'll come after you with a shotgun sure as hell—"

"He already did," Ben told him.

Johnny swore eloquently.

"Johnny, there's a lady present," Ben reminded him.

"Oh, sorry," he muttered, glancing at Molly and turning beet red. Then he remembered his outrage. "You faced down Wade alone? Without me? What if you'd run into trouble? What if he'd—"

"I didn't need any help, or I wouldn't be here."

Plainly Johnny was not pleased to hear this news. "You should've taken me along," he insisted.

"Johnny, it's over. Molly and I are married." He grinned. "Don't you want to kiss the bride?"

Molly would have objected, but Johnny looked so aghast at the suggestion she knew she wouldn't have to. He actually backed up a step and turned an even deeper shade of red, something she would have thought impossible.

"At least shake my hand and congratulate me," Ben said.

Weakly Johnny did so, stealing several secretive glances at Molly in the process. Why was he looking at her so funny?

"How'd you get married?"

"We went to town yesterday, and Reverend Bates did it."

Johnny started to swear again and caught himself just in time. "I didn't see you in town. I was worried sick."

"If you were so worried, why didn't you come back last night?"

Johnny shot Molly another look. "I was . . .

well, I was worried until about suppertime. I don't recollect much after that."

Ben coughed discreetly. "I suppose you came right home as soon as you woke up this morning, though."

"That's right, just as soon as I heard you never showed up."

"I'm sorry I didn't let you know my plans, but they came up kind of sudden."

Johnny glared at Molly, and Ben slipped his arm around her protectively. "Johnny, Molly's my wife now. She's gonna be living here with us. I'd like it if you two got along."

Molly could see Johnny didn't like the idea. Her senses had been finely tuned to detect the slightest changes in her father's moods, and those senses were giving her a strange message about Johnny McGee.

"I got nothin' against her personal," Johnny allowed.

Ben looked at her, waiting for her response. "I'm perfectly willing to give Mr. McGee a chance," she replied.

"Well then, if Johnny's too shy to kiss you, why don't you at least shake on it?"

Molly extended her hand. Johnny looked as if he would have much preferred petting a rattlesnake, but he took her fingers in his for the briefest instant and shook them once.

Ben smiled proudly, as if he had been personally responsible for bringing peace to two warring nations. "There now, you're friends."

Molly doubted this, but she wouldn't give Johnny McGee the satisfaction of knowing she distrusted him.

"Where's Tom and Billy?" Ben asked, naming his two new hired hands.

"They'll be along directly, I reckon."

"I bet you could use a little shut-eye. Why don't you go get some."

"I could use a little coffee first," Johnny said. "I don't suppose you've got any made."

Molly couldn't help smiling. This was probably the first time Johnny McGee had ever had to ask for coffee since he'd been at Ben Cantrell's ranch. Surely he was used to simply walking into the house and taking what he wanted. At least he recognized the house had become her domain. "I've got some hot," she told him. "Come on over and get it."

"I like my coffee strong," he warned. "It has to kick up in the middle and pack double."

"Don't worry, partner," Ben assured him. "Molly knows how to make coffee."

"That's right," she bragged as the three of them started back toward the cabin. "I just use enough water to wet the grounds good."

Johnny rolled his eyes skeptically, so she decided to really get his goat. "Ben, I was on my way out to ask if you want me to make you some apple pie. I know you liked my pie the night of the box supper."

Ben grinned, delighted. "How long since we've had apple pie, Johnny?"

"*We* don't never have it," he replied sourly.

"Don't you like pie, Mr. McGee?" Molly asked.

"I reckon I do," he admitted grudgingly.

Ben chuckled. "I bet Johnny could eat his weight in pie if you gave him a chance."

"We don't have enough pie pans to find out for sure," Molly said, "but I'll be glad to bake Mr. McGee his own pie. That is, if he wants me to."

She waited, knowing how difficult it would be for him to say so. "That . . . sounds . . . fine," he said as if each word were a tooth being yanked from his mouth.

"Come on in and get your coffee while I start soaking the apples, then," she invited cheerfully.

Later, when Johnny had carried his coffee back to the bunkhouse, Ben came up behind Molly and slipped his arms around her waist. "Be patient with Johnny. He's a little nervous around women."

"He's jealous," Molly informed him.

"Jealous?" He spun her around to face him. "Of *you?*"

The idea was so absurd, Molly almost laughed aloud. "No, silly, of *you*. He's had you to himself for a long time now. He doesn't want me messing things up."

"What would you mess up? Johnny and I will always be friends."

Molly decided not to voice her theories. For all she knew, Johnny McGee had nothing to worry about. Maybe having a wife wouldn't change Ben in the slightest. Maybe next Saturday night he and Johnny would go to town the same as they always had. Maybe *she* was the one who should be jealous. "Of course you and Johnny will always be friends," she said.

Ben leaned back in his chair, watching Molly scrape the supper dishes. He, Johnny, and his two hired men were still sitting around the table, too full to consider moving just yet.

"You know, Miz Cantrell, I ain't never worked anyplace where they had better grub than this," Tom said. Tom was a homely fellow in his early twenties, tall and painfully thin, in spite of the prodigious amounts of food he put away.

Molly flashed him a grateful smile over her shoulder and went back to scraping dishes. Ben wondered idly how she could look so sexy bending over the slop jar.

"Yes, ma'am," said Ben's other hired hand. Billy was younger than Tom, probably only eighteen or nineteen, and shorter but no less thin. He would have been fairly handsome if he hadn't lost his two front teeth to an angry steer. He whistled slightly when he talked. "The grub here sure is fine. You're a mighty good cook."

"Thank you," Molly said with another smile, and Ben bit back a grin of his own. They had said practically the same thing to her after each and every meal she had fixed them all week. He supposed it was because they couldn't think of anything else to say, and the urge to converse with such a gorgeous creature as Molly was simply too strong to resist.

Ben let his gaze stray to the curve of her hip where her body bent slightly to the task at hand. He knew what that hip looked like beneath the fabric of her skirt. He knew how her skin felt, soft and warm and vibrant. He knew how her body came alive in the dark comfort of their bed.

"*Ben.*"

Ben jumped at Johnny's voice, drawn reluctantly back to the present. From Johnny's disgruntled frown, Ben guessed he'd tried more than once to get his attention.

"I was just saying we ought to think about fencing off that seep. We lose a lot of cows in it, and it hardly ever has enough water to be useful."

"I reckon you're right. I'll order some posts next time I'm in town."

"You're going tomorrow like always, ain't you?" Johnny asked, giving Molly a suspicious glance.

"I don't know," Ben replied, following Johnny's gaze. "Depends on if Molly needs anything or not."

"But we always got to town on Saturday night," Johnny argued, color rising on his neck.

Ben shrugged. "I'm a married man, Johnny. I can't go gallivanting off and leave my wife all alone, now, can I?"

He noticed Molly straighten abruptly, but Johnny's snort of disgust distracted him. "I'd think the two of you saw enough of each other."

Tom and Billy rose abruptly. "Reckon we'll catch a smoke," Billy said as they hastily exited the cabin. Ben supposed they sensed the trouble he'd been expecting for several days now.

"Maybe you and me oughta go outside, too," Ben suggested to Johnny. He didn't want to have this conversation in front of Molly.

Apparently Johnny felt the same way. He stomped ouside with Ben at his heels, not stopping until he was a safe distance from the house. Then he wouldn't look directly at Ben. He busied himself rolling a cigarette and offered the makings to Ben, who accepted them wordlessly. They smoked in silence for a minute or two while Ben tried to decide the best way to bring up the subject he didn't even want to think about.

"Johnny, Molly is my wife."

"So you've reminded me about a hundred times since last Sunday. That don't mean you've got to tie yourself to her apron strings. Hell, you don't even want to play cards at night anymore."

Ben looked away, embarrassed by the rebuke. It was true. He always used to join Johnny and whoever was currently working for them after supper in the evening for a friendly game of poker. Now, of course, he had more interesting things to do after supper. "Johnny, you know how it is."

"Yeah, I know," Johnny snapped. "I see the light go out about five minutes after we leave."

Ben thought he and Molly waited a little longer than five minutes, but he wasn't going to argue.

Some nights even five minutes seemed like an eternity to wait until he could hold Molly in his arms. "Johnny, Molly thinks you're jealous."

"*Jealous!*" he scoffed. "Ain't that just like a woman. They think every man wants 'em."

"No, she thinks you're jealous of me, because I'm spending all my time with her now instead of you."

Johnny muttered an imprecation against women in general, took a deep drag on his cigarette, and threw it down. "I don't see why you can't at least go to town. Would it kill her if you left her just once?"

"But I don't *want* to leave her. I *want* to be with her. I don't expect you to understand, and I don't reckon you can like it, either, but it's true."

Johnny's eyes were bleak. "Maybe you'd like me to leave here and find another job."

"Don't be a jackass! You're the best friend I ever had, the *only* friend I've had in a long time."

"Maybe you don't need a friend anymore now that you've got her."

"Dammit, Johnny, you even *sound* jealous."

Johnny glared, refusing to respond to such a ridiculous charge.

"Johnny, look, we haven't even been married a week yet. We're still on our honeymoon."

Unmoved, Johnny stared out at the setting sun.

"I know what you need," Ben said. "You need a woman of your own."

Johnny grunted contemptuously.

"I know what you always said, but you're

wrong about nice girls, Johnny. They can be more fun than the other kind, if you pick the right one."

This was as near as Ben would come to discussing his love life with Johnny, but Johnny was perfectly capable of filling in any blanks and getting the full picture. "Oh, hell," he muttered, shoving his hands into his pockets. "You've got *everything* now, Ben."

"Everything?"

"Yeah, you've got your ranch and your home and your woman, and pretty soon she's gonna have a baby. Then there you'll be, all settled down, while I'll still be bumming around, sleeping alone in somebody else's bunkhouse."

No wonder Johnny looked so woebegone. "It doesn't have to be like that," Ben assured him.

"Oh, no? How's it gonna change? You think some nice girl's gonna even look twice at me? You think some girl'll come out here to live in the bunkhouse with me on my wages?"

Ben had no answer. "I'm sorry, partner." The words seemed woefully inadequate. Ben was beginning to feel guilty for his own good fortune. Still, neither his guilt nor Johnny's unhappiness negated the problem at hand. "Could you try not to take it out on Molly? She can't help it that she's making you miserable."

Johnny sighed. "All right." He glanced toward the house where Molly sat on the front porch, her lap covered with rose taffeta. "You better get on back. She's waiting, and I don't wanna cause trouble between you two."

"You aren't causing any trouble."

Johnny grinned mirthlessly. "Then get on back 'cause she's waiting. You wanna be there when she puts out the light, don't you?"

Ben walked slowly back to the house, troubled more than he wanted to admit by his conversation with Johnny. He never would have guessed how much his marriage would interfere with their long-standing friendship. The problem was, he really did prefer being with Molly, at least for right now. Maybe the intoxication would wear off in time, but he was perfectly willing to indulge himself to the fullest while it lasted. And he couldn't forget she was pregnant. Ben couldn't upset her now, even if he'd wanted.

Molly had watched the two men from her chair on the porch, wishing she could hear what they were saying. This was what she had been dreading all week, the moment when Ben would have to choose between her and Johnny. Oh, she knew Ben wouldn't throw her out. He enjoyed their times in bed together far too much to even consider such a thing, and besides, she carried his child. No, she need not fear losing her home, but what she feared almost as much was losing Ben's devotion.

The past week had been a dream. Each morning Ben woke her with kisses, arousing her mindless ecstasy before reluctantly leaving their

bed for the day's work. Each evening he greeted
her with a lusty kiss and followed her every
move with hungry eyes until the others finally
left them alone. Then the passion would begin
again. Sometimes they couldn't even wait to get
undressed. Molly had never imagined such a
driving need existed, and even if she had, she
would never have imagined feeling it herself,
much less inspiring it in someone else.

The only shadow clouding her idyll was
Johnny McGee. He and Ben had been together a
long time, and Johnny had stood by him when
Ben felt the whole community was against him.
How could she fight him?

Yet fight him she must, as terrifying as the
thought of conflict was to her. She couldn't let
Ben continue in his role of innocent victim, shun-
ning the company of everyone else. Molly knew
what it was like to be different, to carry the burden of a secret shame, and she didn't want her
child to bear that burden, too. She had to make
Ben see he must make a place for himself in the
world, a place where they could raise their child
in some semblance of normalcy.

She drew an unsteady breath when she saw
Ben walking back toward the house again. Lowering her eyes to the sewing in her lap, she
prayed for the wisdom, and the courage she so
deperately needed.

Molly was stitching doggedly on the rose taffeta when Ben approached her. She didn't look
up until he stopped beside her chair. When she

did, her blue eyes were as troubled as Johnny's had been. "You can go to town with him tomorrow," she said. "I don't mind."

"I don't want to go without you, and I for sure don't want to leave you here alone."

"Why not?"

"Because . . . because I don't, that's why," he hedged, not knowing exactly how to express the protective feelings he had for her.

"I said I don't mind. I hardly ever got a trip to town when I lived with my family, so I won't miss it. Besides, I want to finish my dress."

He smiled tolerantly. "You been working on that every time you sat down this week. What's your hurry?"

"I want to have it ready to wear to church on Sunday."

Church? Ben shouldn't have been shocked. He knew she was a churchgoing woman. He simply wasn't used to thinking of Sunday as anything except a day in which to sleep off a hangover. "I reckon you'll want somebody to take you to town, then."

"I thought . . . that is . . ."

"What?"

"I expected you'd go with me. I mean, I know you don't usually go to church," she hurried on when he frowned, "but I thought, now we're married . . ."

Good God, what had he gotten himself into? "Molly, I don't think you want me along with you when you go to church."

"Why not?"

"Because I'm the town outcast. Don't tell me you've forgotten already."

Her lovely eyes grew wide with astonishment. "You don't think anybody'd treat you mean at *church*, do you?"

"All the men who hanged my pa were good Christians, Molly. I learned a long time ago not to trust a single one of them."

"Ben, most of those men are sorry for what happened."

"How do you know?" he challenged.

"I . . . I just know. . . ."

"How about your pa? Is *he* sorry?"

She started at the question, but she had no answer for him, just as he'd suspected.

"Molly, I'm not going to walk into that church and have people pointing and whispering behind their hands—"

"What makes you think they'd do that?"

"They always do it, wherever I go."

"They most certainly do not!"

"And what makes you think they don't?" he mocked.

"Because I've been one of them most of my life." She jumped to her feet, carefully laying the dress she was working on back down on the chair. "I *know* what they talk about, and it's not what you think."

"Then what is it?"

Molly took him by the arms. "Mostly they talk about how unfair it was that your pa got killed and how much they admire you for making the ranch a success and . . ."

"And what?"

"And they wonder why you won't let any of them make friends with you."

Ben snorted derisively. "They don't want to be friends. They just want to ease their consciences."

"You're wrong! They want to make amends for what happened. They want you to be one of them again."

"Why?"

"So they can make it up to you."

Ben swore. "Do they think being nice to me can make up for murdering my father?"

"Of course not!" she said, giving him an impatient shake. "But they don't think you ought to still be suffering for it six years later."

He jerked out of her grasp and turned away. Fury bubbled up in him, the same impotent rage he felt whenever he thought of the injustice of it all. How dare they feel sorry for him! How dare they try to "make it up"! Only one thing could ever accomplish that: clearing his father's name once and for all. He almost laughed out loud when he tried to imagine any of *them* attempting to do such a thing. In spite of their guilty consciences, they had never even hinted they believed in his father's innocence. If they already felt bad, think how miserable they'd be when they knew the truth.

"Ben," Molly said in the soft voice she used when they were alone in the dark, "you can't only think of yourself. What about our baby? Do you want your son to be an outcast, too?"

He whirled on her, making her flinch, but she stood her ground with the assurance of rightness. "No, I don't want my son to be an outcast."

"Then you'd better start mending your fences while you still have a chance." Her eyes grew soft and pleading. "Please, Ben," she said, moving closer and placing a hand on his chest. "Just come with me this one time. If anybody does anything you don't like, you never have to come again."

Unable to resist her nearness, he slipped his arms around her waist. "I don't know," he said, pretending to consider as he pulled her hips to his. "What's in it for me?"

"Ben!" she protested, pulling out of his grasp. "Not out here where anybody could see us!"

"You didn't answer my question," he reminded her with a grin.

She smiled back enticingly. "Come inside and I will."

Chapter Eight

✦ ✦ ✦ ✦

"WELL, THERE THEY are," Ben said as their buck-board rattled up to the churchyard on Sunday morning. Those who had arrived early were standing out front, clustered in small groups. All eyes turned to watch as Ben reined the team to a halt and jumped down to help Molly out.

While she waited, Molly placed a hand over the nervous flutter in her stomach. She'd expected to be the center of attention, of course. Word of her elopement with Ben would have spread far and wide by now, and the fact that Ben had not been seen at the Holy Trinity Church for six years made their presence now a double curiosity. Thank heaven she'd finished her dress in time. Without the confidence of knowing how perfectly elegant she looked in the rose taffeta, Molly didn't think she would have had the courage to face all these staring eyes.

"Why do you look so scared? This was your idea," Ben whispered as he lifted her down from the wagon.

"I'm not scared," she said. "Is my dress all right?"

Ben rolled his eyes. He'd told her at least three times already how beautiful she looked. "It's not too late to go home."

"Don't tempt me," she replied, turning abruptly at the sound of a female squeal.

"Molly Wade, you sly thing!" Daisy Ferguson

cried, hurrying over to give Molly a hug. "Imagine, eloping and never telling me a thing! I had to hear it in school, from one of the children, no less." She released Molly and turned to Ben. "Now I know why she wouldn't introduce me to you!"

Ben gave her a bewildered smile and sent Molly a silent plea for rescue.

"Daisy, this is my husband, Ben Cantrell." *Husband.* How wonderful it sounded. "Ben, this is my friend Daisy Ferguson."

Daisy gave Ben her hand as she babbled on about how thrilled she was to finally meet him. Suddenly Molly found herself surrounded by female friends eager to give her their best wishes. From the corner of her eye, she saw Ben moving cautiously away from the group only to be surrounded by young men come to tease him and shake his hand.

"Did you really faint?" one of the girls asked Molly.

"Let's see your ring!"

"That taffeta looks positively gorgeous on you!"

"I tried to get Mama to buy me some, but she said it cost too much!"

"What's your house like, Molly?"

Only the peal of the church bell ended the barrage of comments and questions. Ben found her again, and she slipped her arm through his. "That wasn't so bad, was it?" she asked as they followed the others into the church.

Before he could answer, they caught sight of

Harry Hoskins glaring at them from across the yard. "No, but it might get a whole lot worse," he said grimly.

Oh, dear, Molly thought. She had forgotten about Harry. If he had been angry when he thought Ben had burned his barn, he must be absolutely furious now that she had run off with Ben. Were people laughing at Harry behind his back? Or worse yet, to his face? As much as she hated to think of it, she knew she would have to apologize to him. Only when Ben and Harry had made their peace could she and Ben have any hope for a normal life.

Inside the church, Molly slipped into a pew near the middle of the room. So far, she had not seen a sign of her family. Although she wasn't looking forward to confronting her father again, she longed for the sight of Julie and their mother. She also wanted them to see her so they would know she was being well taken care of. The instant they saw her dress, they would understand exactly how much Ben Cantrell cherished his new bride.

At last, just as the service was about to start, her family walked in. Molly knew a moment of relief. Their absence would have meant that her mother had been too badly beaten to appear in public. But their presence meant entirely new problems. An expectant hush fell over the room as the Wade family became aware of the Cantrells.

Elijah's weathered face screwed up in outrage as he directed his wife and daughter to the opposite side of the room, as far away from Ben and Molly as possible. Molly managed a small smile for her mother, who dared a series of surreptitious glances, and for Julie, who stared openly. When the congregation rose for the opening hymn, Molly blinked at tears. She was almost sorry for having come. How could she have known how painful seeing them would be? But, she told herself, not seeing them at all would have been far worse, and at least they had gotten to see her.

Ben found her hand and squeezed it comfortingly. She flashed him a grateful look and managed a smile. By the time the hymn was over, the danger of tears had passed, and Molly was able to settle into the familiar rhythm of the service.

Reverend Bates asked them to open their Bibles to Genesis chapter 37 and read the story of Joseph, whose jealous brothers sold him into slavery and told their father he was dead. Then Reverend Bates began to preach, enumerating the further disasters that befell hapless Joseph and eventually landed him in prison until, at last, his special talents brought him to the attention of the pharaoh, who made him ruler over all of Egypt. Then the time came that Joseph's brothers went to buy food in the land of Egypt, and Joseph recognized them.

"He recognized them, but they did not know him," Reverend Bates shouted from the pulpit. "And how could they? He was the second-greatest man in the greatest country of the world they lived in. Would they be likely to recognize him as the boy they had thrown in a pit to die? Certainly not, and if they had, what treatment could they expect from him? He had the power to do whatever he liked, the power to take their very lives in revenge for the injustice they had done to him.

"But did he? Did he kill them, as they deserved? Did he punish them in any way? No, he didn't, brothers and sisters, he didn't. Oh, he tested them. He wanted to know if they were still the heartless wretches who had thrown their own brother in a pit. He tested them by testing their love for their youngest brother, Benjamin, and he found that they had changed. He found that they had repented of the evil they had done to Joseph, even to the point of offering their own lives to protect the life of Benjamin. And then, brothers and sisters, *then*—in spite of the terrible thing they had done to him and all the terrible things that had happened to him as a result— Joseph *forgave* them!"

Molly felt the sting of gooseflesh forming on her arms, and she hazarded a quick glance at Ben. His frown told her he was listening and that he didn't like what he was hearing one bit. She clenched her hands together as Reverend Bates continued.

"He forgave them, even though what they had done was unforgivable, even though they had intended to destroy his very life. His brothers had meant to strip him of everything, yet God blessed him above all other men. His

brothers had intended evil to him, yet God used
the evil for good because Joseph was patient.
Joseph waited through what must have seemed
like a nightmare, through suffering and prison,
never losing his faith. And God rewarded his
patience and his faith.

"But why did he forgive his brothers? Not
because they deserved it; oh, no. We *know* they
didn't deserve it. And he didn't forgive them
because he was a good man, either, although we
know he was. He forgave them, brothers and
sisters, because he knew that the hate and the
bitterness would eat him alive, would destroy
his very soul, the way his brothers had once
sought to destroy his life. He knew he must let
go of his anger. He knew he must leave ven-
geance to the Lord God almighty, who claims
that privilege for Himself alone, and he must
make peace with his fellow man."

There was more, but Molly was too frightened
to listen. Beside her Ben sat as stiff and straight
as a poker, hardly even blinking as he listened to
the minister's words. Was he furious or moved?
She could tell nothing from his grim expression.
If he was furious, what would he do? Would he
blame her for making him come? She shivered
slightly.

So much for her plan to ease Ben back into
community life. Why couldn't she have left well
enough alone?

Ben's expression didn't alter when they rose
to sing the final hymn, but if he had anything to
say to her, he had no chance. The moment the

service ended, they were surrounded once again. This time the older members of the congregation hurried up to greet them. From the corner of her eye, Molly saw her father ushering Julie and her mother out. She sent them a silent message of love, which they returned.

Slowly Ben and Molly made their way to the door, pausing every few steps to reply to someone else's good wishes. Then they were on the church steps where Reverend Bates stood shaking hands with the members of his congregation.

"Molly, Ben, I'm awfully glad to see both of you here today. It seems marriage has already had a good effect on you, Ben," he said, pumping Ben's hand vigorously. "I can't recall the last time I saw you in church."

"It's been a while," Ben acknowledged. "That was a real interesting sermon this morning."

Reverend Bates continued to smile. "I changed my topic at the last moment. Somehow I thought this message would be more appropriate than the one I had originally prepared."

"I guess you figured you might not get another chance at me."

"Something like that," the minister admitted cheerfully, "although I do sincerely hope you'll be back. It's been entirely too long, and now that you're a family man . . ." He gave Molly a significant glance, which brought the color to her cheeks.

"That was the same argument Molly used on me."

"I'm glad it worked."

Ben and Molly strolled on out into the church-yard, momentarily alone.

"I'm sorry, Ben," Molly whispered. "I had no idea—"

"It's all right," Ben replied. She looked up in surprise to discover a quiet amusement in his azure eyes. "I reckon I needed to hear that sermon again. You preached it to me once already this week, if I recall."

Fighting the urge to throw her arms around him, she settled for giving him the most adoring look she could muster. Then, over Ben's shoulder, she caught sight of Harry Hoskins. If looks could kill, she and Ben would be stone cold dead.

"Oh, Ben, I have to talk to Harry," she said.

Ben turned to receive his share of Harry's rage. "No, Molly. Come on. We're going home."

"I can't, Ben, not until I've told Harry how sorry I am. Don't you see, he's been humiliated, and I owe him that much. We both do!"

"Then we'll both talk to him."

"No, I have to talk to him alone, first. Please, Ben." Without waiting for his reply, she hurried away.

Harry could not conceal his surprise at her approach, but he recovered quickly. "If you came over here to get congratulated, you're wasting your time," he informed her stiffly.

"I came over to apologize, Harry. I can't tell you how sorry I am. I know I should have told you about me and Ben, but there just wasn't time—"

He gave a bark of mirthless laughter. "No, I guess there wasn't, since you've been avoiding me like I had the plague ever since Cantrell's trial. Is that when you made up your mind, Molly? Did you see him as some romantic figure who burned people's barns and got women to lie for him?"

"Harry! Ben didn't burn your barn!"

"I expected you to defend him."

"I'm not defending him. I *know* he didn't burn the barn because *I* was the 'mystery woman.' He was with me that night, so he *couldn't* have burned your barn."

"You? You mean the story was true? Then why didn't you come forward at the trial?"

"I couldn't. You know how my pa feels about Ben. He would've killed me."

Harry frowned, but before he could speak, Ben said, "Molly?" He was beside her, his eyes blazing with a mixture of jealousy and anger.

"It's all right, Ben. I was just telling Harry why you couldn't have burned his barn."

"But don't expect me to shake your hand and wish you well, Cantrell. You stole my girl."

"Harry," Molly chastened gently. "Please don't try to pretend your heart was broken when I married Ben. I know I wounded your pride, but I also know you weren't in love with me."

Harry opened his mouth to protest but then closed it with a snap. His disgruntled gaze went from Molly to Ben and back to Molly again. She'd given him a way to salvage some portion of his pride, and he was thinking it over. The fact that he really hadn't loved her would work to her advantage.

Now she had to take this one step further. Thank heaven for the experiences she'd had trying to manipulate her father's unstable moods. Handling these two rational creatures was like child's play in comparison.

"Harry," she continued with a secretive smile, "I think you and Ben ought to be friends."

Both men scowled at her in disbelief, but she ignored them. "Think about it, both of you. Harry, somebody burned your barn, and you want to find out who it was. Ben, somebody burned Harry's barn and tried to blame you for it. You both want to find this person, and you'll have a much better chance if you work together . . . as friends."

She could see they were intrigued by the idea, but were they convinced? They simply had to be. She knew that if they worked together, they would soon discover the identity of the barn burner, just as she and Julie had. Then Ben's name would be cleared, and her father would get what he so richly deserved.

"Just think," she tried, "the guilty person might be here today. He might be watching you right now. Imagine how he'd start sweating if he saw you shaking hands."

She held her breath as they eyed each other warily, then decided to use her final argument. "Harry, if you shake Ben's hand, everybody'll know your heart's not really broken. You don't want people feeling sorry for you, do you?"

That did the trick. Harry jerked his hand out of his pocket and thrust it at Ben. Ben blinked in surprise but hesitated only a second. The two men shook solemnly.

"Smile, for heaven's sake," Molly urged, eliciting grudging grins. She sighed with relief, glad no one had overheard the conversation. Word of the apparent reconciliation would be all over the county within twenty-four hours, and Harry would not have to endure another moment of sympathy. It was the least she could do for him.

"You're a lucky man, Cantrell," Harry was saying, his stiff grin still firmly in place.

"I know it," Ben replied, his smile growing more genuine at mention of Molly.

"Harry," Molly said when they stopped shaking hands, "why don't you come over to the house this afternoon for some pie and coffee. You and Ben can talk things over and see if you can figure out who might be behind all the trouble."

Harry's wariness returned, but Ben said, "She's right, Hoskins. We've both got a stake in finding out who really set the fire. Maybe we oughta work together."

"I suppose you're right," Harry allowed after a moment's thought.

"Good," Molly said, delighted, and then another possibility occurred to her. "Harry, I have an idea. Why don't you stop by and pick up Julie on your way to our place."

"Julie? Your sister?"

"Yes. Don't you see, word'll get out that

you're courting her now, and everyone'll see how easily you forgot about me."

"Courting *Julie*? She's just a kid!"

"You haven't looked at her lately," Ben said with a knowing smile that annoyed Molly. When had Ben been looking at Julie?

Harry was still doubtful.

"Please, Harry," Molly said. "My pa won't let me come to the house anymore, and he sure won't let Julie visit me, but if you came to take her for a buggy ride, he'd never even ask where you were going."

"All right," he said grudgingly, "but just this once."

"Good. We'll see you this afternoon," Ben said as they turned away, surprising a whole gang of curious onlookers who had suspended their own conversations to observe this one. The gawkers quickly resumed their talk and allowed Ben and Molly to slip away.

They were halfway home before Molly found the courage to speak about their experience. "The preacher was right, you know," she ventured. "All that hate hurts you worse than anybody else."

"He also said Joseph tested his brothers before he forgave them," Ben reminded her.

"Then test folks. At least give them a chance to prove themselves instead of just assuming they have a grudge against you."

Ben sighed with mock despair. "I never expected you'd try to turn my life upside down, Molly Cantrell."

Molly slipped her arm through his and rested her head on his shoulder. "Don't you like surprises?"

Ben wasn't sure whether he did or not.

Molly had been out on the porch, anxiously watching the road, for over an hour when she finally caught sight of Harry's buggy approaching the ranch. Squinting into the afternoon sun, she strained to see if he carried a passenger. She cried out joyfully when she saw Julie's eager wave.

Ben and Johnny watched the arrival with slightly less enthusiasm. They were leaning against the corral fence, smoking. Johnny had returned from town that morning while the Cantrells were still at church and had been lecturing Ben about his foolishness ever since they got back.

"I swear, you're turning into a regular pillar of the community," Johnny scoffed. "Going to church! Next thing you know, you'll be running for mayor."

"I'd have to make friends with a lot of folks before I could get elected," Ben pointed out.

"That what you're planning to do? Make friends, I mean? That why you invited Harry over here today?"

Again Ben heard what sounded like jealousy in Johnny's tone, but he knew better than to accuse him. "Harry and I have some business. I told you, we both want to find out who burned his barn."

"I don't see how you two talking it over can solve anything. If either one of you knew who was guilty, he'd already be behind bars."

"Molly figures we know more than we think we do. She says if we start talking and thinking, we might discover who'd like to do us both harm."

"Maybe Molly oughta get a job as sheriff."

"Johnny," Ben said in warning.

Johnny shrugged apologetically. "Reckon we oughta go over and say hello to your visitors," he said to change the subject.

"John, I want you to help me today. We need somebody with a clear head to listen and help us figure this thing out."

Johnny covered his surprise well. "You know I'll do whatever I can."

"I'm counting on it."

They walked over to greet the guests. Molly had already run out to the buggy and was hugging Julie even before the poor girl had a chance to get out. They were laughing and crying at the same time as the men watched helplessly.

"Oh, Harry, thank you," Molly managed after a few minutes. "I can't tell you how grateful I am."

"It was no trouble to get her. It was right on the way," he demurred, obviously proud of having pleased her so much.

"When you've got the buggy put up, come on over to the house. The pie's still warm." She and Julie hooked arms and headed for the cabin, both of them talking a mile a minute.

Belatedly and with far more reserve, Ben and Johnny greeted Harry and helped him put his horse and buggy in the barn. Molly had set chairs out on the porch, and the men sat down on them to enjoy the shade. They muttered a few inconsequential remarks about the weather and cattle prices before Ben got down to business.

"Well, Harry, who do you think wanted to burn your barn?"

Harry shrugged. "Who do you think wanted you to get the blame?"

"I don't know, but it seems kinda funny to me that this is the same thing happened to my pa six years ago."

"Same thing? What do you mean?"

"I mean my pa never burned Fletcher's barn. He was home with me all night that night until the posse came for him."

"The hell you say! Why didn't you ever tell anybody?"

"I did, but nobody paid me any mind. After he was dead, nobody wanted to talk about it, so I stopped trying to get folks to believe me. Anyway, Molly thinks . . . Molly and I think," he corrected when he caught Johnny wincing, "that the same person is responsible for both crimes."

"Six years apart? Why would anybody have it in for both you and your father? And why would he wait so long to try something again?"

"I don't know, but I've never been able to find a reason why somebody wanted Fletcher dead, and I'd bet money you can't think of anybody who'd want to burn your barn."

"You think I was a convenient victim, just like Fletcher, then?"

"Yeah, it makes sense. Until my pa had the fight with Fletcher, he didn't have an enemy in the world, and until we had the fight at the social, I'd never done anything to make anybody mad at me, either. The minute we did, though, something happened to that person, something folks thought my pa and me did."

"Damn," Harry murmured. "Any idea who it might be?"

"I reckon that's what we're here to figure out."

Inside the house, Molly and Julie were trying to dish up pie and catch up on news at the same time. The pie was sitting forgotten on the table.

"Oh, Molly, your house is so nice," Julie said, gazing enviously around the single room.

"Ben says we have to add on before the baby comes. I know," she added, seeing Julie's amazement. "I tried to tell him he shouldn't spend so much money, but he doesn't seem to mind a bit. You'd die if you knew how much this dress cost, and he *made* me get it. He bought me two other outfits, too, and he said he was going to burn my 'rags' if I ever tried to wear them again."

Julie's eyes were wide with wonder. She moved closer, checking the door to make sure no one would overhear. "How does he treat you? Otherwise, I mean."

She didn't have to explain. Both girls shared

the same concerns. "He's never raised his hand to me, not once. Of course, it's only been a week, but he . . . he's always telling me he won't ever hurt me."

Molly knew better than to trust completely in a man's promises, but she managed to conceal her own doubts from Julie, who sighed with relief. "I've been so worried, wondering if I did the right thing by telling Ben."

"How did Pa act after I left?"

"Strange, real strange. For a couple days he just laid around and drank, but he didn't get mean. It was like the fight had gone clean out of him. Then he sobered up and started complaining about what a worthless ungrateful thing you were and all that."

Molly nodded. She could just imagine.

"Then when he saw you all in church this morning, he got mad. He dropped us off at home and went right back to town. I figure he'll come home mean drunk tonight."

"Oh, I'm so sorry, Julie!"

"He would've done it sooner or later. He was probably only waiting for an excuse. Don't worry. I'll take care of Mama."

Molly only wished it were possible. "If he gets too bad, you can bring her over here."

Julie stared at her in horror. "Are you crazy? He'd kill us all if she tried to leave him."

"But Ben would—"

"He'd kill Ben, too, and you know he would. I can't figure it out. He calls her all kinds of names and tells her how worthless and ugly she is, but then he tells her all the horrible things he'll do if she ever tries to leave. If he hates her so much, you'd think he'd be glad to get rid of her."

"I know," Molly said in despair. "I gave up trying to understand it a long time ago."

"I wish . . ."

"What?"

"I . . . No, I can't say it. It sounds too awful."

"You wish he would die," Molly guessed. "Don't look so shocked. I've wished it myself a hundred times. I've wished that one time when he was hitting Mama his heart would stop or his brain would start bleeding or something. I've even thought of killing him myself."

"Molly!"

"Don't worry. I wouldn't risk hanging over the likes of him. But that doesn't stop me from wishing all the same."

"Ladies," Ben called from the doorway, startling them both. "I thought you promised us some pie and coffee. When Harry sees how bad you treat me, Molly, he'll be glad he didn't marry you."

Molly stuck her tongue out at him and got up to find the plates and cups. When he had gone, she noticed Julie's expression. "He's only teasing, Julie," Molly assured her.

"I know," she replied in amazement. "It just . . . it seems so strange."

As she was cutting the pie and transferring the slices onto plates, Molly said, "What did you think when you saw Harry today?"

"I didn't know what to think. I could hardly believe he really wanted to take *me* on a buggy ride. . . ."

Her voice trailed off, and Molly glanced up to find her blushing furiously. "Julie! You like him, don't you?"

Julie nodded in an agony of embarrassment.

"Since when? I mean, you never said anything."

"Since always. I couldn't say anything because he was your fellow."

"But Julie, you were going to let me marry him. How could you stand it?"

"You said I could come live with you. I knew he'd never look at me. I'm too young and not nearly as pretty as you—"

"That's not true! You're as pretty as anybody!"

"Anyway, I figured having him as a brother was better than not having him at all."

"Oh, Julie!" Molly put down her knife and hurried over to take Julie in a comforting embrace. "Julie, I never said anything, but . . . I'm afraid of Harry. You remember how he hit Ben at the social, and he's a lot like Pa—"

"No, he isn't!" Julie protested, pulling out of Molly's arms. "He's nice, and he's polite, and he'd never hit a woman. I know he wouldn't."

"I . . ." Molly didn't know what to say. For Julie's sake, she wanted to agree, but she simply couldn't.

"I don't think you need to worry, though. He made sure I understood he was only bringing me today because you asked him to. I doubt he'll ever think of me as anything but your baby sister, anyway."

Molly couldn't stand seeing Julie's despair. "He's bound to notice you've grown up. Ben did," she remembered, still a little annoyed at the thought.

"He did?"

"Yes, and he told Harry, too. I think . . . I'm sure Harry will see it, too, in time. . . ." She frowned, wondering whether she was doing the right thing, and then said, "I could ask Harry to bring you over next week, and—"

"No! Don't you dare. If he ever comes for me again, I want it to be his idea."

"Well, all right," Molly agreed with relief. Maybe Harry wouldn't notice her sister after all. Or maybe Molly was wrong about him. "But if he starts getting interested in you, be careful."

"Don't worry. I won't make the mistake Ma did."

Molly sighed, wondering how a woman could ever be sure about a man. She'd lived with Ben for a week, and she still wasn't certain. "Here," she said, handing Julie a plate. "At least take him his pie."

When Molly and Julie joined the men on the porch, Molly noticed they looked much more friendly than they had at first. "Have you all come to any conclusions?" she asked, taking a chair beside Ben.

"No," Ben replied, "but at least we've managed to convince Harry I'm the reason his barn was burned."

"The funny thing is, I was planning to tear it down anyway," Harry said, taking a bite of pie. "Mmm, this is good, Molly. I'd just been telling my father a few days earlier how I was afraid it was going to fall on someone's head one day soon. I didn't even have any stock in it, and whoever set the fire turned loose the horses in the corrals so they wouldn't get burned." Harry shook his head in wonder.

"Mighty considerate of him," Johnny remarked acidly.

"He might've somehow got wind of your plans," Ben said.

"Or else he just took one look at the barn and came to the same conclusion I did," Harry said.

"Anyway, he didn't want to hurt you too bad, or he would've set fire to the house."

"And he wouldn't've let the horses go," Johnny added.

Molly listened with growing apprehension. "Then the person who set the fire was somebody who liked Harry or at least wanted to be considerate of him, but who doesn't like Ben," she said.

Ben and Harry both turned to her, and from the looks on their faces, she was certain they must know the truth. Her breath lodged in her throat.

"That's right," Ben said thoughtfully. "What we can't figure out is what I've got that anybody'd want."

"Well, it has to be the same thing your pa had, so it must be this ranch," Johnny said.

Molly didn't dare glance at Julie for fear she was thinking the same thing Molly was. Did Julie remember their father had disappeared from the schoolhouse the night of the fire? Did she remember how many times Elijah Wade had coveted Ben Cantrell's land?

Ben's gaze was riveted on her, as if he were trying to search her soul. Did he know? Had he figured it out yet? His eyes narrowed speculatively, and she wondered if he could sense her inner turmoil.

"And speaking of my poor barn," Harry said between bites of pie, "I'm going to have a barn raising next Saturday, and you're all invited."

To Molly's relief, this effectively changed the subject. After an hour or so of pleasant conversation beginning with how the barn should be constructed and ending with even more innocuous topics, Harry said, "Well, Julie, I guess I'd better be getting you back. I wouldn't want your father to think his other daughter had been stolen."

"Stolen?" Ben echoed in amazement.

"Sure, that's what he's telling people. Say, Ben, did you really hold a gun on him when you took Molly away?" Harry asked with a twinkle.

Molly sputtered in outrage, but Ben chuckled. "Harry, *he* held a gun on *me*, or at least he tried to. I had to take it away from him so he wouldn't hurt anybody."

Harry glanced at Molly and then at Julie, who nodded their confirmation. He whistled softly. "I suppose it's my duty to tell folks the way it

really happened, isn't it?" he asked of no one in
particular. "Well, let's get going, Julie."

In a few minutes Ben and Molly stood in the
yard, waving farewell to their guests. Ben slid
his arm around Molly's waist and gave her a
smile of admiration. "I do believe you're a witch,
Mrs. Cantrell."

"A witch? What are you talking about, Mr.
Cantrell?" Molly asked.

"You must have some kind of magical powers.
Somehow you managed to get me to church,
you made Harry Hoskins forget you jilted him,
and you've got the two of us thinking we're
friends. You're an amazing woman."

She smiled at his praise, but inside she knew
a tiny fear. Had she made a mistake in bringing
him and Harry together? Would Ben still think
she was wonderful when he finally discovered
the identity of the barn burner?

The morning of the barn raising dawned bright
and clear. Molly had been cooking for two days in
preparation for the event. Friends and neighbors
from miles around would come to Harry's ranch,
and each woman would be expected to bring
plenty of food to feed the men doing the work.

Ben and Johnny carefully loaded her pies and
cakes and laden pots into the back of the wagon
along with the tools they would take along. The
sky was not yet fully light when they pulled into
Harry's ranch yard, but still they were not the
first to arrive.

Harry greeted them with a shout and a wave from atop a pile of lumber he was inspecting. By the time he climbed down and made his way over to them, they had begun to unload the wagon.

"Good Lord, Molly, you brought enough food to feed the whole county," he protested, picking up a huge pot of beans.

"I thought you invited the whole county," she replied with a laugh. "Besides, I know how much Johnny McGee and my husband eat."

"Just be sure you put back one of your pies for us," Ben warned.

"*Two* of your pies," muttered Johnny.

Molly stared at him in astonishment. "Why, Mr. McGee, are you admitting you like my cooking?"

"Never said I didn't," he replied, hefting an armload of tools.

"Never said you did, either," she reminded him.

Blushing furiously, he turned away, carrying the tools over to the work area. Molly flashed Ben a look of exasperation, but he only grinned and, taking a cake in each hand, moved off toward the row of plank tables where the food was being spread out.

Miriam Hoskins was serving as Harry's hostess. She directed everyone where to put the various items of food. When Molly had donned her apron, she asked Miriam what else needed to be done, and Mariam set her the task of organizing the dishes and silverware each family had provided.

"That's a pretty dress," Miriam remarked during a momentary lull in new arrivals.

Molly fiddled self-consciously with the collar of her violet calico, knowing how much a compliment from someone as grand as Mrs. Hoskins meant. "Thank you. Your dress is pretty, too."

Miriam smiled ruefully. "It's hardly practical for a job like this, but I really don't have anything more suitable. Franklin refuses to buy me practical clothes. He says I don't need them."

Eyeing the pale green dimity gown, Molly could understand Miriam's concern. By the end of the long hard day ahead, the fine fabric would probably be ruined. Still, "It must be nice not to need work clothes."

Molly did not understand Miriam's troubled frown, but before they could say more, another family arrived, and Miriam went over to welcome them.

Johnny McGee watched her through narrowed eyes, admiring the unconsciously graceful way she moved. Miriam Hoskins was about the finest-looking woman he had ever set eyes on, and he had set his eyes on plenty of them. In the early morning sunlight, her black hair glistened like a raven's wing, and her dark eyes sparkled like stars. Earlier, she'd laughed at something one of the women said to her, and the sound was like music.

She walked right by without giving him so much as a glance. Didn't she recognize him? Didn't she remember how he had bid for her at the box supper? Of course she didn't. Why should she remember an insignificant cowboy? Bitterness left an acrid taste in his mouth as he continued to follow her with his eyes. She was helping some rancher's wife carry her food offerings over to the table. She was bringing a big pot, coming right toward him again. Frowning, she stopped and shifted the pot. The lid was slipping off. She tried to juggle it, but the lid slid farther, and the contents of the pot sloshed onto her hand.

Johnny was beside her in an instant. "Whoa, careful," he said, catching the lid and taking the pot from her. "Did it burn you?"

"No, I . . ."

Their gazes met, and he saw the flash of recognition in the second before it turned to despair. The bloom vanished from her cheeks, leaving them pale, but before he could do more than register her distress, someone called her name.

"Miriam!" Franklin Hoskins shouted from across the yard. "Miriam, you have guests to greet over here." His expression was murderous as he glared at Johnny McGee.

"Please," she whispered, "don't talk to me again." She snatched the pot from him and whirled away in a flurry of skirts, leaving Johnny to stare after her in astonishment.

God almighty, he mused, she's terrified of the old bastard. The thought turned his bitterness to gall.

Molly kept watching the new arrivals, and as the flood slowed to a trickle, she began to won-

der if her family was coming. The Wades were
Harry's nearest neighbors. For Elijah to miss
Harry's barn raising was unthinkable, but just
when she was beginning to think he might, she
saw their wagon.

Restraining herself with difficulty, she waited
while Harry went over to welcome them and
Miriam helped her mother carry her food over to
the table. Hannah had a warm smile for Molly,
but neither of them made any move to embrace,
although Molly's arms ached to hold her mother
close. With Elijah watching, they would have to
be circumspect. The mere fact that they would
have ample opportunity to talk while they were
with the women today was blessing enough.

From the corner of her eye, Molly saw Harry
helping Julie down from the wagon. Had Harry
already noticed that Julie was grown up? After
all, she'd recently turned sixteen, and many
women married even younger.

Before she could decide how she felt about
Harry really courting her sister, she heard her
father's strident voice. "What's *he* doing here? If
it wasn't for him, you wouldn't *need* a new barn!"

Molly's gaze found Ben where he was standing with a group of men. His face was red with
suppressed rage, and one of the men put his
hand on Ben's shoulder and spoke quietly to
him. Molly's breakfast formed a hard lump in
her stomach, and for the first time in two weeks
she feared an attack of the morning sickness that
had vanished the day she'd married Ben.

"Ben is here because I invited him and Molly,"

Harry replied, loudly enough for everyone to hear. "You heard the evidence at the trial. Ben wasn't the one who set the fire."

"Since when do you believe that? You was fit to be tied when he got off on the word of some 'mystery woman.'"

"I've spoken to the mystery woman myself and to Ben, too. I believe he's innocent. Ben is my guest today the same as you. I expect *everyone* to treat him with courtesy." The message was clear, but would Elijah care? Beside Molly, Hannah drew a shaky breath and held it while they awaited his reply.

"Well, *I* don't have to be polite to him, not after he stole my girl," Elijah muttered, stomping off.

Ben made a move as if to go after him, but several of the men closed ranks around him. All of them started talking at once, and after a few moments Ben seemed to calm down. Molly felt a surge of relief and instinctively found her mother's hand.

"I wish you'd leave him and come live with me, Mama," she whispered.

"Hush. You know what your pa'd do if I ever left him. Besides, I'm his wife, Molly. I can't forget that. I'm just glad you found a good man." Her eyes searched Molly's. "Julie says you're happy."

"I am, Mama. Ben's real nice to me."

"I can see," she said, taking in Molly's dress. "He doesn't . . . ?"

"No," Molly assured her.

Her mother sighed. "I'm happy for you, honey. Now, if we can just get Julie settled."

Molly smiled sadly. "She's got her eye on Harry."

"I know. I hope she don't get hurt."

"I hope so, too," Molly replied as Harry escorted Julie over to her mother. He was still fuming from his run-in with her father, and Julie was speaking softly to him, trying to soothe him.

"I'm sorry, Harry," Molly said when he approached.

"There's nothing for you to be sorry for . . . either of you," he added when Ben came up behind her.

But Ben was shaking his head. "Maybe we oughta leave, Harry."

"Don't talk crazy. Besides, if somebody ought to leave, it's him. Oh, I'm sorry, Mrs. Wade. I didn't mean—"

"That's all right, Harry," Hannah said. "I just hope we didn't spoil the day for you."

"No, no, of course not. Ben, let's get these men organized so we can get started."

Before Ben could protest again, Harry took his arm and led him away. Molly gazed after them, trying to ignore her growing feeling of apprehension. Would others scorn Ben the way her father had? Would he be sorry he came? Last Sunday he'd seemed ready to start giving people a chance to get to know him. Now she could see his guard was back up again. Feeling helpless against the forces she had sent in motion, she said a silent prayer and turned to follow her

mother over to where the women were gathered
in the shade of Harry's front porch.

Some of them had brought knitting or needle-
work with which they busied their hands while
they gossiped and exhausted every conceivable
topic of small talk. Molly came in for a little
teasing as the most newly married woman, and
Julie received her share of comments for the attention Harry had paid her earlier.

Slowly the barn walls took shape, and the
women carried water and coffee to the workers
at intervals. When it was Molly's turn, she
stopped in front of Ben, trying to read his mood.
His expression was set, and she could see he still
nursed a fierce anger. The men who had been so
open to him that morning were now avoiding
his apparent hostility.

"Ben," she said in frustration, "you've got to
give people a chance. They want to be friendly to
you."

"What's the use?" he replied coldly. "They're
all thinking the same thing your father is."

"That isn't true!"

But of course she had no proof, as Ben's unblinking gaze reminded her. She turned away in
defeat, carrying the water to the next man.

The noon meal was a pleasant time for everyone, it seemed, except the Cantrells. Elijah had
wandered back sometime during the morning,
his face flushed from alcohol, and although he
had avoided Ben, he continued to give his son-
in-law evil looks.

Molly recalled telling Julie how she wished

their father were dead. She had thought his beating their mother was his greatest sin, but now she realized he was capable of hurting people without laying a hand on them. Her heart ached when she heard him saying something about barn burners, and for the first time she wished she had the courage to reveal Elijah Wade for what he was.

When the men had gone back to work, the women began cleaning up the mess. As Molly set down a stack of dirty dishes near the washtubs, Miriam Hoskins stopped beside her and gave her arm a comforting squeeze. "I'm so sorry, Molly."

Molly opened her mouth to reply, but when she saw the naked agony in Miriam Hoskins's dark eyes, she was struck dumb. How could the wife of the richest man in town understand the depth of her suffering? Yet in that instant, Molly knew beyond a shadow of a doubt she did.

On the verge of tears, Molly hurried away, seeking the privacy of the privy in which to compose herself. When she was in control of her emotions again, she made her way slowly back to where the women were still working. As she passed the house, however, the sound of an argument inside stopped her. Was Ben . . .?

But no, it was Harry and his father. She would have gone on except she heard Mr. Hoskins say, "You mean you actually spoke to this 'mystery woman'?"

"That's right, and I believe her story."

"She's someone you know? Someone whose word you trust?" Hoskins pressed.

"Yes, I know her very well, and believe me, she had a good reason for keeping her identity a secret."

"I'm sure she did," Hoskins said, and the fury in his voice shocked Molly.

"You seem awfully reluctant to believe Ben is innocent, Father. Why can't you be satisfied with my word . . . or do you know something you're not telling?"

"What could I possibly know? I'm simply interested in finding out the facts. This is still my ranch, something you tend to forget. It won't be yours until you marry, and now that you've let Molly Wade slip through your fingers, you aren't likely to have it anytime soon."

"I can wait. Maybe I've decided I'm not as anxious as I thought I was to get the ranch, not if it means a loveless marriage."

"What does that mean?" Hoskins snapped.

"You know what it means."

Molly heard the back door slam, telling of Harry's hasty exit, and she hurried on before he could catch her eavesdropping. Suddenly Miriam Hoskins's empathy for Molly's problems was starting to make sense. And why was Harry so put out with his father? Anyone would think . . . Then she remembered: long ago, when she had discussed the burning of Fletcher's barn, Harry had seemed to think his own father had a reason for wanting Ben's father out of the way.

It was crazy, of course, and Molly knew Mr. Hoskins couldn't possibly be the guilty party because she knew perfectly well who the guilty party was.

But poor Harry. How she wished she could tell him the truth and put his mind at ease; but she could never let anyone know she suspected the truth. Ben would be upset enough as it was without thinking she had kept it from him.

By suppertime, the barn was finished except for shingling the roof, which Harry and his men could do themselves. As soon as the meal was over, Ben found her and helped her carry their dishes to the wagon. Neither of them was eager to prolong what had been an ordeal. Although Elijah Wade had disappeared again around mid-afternoon, Ben's mood had not improved, and Molly's apprehension had grown accordingly. Would he blame her for the way things had gone? If she hadn't encouraged him to find a place for himself in the community, he would never have attended the barn raising at all, never subjected himself to the unpleasantness.

Ben hardly spoke a word during the trip home, but as soon as they had finished unloading the wagon, he said, "I reckon I'll go into town with Johnny tonight. He's feeling kind of low, and I don't like to let him go alone."

Molly bit her lip. Only last week he had told her he couldn't bear to leave *her* alone. As she had feared, Johnny McGee had won.

Chapter Nine

✦✦✦✦✦

BEN STOOD AT the end of the bar nursing a beer.
The saloon was crowded with cowboys enjoying
their Saturday night, but he might as well have
been alone. He sought no one's company, and
no one sought his. Even Johnny had deserted
him for one of the girls. So much for Ben's concern for his friend's welfare. Johnny had been so
depressed after the barn raising that Ben had
been afraid to turn him loose in town on his
own. Now here Ben was, in town when he
would much rather be home in his own bed, and
he hadn't seen Johnny in over two hours.

But Ben had more than enough other troubles
to occupy his mind. For the past six years he'd
wanted nothing so much as to clear his family's
name. Not only had he failed in that, he had
seen it blackened even more when he himself
was implicated in a crime he hadn't committed.
The situation had been unpleasant enough when
he was the last of the Cantrells, but now he had
a wife and a baby to consider. What kind of
future would they have under the stigma of the
Cantrell name?

To make matters worse, the new clues he had
gathered since Harry's barn was burned only
confused the issue, and he found himself farther
than ever from a solution. What did he have that
anyone could want badly enough to frame his
father and then wait six years to frame him?

Who would do such a thing, and why? *Why?*
The question resounded in his mind like a ma-
licious taunt, and he downed the rest of his beer
in one gulp.

"Ben?"

He looked up to see the girl with whom
Johnny had disappeared earlier. She looked
much the worse for wear. Her dark hair was in
tangles, and her gaudy red dress was wrinkled
and mussed. "Ben, can you come up and get
Johnny out of my room?"

"What's the matter?"

She glanced around, obviously embarrassed
for anyone to overhear. She leaned closer to him,
and he caught the unmistakable odors of cheap
perfume and sex. "He just keeps wanting more,
but he's out of money, and he's . . . well, he's
dead drunk, and he couldn't do anything anyway. I like Johnny, and I wouldn't mind if he
slept it off up there, but I've got other custom-
ers." She made a beseeching gesture, and Ben
pushed himself away from the bar.

"I'll take care of him. Where is he?"

"Come on, I'll show you."

Ben followed her up the stairs, oblivious to the
presence of Elijah Wade, who sat in a far corner
of the room, watching their progress through
narrowed eyes. Upstairs Ben found Johnny
asleep in the girl's bed, snoring loudly.

"Come on, partner, you're making a nuisance
of yourself," Ben said when he had finally
roused his friend.

"Ben, she's scared to death of him," Johnny said urgently, grabbing Ben's arms.

"Who's scared of who?"

"*She* is, of *him*," he insisted.

Ben looked to the girl for an explanation, but she shook her head in bewilderment. "I don't know what he's talking about. He's been saying that all night."

"Well, help me put his clothes on, and I'll get him out of here." When Johnny was dressed, he looked even more disreputable than the girl did, but at least he was decent enough to go outside. Ben took him out the back way, since it was closer to the horses.

The night air revived Johnny enough so he was able to sit his horse. They did have to stop twice for him to empty his stomach, though, and by the time they reached the ranch, Johnny was threatening to give up alcohol for good.

When Ben had put him safely to bed, Johnny caught his sleeve before he could leave. "Thanks, partner."

"For what?" Ben scoffed good-naturedly. "I've gotten you out of a lot worse."

"For going to town with me tonight. I didn't want to be alone."

Ben frowned. "What is it you've got stuck in your craw? Is it Elijah Wade? 'Cause if it is—"

"No, it ain't him. I reckon you can fight your own battles. It's *her*."

"Her who?" Ben asked impatiently.

"Miz Hoskins," he said reverently. "Miriam."

Ben swore. "Can't you forget about her? She's a married woman, Johnny, and her husband is—"

"The meanest sonofabitch in creation," Johnny concluded. "She's scared to death of him. I'll bet he beats her."

"Even if he does, it ain't any of your business." Ben stared down at him in exasperation. "Johnny, why are you doing this to yourself?"

"I don't know," Johnny said morosely.

Ben decided he'd better end this futile conversation. Johnny was still pretty drunk, and he just might start blubbering. "Go to sleep, partner. We'll talk about it tomorrow." Fortunately Johnny was too miserable to argue.

Ben made his way to the dark cabin, wondering if Molly was going to be mad at him for leaving her tonight. She'd seemed pretty disappointed, but she hadn't tried to stop him. He almost wished she had.

Molly woke up the instant Ben opened the cabin door. She lay perfectly still, listening for any telltale sound that would betray his condition. Was he drunk? Was he angry? He moved through the darkened house with the surefootedness of a cat, so he couldn't be drunk.

She heard the faint rustle of cloth as he undressed. Seeing his dark shadow looming closer as he moved toward the bed, she braced herself. She'd known her father to drag her mother out of bed in the dead of night when he came home in a rage. Would Ben . . . ?

He barely lifted the cover as he slipped in beside her, moving carefully. She realized with a start that he was trying very hard not to waken her. He rolled over on his side with his back to her, and in a few minutes his breathing told her he was asleep.

She caught a whiff of beer. He had been drinking, but he wasn't drunk. He wasn't too very angry, either, if his consideration was any proof. But he hadn't reached for her. He always reached for her the moment he got in bed.

Molly decided to bake some pies. Ben loved her pies. Besides, she needed something to keep her hands busy so she wouldn't wring them while she worried about her marriage falling apart. Sunday had been a disaster, and Monday hadn't started out much better.

The day before, Ben had offered to take her to church, but he'd flatly refused to go himself, so Molly had stayed home, too. Johnny had been even more cross than usual, probably because he was nursing a hangover. Ben had managed to find some things to occupy him out in the barn, so Molly had hardly seen him all day, and when she did he had little to say.

That night he had reached for her, but while they usually made love with abandon, this time Molly just couldn't respond with her usual fire.

Ben had also seemed restrained, as if his mind were on something else. Afterward Molly had lain awake for hours wondering if he could have lost interest in her so soon. Even now the thought made her blood run cold.

The Monday morning washing for two people hardly took any time at all, and now time lay heavy on her hands until the men returned for dinner. If she hurried, she could have at least one pie ready for the noon meal, she realized, finding a bowl in which to soak the apples and remembering the absent way Ben had kissed her good-bye that morning before going out with the other men. Maybe a pie would bring a smile to his lips and bring some enthusiasm back to his kiss. Later on she would scrub the cabin floor, and then . . .

The sound of a horse approaching brought her head up. Could Ben have come home? She raced to the door but stopped short when she saw the all-too-familiar figure of her father astride the approaching horse. Her breath caught, and her heart lurched painfully in her chest. Why was he here? What did he want?

Did he mean her harm? She thought vaguely of the shotgun inside the house, the gun Ben kept loaded, the gun he had instructed her to use in an emergency since she didn't have to be an accurate shot to use it to effect. She wanted to fetch it, but panic had paralyzed her. Like a bird trapped in the mesmerizing gaze of a snake, she stood and waited as he walked his horse right up to the front porch.

"Mornin', Miss Molly, or should I say 'Mrs.'?" he asked snidely, taking her in from head to toe. Then he let his contemptuous gaze wander over the ranch buildings, the buildings Ben was so proud of and maintained so well, the buildings that made the Wade ranch look poor by comparison. "Looks like you fell into the honey pot, girl. Yes, sir, I been hearing how much money he's spent on you already. He's even planning to add onto his house so's he'll have more room for your little bastard."

"Get out of here," she tried, but the words were deathly faint. He didn't appear to have heard.

"But don't you go thinking he likes you special. Oh, no, he pays *all* his whores real good."

"What are you talking about?" she asked, knowing he was baiting her and hating herself for taking the bait.

"I seen him in the saloon on Saturday night. He was with one of them fancy women who works there. They was laughing and talking and drinking, and then he took her upstairs. I don't reckon I gotta tell you what goes on up there. A whore like you knows all about them things."

"You're lying!"

"Am I? You ask him, then. You ask him if he didn't have himself another woman. I coulda told you it would happen. Did you think he was crazy in love with you? Did you think he'd look up to you like you was some kind of fine lady? A man don't have no respect for a woman who spreads her legs for him before they're married. He counts you as just one more of his whores, the one who keeps his house, too." He pointed a shaking finger at her. "You mark my words, little girl, soon as that baby comes, he'll throw you out so fast—"

"Get out of here! Now!" Molly dashed into the house and snatched up the shotgun, but by the time she got back to the doorway, he was riding away.

"You mark my words!" he shouted back over his shoulder before kicking his horse into a gallop.

Molly wanted to shriek her protest. It wasn't true, she told herself over and over, but she couldn't forget Ben hadn't made love to her when he'd returned from town on Saturday night. She couldn't forget how distant he had been ever since, either, or her own fears that he had already tired of her.

She kicked the door frame in frustration and then turned to put the shotgun away. How she wished she'd gotten it earlier, how she wished she'd driven him off before he'd told his filthy lies!

But *were* they lies? And how could she ever find out?

Molly had no pie ready when the men came in for dinner; she was lucky to have any meal at all prepared. They didn't seem to notice how little time she had put into it, though, and when they were done they left again. Ben had barely spoken to her, barely even looked at her, but as he was leaving he bent for a quick kiss and seemed to notice her for the first time.

"Are you feeling all right? You look kinda pale."

"I . . . I have a headache," she said. That was certainly true.

"Maybe you oughta lay down, then." He smiled at her for the first time in days. "You have to think of the baby, you know. Can't be too careful."

His lips brushed hers, and then he was gone. *The baby.* Her father was right. The baby was all Ben cared about!

The pain in her skull started pounding, but she ignored it. She couldn't go to bed, not when there was so much to do. With almost frantic haste, she cleaned up the mess from dinner and began assembling the ingredients for pie dough. Working mechanically, she rolled out crust after crust, filling the pans in a mindless frenzy and sliding them into the oven.

Ben cared about *her*, too, she knew he did. He thought she was a good wife, and she would be the best wife any man ever had. He would see the pies, and he would see how clean the house was and how well she did all her chores. Then tonight, when he came to bed, she would respond the way she used to, and everything would be just the way it was before.

Except she burned two of the pies and had to throw them out. She only got half the cabin swept before the room started spinning and she had to sit down and rest for a while. Then she remembered the clothes still on the line and had to rush out to get them down. The sun made the pain in her head pulse and throb, and by the time she got back to the house again, she was nauseated.

But she couldn't stop. She had to get supper ready, even though the smell of beans and fatback made her stomach roil. When she set the food on the table, the men dug in enthusiastically, even though the biscuits were black on the bottom. Molly sat at the table in a kind of stupor, watching the men eat while barely touching her own food.

Had Ben noticed the half-swept cabin, the burned biscuits, the wasted pies? If so, he said nothing. He inquired about her headache, but she assured him with a smile that she was fine. When everyone else had finished eating, she washed the dishes, performing the task by rote as the pain clawed at her brain like a giant talon, all but blinding her.

At last she could resist it no longer. She swayed, and a groan escaped her as she caught herself on the side of the dry sink. Ben was beside her in an instant.

"Molly, what the . . . You're sick!" he accused, and she knew once again she had failed in some way. "Why didn't you say something? I could've washed the dishes."

She stared at him, horrified. Didn't he know she couldn't ask him to do her work, not if she wanted to prove herself to him?

"Don't look so shocked," he was saying with a tolerant smile. "I washed plenty of dishes before you came, and I can do it again. I told you this afternoon to take it easy. We don't want anything to happen to the baby."

The baby, she thought numbly, allowing him to seat her on their bed.

"Lay down now, and I'll finish up. When I'm done, I'll help you get ready for bed."

She lay back against the pillows, thinking she had to get hold of herself. So far she'd ruined every other aspect of her plan, but she could still be the passionate wife. She only needed a little rest. If she closed her eyes for a minute, the pain would subside, she knew it would.

The next time she opened her eyes, the room was pitch dark, and the bed was shifting.

"Ben?"

"I'm sorry. I tried not to wake you." He slipped into the bed beside her. "Are you feeling any better? You were dead to the world when I undressed you before."

Her hand went to her bosom, and she discovered she was clad in her nightdress. How could she have slept through it all? "Ben, I . . . if you want . . ."

"Hush now, and go back to sleep. I'll try not to bother you."

True to his word, he turned his back to her just as he had on Saturday night, the night he'd been with the whore. She'd failed again. In a few minutes he was asleep, and Molly surrendered to the tears she'd been fighting all day. Smothering the sounds in her pillow, she wept out her fears and frustrations while her husband slept peacefully beside her.

Molly thought things could not be any worse until she awoke the next morning. Dawn had barely lighted the sky, and for a moment she lay there wondering what was wrong and knowing something was, something terrible. Then she felt the pain, the vicious, viselike cramping that convulsed her body into a protective ball.

No! It can't be! she thought frantically, but then she felt the warm liquid streaming out between her legs.

"*No!*" She threw back the bedclothes and screamed at the sight of the bright-red blood pooling beneath her. "No! Ben, help me!"

But he was already up beside her. "My God, what is it? Is it the baby?"

She couldn't even nod, couldn't acknowledge the unthinkable. "Help me!" she begged, not even knowing what kind of help she needed.

He was out of bed in an instant, pulling on his pants as he ran for the front door. "Johnny!" he shouted. "Johnny, wake up!"

Johnny was already awake and running toward the house, having heard the scream. "What the hell is it?"

"It's Molly. She's bleeding bad. I think it's the baby. Can you go to town and find the doc?"

"Sure, I'm already gone. Tom, Billy, saddle me a horse while I get dressed," he cried, hurrying back to the bunkhouse.

Molly listened, but all the while she was staring hypnotically at the bright-red blood and thinking, No, no, no! But the pains didn't stop, and with each new one more blood seeped out of her. She was sobbing hysterically when Ben came back.

"What should I do, honey? Just tell me. What should I do?"

She stared at him helplessly. "I . . . I don't know . . . I . . ." She wanted her mother, but of course her mother couldn't come, and she couldn't think of any other woman she could ask. She took a deep breath, fighting the hysteria, willing herself to think rationally. "I . . . maybe we should try to stop it. I . . . bring me some clean rags."

With Ben's help, she bound herself and changed into a clean nightdress. Ben stripped the soiled bedclothes and remade the bed while Molly held herself as still as possible, praying it wasn't already too late and that the pains would stop before her baby died. Back in bed again, she curled herself into a ball, cradling the precious life she hoped still lay within her.

Time crawled by. Ben brought her some tea, which she sipped obediently, but despite her care the pains still wrenched her, soaking the rags and draining her life's blood. By the time she heard the doctor's buggy outside, her initial panic had settled into a paralyzing terror.

Dr. Logan was a short, stocky man with white hair and a distracted manner. His mustache drooped, giving him a melancholy appearance that his pale blue eyes did not dispel. "Well, now, what seems to be the trouble, little lady?" he asked the moment he came into the room. "Johnny McGee had you bleeding to death, but you can't trust those Irishmen. They cry over every little thing."

As best she could, Molly told him everything, answering even his most embarrassing questions with complete candor and enduring his examination stoically. When he had looked at the soiled bedclothes and asked a few more questions, he fell into a thoughtful silence.

"Doctor? What's wrong?" she asked when she could stand the suspense no longer. "Am I going to lose the baby?"

"Honey," he said, patting her hand and giving Ben an apologetic look, "I don't know if you ever even had a baby. If you did, it's gone now. As near as I can tell, this bleeding is your menstrual blood. I don't see any sign of a miscarriage today, and from what you told me, if you did lose the baby, it was a while back."

"But I missed my monthly twice! That means I was expecting, doesn't it? What could've happened?"

"I don't know. Like I said, there's no way of knowing now, and there's lots of other reasons you might've missed your monthly. I wish I could tell you more, but all I know is this bleeding is completely natural and there's not a thing wrong with you. Don't worry yourself about whether you lost a baby or not. You're a healthy young woman, and there'll be lots of babies in your future." He patted her hand again, then gathered his things and left, telling her to rest for the next few days.

"How is she?" Johnny demanded the instant Ben and the doctor stepped outside.

"She'll be fine," the doctor told him.

"But she lost the baby," Ben added.

"Damn, I'm sorry, partner," Johnny said, clapping a hand on his friend's shoulder.

Inside, Molly heard the exchange and began to weep again, slowly and silently. She'd failed completely, losing the child Ben wanted more than anything else in the world.

Ben walked the doctor to his buggy, and when they were alone, the doctor said, "Now, Ben, like I said, I can't say for sure whether she miscarried or not, but just in case she did, you ought to stay away from her for a couple of weeks."

"Stay away from her?" Ben asked in confusion.

"Yes, no marital relations."

It took Ben a moment to comprehend. "Oh, sure," he said, flushing. "I'll stay away." God, it was the least he could do. He knew how miserable Molly was going to be. She'd wanted that baby in the worst way. He'd wanted it, too, of course, but he was selfish enough to want Molly all to himself for a while, too. There'd be plenty of time for a family later. "You won't tell anybody we had to get married, will you?"

Doc Logan sniffed. "You want my opinion, you *didn't* have to. If anybody asks, that's what I'll say. Now get out of my way. I've got sick people to look after."

At Ben's insistence, Molly spent the next two days in bed. After the cramps subsided about midway through the first day, the rest of the time was pure torture as she watched Ben cooking and cleaning up—jobs she should have been doing—and waiting on her hand and foot to boot. She felt worthless and miserable, and she wept almost as much out of self-pity as she did out of grief for the child she had lost, the child who had been very real to her no matter whether it had ever really existed or not.

Compounding her loss was the nagging memory of her father's prediction: "Soon as that baby comes, he'll throw you out so fast. . . ." Now there was no baby, and Ben needn't have married her at all. He might even think she had lied about the baby in the first place. Heaven knew he never would have married her otherwise. What would he do now?

On the third day, she got up and dressed when he did, ignoring his protests. She fixed breakfast for the men as she had before her illness, and they all commented on how well she looked. Even Johnny was civil for once, which frightened her more than anything. Did she know something she didn't? Did he know he had nothing more to fear from her?

Ben kissed her lightly as he was leaving. When was the last time he had given her a real kiss?

"Just take it easy today," he said. "Don't overdo."

His tender tone brought tears to her eyes. "I won't," she lied, knowing she had to start atoning for the lapse in her wifely duties. She would show him what a good wife she was, baby or no baby. She would show him how much he needed her.

But her efforts only made him frown when he came home that evening. He told her she shouldn't have cooked such a fancy meal. He told her she shouldn't have worked so hard around the house. After supper, he went to play cards with the other men and didn't come back until after she was asleep.

So the next day she made an even bigger meal and worked even harder, and his frown was even deeper. But when he came back from playing cards, she was still awake.

"My bleeding stopped," she whispered when he lay beside her, knowing she still had one hold over him.

"Did it? That's good," he replied gruffly, and turned away.

Mortified, she stared at his back in the darkness as terror wrapped its slimy tentacles around her heart. Now he didn't even want to make love to her anymore. What on earth was she going to do?

As the days went by, all hope died within her. On Sunday she didn't even suggest going to church. The next morning she went numbly through the motions of life, preparing breakfast, eating it, and accepting Ben's obligatory kiss. She had one last hope. She had to find out what she was doing wrong, how to win Ben's love, and she knew one person who had devoted her life to pleasing a man. Her mother had failed, since no one and nothing would ever please her father, but her mother knew how to try better than anyone alive. Molly had to see her mother, and right now she was desperate enough to risk even her father's wrath to do so.

As soon as Ben and the others were out of sight, she went to the corral and caught up the gentle mare Ben had designated as her horse. She saddled the animal and rode as rapidly as possible out to the road, toward the Flying W ranch.

She knew she was unlikely to encounter her father at home on a weekday morning, but she watched the ranch for several minutes before riding in, just to be sure he wasn't anywhere around. Julie came out at the sound of her approach and shouted the news to their mother, who appeared instantly in the doorway.

The three hugged and kissed, and all talked at once. Yes, Pa had gone out with the other men. No, they didn't expect him back 'til evening. They could have a long, cozy visit in safety.

When the three of them were seated around the table drinking coffee, Hannah asked, "How are you keeping yourself, Molly? You feeling poorly at all?"

"Mama, I . . . I lost the baby," she said, deciding not to complicate matters by telling the whole story.

Julie uttered a sharp cry of disappointment, and Hannah covered Molly's hands with her own. "Oh, darlin', I know how you feel. There ain't hardly nothing so bad as losing a little one. Oh, I wish you could've called for me. Did you have anybody at all?"

"Ben sent for the doctor. He said I was fine and that I'd have lots of other babies."

"That's a comfort," Hannah said. "And think of it this way, now nobody'll be counting on their fingers when it does happen."

If it happens, Molly thought grimly, wondering how she could broach the subject in front of Julie. But she did not need to speak her fears aloud. Years of vigilance had taught her mother every nuance of human expression.

"Julie," Hannah said, "there's some things your sister and me need to discuss that ain't fit for an unmarried girl to hear about. Would you step outside a minute?"

Plainly, Julie did not want to miss one word of this conversation, but she had also sensed Molly's reticence. "All right, but call me as soon as you're done. I want to visit with Molly, too."

"Sure we will." Hannah waited until Julie was out of earshot. "Now what is it?"

"Mama, Ben won't . . . Ever since I lost the baby, he hasn't laid a hand on me except a kiss or two. Oh, Mama, what am I going to do?"

"Now don't cry, honey. Tell me, how long has it been?"

"Since Tuesday."

"Tuesday? Honey, that's less than a week."

"But before he always . . ."

"What, dear?"

"He always . . . he did it *every night* before."

"Oh, my," her mother said, slightly flustered. "Well, I mean, you were only just married. You can't expect . . . I mean, a man works hard all day, and sometimes he needs his rest. He was bound to slow down some."

"Oh," Molly said, wondering if she was being silly. "But he really wanted that baby. Wouldn't he want to make another one as quick as he could?"

Hannah was shaking her head when a noise from outside distracted them.

"Pa!" Julie shouted, loudly enough to warn them of his arrival. "What are you doing home?"

"Catching a rat. I knew that whore had men coming here when I wasn't around. Who is he? Who's in there with your ma?"

"Nobody, Pa. It's just Molly, come for a visit. . . ."

Hannah and Molly jumped to their feet as Elijah appeared in the doorway. "God damn you, you little bitch. I told you never to set foot in this house again!"

Hannah instantly stepped in front of her. "She was only visiting. She's not doing any harm."

Elijah cackled, and the sound sent shivers of alarm racing down Molly's spine. She'd never seen him look so strange, so wild, not even during his worst rages. Now she noticed what she had been too frightened to notice last week when he had come to her house. As thin as he had always been, he was even thinner now, his skin a sickly yellow and his eyes red-rimmed and bloodshot. The tremor she had noticed before was worse now. His whole body seemed to quiver.

"Pa, I'm sorry. I'll leave right away," she said, edging around her mother. "Mama didn't even know I was coming—"

"Well, ain't this nice, a tea party," he said contemptuously, striding over to the table and flinging it over on them. Cups and saucers and hot coffee flew everywhere, and Molly and Hannah scrambled out of the way.

"Pa, don't!" Julie cried from the doorway, but he paid her no mind.

Smack! He sent Hannah careening into the wall, clearing his path toward Molly.

"*Pa!*" Julie screamed again, and ran for him.

"Don't Pa, I'm warning you!" Molly reached for the cast-iron skillet hanging nearby. "I'm not like Ma. I won't take a beating."

But he didn't hear her, either. He just kept coming, his eyes unblinking and filled with an unspeakable rage. Molly lifted the skillet with both hands, but Hannah and Julie lunged for him, bringing him down.

"Elijah, don't! You never beat the girls before, never!"

"She's a whore, just like her mother," he said, struggling free of their clinging hands. With superhuman strength, he shook them off and rose again. "I won't have a whore in my house."

Julie grabbed his arm and hung on, but he lifted his free hand and brought his fist down in her face. She sprawled backward with an agonized cry, spurring Molly to action. She swung the skillet, connecting with his shoulder. His grunt of pain was the only indication she had scored a hit. In an instant he was on her, wrenching the skillet out of her hands and backhanding her. She fell to the floor, and the breath *whoosh*ed from her lungs. Fighting for breath and unable to move, she watched him advance on her.

"I'll take care of your little bastard, you whore. I'll kick it out of you like I did before—"

"*No!*" Hannah screamed, and lunged for him again. This time she brought him down alone and refused to let go. "No, you won't hurt her, you won't!"

They wrestled for a moment, only inches from where Molly lay struggling for breath, and then his hands closed around Hannah's throat. "I'll teach you, you bitch! Nobody tells me what to do! Nobody!"

Julie jumped on his back, fighting with all her strength to loosen his grip, but he hardly seemed aware of her. In his maniacal fury, he shook her off as he would have shooed a fly while Hannah's face reddened and her breath wheezed. She clawed frantically at his hands, drawing blood, but he was oblivious to pain.

Julie was on him again, pulling, punching, scratching, and screaming, but she no longer existed for Elijah. Hannah's eyes were starting to bulge when Molly's lungs finally drew breath again, and she threw her own returning strength into the battle. She and Julie each took one of his hands and tried to pry them loose, but they were slippery now with flecks of blood and sweat and blood and spit and blood . . .

Elijah made a gurgling sound, and blood poured from his mouth. Molly and Julie both screamed and fell back. He flung Hannah away as he lunged to his feet, holding his mouth as if to stanch the flow. He staggered backward, staring in wide-eyed horror at the crimson flood following his footsteps.

Molly clapped both hands over her own mouth as she felt the gorge rising in her throat. Dear heaven, it was her dearest wish coming true, but the reality was nothing like the dream.

Hannah lay gasping on the floor, sucking in air with the desperation of one near death, but after a moment even she saw what was happening. " 'Lije?" she croaked, pushing up on one elbow. "My God, Elijah, what's happening?"

Elijah made a choking sound and fell to his knees.

"Help him, girls! Help him!" Hannah cried hoarsely, but neither Julie nor Molly moved as he pitched forward onto his face.

"Elijah?" Hannah scrambled over to him, her breath still coming in ragged gasps. Heedless of the gore soaking her clothing and the floor, she rolled him over. "Elijah, speak to me! What's wrong?"

He groaned, and more blood gurgled from his mouth.

"Girls, quick, go hitch up the wagon!" Hannah cried. "We'll make him a bed in the back and carry him into the doctor. Hurry now!"

But neither girl moved. Elijah's eyes had rolled back in his head. He gurgled once again, and then his heaving chest stilled.

"Elijah?" Hannah shook him, but to no avail. *"Elijah!* Molly, Julie, hurry! Get the wagon! Your pa's real bad sick. Elijah!"

Molly got up slowly and walked over to her mother, stepping carefully to avoid the mess. "Mama," she said softly, placing a hand on Hannah's shoulder. "He's gone, Mama."

"No! It's not too late! If we hurry, we can—"

"*Mama*, he's dead! Look at him. He's not breathing."

Julie had crawled up beside them, too. "Mama, she's right. Look at him."

Hannah stared at her husband with wide, panic-stricken eyes. "No! It can't be. Elijah! Elijah, speak to me." He only lay there, unblinking and unmoving.

Hannah screamed, a shriek that became a bloodcurdling wail denoting an agony too deep for the human spirit to endure.

Molly stared at her mother incredulously as Hannah clasped the bloody corpse to her bosom and rocked it as one would soothe a beloved child. "Mama, stop it!" she commanded, but her mother only hugged him more fiercely and moaned more loudly.

Molly wanted to grab her and shake her, to tear the hated body from her arms. She wanted to shout at her mother and remind her this was the man who only moments ago had very nearly killed her, had surely *intended* to kill her. But how could she penetrate such grief? Hannah's wail went on and on, chilling Molly's very soul.

Molly glanced at her sister to see her own confusion mirrored in Julie's face. What was wrong with their mother? How could she grieve so when Elijah Wade's death meant an end to the hell he had created for them all, his wife most of all?

The keening rose in pitch again, and Molly could bear it no longer. *"Mama, stop it!"*

The wail strangled on a sob, and Hannah raised anguished eyes to her eldest daughter. "Oh, Molly, what'll we do now? Who'll take care of us?"

Molly could hardly believe her ears. She might well have asked, "Who'll beat you now, Mama? Who'll drink up all your money so you don't have a decent dress to wear in public on the rare occasions when your face isn't too bruised up to show? Who'll treat you like dirt and call you names and make you feel worthless?"

But of course she loved her mother, so she said none of those things. Instead, she patted her shoulder and said, "I'll look after you, Mama, you and Julie. And Ben will, too. We'll see you get along all right."

It took the girls a long time to pry their mother loose from Elijah's body. Molly found an old sheet and covered him while Julie took Hannah into the other room to get her cleaned up and try to calm her growing hysteria. There was so much to do, Molly could hardly decide where to start. The house was a mess, and the body would have to be cared for, and . . .

But Molly knew she couldn't stay in this house another minute. She had to get away. "I'll go into town," she told Julie. "I'll tell . . . I don't know who I should tell, but I'll find Sheriff Bigelow. He'll know."

"Tell Reverend Bates," Julie suggested. "He'll take care of the funeral, and Mrs. Bates will get some ladies out here to help."

"Yes, I will," Molly said, feeling simple for not having thought of it herself. Reverend Bates would take care of everything.

The air outside smelled blessedly clean, free of the sickly-sweet stench of death. Keeping a tight rein on her emotions, fighting the urge to react to the horrors she had witnessed, Molly caught up her mare and rode swiftly into town. She went straight to the minister's house. Mrs. Bates answered the door.

"Molly, how nice to . . . What's the matter? Is that blood on your sleeve? Are you hurt?"

"No, it's . . . it's my father. He died." Molly told the story quickly, barely pausing for breath.

Mrs. Bates was suitably shocked and took Molly into the house for some tea while she summoned her husband from the church. As Julie had predicted, the Bateses knew exactly what to do from their experience with past tragedies. Within an hour, a group of ladies was on its way to the Wade ranch armed with food and comfort.

Molly accompanied them as far as the turnoff to the ranch, but she was still not quite ready to face that bloodied room again. Telling the others she must notify her husband, she rode on to what she now realized was her true home.

"There she is!" Johnny McGee shouted as she rode into the yard. In an instant, Ben appeared from the far side of the barn, running toward her full tilt.

"Where have you been?" he demanded, grabbing the reins from her hands. "I was worried sick when I got back and you weren't . . . My God, is that blood? Are you hurt?"

He plucked her from the saddle before she could utter a word. "No, I'm fine," she protested as he searched for a wound. "It's Pa. He's dead."

"Dead?"

"Yes, he . . . I went over to visit Mama this morning, and he came home and caught me there, and . . . Oh, Ben, it was terrible!" The terror and horror and grief she had not allowed herself to feel before came flooding up, choking her.

He muttered something she didn't understand and scooped her up into his arms so she could muffle her sobs against his shoulder. "Johnny, get her mare, will you?" he called as he carried her into the house.

He settled on the bed, draping Molly across his lap and cradling her while she wept inconsolably. Even when she had managed to regain some of her self-control, she could not have said why she was crying. Surely she felt no grief for the man she had so often wished dead. Surely she felt only relief and joy for her mother and sister, who were now free of his tyranny.

Ben gave her his bandanna to wipe her face. "Now tell me what happened, for God's sake."

Hiccuping, she swabbed her face and drew several calming breaths. "Like I said, I went over to Mama's for a visit." She couldn't tell him why, not now. That would have to wait until later. "Pa came in, yelling and screaming and calling me names, and when Mama tried to protect me, he started strangling her—"

"God almighty!"

"Julie and I tried to get him off, and then he started choking and spitting up blood. I never saw anything like it." She shuddered at the memory. "He fell down on the floor and died, just like that."

Ben muttered another curse. "How's your mother?"

"She was taking it pretty hard, but Julie stayed with her while I went for help."

"We'd better get on over there, then."

"Oh, I went to town first, and Reverend and Mrs. Bates got some ladies together. They're at the house now. Then I came here to tell you."

Ben pulled her close, pressing a kiss to her temple and murmuring words of comfort. Molly surrendered to his tenderness, savoring the closeness he had denied her for so long, but her joy was bittersweet. While his hold was loving, there was nothing passionate in the kisses he gave her.

After a while, Johnny came to the door and cleared his throat discreetly. "Mind telling the rest of us what's going on?" he asked.

Ben did, in a few short sentences.

"I'll be damned," Johnny said, and then, "Oh, excuse me, Miz Cantrell. I reckon you two'll want to go on over there."

"I'll get you some dinner first," Molly said,

reluctantly leaving the solace of Ben's arms and struggling to her feet.

"Don't worry about us. We can manage," Johnny said. "I'll go hitch up the buckboard for you."

"Thank you," she said, wondering at his consideration. He'd been remarkably nice to her ever since he'd found out she lost the baby. Once again she knew a pang of worry. Did he know Ben didn't plan to keep her around much longer?

"Do you want to change your clothes before we go?" Ben asked.

"No, there might . . . I might need to help clean up," she said, shuddering again. "I'll take something to change into later, though."

When she'd gathered her clothes and a few items of food to add to what the other women had taken, Ben helped her load it all into the wagon and drove her over to the Flying W ranch. Molly was glad now that she had not come straight back. The gruesome scene in the house had already been cleansed away by the other women. Elijah Wade's body now lay on the table, stripped of its soiled clothes and decently covered, awaiting further burial preparations.

The only thing to remind her of the earlier horrors was the sound of her mother's keening. It was fainter now, muffled by the closed bedroom door. She didn't hear it until she came into the house. The women working at the stove cast her sympathetic looks as she braced herself and entered the bedroom.

Julie and her mother sat side by side on the

bed. Julie had her arms around Hannah and was crooning words of comfort that Hannah did not seem to hear. She simply sat rocking back and forth, wailing and weeping, while several other women tried to calm her down. They looked to Molly hopefully, apparently feeling she might be able to get through to Hannah where they had failed.

Resolutely, Molly walked to the bed and put her hand on her mother's shoulder. "Mama, it's over now. Please stop. You'll wear yourself out."

The wail died mournfully, and Hannah looked up at her eldest daughter, her eyes wild with grief. "If you hadn't come back and made him mad, he'd still be alive!"

Chapter Ten
+ + + +

EVEN NOW, TWO days after her father's death, Molly still couldn't believe her mother's reaction. In all the times she had imagined her father's demise, even when she had dreamed of murdering him herself, she had never imagined her mother *blaming* her for what would be the most blessed event in their lives.

And she simply could not reconcile herself to the overwhelming grief her mother was still ex-

periencing. Anyone would think Elijah Wade
had been the kindest, most loving of husbands
instead of the Devil incarnate. Even Reverend
Bates had been hard-pressed to think of something nice to say about him at the funeral. Still,
Hannah had stood beside the grave, the bruises
from Elijah's fingers black upon her neck, and
sobbed uncontrollably.

"She didn't really mean it," Julie had assured
Molly over and over. "She doesn't know what
she's saying." The other women had agreed, but
Molly took small comfort in the knowledge. The
mother who had defended her from him for
eighteen years had taken his side in the end.
Molly should at least have been able to turn to
her husband for solace, but now she was afraid
of his rejection, too.

Molly stood in the doorway of their cabin and
watched Ben and Johnny standing beside the
corrals beneath the shade of a cottonwood,
smoking their after-supper cigarettes. She and
Ben had barely spoken, indeed had hardly been
alone, since she had fetched him from the ranch
two days ago. During the ordeal of the wake
yesterday and the funeral that morning, he had
been solicitous of her comfort and helpful in
every way, earning the praise of the other
women, who complimented her on her good
fortune at having such a thoughtful husband.
While she had smiled outwardly, inwardly she
had cringed at the thought of what she would do
if Ben were to send her away.

Even now fear churned within her, fear of the

future and of what Ben might do, fear of knowing and fear of not knowing. She had always dreamed that when she married, her life would be different, that she would leave the fear behind in her father's house, but she found herself living exactly the way her mother had always lived, in constant vigilance against the unexpected.

The realization stunned her. *She was becoming just like her mother.* For one awful moment she pictured her life stretching before her in a pattern of uncertainty and terror as she pampered and tried to please a husband who could never be pleased.

No! her mind screamed in rebellion. She wouldn't live like that, *couldn't* live like that. But could she change things? Had she already set the pattern with her fruitless efforts to please Ben? *No!* She wouldn't let it be too late.

Outside, Ben and Johnny threw down their cigarettes and started for the bunkhouse. If she let him go, Ben would not return to the house until he knew she was asleep, and another night would go by during which they didn't even touch. "Ben!" she called impulsively.

He looked up in surprise. She saw him say something to Johnny, and then he came over to her, moving quickly, as if he sensed the urgency of her summons.

She backed into the house as he approached, as much in trepidation at her own boldness as in a desire for privacy. Was she making a mistake? And what on earth was she going to say to him?

His wonderful blue eyes narrowed in concern when he came into the house. "What's the matter?"

"I . . . we . . . Why don't you make love to me anymore?" she blurted, covering her mouth the instant the words spilled out. What a thing to say!

His jaw dropped in astonishment, but he recovered quickly. He closed the door behind him, ensuring they would not be disturbed. "I can't. You know that," he said, frowning in confusion.

"What do you mean, you can't?" she demanded, summoning the courage for which Julie had always praised her.

"The doctor said . . . you heard him yourself. He said just in case you'd really had a miscarriage, we shouldn't do anything for at least two weeks."

"He never said anything like that!" she said, tears stinging her eyes at the lie. "He only said I should rest."

"Yes, he did. Don't you . . . Oh, wait a minute! I just remembered. He told me outside, when I walked him to his buggy. It shocked me so much, I guess I forgot to tell you."

Molly blinked fiercely at the tears. "You don't have to lie, Ben. If you don't want me anymore—"

"Don't want you? Where'd you get an idea like that?"

"The way you go off with the other men after supper. You can't stand to even be in the same room with me anymore."

"You're damn right I can't! It drives me crazy, knowing I can't touch you."

She saw it now, the anguish she'd been too distracted to notice before, the pain she'd identified as indifference. "Ben?" she whispered, hardly daring to believe. She lifted one hand beseechingly. In an instant, she was in his arms.

His mouth was hot and hungry, devouring the feast denied him for so long. Molly clung to him with all her strength, freely offering the love she had so carefully hidden. When they were both breathless, he held her close and rested his forehead against hers.

"God, Molly, how could you think I didn't want you?"

This time she didn't fight the tears. "I was so afraid. . . ."

"Afraid of what?"

"Afraid because I lost the baby. You wanted it so much, and I knew you never would've married me otherwise. I was even afraid you'd think I lied about it just to get you."

He drew back in amazement. "The main reason I was so happy about the baby was because it gave me an *excuse* to marry you." His lips twitched into a grin. "In fact, I kind of like the idea that you wanted me enough to lie to get me."

She gave him back a watery smile. "I didn't lie, but I do want you that much."

He murmured her name as his lips came down to hers again. This time the kiss went on and on as eager hands explored remembered delights.

"Molly," he gasped at last, "we'd better stop."

"Why?" she asked, seeking his mouth again.

"Be . . . cause . . . Doc said . . . two weeks . . ."

"Ben, please . . . I'm fine . . . but if . . . we don't . . . make love . . . *right now* . . . I'm going to *die*!"

With a groan, he picked her up and carried her to the bed, never lifting his mouth from hers. They tumbled together on the feather mattress in a tangle of arms and legs and petticoats, and for a while they simply kissed and fondled.

Ben's searching fingers plucked the pins from her hair until it spilled across the pillow in a honey-colored wave. He buried his face in it, inhaling the sweetness of her scent while she nibbled at his ear.

When that was no longer enough, Ben sought the fastenings of her dress. She was wearing her blue gown, the one she'd worn the night of the box social, and once again he was baffled by the hidden closures.

Laughing, she showed him, and soon she was bare to the waist and struggling to help him out of his vest and shirt. She moaned aloud when his naked flesh touched hers. Her breasts swelled against the hair-roughened plane of his chest, and she greedily ran her hands over his back, reveling in his strength.

His callused palms found her aching nipples, chafing them to awareness, then soothing them in the moist haven of his mouth. When such torture became too much to bear, they stripped

off the rest of their clothes with clumsy haste.
When Ben took her in his arms again, she felt the
hard evidence of his arousal against her thigh.

"Still think I don't want you?" he teased.

"I'm still a little worried. I don't suppose you'd
like to prove . . . Omph!"

He smothered her words with his mouth and
rolled her over on her back beneath him. "I'll be
more than happy to prove anything you want,"
he whispered into the sensitive hollow behind
her ear, sending delicious shivers racing over
her.

With hands and lips, he began working his way
down her body, stroking, kissing, caressing, nip-
ping, as if he would touch and taste every square
inch of her naked flesh. He lavished his attentions
on her breasts again, until the nipples throbbed
wantonly from his avid suckling. Then he moved
downward, laving her belly button before moving on to nibble at the inside of her thighs. He
found a ticklish spot behind her knee and another
on her ankle. When she was fairly writhing, he
slid back up and began to explore the secrets
concealed beneath the nest of russet curls at the
apex of her thighs.

"Ben, what on earth . . . ?" But her protest
became a moan of pleasure as sensation
screamed along her nerve endings. He lingered
over her, teasing and tormenting, until she
begged for the release only he could give. Then
he rose up, breathing her name and claiming her
as his own. She wrapped her legs around him,
knowing she needed him close and closer still.

He tortured her with gentle thrusts, fueling the fire but never allowing it to rage out of control until Molly thought she would go mad with longing.

"Ben, please," she begged again, and this time her plea snapped his control. No longer able to resist her frantic urging, he let the fire race. His hips churned against hers, flint to stone, sparks to tinder, faster and faster, until the flames crackled, roaring up into a blaze that melded them into one glorious being.

Ben collapsed on top of her, and for a long time they clung together, sobbing for breath and shuddering out the last sweet flickers of their passion.

For a time she could do nothing more than stroke the golden silkiness of his hair.

"Oh, Ben, I love you so much," she said when she was finally able to speak.

His body shuddered once more, pulsing within her. With great effort, he pushed up on one elbow so he could see her face. "I love you, too, Molly, more than I ever thought I could love anybody. Finding you was the best thing that's happened to me since . . ." A shadow from the past clouded his brilliant eyes but was gone in an instant. "Since I can remember."

Reluctantly, he levered his weight off her and drew her close to his side as they let their bodies cool. But Ben's remark had pricked Molly's conscience, and she knew she would never be able to truly enjoy his love until she had told him everything she knew about the past.

"Ben, it's very important to you to clear your father's name, isn't it?"

"Until you came along, it was the most important thing in the world to me," he said, idly stroking the softness of her hair.

"Ben, I . . . I think I know who did it."

His hands ceased its stroking, and his whole body went still. "Who?"

His eyes were like blue fire. Would his fury turn on her when he heard the truth? By an act of will, she resisted the fear she had sworn to overcome. "I think . . . I think it was my father."

"Why would you think that?"

She swallowed against the lump forming in her throat. "Well, I didn't want to think it, but even six years ago . . . He always used to complain about your father, about how lucky he was and how he had better grass and water than we did."

He pushed himself up on his elbow. "But your father was here first."

"I know. That didn't make any difference. He just hated anybody who was more successful than he was. I always thought he wanted your ranch, and after . . . after your pa was hanged, that's all he talked about, about how you'd hightail it and then he could have your place."

"Molly, that doesn't really prove anything."

"Then, the night of the box social . . ."

"What?"

"He wasn't at the school when the fire broke out. Nobody saw him, not Julie or Mama, but he was at Harry's when they got there to fight the fire."

"That doesn't prove anything, either. Maybe he was just off somewhere, drinking. Julie said he'd been drunk almost all the time for the past few months."

"Ben, he wanted to hang you! He tried to get everybody all riled up that night, and when he couldn't, he was hoping you'd go to prison. That's why I had to go talk to the sheriff. Don't you see? He's the only one who had something to gain, and the only one crazy enough to wait six years for an opportunity to get rid of you, too."

"Shhh, don't cry," he said, brushing a stray tear from her cheek. "How long have you suspected this?"

"Since I was twelve years old, but I was afraid to tell you. I thought you might hate me if you found out I'd known all this time and didn't say anything. That's why I got you and Harry together. I was sure the two of you would figure it out for yourselves sooner or later. Oh, Ben, I'm so sorry!"

"Sorry? Why?"

"Don't you see? If I'd told you before, you could've made him confess, and your father's name would've been cleared. Now it's too late!"

Ben sighed and slumped back onto the pillow. She waited, tensed for the explosion of anger, but nothing happened. He simply lay there, staring up at the ceiling.

"Ben?"

"Hmm?"

"Do you . . . are you mad?"

He sighed. "No. How could I be mad at you for keeping it a secret when I've been doing the same thing myself?"

"What do you mean?"

"I mean ever since the night of the box social when we talked about this, I thought you knew more than you were saying. The day Harry came over here, I was *sure* you did. I didn't know about your father wanting my land, but he sure hated me and my pa enough. He wouldn't want to hurt Harry, so he'd be considerate about the fire. He was on the posse. . . . Everything fit."

"If you knew, why didn't you say anything?" Molly asked, struggling up so she could see his face.

"Because he's your father, Molly. I know what it's like being the son of a murdering barn burner. I didn't want to put you through it, too."

"Oh, Ben, I wouldn't care about that. I only care about *you*, but now I've ruined everything! Now you can't tell anyone the truth because my father's dead and no one will believe you—" Her voice broke on a sob, and he gathered her to him.

"For God's sake, don't cry, Molly. It's as much my fault as it is yours. I knew, too."

"You didn't know for sure."

He didn't argue. He simply held her while she wept, stroking her hair and her back and pressing kisses to her wet face. At last she regained control and wiped away the tears with the corner of the sheet. "I wish you'd yell at me or something," she said, surprised to realize it was true. His somber silence frightened her even more than a rage would have.

"Molly, why did you run away that night at the school?" he asked suddenly.

"Run away? You mean after . . . ?"

"No, before. Why did you run to the woods instead of to the school where you would've been safe?"

"I . . ." She didn't know what to say.

"Molly," he said, turning her to face him again, "you were angry and scared of me, or at least I thought you were, and you ran, except you ran *away* from safety instead of toward it. I asked you why that night. Do you remember?"

She shook her head. There were so many things about that night she had forced herself to forget, and this was one of the most painful memories of all.

"You could've screamed when I started kissing you or when I started touching you or when I took your clothes off. Someone would've heard. Why didn't you?"

"I . . . I didn't want to."

"Why not?" he demanded.

She saw a flash of the anger she had expected earlier, and she began to tremble. "I don't know."

"Was it because you felt sorry for me? Because you wanted to make up for keeping the secret all those years?"

"No!" she cried, pushing out of his arms. "How could you think a thing like that?"

"What am I supposed to think? You tell me

how sorry you are for keeping this secret, and God knows you've been killing yourself around here, cooking and cleaning like there's no tomorrow, or like you're trying to make up for something—"

"That's not why!"

"And now I'm starting to wonder if the whole thing hasn't been an act, even this part," he said, gesturing to indicate their naked bodies.

She stared at him in horror. "I love you, Ben! I told you that. I even told you that the night of the box social."

"I thought you didn't remember."

She felt the color coming to her cheeks. "I remember," she admitted.

"Then do you remember why you ran to the woods? Why you didn't scream?"

"Yes." The word was little more than a rasp.

His hands closed over her shoulders. "Why, Molly? Why?"

"Because I . . . because you were the man I'd been waiting for."

"Waiting for? What are you talking about?"

How could she explain? "I'd loved you for a long time, Ben, but I was scared of you. Then when you wouldn't fight with Harry, I knew you were the one, the man I'd been looking for all my life."

"So you ran off into the woods with me and lay down on the ground and—"

"Don't make it sound ugly!" she pleaded. "I wanted you, but I couldn't tell you! I couldn't even talk to you, not with Pa watching me every minute. We might never be together again, and I thought . . ." She stopped as she saw her own emotions clearly for the first time. "I thought if we were together, then maybe . . . Oh, Ben, I thought maybe I'd have a baby and then nobody could keep us apart! Don't you see, I made the baby up in my mind. I was never expecting at all, just like Doc Logan said!"

"You wanted me that much?"

She saw his wonder and the feeble hope he dared not admit glistening in his azure eyes. She nodded. "I was so afraid we'd never, ever be together."

"Molly, you don't have to be afraid anymore."

His kiss was fierce and possessive, as searing as a brand. He claimed her, marking her with the heat of his love, and the heat scorched away the last of her lingering doubts. He loved her, and he would never let her go.

She opened to him, welcoming him into her body as she had welcomed her into her heart so long ago. They had no use for tenderness, no need to cuddle or cajole. Desire flamed quick and hot between them, igniting their very souls so that when the final explosion came, it seemed to rock the ground beneath them.

The sky was barely dark when they fell into an exhausted slumber, too tired even to turn back the bedclothes. Molly's last thought was a brief, incoherent prayer that now, at last, everything would be all right.

The next day began promisingly enough. Ben woke her with kisses and greeted her with a smile. They went through their morning routine with the easy camaraderie they had known before she'd "lost" the baby, and Molly finally realized that Ben's frustration had caused the tension she had misinterpreted. He kissed her before he left, a long lingering kiss full of promises, and she flew through her morning chores, eagerly anticipating his return at noon.

He kissed her even more enthusiastically then, and she set out the meal with a renewed sense of purpose. She was dishing up the stew when Johnny McGee stepped into the cabin.

"It smells good in here," he remarked, stuffing his hands into his pockets and looking around. "It always smells good in here."

Molly bit back a smile. Johnny would probably die before paying her a direct compliment, but she couldn't be mad at him, not today.

"Where's Ben?" he asked after a moment.

"Out back," she said, referring obliquely to the privy.

"Oh." He shuffled his feet and looked around again. "It's too bad about your pa."

She glanced up in surprise. Was Johnny McGee offering her sympathy? "I don't think he'll be missed much."

Johnny shrugged. "It's hard on your ma and all, though." He'd seen Hannah crying at the funeral.

"Yes, it is," Molly replied, still puzzled over his uncharacteristic behavior.

Ben came in then. "Look, Johnny, Molly made your favorite," he said with a grin. Molly, of course, had no idea her stew was Johnny's favorite. "Say, I just remembered. Mr. Wells said the lumber I ordered for the new room would be in this week. We'll have you a bedroom before you know it, Molly."

Molly smiled at the prospect. "We can have a 'room raising.' "

"A what?"

"A 'room raising,' like Harry had a barn raising. We can invite all the neighbors and—"

"Are you crazy?" Ben looked as if he thought she really had lost her senses.

"The room'll go up so much faster than if just you and the men work on it, and it'll be fun. Maybe we could even have dancing afterwards." Her smile faded in the face of Ben's scowl.

"Molly, I'm not going to ask those people to help me."

"Why not?"

"Because I'm not going to give them a chance to say no."

"They wouldn't say no!"

Ben opened his mouth to reply, but Johnny beat him to it. "She's right, Ben. Most of 'em would be glad to help."

Both Molly and Ben gaped at him.

"I been thinking," Johnny said defensively. "I mean, we used to laugh about it sometimes, about how folks acted like they wanted to be friends with you. Maybe they wasn't just acting. Maybe they really meant it."

"They hanged my pa, Johnny," Ben reminded him.

"Not all of them did, only a few, and most of them are sorry for it now."

"But they're not sorry because they think he was innocent."

"Does that matter? Oh, I know it matters to you, but when you think about living out here all alone, without any friends, it doesn't count for much. It was kinda fun being the town outcasts when it was just you and me, but I don't reckon your wife likes it much."

Molly didn't bother to hide her astonishment. Johnny McGee was the last man on earth she would have expected to champion her cause, but she wasn't about to leave him unaided. "He's right, I don't like it. I want a normal life, Ben. I want friends."

Ben snorted. "You saw the way they treated us at the barn raising."

"That was my father, and he's dead now."

"Molly," Ben said in warning as the other men came in. They paused in the doorway, sensing the tension, but Ben jerked out his chair and sat down at the table, pretending nothing untoward had happened. Johnny followed his lead, so Tom and Billy sat, too. They ate in silence, as usual, but this silence was much weightier than usual.

Molly kept stealing glances at Johnny, wondering what on earth had come over him. She suspected Ben was wondering the same thing. Johnny had always stood by Ben, defending him against every imagined slight. Now, for no apparent reason, he had gone over to the other side. *Her* side. The knowledge touched her, and she began to wonder about herself. Had she misjudged Johnny McGee?

When Ben was finished eating, he got up and left without a word. Tom and Billy soon followed, but Johnny waited until they were gone. When he and Molly were alone, he said, "Ben's a little hardheaded sometimes."

"I've noticed," she replied with a sad smile.

"He'll come around."

"He'll have to. I don't think he can fight both of us for very long."

Slowly, tentatively, Johnny grinned back at her. "No, I don't reckon he can."

"Johnny," she said, calling him by his given name for the very first time, "do you have any other favorite foods I don't know about?"

His cheeks flushed like a schoolgirl's. "I . . . I do like your pies, Miz Cantrell."

"Then I'll bake some this afternoon. And you can call me 'Molly,' if you like."

"Well," he said, and his face turned absolutely scarlet. "Well, I'd be much obliged . . . Molly."

He bolted from the room, reminding Molly of Ben's warning that Johnny was shy around women. Maybe that's what the problem had been all along. Maybe he didn't really dislike her. Maybe he was just shy and a little scared of her. She'd certainly been scared of him. But she wasn't going to be scared of anything anymore.

Ben didn't kiss her good-bye when he and the others left after dinner. Molly reminded herself

he was still annoyed with her, and since she
knew the reason for his annoyance, she tried not
to brood. Instead, she planned.

After last night, she'd almost imagined her and
Ben's life together would be a downhill slide.
Now she realized their confrontation and reconciliation had been merely the very first step on a
long steep climb, and already she had reached a
fork in the road. On the one hand, she could yield
to Ben's wishes and let him continue to play the
martyr. Heaven knew he had every right to do so
since he had been a perfectly innocent victim of
terrible injustice. By letting him have his way, she
would spare herself a lot of unpleasantness, too.
Already her heart was aching because he hadn't
kissed her when he left. She didn't even want to
imagine how awful a full-fledged argument
would be. The temptation to give in and make
everything all right again was great, especially for
a girl who had learned early the terrible consequences of arousing a man's anger.

But she also knew this was the path her
mother had chosen, the path of least resistance.
Give in to him to keep the peace, never cross
him, never say what you really think. Hadn't
she already decided she couldn't live the way
her mother had?

So her other choice was to challenge him, let
him know she disagreed and try to make him see
how wrong he was. Remembering how stoically
he had faced down her father and his Winchester, she shivered. Ben would be a difficult adver-

sary, and he would certainly not be too eager
to admit he had wasted six years of his life
taking offense from neighbors who had meant
none.

She might lose the battle and crush the delicate bond of trust growing between her and Ben.
She might even destroy the love she cherished
above all else. Even if she won, things might
never be the same between them. What if Ben
didn't approve of assertive women? What if he
hated them? What if . . . ?

But she couldn't dwell on the "what if's" because she simply couldn't live the way her
mother had, no matter what the consequences.

By the time the men got back that evening,
Molly had baked half a dozen pies and worked
herself into a state of nervous apprehension.
Ben's muttered greeting did not improve her
mood, but she smiled cheerfully, gave him a
hug, and put supper on the table as if nothing in
the world were wrong. As if her whole world
did not hang in the balance.

When she had finished the dishes, she found
him sitting alone on the porch, his chair tipped
back against the wall. She sat down beside him,
and he tossed away the cigarette he had been
smoking.

"It'll be nice to have another room in the
house," she remarked.

"I figured you'd like some privacy. With the
men going in and out all the time, you don't
have much," he replied, his expression guarded.

He knew she was up to something. She gave him what she hoped was a disarming smile.

"You're awfully good to me, Ben. How long do you think it'll take to build the room?"

He frowned. She wasn't fooling him a bit. "Probably most of the summer since we'll only be able to work on it now and then."

"Oh." She stared off into the distance and waited until she sensed his guard had relaxed a bit. "You know, some people might be offended because you didn't ask them to help."

He made a rude noise. "Who?"

"Oh, Mr. and Mrs. Wells. They've always treated you real nice. And Harry. I'm sure he feels obliged to you for helping with his barn. And Reverend and Mrs. Bates—"

"Molly, I don't want to talk about this." He lunged out of his chair, but to her relief he went into the house. She didn't think she wanted to continue the discussion outside anyway.

She followed him inside. "Would you like some coffee?"

He was standing by the fireplace, arms akimbo, staring at the cold hearth. He nodded absently. She poured a cup from the pot on the stove and handed it to him. He watched her warily over the rim as he sipped, and she tried to keep her expression innocent.

"Nothing you do can bring your father back, Ben."

"Dammit, Molly!" He slammed his cup down on the mantel.

She flinched automatically, backing up a step

at his fury, but she forced herself not to cringe or
run. "I mean it, Ben. I think that's what you
want. You want everybody to be sorry they
killed your father, and you want everything to
be like it was before, but it never will—"

"Stop it!" He reached for her, and she dodged
instinctively, making him swear again. "What's
wrong with you?" he demanded in exasperation. "Every time I come near you, you act like
I'm going to take a stick to you."

"I can't help it," she said, placing a hand over
her pounding heart and reminding herself Ben
had promised never to hurt her. "I'm used to it,
I guess."

"Used to what?"

"My father, he . . ."

"He what?" But she didn't need to answer.
She saw the shock of understanding darken his
eyes. "Did he beat you?"

She shook her head. "No, not me. My mother."

"Often?" he asked incredulously.

"Whenever he drank."

"My God." Ben ran a hand over his face. "I
thought . . . what you told me about him strangling her that last day, I thought it was just
because she tried to defend you."

"It was, but it wasn't the first time."

He stared at her for a long moment as the
horror of it sank in. She could see him trying to
imagine what her life had been like and hating
the very thought.

"But why do you act like you're afraid of *me*?"
he asked at last.

"Because I *am* afraid, Ben. Your anger scares me."

Shock widened his eyes. "You know I'd never hit you."

She hadn't known that for certain, of course, but she'd wanted to believe it with all her heart. "I don't really think you'd hit me, but I still get scared when you're angry."

He drew a calming breath. "Then don't make me mad. You know how I feel about all this. Just leave it be."

"I wish I could, but I've already hurt you once by not telling you the truth. I stole your chance to clear your father's name, but I'm not going to stand by and watch you throw away your chance to lead a normal life. It's my life, too. Don't you even care about that?"

"Of course I care!" he said, pacing away from her. "I don't want to give those hypocrites any more opportunities to snub you."

"They've never snubbed me before, and they never will. Give them a chance!"

"I gave them a chance at the barn raising and look what happened."

"That was my father. My father and *you*."

"What do you mean 'me'?"

"I mean if people treated you funny, it was because you acted funny. You've got a chip on your shoulder a yard wide, and you strut around just daring somebody to knock it off."

"Goddammit, Molly—"

"She's right," Johnny said from the doorway.

Ben whirled on his friend. "You stay out of this. It's none of your damn business."

"The way you're yelling, you've made it everybody's business. Hell, we're just putting up one little room. You don't have to ask everybody in the county. Just ask a few, the ones you know'll come."

"I don't need their help."

"Maybe you do. Maybe I don't want to help build your damn house. I hired on to punch cows. I'm not a damn carpenter."

While Ben glared at Johnny, Molly moved closer, laying her hand on Ben's arm. "Johnny has a good idea. We'll only ask the ones we know would want to help." He turned his glare on her, and she fought the urge to flinch again. "Ben, please, just this once. If it doesn't work out, I swear I'll never say another thing about it. I'll let you go your own way, and I'll never nag you about making friends with them again. I promise."

Molly held her breath while he made up his mind. He had a time of it, but at last his expression softened just a tiny bit. "What do you think, Johnny? Do you think she'd keep her word?"

"I don't think she'll have to," Johnny replied.

Ben drew in a ragged breath and let it out in a long sigh. "All right, Molly, you win. I'll try it one more time, but I'm warning you right now, I'm going to hold you to your promise."

She nodded as she went weak with relief. He

didn't even look angry anymore. "Thank you, Ben."

Johnny cleared his throat. "Well, I'll be running along," he said to no one in particular, and pulled the door shut behind him.

"Don't thank me," Ben said when Johnny was gone. "I'm going to be a bear to live with until this is over, and maybe for a long time afterward."

She managed a tremulous smile and ran her hand up to his shoulder. "I'm willing to do whatever I can to cheer you up."

His breath snagged in his chest just before he pulled her into his arms.

They decided they would call on the people they had chosen to invite when they went to town on Saturday to pick up the lumber. Mrs. Wells was delighted, and Mr. Wells asked, "Only one room, Ben? If you're going to all this trouble, why not let us put up a whole new house for you?"

Ben smiled knowingly. "What makes me think you're just trying to sell me more lumber?"

They were still chuckling when Mr. Riggs came in. "Did I miss a joke?" he inquired.

Molly felt Ben tense beside her, and then she remembered Riggs had been on the infamous posse. He was one of the people Ben was certain would refuse to help him, but before anyone else could speak, Mr. Wells was telling him about Ben's project. "Next Saturday's the day, right, Ben?"

Ben nodded stiffly.

"We'll be there for sure, then," Riggs said, apparently oblivious to Ben's unease. "I'm not much good with a hammer, but my boys'll be a big help."

Ben was speechless with surprise, so Molly came to his rescue. "Would you ask them to bring their fiddles? We figure it won't take as long to put up the room as it did to put up Harry's barn, so maybe we can have a little entertainment afterwards."

"They'll be tickled," Riggs assured her.

"We'll spread the word," Mrs. Wells promised later as Ben and Molly left the store.

Ben was muttering something Molly couldn't make out, but they encountered Reverend and Mrs. Bates before she had a chance to ask. When they had greeted each other, Molly quickly invited them to the room raising, not giving Ben a chance to change his mind. The Bateses were as delighted as the Wellses had been.

"I'll make sure everybody hears about it tomorrow at church," Reverend Bates said, "but of course, you'll probably be there yourselves, won't you?"

Molly didn't dare glance at Ben. "We certainly plan to be," she said, and hustled Ben away before he could contradict her. Seeing Harry Hoskins on the opposite side of the street, she hurried over, dragging Ben along with her.

Harry was waiting for them and was also glad to hear about the plan. "I'll tell all my men to spread the word. A week is short notice, but I think we should be able to get a pretty good crowd together.''

"Thanks," Ben said, and Molly stole a glance at him. He didn't seem angry, only a little disgruntled. She tried not to look too smug.

When they had parted company with Harry, Ben said, "Did you plan this?"

"Plan what?"

He stopped right in the middle of the sidewalk. "Did you know that everybody would get invited whether I wanted them to or not?"

"No," she said quite honestly. "I wish I had, though. I would've worried a lot less."

He pursed his lips, and she couldn't tell if he was trying not to smile or if he was just disgusted.

"Hey, Ben," Sheriff Bigelow called from across the street, "I hear we're putting a room on your house next Saturday."

The rest of the afternoon was more of the same as everyone they encountered questioned them about the room raising. Ben was ominously silent on the drive home, and Molly did a lot of praying and worrying about the situation. Of course, she had been vindicated by the response of the people in town, but she suspected Ben wasn't too happy about it.

When they were almost home, Ben turned to her. "I expect you want to go to church tomorrow."

"Yes, I would, but only if you go with me."

His only reply was a grunt, but the next morning he got up and dressed as if it were the most natural thing in the world. Molly hid her unreasonable joy as best she could, but she knew she must have been beaming all the same. Everyone in the congregation already knew about the Cantrells's new room, and Ben and Molly were cornered the minute they arrived with questions about what to bring and what sort of entertainment Molly had planned.

The week passed with agonizing slowness, and several times Molly caught Ben brooding. She wondered whether he still had doubts or whether he was worried the people really would show up and prove him wrong. Although she was tempted to ask him which would be the most painful to endure, she bit her tongue and remained silent on the subject. Considering how much preparation everyone on the ranch was doing for the big event, amazingly little was actually said about it by anyone.

Harry Hoskins was the first to arrive that morning, and to Molly's delight he brought her sister and her mother. The sight of her mother brought back the pain Molly had felt at being blamed for Elijah's death, but her mother's greeting was as warm as if no cross words had ever been spoken between them.

"How are you doing, Mama?" she asked when her mother had released her from her hug.

Hannah gave her a sad smile. "I miss your pa something awful, but I reckon I'll survive. I wish you'd come by and see me, though. We half expected to see you Sunday after church."

"When you weren't there, we thought you

weren't feeling well, so we didn't want to bother you," Molly said, telling only a partial truth. She hadn't wanted to hear any more recriminations, either, but apparently Julie had been right: Hannah had no recollection of her accusation.

"Mama needed to get out of the house," Julie explained, giving Molly a silent message. "She's just bored is all. We'll put her right to work, won't we?"

"We certainly will," Molly agreed, conducting her mother over to the tables she had set up to hold the food. "Is that a new dress?"

"Yes," Hannah said, fingering the black bombazine self-consciously. "Julie stitched it for me. I thought I should have a black dress now that I'm a widow." Her eyes clouded, but Julie deftly changed the subject and distracted her, leaving Molly to marvel at how her mother could still be mourning the man who had terrorized her for so many years.

Ben was showing Harry where the new room would go when the others began arriving. Wagon after wagon pulled up, and people spilled out bringing tools and food and laughter. Molly tried to watch Ben without appearing to. She supposed she was the only one besides Johnny McGee who truly understood what a momentous event this was for Ben, and she hoped they were the only ones who knew how forced his smiling welcomes were. To Molly's eye, he seemed slightly dazed, as if unable to believe what was happening.

When the arrivals had slowed to a trickle, Mr.

Wells shouted, "Ben, are you going to tell us what to do or not?"

Since the number of hands far exceeded the amount of work, Ben divided the men up into teams for different tasks. One group set about raking a spot clear for dancing later on.

Molly watched, taking careful note of who was present and who was not. There had been five men on the posse that hanged Sam Cantrell. Three of them were there today, looking even more relieved than Molly felt. Whether Ben wanted to believe it or not, Molly knew they had suffered because of their actions that night, too. Of the remaining two posse members, one was dead and the last one was Franklin Hoskins.

"My father wouldn't come," Harry said from behind her. She turned, wondering if her thoughts had been so obvious. "I tried to convince him, but he prefers to believe Ben burned my barn."

Molly could see the situation pained him. "He'll come around," she said, but she knew she was speaking an empty platitude. Franklin Hoskins was not the type of man to "come around." Like her own father, he would justify his actions in his own mind and refuse to let facts convince him otherwise.

Harry's rueful grin told her he, too, knew the truth. "Miriam said to tell you how sorry she was. She really wanted to be here."

"Thank her for me, will you?" Molly replied. "And tell her I understand." Harry nodded and hurried off to his assigned task.

As the day wore on, Molly began to sense an undercurrent of emotion. At first she thought it was only her own feeling of triumph, but she soon realized the others shared her sense of accomplishment. The building up of the house walls seemed to symbolize a tearing down of the invisible walls that had separated Ben from the community. No matter who had been responsible for erecting those walls, everyone was equally happy to see them coming down at last. As the room took shape and the roof was set in place, the crowd's good humor swelled into hilarity. When someone made a joke, everyone roared. The men began a competition to see who could issue the most outrageous insult. The women teased and taunted, spurring them on. The children raced around like Indians, and for once no one even thought of telling them to settle down.

At last the room was finished, the doorway cut, and the crowd gathered around while Ben found Molly and escorted her over to admire it. She assumed she would just peek in the window, but as they approached the house, Ben scooped her up and carried her inside, through the old part and straight into the new amid the raucous cheering of their audience. Once inside, he set her on her feet, stirring up a cloud of sawdust, and placed a very proprietary kiss on her startled mouth.

The crowd went wild, but Molly was barely aware of them. All she could see was the look of adoration in Ben's eyes.

"Thank you, Molly," he whispered. "You gave me back my life."

Chapter Eleven
✦✦✦✦

FOR THE FIRST time since he could remember, Ben walked down the main street of Hoskinsville without a thought as to who might be watching him and whispering behind his back. Oh, he knew there were still a few diehards who would never believe he or his father were innocent, but Molly and Johnny had finally convinced him they no longer mattered. In fact, Ben now considered facing them an amusing diversion rather than an act of defiance.

Today would be even more than amusing because his mortgage payment was due and he would have to face the most influential of his remaining enemies, Franklin Hoskins. In anticipation of the meeting, Ben had taken Molly on a belated honeymoon trip to San Antonio, where he'd withdrawn the cash he would need for the transaction. Molly had been astonished to learn he kept the bulk of his money deposited there in order to keep his true financial status a secret from Franklin Hoskins.

Ben was whistling when he walked into the

Hoskinsville Bank. The clerk looked up. He was a young man wearing paper cuff protectors and a green eyeshade. He smiled a greeting.

"Hello, Dave. I'm here to make a loan payment," Ben said, and the clerk announced him to Mr. Hoskins.

Hoskins's inner office was as austere as the man himself, containing his desk, two straight chairs for visitors, and little else. A calendar was the only adornment on any of the walls, and the windows looked out into the alley. Hoskins rose but did not offer to shake hands. "Good afternoon, Cantrell. Have a seat."

Ben did so, feeling more smugly confident than he had ever felt in all the six years during which he had made the interest payments on the loan his father had procured before his death. "I'm here to—"

"I know," Hoskins interrupted. "I'm sorry to say this, but I'm afraid I'm going to have to call in your loan this time."

"Call it in?" Ben echoed in astonishment.

"Yes, I believe I explained the terms of the loan to you before, but to refresh your memory, I hold a mortgage on your ranch. According to Texas law, I cannot touch your original homestead—the house and the property on which it sits—but the rest of the ranch is subject to repossession if you cannot pay off the loan in full."

"But the only thing due right now is the interest payment."

"Ordinarily, yes, but as I said, I'm calling in

your loan, as the law entitles me to do at any time, so the entire balance is due in thirty days. If you cannot pay, we will auction the ranch. If the amount of money received from the auction exceeds the loan balance, the excess will, of course, be yours."

Ben frowned, knowing that although the loan balance was less than $200 and his ranch was worth far more, there was little chance he would see a penny of profit. Bankers all over the state had used this law to cheat men out of their property since the bankers or their friends were usually the buyers in these bargain sales.

"Why are you calling in the loan now?"

"Because . . ." To Hoskins's credit, he looked a little uncomfortable. "These are difficult times for everyone, and the bank needs some working capital, I'm afraid."

Ben wasn't fooled. "So you're going to steal my ranch to get it, is that it?"

Hoskins stiffened visibly. "The transaction is perfectly legal, I assure you."

"Legal doesn't make it right," Ben said. "How many other loans are you going to call in?"

"I . . . I don't know just yet." Hoskins was a nervous liar. Ben knew his was the only ranch currently in danger.

"Well, then, I reckon I'll have to come up with the money. How much is it?"

"One hundred seventy-six dollars and twenty-seven cents."

"Exactly?" Ben asked sarcastically.

"Yes," Hoskins replied with annoyance.

Ben pulled a small sack out of his vest pocket. "I suppose you can make change, then, this being a bank and all." He counted out ten gold double eagles and flung the handful onto Hoskins's desk. They landed with a magnificent crash, skidding and sliding and clattering to the floor.

Hoskins swore, jumping up and making a very undignified attempt to catch as many as he could. His face turned red as he gathered up the coins and bent to retrieve those on the floor.

Ben leaned back in his chair and crossed his legs, glad he'd responded to the impulse to end this charade once and for all. Years of frugal living had swelled his distant bank account, but pure stubbornness had prevented him from paying off the loan. He had taken a perverse delight in allowing Hoskins to think he had a hold over the Cantrells all these years, but Molly had shown him he no longer needed the satisfaction of such petty pleasures. Indeed, seeing Hoskins's beady-eyed resentment, he wished he'd done this years ago.

"David!" Hoskins called when he had the coins in neat little stacks. The clerk came in and took the money Hoskins handed him. "Mr. Cantrell is paying off his loan. Would you write him a receipt and bring him his change, please?"

By the time the clerk left, Hoskins had regained his normal dignity, although his face was still dangerously flushed. "I'm surprised you have so much ready cash after all the money you've spent lately," he said, giving Ben an insight into why his loan had been called at this particular time.

Ben smiled enigmatically but refused to respond to the leading question. His finances were certainly none of Franklin Hoskins's business, especially since he chose not to deposit them in Hoskins's bank.

The silence stretched between them. Ben didn't mind, but Hoskins grew increasingly uncomfortable. He was drumming his fingers on the desk by the time the clerk returned with Ben's change and receipt.

Ben thanked him and rose to leave. He was almost to the door when Hoskins said, "By the way, did you know Elijah Wade took out a mortgage on his place, too?"

The warning was no less real for being unspoken. "Foreclosing on widows and orphans now, Hoskins?" Ben asked, not bothering to hide his contempt.

But Hoskins was unfazed. "If I have to, Cantrell."

Ben called a family meeting with Molly, Hannah, and Julie, during which he explained the problem of the loan. Although the balance on the Wade loan was even smaller than Ben's, Hannah had no more than thirty dollars in ready cash with which to pay it should Hoskins call it in. Since the interest payment was not due for a few months, they decided to throw together a trail herd of cattle from both ranches and drive them north to Dodge City for sale. With any kind of luck, Hannah, too, would be able to pay her loan in full when the time came.

The next few weeks were filled with back-breaking labor as Ben tried to bring the same kind of order to the Flying W ranch that he had long maintained on his own. Noon meals were now packed in flour sacks and eaten on horse-back, and too many nights Ben fell asleep before he could show Molly how much he'd missed her all day.

"We've almost got it licked now, partner," Johnny informed him one afternoon. "A few more days and I'll be heading north."

Ben grinned. "You don't know how much I appreciate you taking this job for me."

Johnny grinned back. "Oh, yes, I do, and don't think I won't call in my markers when the time comes. You owe me big for this one."

"Don't pull that martyr act with me. You've been dying to find out if Dodge is still as sinful as it used to be."

Johnny didn't deny it. Instead, he pulled off his hat and wiped his brow with his shirt-sleeve. "Damn, it's hot enough to boil your sweat today."

"Yeah, and summer ain't even settled in good, yet. Looks like we're in for a bad one this year."

The two men had just finished pulling a cow and her calf out of a mud hole that had once been a pond. Ben checked the position of the sun. "It's getting late, but I reckon we'd better take a look at the creek before we head on back."

Johnny had swung down to tighten his cinch strap. "You go on home. I'll check the creek."

"I can't let you—"

"The hell you can't. You got a reason to hurry home. I don't. It won't take more than a few minutes, anyway. Just tell Molly to save me some pie."

Ben laughed out loud. "Molly always saves you some pie. Sometimes I wonder if I oughta be jealous of the two of you."

"Can I help it if women just naturally love me?" Johnny asked innocently, and ducked as Ben took a swipe at him with his Stetson. He was still chuckling as he bade Ben good-bye and headed for the creek.

As usual, he was watching the ground for "sign," tracks indicating whether and how recently cattle had passed that way, when he cut across hoofprints he didn't recognize. Johnny knew the prints of every horse on the ranch, and these belonged to an outsider.

He climbed down to take a better look and noticed how fresh they were, not more than an hour old judging by the clarity of the prints. The Texas wind would blur them shortly. Intrigued, Johnny forgot all about going to the creek and turned his horse to follow the tracks. In a little while he saw where the horse he was following had stopped to relieve itself. He was following a mare. Not many men rode mares, but what would a woman be doing out here all alone?

A little farther on he saw where the rider had spurred the mare into a gallop, although he could see no apparent reason for the sudden change of pace. Then he saw where the mare had stumbled in a hole, knocking the rider from the saddle. He got down again and examined the prints. Now the rider was walking beside the limping mare, and the small bootprints told him beyond a shadow of a doubt the rider was a woman.

He jumped back into the saddle and spurred his own horse, following the ever-fresher trail with ease until he caught sight of his quarry. At the sound of his approach, she stopped and turned, shading her eyes as if she were trying to make out his identity. He knew her instantly.

"Miz Hoskins, what're you doing out here?" he asked as he reined up beside her.

She managed a sheepish smile, although he could see she was upset. Her green riding habit was dirty from her fall. "I'm afraid I had a little accident. I was out riding, and my mare stepped in a hole—"

"I saw the tracks," Johnny said, swinging down from his saddle. "Did you get hurt?"

"No, nothing serious, but Lady is limping."

Johnny bent to examine the mare's left foreleg. "Looks like a sprain."

"Do you think she'll be all right, Mr. McGee?"

Johnny looked up in surprise. "You know my name?"

She was equally surprised by his question. "Did you think I wouldn't try to find out who you were after the box supper?"

He'd tried not to think about the box supper at

all. He could feel the heat crawling up his neck and hoped his deep tan would disguise his blush. "I've got some liniment back at the ranch that'll fix this right up, but she shouldn't be walking on it," he said briskly, rising to his feet.

"Oh, dear." Miriam glanced at the setting sun apprehensively. "I really need to get home. My husband will be . . . worried."

"I'll get you home. That is, if you don't mind riding double."

"Oh, I couldn't do that!" she cried in alarm.

Johnny's face felt like it was on fire. "You don't have to be afraid of me," he said stiffly.

"I'm not," she assured him hastily, placing a reassuring hand on his arm. "I know you wouldn't . . . It's not that at all. You see, my husband is a very jealous man, and if he saw us together . . ."

"He'd never think you'd be mixed up with a common cowboy," Johnny scoffed.

"I'm afraid he already does." Suddenly realizing her hand was on his arm, she snatched it away self-consciously. "You see, when I go riding, I usually take Hector with me. He's the Negro man who cares for our horses, but Hector wasn't feeling well today so I went out alone. My husband doesn't like for me to go alone, but I thought I would be back before he got home. But I forgot how far it is out here. It's been so long since . . . Anyway, I'm sure Franklin is already looking for me, and if he found us together, I don't know what he'd do."

"Then he won't find us. I'll sneak you back. I can't just leave you here. It'll be dark in a few hours. What if nobody else finds you?"

He was right, of course, but she didn't like it one bit. She kept glancing around nervously as if expecting her husband to appear at any moment. "What about Lady?" she asked, gesturing to the mare.

"I'll picket her over there in the shade, and I'll come back and doctor her leg later."

"I don't know," Miriam was saying, but Johnny had already caught up the mare's reins.

"What choice have you got?" he pointed out reasonably, and was relieved to see her following, bringing his own horse along.

He'd just finished hammering in the picket pin with a rock when Miriam whispered, "Oh, my God!"

Johnny followed her stricken gaze to see Franklin Hoskins bearing down on them on a lathered horse. He reined to a halt only a few feet from them and vaulted from his saddle. "You whore! I caught you red-handed this time!" he shouted, advancing on her menacingly.

Johnny jumped in front of her. "Wait a minute, Hoskins. You got this all wrong."

"Do I?" he asked contemptuously. "Don't think you're the first, McGee. She's spread her legs for half the men in the county."

"Franklin, don't!" Miriam cried, but he ignored her.

"Where's Cantrell? I figured the two of you liked to share her."

"You sonofabitch," Johnny snarled, pushing the banker away. "She was just out riding, and her mare went lame. I happened to find her a few minutes ago and was going to take her home when you showed up. You don't deserve a woman like her!"

"Neither do you," Hoskins replied. Before Johnny could guess his intention, he reached inside his coat, jerked out a pistol, and fired.

The impact spun Johnny around, and he fell to one knee. Oddly, he felt no pain at first, only the warm gush of blood from his side.

Miriam was screaming, and for a moment he thought she might be hit, too, since she'd been standing behind him. But she was fighting with Hoskins, struggling for the gun. Johnny saw him lift his hand and smack her. The sound of the blow and her cry of pain echoed in his head as she slumped to the ground. Johnny lunged to his feet or was trying to when Hoskins's gun exploded again. Something struck him in the chest, and he was falling, down and down, into a very dark hole.

"Franklin, you've killed him!" Miriam screamed, scrambling up. She was halfway to Johnny when Franklin grabbed her riding jacket and jerked her backward.

"He's not the first man I've killed for you, Miriam, and I'll kill every one of them before I'm through, Ben Cantrell and all the rest."

"What are you talking about?" she asked as her terror hardened into an icy dread.

"I'm talking about Sam Cantrell," he said, his

eyes glittering dangerously. "Sam Cantrell, your very first love. I hanged him, Miriam."

"I know," she said, the knowledge sending a familiar shaft of pain through her. How many times had he reminded her down through the years?

"What you don't know is that I was the one who killed Fletcher, too."

Her eyes widened in horror.

"That's right, Miriam. I waited and waited, knowing that sooner or later the time would come when I could repay Sam Cantrell for what he had done to me."

"He didn't do anything to you—"

"You call despoiling my wife nothing? Do you call giving her his bastard child nothing?"

"Franklin, please, that man is bleeding to death—"

"Good! I want him to die just like Cantrell died. It's so easy. It's always easy. At first I was only going to burn Fletcher's barn, but he caught me so I had to shoot him. That made everything even easier because then the others wanted to lynch Cantrell as much as I did. They were like sheep, stupid sheep. All I had to do was suggest it, and Elijah Wade did the rest."

Miriam uttered an agonized cry, and Hoskins smiled.

"Then I found out you'd gone after Cantrell's boy, and he made it easy, too. When he got into a fight with Harry, all I had to do was burn Harry's barn."

"Franklin, let me go!" Miriam sobbed.

"Never!" He jerked her to her feet and slapped her again when she tried to struggle. "Come on, I'm taking you home."

"No! What about that man? Look, he's still breathing. You can't leave him here to die."

"Yes, I can." He began dragging her over to her horse, using his fist when she kept resisting.

Her ears rang and stars danced before her eyes, but she dug in her heels and refused to budge. "No! I won't leave him!"

"Then I'll put him out of his misery so you won't have to worry about him anymore." Hoskins raised his gun, but Miriam threw herself at him. The pistol exploded as they fell.

"Franklin, they'll hang you for murder," she cried, fighting for the gun.

"Not for killing my wife's lover." He overpowered her, wrestling her to the ground. "Now we're going home. Will you come quietly, or do I have to put another bullet in him?"

Miriam stared up into his glittering eyes and knew a fear far worse than any she had ever known. "I'll go if you don't shoot him again."

Without another word, he got up and yanked her to her feet, shoving her away when he caught her glancing anxiously at Johnny's unconscious form. With great effort, she resisted the urge to go to Johnny, knowing she would surely cause his death if she did. She covered her mouth with both hands to stifle her sobs and watched helplessly as Franklin pulled loose the picket pin holding the mare.

He cursed when he saw the mare limping, and she wondered vaguely if he would let the proof convince him Johnny had been telling the truth. But of course he didn't. Instead, he simply forced her onto his own horse and mounted behind her. They rode away without a backward glance.

When Molly had finished up the supper dishes, she wandered outside where Ben was smoking by the corral and staring off into the distance. "Where do you suppose Johnny could be?" she asked.

"He said he was going to check the water level in the creek. He shouldn't have been more than a few minutes behind me."

"Do you think you ought to go looking for him?"

Ben sighed. "It'll be dark soon. I wouldn't be able to find him even if I did."

"He'd probably be insulted if you came looking for him anyway," she said, hoping to cheer him up a little.

He forced a grin. "Yeah, I keep reminding myself he's a big boy and he's slept out plenty of nights before now. Probably his horse came up lame or something, and he's taking shank's mare back."

"That's right," Molly said, disguising her own worries. "He'll show up here around midnight, limping, half-starved, and fit to be tied."

Ben nodded, but she noticed his smile faded as he continued to stare out at the horizon.

*   *   *

Miriam lay on her bed in the darkness, huddled into a protective ball and as far from sleep as she had ever been. She was still fully dressed, even to her riding boots, because she wanted to be ready to go the instant Franklin left the house.

The pattern was always the same when he went into one of his rages. He would yell and rant, calling her filthy names and accusing her of every conceivable kind of degradation, until he was exhausted and she was sobbing in hysteria. Then he would start to drink, slowly, steadily, until he was relaxed enough to appear in public so he could take his drinking to the saloon.

She'd often wondered what he did there, whether he bragged to the men that he had just totally humiliated his wife. Of course she knew he'd never reveal their filthy little secrets to the citizens of Hoskinsville. He'd never let anyone know what a farce their marriage truly was. No, he much preferred having the world see them as the perfect couple, wealthy and content, the picture of marital bliss.

Miriam actually laughed out loud at the thought. The sound was harsh and bitter in the darkened room. She quickly covered her mouth, hoping Franklin had not heard. He might come to investigate. But no, she sat upright as she heard the heavy front door closing. He was leaving at last. She waited, heart pounding, until he'd had time to get to the saloon. Then she wasted no time in gathering the things she would need and slipping out to the stables to saddle a horse.

She prayed all the way out to Ben Cantrell's ranch, knowing she would need a miracle to find Johnny McGee in the darkness. Someone heard her prayers and answered them. She spotted the firelight several miles away, and the hope she'd denied herself burst full blown within her. If he'd built a fire, he wasn't dead. Perhaps he wasn't even as seriously wounded as the blood-stains had indicated. Recklessly, she spurred her horse toward the distant flames.

Her hope turned to dread when she caught sight of him lying deathly still beside the fading fire. His clothes were soaked with blood, and his face was chalk white. Somehow he had dragged some sticks together and kept the fire going, at least for a while. The howl of coyotes told her why the fire was necessary.

She jumped out of the saddle even before her horse was completely stopped. "Johnny! Mr. McGee!" Kneeling beside him, she felt his face. His skin was clammy but not cold. She shook him slightly, and he groaned.

"Thank God," she murmured. "Johnny, can you hear me?"

His eyes flickered open. "Water," he rasped.

"Yes, of course." She hurried to her horse and retrieved the sack of supplies she had tied to the horn. In it was a canteen, which she held briefly to his lips. "Only a little until I see how badly you're hurt."

"Not bad," he said vaguely, then seemed to

notice his surroundings. "It's dark. You'd better get home."

"We'll go in a minute," she said to reassure him. "I'll build up the fire a little first." Luckily there were plenty of dead sticks under the old live-oak tree. She fed the fire with trembling hands until the flames roared high enough to discourage any skulking scavengers. By its light she opened his shirt and examined his wounds.

There were two. One was low on his left side, just above his hipbone. The bullet had gone straight through, and Johnny had managed to stuff pieces of his bandanna into the gaping holes to stop the bleeding. The other wound was directly over his heart, but miraculously the bullet had deflected on one of his ribs, cutting a furrow halfway around his body but doing no serious damage. "My God," she whispered, awed by the miracle for which she had prayed.

"I guess . . . it knocked the wind . . . out of me. My chest is . . . sore as blazes," Johnny explained, breathing carefully around the pain.

"You might have a broken rib. I'll bind you before you try to move." Her hands ceased trembling as she washed and bound Johnny's wounds the best she could under the circumstances. He bore up well, although she knew he was suffering tremendously from her ministrations. When she was done, she saw his eyes had cleared. He was staring at her.

"You came back."

"Yes, I couldn't leave you out here. I'm only sorry I couldn't get here sooner."

"He'll come after you."

"Not tonight. He won't realize I'm gone until morning, and by then I'll have told the sheriff what happened. Do you think you can get on a horse?"

"You came back," he repeated as if that were the most important consideration.

"Yes, but it's time to go now. I'll bring the horse over and help you up." As she had expected, both Johnny's horse and her own mare were long gone, probably scared away by the coyotes. She brought her horse over as close as possible and somehow got him up into the saddle. Only the beads of sweat on his face told her what the effort had cost him. "You'll have to hang on and try to stay awake because you're too heavy for me to hold," she warned when she had mounted behind him.

"You came back," he said again. She smiled in spite of herself.

The ride to Ben's ranch was a nightmare. Several times Johnny slipped into unconsciousness again, and Miriam had a time keeping both of them in the saddle. She was almost as happy to see the ranch buildings as she had been to find Johnny still alive.

"Ben! Molly! Somebody!" she cried as she walked the horse up to the house. She recalled the last time she had ridden here in the dark of night to tell Sam Cantrell she was going to marry Franklin Hoskins. The pain of her memories ripped through her like Franklin's bullets had ripped through Johnny. The door opened, as it had that night, but this time Ben Cantrell stood there instead.

"What the hell? Who's there?"

"It's Miriam Hoskins. I have Johnny McGee, and he's badly hurt."

Ben rushed out, wearing only a pair of pants, and Molly followed him, pulling on her robe as she came.

"Johnny?" Ben said as he approached the horse with its double burden. "What happened?"

"Franklin shot him," Miriam explained, helping as Ben assisted Johnny in dismounting. "Be careful. He may have a broken rib."

"Shot him?"

Ben was having a hard time believing this wasn't a bad dream. How could Johnny have gotten himself shot? And by Franklin Hoskins, of all people? And why was Miriam Hoskins bringing him home in the middle of the night? Several unpleasant possibilities occurred to him, but he rejected them. There would be plenty of time for questions when he had taken care of Johnny. His friend groaned, and Ben didn't bother asking if he could walk.

"Bring him in the house," Molly said, running ahead to light the lamp. "Put him on the bed." She pointed to the bed in the front room that she and Ben had shared in the early days of their marriage. Now, of course, they slept in the new brass bed in their new bedroom.

"My God," Ben said when he had laid Johnny down and gotten a good look at him.

"I don't think he's seriously hurt, although one of the bullets went right through," Miriam explained, following Ben inside. "He's lost a lot of blood, though."

"What's going on?" Tom and Billy demanded, hurrying up to the cabin partially dressed.

"My horse went lame out on the range this afternoon," Miriam told them all. "Mr. McGee found me and offered to take me home, but before he could, my husband came up. He had been looking for me for several hours and had found my trail. He . . . he's a very jealous man, and he thought Mr. McGee and I . . . well, Franklin shot him."

Molly gasped.

"When did this happen?" Ben asked.

"Late this afternoon."

"Then where have you been all this time?"

Miriam swallowed with difficulty. "Franklin made me go home with him. He left Mr. McGee out on the range to die." She flinched at the exclamations of disbelief but went on. "I waited until he went out to the saloon tonight, and then I saddled a horse and went looking for Mr. McGee and brought him here."

"She came back for me, Ben," Johnny said faintly.

"Ben," Molly said, "somebody ought to go for the doctor."

"I'll go," Tom offered, but Ben shook his head.

"It's my responsibility. I'll get the sheriff, too."

"Wait, Ben," Miriam said when he would have gone into the bedroom to finish dressing.

"Please, don't get the sheriff yet, not until you've heard the whole story."

"I want to hear it now, then," he said.

"It's too long, and . . . well, it's already kept for six years. It'll keep a few more hours. Please, hurry for the doctor now. Franklin will still be there when you're ready for him."

Ben frowned, but he nodded his agreement.

"Anything we can do?" Tom asked.

"Yes," Molly said, realizing there was work to be done. "Pump me a couple buckets of water, will you? And Billy, pull Johnny's boots off."

Ben was dressed in a matter of minutes. "I'll be back as quick as I can," he promised as he raced out the door.

Molly tested Johnny's forehead, relieved to find he had no fever yet. "How do you feel?"

"Lousy," he said with a shadow of his normal grin.

She shook her head in mock despair. "I always said you'd come to no good, Johnny McGee. Now let's see how bad these holes are."

"What are you doing?" he asked in alarm when she started to remove his shirt.

"I'm undressing you. You don't think I'll let you on my clean sheets in these filthy clothes, do you?"

"Molly!" He was appalled. "Just leave me be. I can wait for the doc."

"Don't be an idiot. He won't be back for hours, and I'm sure those wounds need to be washed out with hot water, don't they?" she asked Miriam.

"They certainly do. We should probably use some whiskey, too, if you have any."

Reluctantly, Johnny allowed Molly to relieve him of his shirt, but he yelped when she started on his pants. Molly winked at Miriam. "Johnny's trying to make us think he's never taken his clothes off in front of a woman before."

"I never did in front of you, and I don't plan on starting now," he informed her indignantly.

"Don't worry, I'll let you keep your drawers."

He flushed scarlet beneath his tan. "I'm not wearing any," he said through stiff lips.

"Johnny!" she cried, pretending to be shocked.

"It's hot as Hades. You don't expect me to wear any clothes I don't need, do you?"

Molly supposed not, but she still didn't want those filthy, bloody pants staining up her bedclothes. With the judicious use of a blanket, she managed to preserve Johnny's modesty and still accomplish her purpose.

By the time he had been stripped, Johnny was too tired to protest any more, so Molly was able to unwrap his wounds while the other men brought in the water she had requested and put it on to heat.

"Good heavens," she said in awe when she saw the wound over his heart. "Your guardian angel was busy tonight, Johnny McGee."

She heard an agonized gasp behind her and turned just in time to keep Miriam from falling. Molly set her on a chair and forced her to put her white face down between her knees until the faintness passed.

When Miriam lifted her head, her eyes were full of pain and remorse. "Franklin tried to kill him, and he killed Ben's father, too."

"It's all right, Miriam. Johnny's going to be fine," Molly soothed her. "But I need your help. Can you tear up a sheet for some bandages?"

Miriam nodded, and although she was still alarmingly pale, Molly put her to work. In a few minutes, Johnny's wounds were cleansed and wrapped in fresh bandages. Molly allowed him a liberal dose of whiskey internally to ease the pain and help him sleep. When he was resting quietly, she turned her attention to Miriam after sending Tom and Billy back to get a good night's sleep, or what was left of it.

Molly put a pot of coffee on to boil, and when it was done she poured some for herself and Miriam. Miriam drank it gratefully.

"How are you feeling?" Molly asked, noticing that for once Miriam Hoskins didn't look like the wife of the richest man in town. Her custom-made riding habit was bloodstained and dusty, her beautiful hair was hanging in limp strands, and her lovely face was bruised and dirty.

"I'm better now, thanks. I'm sorry I almost fainted. I don't know what came over me."

"From what you said, you've had a bad time of it today. It's a wonder you didn't keel over long before now."

Miriam laughed mirthlessly. "You don't know the half of it. I found out things today . . ." Her voice trailed off, and she shuddered.

"You said there was more to the story than what you told Ben."

Miriam nodded.

"Would you like to talk about it? We've got a long wait ahead of us."

Miriam stared into her coffee for a moment, and then she looked to make certain Johnny was asleep. She sighed. "Franklin killed Ben's father."

"I know. My father was on the posse, too."

"No, I don't mean just that he was on the posse. I mean he was the one who burned the barn and shot Mr. Fletcher so Sam would get the blame."

Stunned, Molly could barely speak. "How . . . how do you know?"

"He told me today, after he shot Johnny. He said Johnny wasn't the first man he'd killed because of me. For years he's been reminding me he hanged Sam, but today he told me the rest."

"Why would he do a thing like that? What did he have against Ben's father?"

Miriam's dark eyes clouded and then filled with tears. "Because I was in love with Sam. We were lovers before . . . before I married Franklin." She brushed away a tear. "I loved Sam, but I thought Franklin's money was more important."

"And when you got married, he realized that . . . that he wasn't the first?" Molly prompted when Miriam paused, lost in her bleak memories.

"Oh, no. I fooled him, at least then. I was so

frightened on our wedding night—'scared stiff,' as they say. It was awful, and I even bled, so he thought . . . Anyway, he didn't know until I lost the baby."

Molly murmured her sympathy, putting her hand over Miriam's where it lay on the table.

"Franklin was so excited when he found out I was expecting. Molly, I didn't know I was carrying Sam's child, or I never would have married Franklin."

"Of course you wouldn't," Molly said, patting her hand.

"I even began to think I might fool him about that, too, until I miscarried. The doctor was very reassuring. He told me I could have plenty more, and he comforted Franklin by pointing out how embarrassing it would have been for us to have a baby only six months after our wedding. Of course Franklin knew *he* hadn't fathered a child three months before our marriage. After that . . ."

Molly squeezed Miriam's fingers, thinking how closely the woman's story paralleled her own. How fortunate she was to have found Ben! She knew only too well how awful Miriam's life must have been all these years, living with a man who despised her.

"He got his revenge by killing Sam, and he's still getting his revenge."

"Did he . . . beat you?"

Miriam laughed bitterly. "Oh, no. Oh, he hit me today to convince me to leave Johnny," she said, touching her bruised cheek. "Ordinarily, though, Franklin would never be so uncivilized, but there are many ways to hurt a person without ever lifting a hand against them. Franklin knows them all. And I wasn't the only person he hurt. He was the one who burned Harry's barn, to. He got some crazy idea that Ben and I were lovers just because I spoke to him at the box social. And when Mr. McGee bid on my box . . . Molly, are you all right?''

Molly shook her head, unable to stop the flood of tears coursing down her face. She'd been wrong! Her father was innocent, and she need no longer bear the burden of his guilt. The relief made her dizzy and absurdly happy. Thank heaven she was crying too hard to smile or Miriam would surely think she was insane. "I . . . I'm sorry. You see . . . all this time . . . I thought my father had done those things,'' she explained, trying vainly to wipe the tears from her face.

"Your father! Oh, Molly, how awful.''

Molly nodded, thinking how wonderful it would be to tell Ben, until she realized something else: if her father had been the guilty party, the incident was closed. Indeed, Ben had already put it behind him and started the new life they both wanted so badly. But if Franklin Hoskins was responsible, nothing was settled. Nothing at all.

Chapter Twelve

❖❖❖❖❖

KEEPING HIS PROMISE to Miriam, Ben fetched only the doctor, explaining none of the details of how Johnny had been shot until they were well out of town. On the lonely ride in, Ben had spent a lot of time thinking. If Franklin Hoskins was going to be arrested, the least Ben could do was warn his son. As he and the doctor passed the cut-off to Harry's ranch, Ben took it, leaving Doc Logan to proceed alone.

Harry was less than pleased at being aroused in the middle of the night. "This better be good," he warned Ben, running a hand through his tousled hair and squinting to make out Ben's expression in the shadows of his front porch.

"Johnny's been shot."

"Shot? How? When? Who did it?"

"This afternoon. Your father did it because he thought Johnny was carrying on with Miriam."

"Good God almighty," Harry groaned. "I guess it's too much to hope that this is a bad dream."

"Sorry, partner."

"Come on in while I get my pants on. Tell me the whole story."

Ben filled him in on the details while he dressed. In a matter of minutes they were riding toward Ben's ranch. By the time they got there, the doctor was just finishing up.

"Keep the wound clean, and keep him in bed

for at least a week. If he starts running a fever, send for me," he was telling Molly when Ben and Harry walked in. "You're a mighty lucky man, McGee. If that bullet had been a fraction higher, we'd be laying you out tomorrow."

Johnny gave him one of his grins. "Yeah, it's almost enough to make a man straighten up and try to make something of himself."

Ben felt relief course through him. If Johnny was well enough to joke, he was going to be all right. "I'm just wondering how long until he'll be able to ride," Ben teased. "He's supposed to take a trail herd to Dodge for me next week."

"I'm afraid you'll have to find someone else for the job," the doctor said with a smile, "although I wouldn't let him loaf around more than a month or so before putting him back to work. He looks like the kind of fellow who'd take advantage if you'd let him."

Molly offered the doctor some coffee and breakfast before he went back. He accepted only the coffee, but still he lingered a half hour. By the time he left, Ben and Harry were barely able to contain their eagerness to hear Miriam's story. Johnny had managed to drink some broth and was now dozing again. The rest of them gathered around the table while Miriam told them the sordid tale of her marriage and Franklin Hoskins's mad quest for revenge.

"My God," Ben said when she had finished, rage glittering in his eyes. He had taken Molly's hand the moment he'd learned her father was not responsible for killing Fletcher, and now his grip was so tight her fingers were numb.

Miriam looked at Harry. "I'm so sorry. I wish you'd never had to hear this."

"No, I'm glad I did. I've suspected for a long time that something was very wrong, and now I know what it is. It's almost a relief to finally know the truth."

"What are you going to do now?" Molly asked.

"I guess that's up to Ben."

Molly sensed her husband's tension. "We'll have to go to the sheriff," he said.

Harry nodded grimly. "Yes, and then Father will be tried for murder, among other things." He managed a small smile. "Well, Ben, this is a good day for you. Your father's name will finally be cleared."

"And *your* father's name will be ruined."

"Yes, *his* name, but not *mine*. You've shown me a man doesn't have to bear the sins of his father if he chooses not to."

Molly waited in vain for Ben to acknowledge Harry's compliment. He seemed lost in his own private thoughts, and she felt a quiver of apprehension. "I think we could all do with some breakfast," she announced with false cheerfulness, and proceeded to prepare a meal. Miriam helped, so the work went quickly, but by the time everyone had finished eating, Ben's mood had grown even more dour.

"I guess we'd better go into town," he said to Harry, who nodded solemnly.

Molly followed Ben into the bedroom and

closed the door behind her. She had intended to
comfort him, but she gasped when she saw him
strapping on his six-gun. "What are you doing?"

"I'm putting on my gun," he said impatiently.

"I thought you were going to the sheriff."

"Harry can go to the sheriff. I'm going to see
Hoskins."

"No!" she cried, running to him. She threw
her arms around him and tried to pull him close.
"Don't do this!"

He resisted her embrace. "Molly, the man
killed my father, and he shot Johnny down in
cold blood."

"So if you murder him, then I suppose everything will be fine!" she exclaimed in outrage.
"Ben, haven't you learned anything at all? Revenge destroys the person getting it, too!"

Gently but firmly he removed her hands from
his arms. "This will be the end of it."

"Will it? What about Harry? Don't you think
he'll want some revenge of his own if you murder his father? Ben, think! You're the only one
who can end it, and only if you go to the law.
Please, Ben!"

Deaf to her pleading, he strode to the door
and opened it. "I'm ready if you are, Harry."

"Wait!" Molly called, trying to think of a way
to stop him. "I . . . I think Miriam should go
along. The sheriff will want to hear her story."

Miriam looked up in surprise, but to Molly's
relief she quickly agreed. "She's right. I'll have
to tell it sooner or later, anyway. I might as well
get it over with."

"And I'll go with you," Molly added.

Ben scowled his disapproval. "Who's going to take care of Johnny?"

"Tom and Billy. Go ask them while I get my bonnet." Without waiting for his reply, she hurried back into the bedroom.

Ben drove the women in the buckboard, and Harry rode along beside them. They didn't talk much since they were all lost in their own thoughts, but Molly could feel Ben's anger like a living thing between them. Not long ago, his anger would have terrified her, but now she knew the true danger lay in giving in to it. She wouldn't let him do this terrible thing, no matter how furious he became.

When Ben hesitated outside the sheriff's office, Molly took his arm and forced him to accompany her inside. Sheriff Bigelow immediately sensed the importance of the visit of the grim-faced group and listened solemnly to Miriam's story.

"I'll be da . . . hornswoggled," Bigelow said when she was finished. "Harry, what do you think about all this?"

"I believe her, and I can certainly vouch for how jealous he's always been of her. He hated Sam Cantrell, and even after Ben's name was cleared, my father refused to acknowledge his innocence. I suppose he was afraid if we started looking for the real guilty party, we might discover the truth."

"What about the night of the box social? Did any of you see him leave?"

"I didn't actually see him leave, but I knew he

wasn't anywhere around," Miriam said. "You see, when Ben was cleared of burning Harry's barn, Franklin accused me of being the woman who was with Ben. Ordinarily he watches me very carefully, but he'd disappeared that night for some reason. I didn't realize until last night where he'd been."

"Can you arrest him?" Molly asked, hoping to see Hoskins safely behind bars.

Sheriff Bigelow shook his head. "I can question him about the crimes. The problem is we've got no evidence. All we've got is Miz Hoskins's word that he confessed, but he probably won't be so eager to tell his story to anybody else, and she's his wife, so she can't testify against him."

Molly watched Ben in alarm, sensing his frustration. What would he do if they couldn't get Hoskins to confess?

"We'll make him talk, then," Harry said, surprising everyone with his vehemence.

"Harry, he's your father," Ben protested. "You shouldn't get involved."

"That's exactly why I *should* get involved. You aren't the only one he's hurt. Miriam and I have suffered from his crazy need for revenge, too. Come on, Sheriff. Let's go face him down right now."

Molly listened in horror as Ben and the sheriff readily agreed. She gripped Miriam's hand in panic as they watched the men go. "Be careful," she called helplessly just before Ben closed the door behind them. How would she ever stand the wait until they returned?

Beside her, Miriam drew a ragged breath, and Molly saw her lips moving in silent prayer. Please, Molly begged in her own heart, keep Ben safe, and don't let him do anything he'll regret!

Ben noticed absently how imposing the Hoskins mansion was. Its tall turrets stood head and shoulders above any other house in the town, and its ornate gingerbread cast eerie shadows across the façade as the sun climbed higher in the sky. How ironic to think his father lay dead these long years while his murderer had prospered. A new rage bubbled up within him, and he fought to maintain his outward calm.

"Do you suppose he knows Miriam is missing?" Harry asked while they were crossing the street in front of the house.

"He may not even be awake if he drank as much as Miriam thinks he did last night," Ben replied.

The three men filed through the wrought-iron gate and up onto the broad front porch with its screen of bright morning glories. The sheriff pounded on the door, and they waited. Several minutes passed, and Harry twisted the doorbell a few times. At last they heard movement inside, and then the huge front door swung open to reveal a Franklin Hoskins Ben had never seen before.

The man was obviously wearing the same suit he had worn the day before, and it was wrinkled enough to indicate he had slept in it. In contrast with his normally perfectly groomed appearance, Hoskins's hair was unkempt, and his face was covered with beard stubble. His bloodshot eyes and sallow complexion gave proof to Miriam's story about his drinking the night before. He gazed at the three of them in frank surprise for a moment before gathering his usual dignity. "Good morning, Sheriff. What brings you out so early?"

"I think you can guess, Mr. Hoskins. Seems Johnny McGee was shot yesterday. Your wife says you did it."

"My wife?" he said indignantly. "I can't imagine when you would have spoken with my wife."

"She's in my office right now."

Something like panic flitted across Hoskins's face, but he quickly recovered his aplomb. "I'm sure you're mistaken. Mrs. Hoskins has not even arisen yet this morning."

"You're wrong," Ben informed him. "She never went to bed at all. She spent the night at my place."

"*Your* place?" Hoskins's face turned red with suppressed fury.

"That's right, Father," Harry said. "And so did I. Miriam took Johnny to Ben's after she found him still alive, and Ben got me because he thought I'd like to hear Miriam's story. She told us *everything.*"

"I don't know what you're talking about," Hoskins tried, but he was starting to sweat.

"I think you do," Ben said. "She told us how you shot Johnny and how you burned Harry's barn so I'd get the blame, and how you killed Fletcher—"

"That bitch!" Hoskins spat. "She lied, Sheriff. She wants to get rid of me so she can have my money."

The sheriff was unmoved. "I just want to ask you some questions, Mr. Hoskins, about where you were the night of the box social when the fire was being set—"

"I was there, with her. She knows that."

Ben played a hunch. "Then why did she tell the judge she was with me?"

Hoskins's shock was profound. His red, sweating face turned purple. "I *knew* it! She's a whore. She's always been a whore!" He moved so quickly that no one even suspected anything until the gun flashed in the morning sunlight.

Ben reached for his own pistol and flung himself to the side just as Hoskins fired.

"Father!" Harry yelled, but Hoskins was gone, running through the house.

Harry took off after him, but Ben guessed Hoskins's intention was to get away. "He'll head for the barn," he told the sheriff, scrambling to his feet. The two of them dashed off the porch and around toward the backyard. Harry slammed out the back door just as they rounded the corner of the house.

"He went in the barn," Harry shouted.

"Is there another way out?" the sheriff asked breathlessly.

"Yes, I'll go cover it."

Harry was gone in an instant. Ben and the

sheriff cautiously approached the large double doors, which were still standing open. They paused outside, guns drawn, one on each side of the opening, listening. Ben had expected to hear the sounds of a man frantically saddling a horse. Instead he heard only the normal sounds of horses shuffling in their stalls. Could Hoskins have already escaped?

"He didn't go out the back," Harry called. "The door's still barred from the inside."

Ben and the sheriff exchanged a puzzled look. Why would Hoskins have backed himself into a corner?

"Hoskins," the sheriff yelled, "give it up. We've got all the doors covered. You can't get away, so why don't you come out with your hands up?"

No answer. They waited, the seconds ticking by with agonizing slowness.

"I'm going in," Ben said, doing so before the sheriff could stop him. He slipped in, stepping quickly to one side into the shadows until his eyes could become accustomed to the dimness. He scanned the interior of the barn, searching for possible hiding places. There were dozens, stalls and dark corners, even the loft above. He listened again. Surely if Hoskins had gone into a stall, the horse would be protesting the invasion, yet all the animals were quiet, poking their noses out curiously to see what all the excitement was about.

"Hoskins! You'll never get away. Come out and—"

A bullet whizzed past Ben's ear. He ducked

for cover even before he heard the explosion from the shot.

"Ben!" Harry and the sheriff both yelled at once. The sheriff was inside in a flash, and the sound of running feet preceded Harry's arrival.

Ben signaled that he was all right, not wanting Hoskins to find him by his voice again, and motioned for the others to get down.

Harry refused to be cowed. "Father, this is crazy! What can you hope to gain?"

"I'm not going to let them hang me!" Hoskins's voice came from the loft.

"Johnny McGee's not dead. Doc Logan says he's going to be fine."

"Fletcher is dead, and so is Sam Cantrell!"

"Are you admitting you killed them?"

"You know I did! That bitch told you, didn't she? But you won't take me alive."

"We aren't going to shoot you, Father—"

The next shot hit the wall behind Harry, and Ben dove for him, bringing him down before Hoskins's gun exploded again.

"He's your son, for God's sake!" the sheriff shouted, but Hoskins's only reply was another shot.

"How many is that?" Ben asked as he and Harry scrambled to a safer spot.

"Four, I think."

"I've got a pocket full of ammunition," Hoskins called.

"What's going on?" someone called from outside the barn. They could hear others running up, drawn by the unfamiliar sound of gunfire.

"Get back!" Ben shouted. "Keep everyone away."

Hoskins obligingly fired another shot that kicked up dust in the barn doorway. Ben could hear Reverend Bates and Mr. Wells urging people to move back. Where was Molly? He prayed she hadn't heard the shooting; she was worried enough already. To his surprise, he saw Harry draw his gun. "You're not going to shoot your own father, are you?"

"I figure if we do some shooting ourselves, maybe we can scare him out," Harry whispered. "Maybe he doesn't have as much ammunition as he says, either." He fired, aiming straight up and well away from where Hoskins was hidden.

Hoskins answered the shot, sending Ben and Harry ducking for cover again. This time Ben slipped away from Harry, thinking his time had come, the moment he'd dreamed of for so long. The man who'd killed his father, who'd ruined his name, was up there just begging to be shot.

He waited, listening for a sound to tell him where his quarry was. The sheriff had caught on to Harry's plan and was firing wildly, too, drawing a volley of shots from the loft. Now, Ben thought, carefully drawing a bead on his target. *Now!*

But nothing happened. His finger froze on the trigger, his vision blurred, and for a moment even the blasts of gunfire faded.

Hadn't he learned anything? The question exploded in his mind, and along with it came a vision of Molly's lovely face twisted in despair.

Once he'd thanked her for giving him back his life, and now he wanted to throw it away again for some mindless urge for revenge. Hadn't he learned *anything*?

Yes, he cried silently, I've learned a lot. Slowly, deliberately, he lifted his pistol again and let his shot go wild.

By now the horses were screaming with terror in their stalls, and the crowd noise outside told Ben most of the town had gathered to see what the commotion was about. Above they heard Hoskins moving to a new position. "Damn you, shoot *at* me!" He exposed himself in the opening of the loft and took careful aim at Ben's head. This time the volley of shots came from below, and Hoskins's own bullet went wild as he ducked for cover. "If you don't kill me, I'll kill you all!"

Again he appeared, and a bullet clipped Harry's hat brim.

"I've got no choice, boys," the sheriff said grimly, and the next time Hoskins appeared, he fired with deadly purpose.

"Hey, what's that sound?" Harry asked after a minute.

Ben listened. At first he heard nothing above the din of the braying horses and the echo of gunfire in his ears, but then he detected it, a faint crackling. He sniffed, but the air in the barn was already clouded with gunsmoke. "Hoskins, is there a fire up there?"

His only answer was a bloodcurdling laugh.

The crackle *whoosh*ed into a roar as the hay in the loft exploded into flame.

"Father!" Harry yelled, but Hoskins only laughed again. The sound sent chills up Ben's spine.

"Come down, Hoskins!" Ben called. "You'll burn to death."

"It's fitting, isn't it? I've burned two barns, and now I'll burn my own!"

"Father, don't be a fool!"

Smoke was billowing down through the opening in the loft now, and the people outside were yelling about the fire.

"Hoskins," the sheriff called. "We don't have any evidence against you, and your wife can't testify against you. You'll probably get off scot free."

"Nice try, Bigelow, but I've already confessed to you. I'm not going to strangle like Cantrell did."

A blast of gunfire sent the three men below ducking frantically. Bullets splintered wood everywhere, and a horse screamed in agony.

Heat from the fire came down in waves, and the men below could see the glow as the flames ate through the floor above.

"Father!" Harry called again, but this time he received no answer. All three of them yelled and then fired a round of shots, but the crackle of flames was their only reply. "I can't let him burn," Harry said as he raced for the ladder.

Ben was right on his heels, and the two of them shinned up the ladder, fighting the smoke and heat that grew more intense with every rung.

"Father! Oh, my God!" Ben heard Harry say when he cleared the edge of the loft. Harry lunged as if to grab his father, but in that instant a beam crashed down, striking him on the forehead.

The flames were racing toward them, and to Ben's horror he saw Harry's shirt catch fire. "Harry!" He grasped Harry's gunbelt and jerked him back onto the ladder, very nearly sending them both crashing to the ground. "Your shirt's on fire!"

Ben slapped at the flames while Harry tried to get his footing on the ladder. Suddenly Ben realized the blow had stunned his friend, slowing his reactions. Harry's foot slipped, and he fell against Ben, sending them sliding down another rung.

Ben became aware of the sheriff bellowing orders down below and other voices drifting up as townspeople poured in to rescue the horses.

"Get him on your shoulder, Ben. We'll help you."

Hands, reaching up, supported him as the smoke enveloped them. With superhuman effort, Ben jerked Harry around to face him. His friend's eyes were glazed, and he tried to fight, but Ben wrestled him over his shoulder. He took one step and then another. Someone helped him, and when his foot slipped, solid bodies broke the fall.

Outside, Molly and Miriam clung to each other and watched in terror as men hurried out of the barn, some leading horses, others helping those who had been overcome by smoke.

"Where are they?" Miriam asked for what seemed like the tenth time.

Molly stared at the barn door with stinging eyes, refusing to give way to tears until she knew what had happened to Ben.

"Ben!" she cried the instant he and Harry staggered out. Breaking free of Miriam's grasp, she ran and threw her arms around him. Several men took charge of Harry and led him away while Ben and Molly simply rejoiced in finding each other again.

"Where's Franklin?" Miriam asked from behind Molly.

Reluctantly, Ben released Molly. "He's still inside."

They all looked up at the barn, which was now fully engulfed in flames. Miriam uttered a little cry of horror, and Molly went to her. She and Ben led her over to where Harry was being cared for as Ben told her as briefly and kindly as possible what had happened inside the barn.

Someone had removed Harry's charred shirt, and Dr. Logan was looking at the burns on his back.

"How bad is it?" Ben asked.

"He'll have a nasty bruise from whatever hit him, but you got the fire out before it did more than scorch him a little. A couple days and he'll be good as new."

"Thank heaven," Miriam murmured. "Harry, did you see Franklin when you climbed the ladder?"

Harry drew a ragged breath and let it out in a long sigh. "I only got a glance at him before the beam hit me, but it looked like he'd shot himself. The barrel of his pistol was in his mouth and . . ." He left the rest to their imagination.

Molly looked at Ben. "You didn't . . . ?"

"I remembered what you said, and I couldn't," he told her simply. Molly went weak with relief and gratefully slipped into Ben's embrace.

"How did the fire start?" Miriam asked.

Ben shrugged. "Maybe a flash from his gun. Maybe one of our bullets caught the hay on fire. Maybe he set it himself. We'll never know for sure."

"All you folks are starting to look kind of peaked," Dr. Logan observed. "I think you ought to find a nice quiet place to lay down for a while."

Molly saw the lines of strain on Ben's face, and Harry and Miriam both looked about to drop. She was wondering how on earth they could make it home when Reverend Bates came over and offered to put them all up at his house until they felt well enough to return to their own homes.

Ben slipped his arm around Molly, and she glimpsed the lingering sadness in his eyes. He'd resisted the urge for revenge, but he was certainly entitled to the justice that had eluded him again.

"I reckon we'll take you up on your offer, Reverend," Ben was saying as they turned to go, but they stopped dead at the sight of what must have been the entire population of Hoskinsville standing in a semicircle around them, waiting expectantly.

Molly couldn't imagine what they wanted, and no one seemed inclined to say. They all simply stared, looking sheepish and uncomfortable. At last Mr. Wells stepped forward as spokesman. "Ben, Molly and Mrs. Hoskins told us that Franklin finally confessed to killing Fletcher and having your father lynched. Of course we knew you didn't burn Harry's barn, but it was an awful thing for you to be accused of. Seems like we've failed you all these years, and we want you to know we're sorry for what you've gone through."

A murmur of agreement rippled through the crowd. Molly could hardly believe her ears. Here it was, the moment of vindication Ben had been waiting six years for, but when she looked up at him, she saw not triumph but only a sad acceptance on his face.

"I reckon there was a time I would've tried to make you all feel bad about what happened to my pa," he said, his voice husky. "But I remember how you came to help me when I needed it, and how you've always treated me fair even when I didn't return the favor. What happened to my pa was a terrible thing, but enough people have already suffered because of it. We can't let it ruin the rest of our lives."

Molly gazed at him in astonishment. The miracle that had begun the day the people came to help build their bedroom was now complete. Reverend Bates patted Ben on the back. "Forgiveness is a blessed thing, Ben, and it blesses the one who forgives most of all."

Ben smiled. "I know."

EPILOGUE

MOLLY GLANCED UP from peeling potatoes. "Here comes Miriam," she remarked to Johnny, who was sitting on the porch beside her, dozing in the late morning sunshine.

"Oh, hell," he muttered, coming instantly awake. "I reckon I'll go inside and get back in bed."

"What on earth for?" Molly scolded. "Miriam will be real happy to see you up and around."

"I guess she'll be happy she doesn't have to keep coming out here anymore to help take care of me, too."

Molly's eyes widened with understanding. "So that's why you've been making such a fuss

369

about getting up. You think Miriam won't come if she thinks you're well."

"Well, she won't, will she?" he challenged.

"I don't know. Let's ask her," Molly teased.

"Molly," Johnny said in warning, and Molly managed to wipe the grin off her face.

"I think you might be surprised at what Miriam would do," she said. "Maybe it's more than a guilty conscience that's been bringing her out here every day for the past two weeks."

"What else could it be?" he asked, glancing apprehensively at the approaching rider. Soon she'd be close enough to see he was sitting on the porch.

"She might like you. You can be pretty charming when you put your mind to it, and you've been putting your mind to it a lot lately."

Johnny made a rude noise. "It'd take more than charm to impress a fancy lady like her."

"She hasn't always been so fancy, and whether she is or not, I happen to think she likes you."

"Why?"

"Because I've told her a dozen times I don't need her help, and any fool can see she only gets in my way when she's here. Do you think she'd ride out from town every day if she didn't have another reason?"

"It's like you said, she's got a guilty conscience," he said morosely.

"All right, I'll make a little bet with you. I say she likes you. If I'm wrong, I'll bake you as many pies as you want."

"What do you get if you're right?"

Molly grinned. "Satisfaction."

"How can you find out?"

"I'll make her admit it. Now go around the side of the house where she can't see you."

"You mean I should eavesdrop?"

Molly gave him a disgusted look, and he hurried away. Humming softly, she continued to peel potatoes while waiting for Miriam to arrive.

Miriam waved a greeting as she rode into the ranch yard, and when she had unsaddled her horse and turned it loose in the corral, she came over to the house. "Good morning. Beautiful day, isn't it?" she asked Molly, not even pausing on her way into the cabin.

"Johnny's not in there," Molly said casually.

Miriam glanced inside to verify the statement, then turned back to Molly in confusion. "Where is he?"

"Doc said he could get up and walk around if he felt like it, so he went for a little stroll."

"Oh, my, do you think it's safe for him to be out alone?" Miriam asked in alarm, scanning the yard for sight of him. "What if he faints or something?"

"I don't suppose Johnny ever fainted in his life, but if he doesn't come back soon, we'll go looking for him. Meanwhile, have a seat."

Reluctantly, Miriam took the chair Johnny had vacated a few minutes earlier. Molly noticed with amusement the way Miriam kept looking around, anticipating Johnny's return. "You like him a lot, don't you?"

To her delight, Miriam blushed. "He's a . . . very nice man," she hedged.

"You ought to know after all the time you've spent with him lately. I'll bet you know more about him than Ben does."

Miriam's lips twitched, and her dark eyes gleamed with mischief. "Ben's never given him a bed bath."

Molly almost choked imagining how mortified Johnny would be hearing this, but she managed to limit herself to a conspiratorial giggle. "Some might not think he's too good-looking."

"I think he's darling," Miriam protested.

"Darling?" Molly echoed skeptically.

"Absolutely. And he's so . . . so . . ."

"Nice?" Molly supplied.

"Yes. You just know he'd never be mean or cruel. He'd always treat a woman with respect and consideration."

Molly wished Johnny could see the longing in Miriam's eyes. "Have you told him how you feel?"

"Of course not. How could I? A lady doesn't declare herself until the gentleman has made his intentions known."

"I don't suppose Johnny's done that, either."

Miriam shook her head.

"He probably doesn't feel right about saying anything since your husband died so recently," Molly suggested.

"I hope that's all it is. I'm certainly willing to wait until a suitable time has passed, although no one expects me to be in mourning under the circumstances."

"Johnny might also be worried about your money. A poor man feels funny about courting a rich widow."

Miriam sighed. "I know. It's ironic. I always thought having money would make me happy, but I was utterly miserable with Franklin, and now I'd give it all away if . . ."

"If what?"

"If I thought it was standing between me and Johnny McGee." She sighed again.

"Well," Molly said in a loud, clear voice, "no man could ask for any more encouragement than that."

Miriam gave her a funny look, which she ignored. She changed the subject then, asking Miriam what she was planning to do about running the bank. Miriam was explaining how she had hired a manager when Johnny came sauntering around the side of the house.

"Johnny," Miriam exclaimed, rushing over to help him, although he plainly didn't need help. "You shouldn't have gone off by yourself on your first day out of bed."

"You're right," he told her, somehow keeping a straight face. "I should've waited so you could go with me."

"Come on inside. I'll help you get back in bed."

Johnny gave Molly a wink and mouthed the word "satisfaction" as Miriam escorted him into the house. From her seat on the porch she could hear Miriam helping him with his boots, and she bit back a smile when Miriam asked if she could get him anything.

"I'd appreciate a glass of water and . . ."

"And what?" she asked.

"Well, a back rub would sure be nice."

Molly covered her mouth with both hands. Had she thought Johnny shy? She would have to rethink her opinions.

While Johnny was drinking his water, Miriam said, "I was wondering if you might be able to come into town on Sunday and have dinner at my house. I'm planning to invite Ben and Molly, and Harry is bringing Molly's sister, Julie. I figured Ben could bring the wagon and make a bed for you in the back if you're not up to riding all that way."

Molly's eyes widened. Harry was bringing Julie? Now wasn't that interesting news? Something must have been going on while she was stuck here taking care of Johnny. Molly no longer feared her sister's relationship with Harry after hearing Miriam describe the way he had defended her from her husband's abuse. Molly'd been wrong about Harry, but she certainly didn't regret not having married him. Now maybe he could find the love he claimed not to believe in. Molly couldn't wait to tell Ben about this latest development.

It was after supper that night before she had the opportunity to speak to her husband alone.

In fact, this was the first evening since Johnny had been shot that they'd had the house all to themselves. Johnny had decided to return to the bunkhouse since he no longer saw any point in maintaining his invalid status.

"Johnny and Miriam Hoskins, who would've thought it?" Ben mused as he pulled off his boots in preparation for bed.

"Or Harry and Julie? I guess Harry decided Julie was grown up after all."

"Just like her sister." Ben grabbed Molly as she walked by on her way to hang up the dress she had just removed and pulled her down onto the bed.

She put up a token struggle just to keep Ben from taking her for granted, but in the end she surrendered to his insistent mouth, parting her own lips in silent invitation. His hands moved over her possessively, tugging impatiently at her chemise and petticoats.

"Ouch!" she complained. "You're going to have to be more careful with me, Mr. Cantrell."

"And why is that, Mrs. Cantrell?" he asked against the curve of her breast.

"Because when a woman is in a family way, she needs special treatment."

Ben went completely still, and when he lifted his head he saw the hope he would be afraid to acknowledge. After all, she had been wrong once before.

"I spoke to Doc Logan when he was here the

other day. He said this time I really am expecting. For sure."

"Oh, Molly." He touched her face with a gentleness bordering on reverence.

"You don't have to be *that* careful," she teased. "You can kiss me if you want to, and you can do a whole lot more, too, if the mood takes you."

With a growl he pounced on her, tickling until she squealed for mercy. When they settled again, she was lying on top of him, nestled close enough to know the mood would take him in just a moment. But for now she would savor the adoration in his sky-blue eyes.

"Just think, Molly," he said softly. "Our baby will have the kind of life both of us always dreamed of."

"Yes, a father he can be proud of and a mother who isn't afraid of anything."

"We'll leave him a different legacy than our parents left us, one he can be proud of."

Molly smiled mischievously. "Or that *she* can be proud of. We might have a girl, you know."

"Mmmm," Ben murmured, rolling them both over until Molly lay beneath him. "Do you think it's too late to try for one of each?"

"I'm willing if you are."

Ben was more than willing.

Author's Note

I would like to acknowledge the dedicated counselors at Family and Children's Services of Blair County—Jackie Sutton, Jo Watts, and Beverly Moss-Oswalt—who gave so generously of their time to help me understand the dynamics of domestic abuse and its effect on all members of the family.

My fondest desire was for my story to have a completely happy ending, which would have included the reformation of Elijah Wade. The counselors explained to me, however, that abusers seldom if ever reform unless they receive professional help. I had thought that perhaps Molly's mother might find a sanctuary in Molly and Ben's home, but this would have been the most dangerous place for her to go since abusers have been known to harm and even kill those who give their spouses sanctuary, especially if those people are close family members. I learned that the only "cure" for abusers during the Victorian era was death or debilitating illness. Since illness would have made Hannah Wade a double victim (because the community would have expected her to care for her sick husband), I chose death for Elijah.

During the Victorian era, women truly had no recourse but to stay with an abusive spouse. Today, most large cities and even many small towns have shelters where abused women and their children can find a safe place to stay and help in dealing with their situations. No one should remain in an abusive situation. In reality, things usually get worse, with abuse occurring more frequently and becoming more severe. In some cases it results in death—the death of a battered woman or of the abuser or both.

I hope you enjoyed this book. I love to hear from my readers. Please write to me c/o the Cherry Weiner Literary Agency, 28 Kipling Way, Manalapan, N.J. 07726.

Reading— For The Fun Of It

Ask a teacher to define the most important skill for success and inevitably she will reply, "the ability to read."

But millions of young people never acquire that skill for the simple reason that they've never discovered the pleasures books bring.

That's why there's RIF—Reading is Fundamental. The nation's largest reading motivation program, RIF works with community groups to get youngsters into books and reading. RIF makes it possible for young people to have books that interest them, books they can choose and keep. And RIF involves young people in activities that make them want to read—**for the fun of it.**

The more children read, the more they learn, and the more they **want** to learn.

There are children in your community—maybe in your own home—who need RIF. For more information, write to:

RIF
Dept. BK-3
Box 23444
Washington, D.C.
20026

Founded in 1966, RIF is a national, nonprofit organization with local projects run by volunteers in every state of the union.

A HISTORICAL ROMANCE TO CAPTURE YOUR HEART!

KAT MARTIN
MAGNIFICENT PASSAGE

Mandy Ashton is fleeing her stifling existence at Fort Laramie and is heading toward California. Travis Langley, a white man raised by the Cheyenne, is hired to escort her, although he mistakenly believes she is the rebellious daughter of the governor. This dangerous deception becomes even more perilous when the two discover they've become captives of a passion as untamed as the wilderness of the American West! Will they be able to overcome their contest of wills and let true love reign?

ISBN: 0-517-00620-0   Price: $3.95